THE LAST SPY

Also by John Griffiths

The Good Spy
A Loyal and Dedicated Servant
The Memory Man
Snake Charmer

THE LAST SPY

JOHN GRIFFITHS

Carroll & Graf Publishers, Inc.
New York

First Carroll & Graf edition 1992

Carroll & Graf Publishers, Inc.
260 Fifth Avenue
New York, NY 10001

Library of Congress Cataloging-in-Publication Data is available.

ISBN: 0-88184-797-6

Manufactured in the United States of America

PROLOGUE

(Gori, Georgian SSR. June 1, 1990)

SHORTLY BEFORE NOON AN OFFICIAL CONVOY, ARRIVING ON THE ROAD from Tblisi, made a stately entrance into the main square of Gori. The convoy consisted of three vehicles; at either end was a black BMW, and, gliding between them like a duchess escorted by her chamberlains, a Zil. Even minus its escort, the Zil would have captured attention. In Tblisi, the republic's capital, BMWs were sometimes to be seen, entering or leaving the courtyards of the ministries or parked outside stores reserved for the Party faithful, but even there, at the highest levels of the *nomenklatura,* there were not very many who rated a Zil. *And a Zil escorted by BMWs . . .* When the convoy drew up, across from the town hall, and parked (illegally) in front of the statue that commanded the esplanade, it was more than the usual handful of idlers who gathered to speculate and stare. People with wheels like these must be hotshots. And not just local hotshots. Politburo, probably. Central Committee, at least. And there was only one reason for people like that to be spending time in Gori; they had come to visit the Museum.

The correctness of this guess was confirmed almost at once. From the buildings at the far end of the esplanade there emerged a caravan of trolleys. On closer approach they were seen to contain the museum director and members of his staff. When this welcoming committee pulled up beside the convoy, the BMWs offloaded their passengers, unsmiling men in hats and trenchcoats whom the crowd identified without difficulty as "state security" people. One opened the door for the Zil's passengers. The others lined up along the curb.

Backs to the Zil, their hands thrust deep into overcoat pockets, they surveyed the crowd with eyes at once indifferent and watchful.

The men who emerged from the Zil presented an interesting contrast in appearance. The first, Ivan Ivanovich Gurov, was in his middle sixties; a short man, heavyset and balding, with a round, good-humored face in which the most striking feature was a pair of very penetrating eyes. He looked, as someone in the crowd observed, like someone who laughed a good deal and thoroughly enjoyed his glass of vodka. His companion, Vladimir Pavlovich Sorokhin, was some ten years older and a dozen centimeters taller. Lean and gaunt, with a narrow, dessicated face and close-cropped iron-gray hair, he looked as if he never laughed and disapproved of drinking. Both men wore suits of diplomatic gray and shoes, clearly foreign, of genuine leather. They moved slowly, Sorokhin seemingly in pain, and they carried themselves like people accustomed to public attention, as if enclosed in a capsule of private space. Ignoring both the crowd and the welcoming committee with its trolleys, they stretched themselves, then, gazing up, inspected the giant statue.

The statue stood more than fifteen meters high. A standing figure, dressed in the uniform of a marshal in the Soviet Army, it seemed not so much modeled as hewn from bronze. The last survivor of what had once been a legion, it looked out over the town with eyes that seemed fixed on a distant, heroic future. The plinth, a block of polished granite several times larger than the average Russian house, bore no inscription and did not need to. There was probably no one —no adult, at least, in the fifteen republics he had formerly ruled with a rod of iron—in whom the stern features and drooping mustache would not have compelled immediate recognition.

"It's strange," Gurov murmured. "I remember him as *bigger.*"

"He was a giant, and we were midgets." Sorokhin nodded. "We are still."

Their conversation was preempted then by the intrusion of the museum director. Descending from his trolley and smiling as if his life depended on it, he approached at a half trot, extending a hand in welcome and performing, at the same time, a kind of bow.

"Politburomember Sorokhin, Politburomember Gurov? . . . Shavdatvashvili, Director of the Memorial . . . Honored, believe me. Incredibly honored." He pumped the cool dry hands they offered, indicated the waiting trolleys. "If you and your party would be so kind . . . Refreshments are waiting at the Museum."

They didn't answer. They were used to conferring honor; refreshments were always waiting. They looked past him, down the esplanade. At the far end stood a building in granite and marble with a circular tower on one wing. In front was a cottage of brick and stucco, protected by a canopy of pale-pink marble held up by granite pillars. The cottage had been home to a Vissarion Dzugashvili, a cobbler and reputedly a drunkard, whose only claim to posterity's attention was the fact that he had fathered a son.

"We will walk." It was Sorokhin finally who consented to notice the director. He turned, with a half smile, to Gurov. "Midgets admittedly, but not yet absolutely senile."

Then icily, after a pause, to Shavdatvashvili: "One pays one's respects to a titan on foot, not resting one's backside in a trolley."

" 'We are to see as indisputable . . .' "

They had paused at the entrance to the final exhibit. Gurov was squinting down his nose at the printed white card in its frame to one side of the doorway. He peered at Sorokhin over his half-glasses. "The quote is, of course, from Comrade Blotface, his speech on the seventieth anniversary of the Revolution. . . . We are to see as indisputable the 'contributions to the struggle for socialism and the defense of its gains,' but as equally indisputable 'the despotism and crude errors committed by this man and his circle.' "

"Blotface . . ." Sorokhin growled. "What the hell would he know about it? When those contributions were being made, when millions of Russians were dying to defend those socialist gains, Blotface was stuck to his mother's tit, drooling and shitting his diaper."

There was no one with them. Three hours before, informed of the honor impending, the director had discovered a need for "renovations" and closed the Museum for the rest of the day. Lunch with his staff and local Party bigwigs had been unavoidable—the inevitable caviar, invariable sturgeon, inescapable Georgian champagne—but afterward, in a tactful departure from protocol, he'd suggested his guests might wish to be alone, "to pay respects to the memorial in private."

They had wished. And pushing now through heavy swing doors, they found themselves in a darkened chamber. It was windowless and circular (perhaps thirty feet in diameter) with a vaulted ceiling, a railed walkway around the perimeter, and a thick carpet to muffle footsteps. But these were features they noticed later. What struck them first, what captured their eye from the moment they entered, lay on a pedestal in the center of the chamber: a cushion of blood-red velvet, lit from above so it seemed to be floating in space, and on it, catching the beam of the spotlight, glowing like a jewel in the surrounding gloom, a deathmask.

Iosif Dzugashvili, son of Vissarion.

Known to the world as Joseph Stalin.

For several seconds neither spoke. Gurov, glancing to his right, saw that Sorokhin had come to attention. He was staring fixedly ahead, his right arm raised in a salute. Compelled by the example, Gurov also saluted. It seemed to him that a chill had entered the air.

"I remember him in the war," Sorokhin whispered. "The speech he made when the Germans invaded: how their finest units were already crushed; how the flower of their army lay dead on the field of battle; how our own forces were like a clenched fist, not retreating but drawing back, gathering to deliver the final blow; how we must suffer to be worthy. It was all lies, of course. Except for the part about suffering. In fact our armies were in headlong retreat, and even at the time I knew it. But when he spoke, the facts seemed somehow irrelevant. His lies belonged to a higher order of truth, a truth he alone was able to show us."

Gurov nodded.

"He showed us ourselves, the truth of the Russian spirit. . . . In '54, when Khrushchev denounced him, people were crying in the streets. They felt they'd been robbed of what they knew. What they knew, what *he* had taught them, was sacrifice for the future, discipline, devotion. And now here was Khrushchev, with his dirty facts, telling them their sacrifice had all been wasted." He paused. "It began there, Volodya. The disease began with Khrushchev. With Brezhnev it went into remission for a while. But now, with Blotface and his clique, it's back. Instead of sacrifice and discipline, they offer us what? Openness so-called, restructuring, democratization. Selfishness, in other words, competition, confusion. And instead of devotion—" He broke off, turned to his companion. "Tell me, Vanya. That face on the cushion . . . When you look at it, what does it make you feel?"

For a moment Sorokhin didn't reply. He had to force himself to turn his eyes back to the deathmask.

"He spoke to me once when I was with the Komsomol in Irkutsk. He inspected us and, afterward, because I was the leader, he spoke to me. He asked me a single question: How much was I willing to sacrifice for the Revolution? I was twenty years old, so of course I said: Everything, *any* sacrifice. He said nothing, he just smiled. He looked at me with those yellow eyes and made my insides turn to water. That *bastard.*" Sorokhin shook his head in disbelief. "Thirty-five years in the ground, and *still* he has the power to make me shiver."

"He would have liked that." Gurov nodded. "That was the secret of his power, the truth he alone was able to show us. To earn their devotion you must make people shiver."

"But now, it seems, nobody must shiver." Sorokin's voice was sour with contempt. "Now we have to be like America. No devotion. No sacrifice. Everybody grabbing for what he can get. We Russians have no talent for that kind of freedom. We need to be disciplined, commanded, marched like soldiers down the highroad of our destiny—"

He broke off. Gurov was staring at the deathmask, his lips twisted into something like a smile.

"You find that funny?"

"Funny?" For a moment Gurov looked blank. He shook his head. "But just now, when you were speaking, it almost seemed I could hear *him* laughing. He would call us cowards, old women making speeches, lacking the courage to act . . ."

"Act?" Sorokhin was suddenly intent. "How should we act?"

Gurov shrugged. "Desperate diseases call for desperate remedies."

"Desperate remedies . . . You mean a coup? . . . To remove Blotface."

"Too late for that." Gurov shook his head. "Even if the Army would support us, which I doubt, the rot is into the woodwork too deep. This isn't a problem of one man, Volodya. Blotface is merely a symptom. We need a cure for the disease."

"But what *is* the cure?"

Gurov looked at him sideways. "What would you say is the disease?"

"Apathy." Sorokhin shrugged. "Selfishness. Lack of discipline."

Gurov shook his head. "The disease is America."

"America?" Sorokhin stared.

"I should have said the *idea* of America. We are—we always have been—locked in a fight to the death with that idea, but our people seem to have forgotten. America looks good to them now. They fool themselves that America is compatible with justice, that socialist ends can somehow be achieved by capitalist means. They don't understand that employing the methods implies, in the end, embracing the values. It surrenders everything we ever fought for, betrays the struggle which has dignified our lives. But how to make them see this? That's the problem."

Sorokhin shot him a penetrating glance.

"What are we talking about exactly? What are you trying to make *me* see?"

"The problem is that ideas have no faces," Gurov said. "People need an enemy they can see. Not an *idea,* but the actuality. Three or four thousand American warheads, pointing at us from all points of the compass. That's what we need to make them see."

Sorokhin frowned. "But the Cold War is over."

Gurov shrugged. "People think so perhaps."

"If they think so, it is."

"Then war is an attitude of mind, you think?"

"Mostly. The weapons make a difference, of course. But what counts is the willingness to use them."

"So peace is also an attitude of mind?"

"Presumably," Sorokhin said. "But what conclusion do you draw from this?"

"That attitudes can be changed," Gurov said.

"Changed . . . How?"

"It doesn't take much . . . An incident. A murder perhaps, or a spy ring uncovered. It doesn't even have to be real. All that is needed is a piece of theater. An illusion to end the illusion that America can be our friend. A fiction employed in the service of truth."

"A fiction." Sorokhin thought for a moment. "And who will be the author of this fiction?"

"I'm not sure." Gurov paused. "Maybe your nephew, Rakowski."

BOOK I
(June 15 to July 6, 1990)

CHAPTER ONE

(Moscow. June 15, 1990)

IN HIS OFFICE ON THE SECOND FLOOR OF THE HEADQUARTERS COMPLEX at Yasenevo, General Rodion Rakowski, Head of Directorate R (Operational Planning and Analysis) of the First Chief Directorate of the KGB, sat at his desk, thinking. The office, which was long and narrow with a double door at one end and a floor-to-ceiling window at the other, looked out over landscaped parkland to the Moscow Ring Road, and in the distance, the city. The view of spreading beeches and an ornamental lake on which migrating wildfowl occasionally settled was considered an amenity by those who didn't share it. Rakowski's desk, however, faced in the other direction. One didn't make general in the KGB by spending one's time looking out of the window. One did it by hard work, by staying out of trouble.

By keeping in with one's connections.

He lit a Camel and sat for a moment, the cigarette dangling from his lips, his eyes resting on the violet folder that lay on the desktop before him.

The contents had come by diplomatic pouch. They were classified, as the color of the folder and the legend stamped on its cover in large black letters revealed, SECRET. They consisted of a two-page report and a covering letter from the KGB's London Residency. The report, obtained from a KGB illegal, codenamed Cobalt, was entitled: "Recent activities of the Ukrainian emigré group calling itself The Knights of Vladimir."

Reports on the activities of Ukrainian emigrés were not normally of much interest to Rakowski. They came to him only for background, and he usually passed them, without much more than a glance, to the Second Chief Directorate (Internal Security), which in turn kept track of them, he guessed, because the activities of Ukrainian emigrés were invariably hostile to the interests of the Soviet Union, and one couldn't quite count on the hostility always being offset by incompetence. But these Knights of Vladimir, it struck him, were different. Or rather the circumstances here were different. And because of this, these so-called Knights, who, if their name was anything to go by, were no doubt as incompetent as all the rest, might very well offer him the tool he needed.

It might do, he thought. It might do very well.

If the Americans could be persuaded.

CHAPTER TWO

(London. June 21, 1990)

"You say you have a message for me?" Martin Rosenthal asked. "From Moscow?"

Turner Meredith nodded.

"From *whom* in Moscow?"

Meredith didn't answer. Instead he let his eyes drift round the room. The private offices of the Director of the Foundation for Freedom, it struck him, perfectly reflected the persona of their tenant. The crystal chandelier, the velvet curtains with their heavy gilt tassels, the French doors leading onto the spacious balcony, the hardwood floors strewn with a minor fortune in Oriental rugs, all were intended to remind visitors that Rosenthal had once been Secretary of State, a man of truly global influence, hailed by *Newsweek* as "the descendant of Talleyrand" and by *Time* magazine as "Statesman of the Decade." Except for the usual array of telephones, there was nothing on the vast mahogany desk to show that it was ever used for business, save a blotter in burgundy morocco and a fountain pen of the massive variety favored by the signers of treaties. The walls were covered with framed and signed photographs, all of them, Meredith noted, variations on a theme: Rosenthal in his days of glory, confidant of Presidents and Kings.

"Has this place been swept for bugs?" he asked. "Since our last conversation, I mean?"

Rosenthal frowned. "Do you think I'm stupid?"

Meredith shook his head. Rosenthal was the last man you'd want to call stupid. Or the last man you'd want to call stupid to his face. Short, plump, bespectacled, with a head too large for his body and a body whose essential dumpiness hundreds of dollars in Savile Row tailoring labored in vain to conceal, he projected an aggressive, arrogant cleverness—the conviction that all problems yielded to brain-power and that his was equal to the most intractable problem. Which conviction, Meredith thought, made him much of the time a royal pain in the ass. But since he was also a necessary pain, it was something you had learned to tolerate.

"Not stupid," he said. "Careless of security on occasion. It seemed only prudent to check."

"Well, now that you've checked, suppose you give me my message."

"Actually I think it's *our* message."

Meredith wasn't going to be stampeded. Rosenthal might once have been Secretary of State, but he wasn't any longer. He wasn't, moreover, Meredith's employer. Indeed, Meredith thought, since the reverse was closer to the truth, he, Turner Meredith, the CIA's deputy director (Operations), would tell this thing his way and take his sweet time in the telling.

"Starrett was the carrier," he continued. "It seems he was in Moscow last week. Negotiating wheat sales, buying up obsolete MIGs for resale to African dictators. Who knows? The point is, he got himself invited to a party."

"*Got* himself invited?" Rosenthal frowned. "Since when does Starrett pimp for you?"

"He doesn't. The chairmen of multinational conglomerates don't pimp for the CIA. If anything," Meredith smiled faintly, "it's the other way around. But Fraser Starrett is in Moscow all the time. He has access to the Kremlin at elevated levels, which sometimes allows him to do us a favor. On this occasion, though, he was doing *them* a favor."

Rosenthal frowned.

"Them? Them meaning who, exactly?"

Meredith ignored the question. "The party itself was nothing special, the sort of bash he's always getting asked to. Weekend party at So and So's dacha. Conversation, caviar, vodka. Sex, of course, in fifty-seven varieties."

"And KGB cameras behind every two-way mirror?"

"Probably." Meredith shrugged. "Though I doubt they'd try anything like that with Fraser. Since he seems to have been born completely without shame, he's not really open to blackmail. In any case, since he's one very bigtime capitalist hyena and since capitalist hyenas are all the rage in Moscow right now, every courtesy was extended. A car was laid on to chauffeur him back and forth. And not the usual Intourist jalopy, a big black Chaika, tinted windows, sound-proof passenger compartment, the whole nine yards. And, of course, when Fraser climbed into it, he found he wasn't alone."

"He had company? Who was it? A woman?"

Meredith restrained a sigh. In Washington Rosenthal was said to have two enthusiasms; when he wasn't thinking about his place in history, he was thinking about women.

"No, not a woman."

"Who then?"

"There were two of them, actually. Ivan Gurov was one. Considered by many the brains of the Soviet Right. A close associate of Vladimir Sorokhin, who, you may recall, was the hardliners' candidate to succeed Andropov."

"Of course I recall." Rosenthal cut in testily. "I know Sorokhin personally, also Gurov." He paused. "Who was with Gurov?"

"A Major General Rodion Rakowski."

"Rakowski?" Rosenthal considered, shook his head. "Don't know him. Don't think I've even heard of him."

"You wouldn't have heard of him," Meredith said. "He goes to some lengths to make sure that one doesn't."

"So who is he? Some intelligence bureaucrat or other?"

Meredith nodded. "He's my KGB opposite number."

"Their Director of Dirty Tricks?"

Meredith smiled faintly. "I think he might prefer to be described as the Head of Directorate R. But in essence your description is correct. He's their Director of Dirty Tricks."

Rosenthal thought about this.

"I wonder what he was doing with Gurov? The two of *them* were going to the party?"

Meredith shook his head. "That's what was interesting, they weren't. They were headed in Starrett's direction and quote-unquote 'bumming a ride.' But glad of the opportunity, Gurov said, for a quiet heart-to-heart with a friend."

"Friend?" Rosenthal queried. "Starrett knows him? Personally?"

"Fraser knows everybody." Meredith grinned.

"And in the course of this quiet heart-to-heart?"

"Fraser was given this . . ." Meredith took an envelope from his pocket, laid it on the desk in front of Rosenthal. "For you."

There was silence for a moment. Rosenthal, Meredith noted, made no move to pick up the letter.

"And although it was addressed to me . . ." Rosenthal's voice had acquired an edge, "Starrett delivered it to the CIA."

"He didn't deliver it to the CIA." Meredith spoke calmly. His face was without expression. "He delivered it to *me.*"

More silence. Rosenthal worked through the implications of this.

"You mean that Starrett . . . ?" He let the sentence trail off unfinished.

Meredith rested his gaze on Rosenthal, then he nodded. "Fraser Starrett is one of us. It's his money, in fact—or his company's money —which, filtered discreetly through various Swiss accounts, mostly supports the work of your foundation."

"So Starrett's company's money helps fund us." Rosenthal, trying not to look surprised or impressed, succeeded mostly in looking ungrateful. "Are you suggesting Gurov knows that?"

"Almost certainly, I'd say. I'd bet my pension Rakowski does."

"So, in other words, they know about *us?*"

Meredith thought for a moment, shrugged. "Perhaps in general terms only. But for them, remember, we're the main enemy. They watch us as closely as we watch them. They'll have files on you, and files on me, and on everyone who's anyone in Washington. Let me put it this way . . ." he paused. "They know who on our side eats lunch with whom."

"And knowing this, they sent me a letter, choosing Fraser Starrett as the carrier. Was there any accompanying message?"

Meredith shook his head. "They talked generalities, Fraser said. Problems of *perestroika,* dangers to world peace inherent in détente. Nothing remarkable in itself, but significant perhaps when taken in conjunction with the letter."

"What's *in* the letter?"

"I thought you'd never ask." Meredith smiled. "It's an invitation. You and me to go hunting next week. In Finland."

"Hunting? In Finland? *Gurov* invited us?"

"Not Gurov. Aage Hakkinen. You must have met him. Used to be prominent in the Peace Movement. 'Businessman-philanthropist' the media call him, usually omitting to add 'fellow traveler.' "

Silence.

"He invited me and *you?* He specified you by name?"

"Odd, isn't it?" Meredith nodded. "You and me to meet Gurov and Rakowski. *They'll* have put Haakinen up to this, of course. There's an intriguing symmetry there, if you think about it. Soviet hardliners meet secretly with US hardliners on neutral ground in Finland."

"Intriguing?" Rosenthal looked dubious. "What do you think they want?"

"I've no idea," Meredith said. "But I think we ought to find out."

CHAPTER THREE

(Taivalkoski, Finland. July 2, 1990)

THIS HAD TO BE, MEREDITH REFLECTED, ABOUT THE ODDEST ENCOUNTER it had been his lot to take part in. The ambience, for one thing, verged on the surreal. It inclined one, he thought, to suspect the Russians of satire. A forest clearing, middle of nowhere, all profound silence and great brooding trees, had been fitted out as if for a diplomatic powwow. On the carpet of dead pine needles someone had plonked down a mahogany round table with chairs to match. Ashtrays in finest Carrara marble, a cut-glass Waterford carafe and tumbler, were thoughtfully provided for each participant. All that was missing were scratch pads and name cards, a chandelier, possibly, suspended from overhanging branches. And microphones of course. But microphones had been the burning issue. At least with Rosenthal they had. There were, Meredith recalled reading somewhere, two basic forms of paranoia: delusions of grandeur and of persecution; Rosenthal appeared to have both. He'd developed, at any rate, a phobia about bugging and stubbornly insisted on meeting outdoors. It appeared this charade was the Russians' response. Meredith tried to imagine the scene from above, from the vantage point of some passing bird. His mind's eye panned up and back till the clearing dwindled to a speck, an island lost in a limitless ocean of trees. . . . Four men at a table in the woods, conspiring to subvert the course of history.

He hoped someone knew the way home.

"You wish to propose a *provocation*?"

Rosenthal looked puzzled. And disapproving. Like a bishop confronting some novel form of sin. A bishop, moreover, very bizarrely clad: tweed jacket and vest, corduroy knee breeches, boots and gaiters, bottle-green Tyrolean hat, and protruding from it jauntily, a pheasant's tail feather; the whole effect only slightly marred by the indispensable thick-rimmed glasses, misting now slightly with suspicion and indignation—Rosenthal *en tenue de chasse,* every inch the intrepid hunter. An improbable vision at best, and all the more ludicrous, Meredith knew, for being also quite unnecessary. In the years since he'd held public office, Rosenthal's celebrity had almost completely subsided. And thanks to arrangements made by Meredith, no publicity had attended his arrival in Helsinki. No one, so far as Meredith had noticed, had spared either of them a second glance, not even the servants on Haakinen's estate, where Rosenthal's Nimrod impersonation was making him stick out like a sore thumb. But in the matter of dress, as in the matter of bugs, Rosenthal had been adamant. It was elementary tradecraft, he'd insisted; if one claimed to be hunting, one should look the part. There was this consolation at least, Meredith thought; in one's private scrapbook of memories one image would certainly endure: Rosenthal in deep cover, courtesy of Abercrombie & Fitch.

"Provocation is the KGB term." Rakowski nodded. "In America you would call it entrapment. I, for example, entice you to sell me cocaine. When the sale has been made I arrest you for dealing, producing as evidence a film I've had made of the transaction. The principle is somewhat the same here."

"The principle is familiar." Rosenthal maintained the note of disapproval. "It's the application that puzzles me. Who would be provoking whom?"

Momentary silence. Exchange of Russian glances.

"We would be provoking you." It was Gurov who responded. "With your full knowledge and consent, for the ultimate benefit of both parties."

"So *we* get to stick our tit in the wringer and you get to crank the handle? For the ultimate benefit of *both* parties?" Rosenthal gave a who-are-you-trying-to-kid look. "I'm glad I'm wearing my boots."

"Boots?" Gurov looked blank.

"For the bullshit," Rosenthal said. "It's six inches deep and rising."

Gurov shrugged, turned to Rakowski. "As you predicted, the issue of trust. What basis for trust can we offer?"

For a moment Rakowski stared at Rosenthal without speaking. He gave, Meredith thought, above all an impression of weight. Gurov, though his senior, was less considerable: a sly peasant, one of those instinctive politicians, ubiquitous wherever the grubby art was practiced, whose principal talent was for getting ahead. Rakowski was different. His appearance seemed to promise what the Romans had called *gravitas:* a broad, heavy-jowled face, strong-featured but slightly fleshy, the chin deeply cleft, the large brow creased with lines of care, the eyes, green-hazel, deepset under thick, bushy eyebrows, the lips compressed in a look of permanent suspicion, the hair receding a little at the forehead but thick and wavy, a fierce foxy red. A formidable man, stern, perhaps even severe, who took himself and his business seriously.

"What basis for trust can we offer?" Rakowski continued to scrutinize Rosenthal. "You've mentioned the most reliable already: an identity of interest between the parties. However, if this is not enough . . ."

He left the sentence unfinished, shrugged, reached into his briefcase. Extracting a violet folder, he placed it on the table. For a moment he sat motionless, considering, then he slid the folder, with a deft backhanded flick, across the table to Meredith.

"Earnest of sincerity." He smiled coldly. "From Russia with love."

Meredith opened it. Inside was a single sheet of paper. Several paragraphs of English text, preceded by all the familiar rubrics: Security Classification. Country of Origin. Date of Origin. Source. He read it twice: skimming the first time, eyes widening slightly in surprise, the second time carefully, giving himself time to memorize the contents. He closed the folder, slid it back to Rakowski.

"Might one inquire," Rosenthal inquired icily, "what *that* was?"

"Verbatim transcript of a KGB report," Rakowski answered him. "Source employed by the US embassy in London, English translation made by myself. But you don't need to take my word for it. The information, which your colleague will know is accurate, will permit him to identify the source. In other words we're giving you a gift, no strings attached, no assurance of return. A valuable asset lost to us now forever." He turned to Meredith. "It was this source, incidentally, who informed us of your contacts with the Knights of Vladimir."

"The Knights of Vladimir?" Rosenthal was losing patience. "Who the hell are the Knights of Vladimir?"

"Ukrainian emigrés in London," Rakowski said. "Aspiring terrorists, would-be assassins. Idiots really. Political romantics, whose notion of patriotism, it would seem, is murdering Communists in the Ukraine."

"Murdering Communists?" Rosenthal stared. "What do they hope to achieve by that?"

Rakowski shrugged. "The mental processes of idiots are notoriously hard for rational people to follow. Their ultimate objective, I gather, is fomenting some kind of popular uprising, but how this will result from what they plan is not at all clear, at least not to me." He turned to Meredith again. "They're realists to this extent at least, that they know their limitations. Presumably that's why they came to you for help."

"You *know* about this?" Rosenthal gave Meredith his episcopal look.

Meredith nodded. "It was London they applied to, actually. There's a kind of emigré mafia there we make it our business to keep tabs on. Exiled Ukrainians, Hungarians, or Balts, all conspiring to some lunacy or other. These Knights are notable mostly for ambition. That and spectacularly lousy timing. They asked us for half a million dollars, not to mention technical support." He glanced at Rakowski, grinned, and rolled his eyes.

"Technical support for *what?*"

"I'm sorry, I thought you'd have gathered. A campaign of terror, PLO-style, intended to lead, as General Rakowski says, to a full-scale Ukrainian uprising. They asked us for weapons, training, transportation. Which prompts one to wonder what the money was for." Meredith shrugged, smiled faintly. "Salaries, no doubt."

"Which requests you, of course, refused." This from Gurov, not a question.

"Did or will. Their Agency contact, quite correctly, undertook to forward their request, but advised them, also quite correctly, not to hold their breath. The Station Chief, consulted, went off into gales of helpless laughter. And there, to my knowledge, the matter rests. No doubt a formal answer will be given in due course, but this isn't, from our point of view, a matter of any great urgency." Meredith paused, continued blandly. "I need hardly assure you that such an operation, running, as it would, totally counter to official US policy, would never for a moment be sanctioned by Langley."

"Since this is not an official meeting"—Gurov's tone was equally bland—"perhaps we needn't spend time discussing what would or wouldn't be sanctioned by Langley."

Rosenthal made an impatient movement.

"Then what should we spend our time discussing? No doubt it's fascinating, all this spook scuttlebutt, but what's the relevance? Where is it leading?"

"I think that's what they're about to tell us. Though, actually," Meredith smiled, "I think I can guess."

"You think you can guess." Rakowski raised an eyebrow. "I'd be interested to hear this guess."

Meredith inspected him for a moment. It still felt unreal to be meeting in person, to be actually facing across a table, a man he'd been imagining all these years. The Agency file on Rakowski, which he'd reread prior to this meeting, was not, after all, very thick. What it chronicled mostly were suppositions, third-hand reports, defectors' defective recollections, the blanks filled in by guesswork and hindsight. A Major Rakowski (first name unknown) had in 1975 delivered at the KGB school in Kiev a celebrated lecture on black operations. A Colonel Rakowski, some time appropriately later, had been listed as second—or was it third?—deputy in the FCD's Directorate S (Illegals). A Rodian Radowski (spelling uncertain), briefly encountered in civilian clothes at a national day reception in Moscow in 1978, was reported by the source (a visiting US businessman, no doubt at the time half smashed on vodka) to speak fluent colloquial English and possess a surprising knowledge of pro football. A Major General Rakowski (the item culled from Isvestiya, the ID positive this time), surprising a mugger in Gorki Park, had drawn his service automatic, shot and killed the fleeing bandit. The file had also contained a picture: third from the left, back row, in the usual blurred enlargement of a tourist's hasty snapshot of some Mayday lineup of Party bigshots. A head-and-shoulders shot this, the face, largely obscured by its officer's peaked cap, circled in pencil by an eager-to-be-helpful defector, but in truth more or less indistinguishable from those on either side. None of which, scuttlebutt or picture, had quite prepared one, Meredith thought, for the powerful, leonine presence, given any inkling of the force of the man. An idea, however, could be gleaned from his operations, those he was *rumored* to have authored, which bore, like chess games of a master, the imprint of a mind. The scam, for instance, with visiting British MPs: self-important parliamentarians, all with known intelligence connections, conned into meetings with "potential high-level defectors" who had subsequently proved to be KGB decoys. The upshot of which had been attempts (unsuccessful) to blackmail the MPs in question and exposure (successful) of the incident in the international press, leading to considerable embarrassment for the British government and the expulsion of half the SIS establishment in Moscow. The signature qualities of a Rakowski operation, indeed, were flexibility with regard to target, a

protean ability to change shape and complexion, the invariably minimal blow-back potential. Among the practitioners of dirty tricks
Rakowski was that comparative rarity: a man never hoist with his
own petard.

But that, Meredith thought, might be going to change.

"Guess," Rakowski repeated.

"I'd guess," Meredith said, "you're going to ask us to reconsider."

He had the satisfaction of seeing Rakowski register, fleetingly, surprise and then approval. Rosenthal, on the other hand, was openly
bewildered.

"What would *that* do for us?" Rosenthal demanded.

"Put our tit in the wringer," Meredith said. "Demonstrate for all
the world to see that the Cold War is over only in name, that whatever politicians on both sides want to claim, the reality hasn't
changed a bit, that the CIA is still meddling in Soviet internal affairs,
conspiring to destroy the Soviet state."

He paused, turned to Rakowski.

"You want us to help these Knights, right? You're going to help us
help them. Some Communist hotshots, specially selected for the
honor, are slated to be martyrs to the cause. Then, at the proper
psychological moment, you're going to make sensational arrests.
There'll be trials, carefully stage-managed. The captured assassins
will sing like so many larks. The CIA will be convincingly implicated,
and at this somber moment in history Politburo members Sorokhin
and Gurov, neglected prophets of the true revolution, will step resolutely forward. 'This,' they'll declare, 'is what comes of *perestroika*.
This is what results from abandoning Lenin. These are the fruits of
trusting America.' "

He paused again, looked in turn at each of the Russians.

"Isn't that more or less what you had in mind?"

"More or less *exactly*." Gurov gave a nod of approbation.
"Rakwoski told me you were clever. Perhaps I could use you to write
my speech."

For a moment there was silence. It was broken by Rosenthal.

"Could we defer the mutual admiration?" Frostily, he turned to
Gurov. "You claimed earlier that *both* sides would benefit. It's easy
to see what you get out of this. What it does for us is rather less
obvious."

Gurov stared in apparent astonishment. " 'If the Cold War hadn't
existed, we'd have had to invent it.' It was you, was it not, who wrote
that, in one of your books?"

Rosenthal shrugged and nodded. "So?"

"We're suggesting that at this point in history the Cold War needs to be *re*invented. And what that does for *you* is what it always did. It assures you the leadership of the West and the economic privileges that go with that position. It guarantees obedient allies, acquiescent foreign lenders, willing holders of your Everest of debt. It keeps your generals and arms manufacturers happy. It enriches people like your friend, Fraser Starrett. It keeps your bureaucrats in jobs, your congressmen in office, your diplomats and spymasters in regular employment." He smiled. "Do I need to go on? We all here know that the Cold War was an industry, stable and lucrative. We all know, too, that, as one of your Presidents said, the business of America is business . . ."

He broke off. Rosenthal was regarding him stonily.

"That all sounds wonderful," Rosenthal said. "But rewards are one thing, what about risk?"

"Risk? What risk?"

"The risk to *us,*" Rosenthal said. "You guys get to lie down and cry 'foul.' We get *stuck* with our tit in the wringer."

"Not really. Not inextricably." Gurov smiled. "Your involvement would be disavowable."

"Disavowable." Rosenthal's sarcasm was savage. "Oh, of course."

He turned to Meredith.

"You mentioned trials. There'd be trials all right, and not all of them would take place in Moscow. Remember what happened with that Contra business? This would make that one look like cake." He paused. "I've no desire to go down in history as the only US Secretary of State to be tried for accessory to murder."

"You wouldn't be tried," Rakowski said.

"Really? Perhaps I lack subtlety. It's hard to see how an operation in which we would be 'convincingly implicated' could be at the same time disavowable. *Convincingly* disavowable, that is."

"What *is* 'convincing?' " Rakowski shrugged. "It depends, doesn't it, on who you're trying to convince? Most people can't be bothered with evidence and logic; prejudice offers more freedom. I will tell you what will happen here: We will accuse you of plotting to unsettle the Ukraine, of conspiring to destroy the Soviet state. We will offer, as evidence, confessions made by the arrested terrorists and other 'facts' of a circumstantial nature, evidence that falls far short of proof but is deeply convincing to the average Russian, whose fears of US duplicity and aggression our leaders have played on for generations.

You, on the other hand . . ." He broke off, smiled quizzically at
Meredith. "You seem to be good at this kind of thing, tell us what
your side will claim."

"That your evidence was fabricated"—Meredith didn't hesitate—
"your confessions extorted, probably by torture. That your so-called
terrorist campaign was a fiction, a piece of theater, conceived by
Stalinist hardliners in the Kremlin and carried out by minions in the
KGB, whose object is to slander the US, to undermine détente, to
restore the Cold War and discredit, in the process, their political
opponents, the reformist faction of *glasnost* and *perestroika.*" He
paused. "How was that?"

"Perfect." Rakowski gave a sudden ferocious grin. "Every word a
vicious lie, of course, but when backed by evidence of a circumstantial nature, deeply convincing to the average American, whose fears
of Russian duplicity and aggression your leaders have played on for
generations."

He paused.

"What follows is the usual war of words, accusation and counter-
accusation hurled back and forth like so many missiles. No one but
us will really know the truth, and by that time the truth will be almost
irrelevant."

"Irrelevant?" Rosenthal stared.

"Certainly," Gurov said. He and Rakowski were alternating
smoothly, as if, Meredith thought, they had scripted their roles in
advance. "No matter who was actually to blame, the incident creates
a crisis. Neither leader can risk seeming weak. Bush, to avoid the
'wimp' reputation, has made himself a prisoner of the redneck right.
As for Blotface . . ." He shrugged. "It was Blotface who withdrew
from Afghanistan, Blotface who surrendered Eastern Europe.
Blotface who dismantled the Warsaw Pact. Blotface is the prisoner of
almost everyone. In particular the Marshals of the Soviet Army."

Silence.

"And the terrorism?" Rosenthal queried. "These murders of high-
ranking Communist officials—they would have to be actually carried
out?"

"Some would, certainly." Rakowski nodded. "The terrorism must
be a fact. Attempts can be covered up, disputed. What we need here
is outraged patriotic feeling, and for that, unfortunately, we need
bodies."

Extended silence.

Rakowski stood up. "I propose we adjourn for the moment. You will wish to talk this over. No doubt you will have questions, both as to concept and details. These can be discussed in due course." He paused, addressed his next words to Meredith. "I've found our meeting enjoyable and enlightening. The extent to which we think alike convinces me we can cooperate in this venture. At moments like this, when it is rational to trust, I'm sure we can all be trusted to be rational."

CHAPTER FOUR

(Taivalkoski, Finland. July 2, 1990)

"WHAT WAS THAT STUFF ABOUT A SOURCE?" ROSENTHAL ASKED. "THAT document Rakowski showed you?"

"Misinformation." Meredith shrugged. "He claimed he was giving us an asset, but I think he was actually trying to protect one."

It was some hours since they had parted from the Russians. Rosenthal and he were taking an excursion in a Land Cruiser borrowed from their host. Turning off the highway some miles from Haakinen's estate, they'd followed a logging road into the forest. A mile or so in they'd parked their vehicle and ventured a little way on foot. These precautions made Meredith feel silly, but not enough to dispense with them. Privacy was important now, concern about bugs entirely appropriate.

"Then what he gave you wasn't genuine?"

"In most respects it almost certainly was. That's the way you do misinformation. Ninety-eight percent of what you give is real, it's that last two percent does the damage."

Rosenthal considered.

"What was he misinforming you about?"

"The Knights of Vladimir. Specifically how he learned that they'd approached us. Since it's obvious he has a source somewhere, either in the Agency or the Knights, he's got to expect we'll be mounting a search. He was hoping to point us in the wrong direction."

"But you didn't believe him, so he didn't succeed."

"Maybe. But good deceptions usually have more than one layer, receding levels of obviousness, so to speak. By offering us Suspect A on a plate, he may hope to direct our attention to Suspect B, while his source may be someone else entirely. Suspect C perhaps, or even D." Meredith shrugged. "The only sure thing is, he doesn't trust us."

Rosenthal frowned. "Do you trust him?"

"Not as far as I can throw him." Meredith grinned. "The beauty is, I don't have to."

The beauty of what? Rosenthal wondered. Evidently he was missing something here. Talking to Meredith made him feel naive, and feeling naive had always bothered him. He, after all, had been Secretary of State. He was the one with the doctorate from Harvard.

"I still don't like it," he grumbled. "It's all very well for you and your Russian friends to talk so glibly about absence of proof and the precise semantics of 'convincingly implicated,' but when this thing happens, shit will hit the fan. People are going to get very steamed up. Congress is going to be holding inquiries. Fingers will get pointed, most of them at me. What am I going to do about that?"

"You're going to lie, I'd imagine." Meredith shrugged. "That's the essence of diplomacy, isn't it? It's not as if you've lacked practice."

"You're missing the point." Rosenthal ignored the levity. "The point is, I could go to jail."

Meredith shrugged.

"Presumably we could both go to jail."

"Maybe so. It doesn't comfort me. It doesn't in the least diminish my risk."

"We're serving our country." Meredith smiled faintly. "We're not supposed to worry about risk."

"Reasonable risk is one thing. I draw the line at hara-kiri."

Reasonable risk . . . Actually, Meredith thought, Herr Doktor Rosenthal would prefer no risk at all. He'd rather lead from behind, sit on his duff in his office in London, pontificating on global affairs and enjoying the fruits of his bygone eminence. But Rosenthal, of course, was a politician, a member of that sorry breed whose unswerving devotion to self-interest had reduced the US to the status of a second rate power. Politicians didn't take risks; risk-taking was for other people. Sometimes, Meredith thought, *most* times actually, politicians made you want to puke.

But you needed this one, so maybe it was time to stop needling him.

"Relax," he said. "You won't be tried. You won't even be suspected."

"I'd like to know by what apology for logic you manage to arrive at that comforting conclusion." Rosenthal's accent, something guttural he did with the letter r, had grown more pronounced, as it always did in moments of stress. "The foundation I happen to head gets involved in a terrorist campaign and I'm supposed to know nothing about it? I can just see people buying that."

"There's nothing the matter with my logic." In spite of their being miles from anywhere and surrounded by nothing but northern pine forest, Meredith found himself lowering his voice. "My conclusions follow just fine. You happen to have the premises screwed up. No fingers are going to point at you for one very simple reason. There isn't going to be a terrorist campaign for you or your foundation to be implicated *in.*"

"You mean nobody's going to be killed."

"I'm not saying that."

"What *are* you saying, then?"

"People are going to get killed, all right." Meredith smiled mysteriously. "But not the ones our Russian friends expect."

CHAPTER FIVE

(Moscow. July 6, 1990)

BACK IN HIS OFFICE AT YASENEVO, GENERAL RAKOWSKI SAT AT HIS DESK, surrounded by files he'd ordered up from Archive. He was pondering the problem of trust.

The problem was that one couldn't afford it.

Not in a matter as delicate as this.

That Americans would try to cheat on the agreement reached in Finland was, it seemed to him, almost axiomatic. Trust and cooperation might be rational, the interests of both parties might run nearly parallel, but after nearly fifty years of more or less reflex hostility, the impulse to treachery was likely to prove overwhelming. To rely on trust would, in the circumstances, be inexcusable folly. One would have to keep an eye on them somehow or other.

Rakowski had been checking into the means available.

The results were not reassuring. Originally he'd had two potential sources of information about CIA contacts with the Knights of Vladimir, but at the meeting in Finland he'd sacrificed one of them in an effort to protect the other, who for present purposes was better placed. The task of keeping an eye on the Americans would therefore fall entirely on the shoulders of one man, an illegal agent, based in London.

Adam Kalugin, code named Cobalt.

Early in his career, in the course of a stint as instructor at the KGB school in Kiev, Rakowski had delivered to an audience of budding case officers a lecture which, in spite of its somewhat downbeat title, "Avoid disaster, aim for second best," had won him instant, if limited, celebrity and achieved, in the KGB's instructional literature, close to the status of a classic. Citing as evidence the Bay of Pigs and other notorious intelligence foul-ups, he'd argued: a) that the majority of black operations did their instigators more harm than good; b) that the more desirable the outcome, the less likely was it to be realized in practice; and c) that conditions envisaged in the planning could almost be counted on *not* to obtain in the event. Distilling his lesson into two homely maxims—"Don't dive off a cliff into three feet of water" and "Half a loaf is a whole lot better than a poke in the eye with a burnt stick"—he'd concluded that when contemplating such operations case officers should be modest in their objectives, careful to allow for the consequences of failure, and above all mindful, in their planning, of life's nasty habit of doing the unexpected and the undependable nature of the human element.

All of which wisdom, especially the last bit, was now uncomfortably echoing in his mind. People *were* undependable; none more than those who, from a variety of more or less disreputable motives, offered themselves for employment as 'illegals.' With the average illegal, however, the problem was at least manageable; when the motivation was fear or greed, one could make educated guesses, at least, about breaking strains and sticking points. But exactly how far could one rely on an illegal when the motivation was self-hatred and revenge?

Motivation aside, as a browse through the files had disclosed, this Kalugin was ideal for the purpose. A twenty-eight-year-old Ukrainian whose family had (or had been made to seem to have) a history of dissidence and support for the Ukrainian separatist movement, he fitted perfectly in the London emigré scene. He had hardly needed, indeed, the fictitious personal history, or "legend," which his KGB masters, weaving fantasy from threads of fact, had tailored for him, and which he had since grown into till it fitted him like his skin. He had graduated from Sleeper School near the top of his class. He spoke four languages, three of them perfectly, and in intelligence tests had placed consistently in the ninety-fifth percentile. In the physical aspects of his training he'd performed with even greater distinction. A report from the instructor in unarmed combat spoke of "impressive athletic ability," and a willingness, "almost masochistic," to tolerate pain. The small arms instructor had gone even further, stating quite flatly that with a rifle Lieutenant Kalugin was "Olympic Medal material" and all round about the best natural shot that he, the instructor, had ever encountered. The reports from his instructors in tradecraft and communications had been almost as complimentary. The only dissonant voice in what was otherwise a chorus of praise had belonged to the school's consulting psychologist.

But *she* had sounded, forte, the note of caution. Describing a personality "surrounded by walls of reserve which, once penetrated, reveal low self-esteem and tendencies, so far probably unconscious, to self-destruction," she'd gone on to comment: "This officer's motivation is weak. His ideological commitment is suspect and may be outweighed by personal loyalties. In a conflict his behavior is unpredictable. I would guess the personal agenda would prevail." Elsewhere she'd added, rather intriguingly: "The subject displayed, at times, traces of a youthful idealism and a surprisingly strong sense of bourgeois morality, qualities apparently stunted by some trauma of his youth, the details of which have not so far emerged."

These reservations had not been ignored. In a handwritten minute at the foot of the memo, Kalugin's official mentor, a Major P.I. Volkov, had commented:

"Recommend polygraph testing and, if indicated, deeper probing. We are dealing, clearly, with a volcano under ice."

The recommendation had clearly been heeded. A polygraph test had been followed, almost at once, by some sessions of question and answer in preparation for which the subject had been hypnotized and dosed with pentathol. The story of youthful trauma that emerged had confirmed, beyond reasonable question, the psychologist's suspicions about motivation. It appeared that in joining the KGB Kalugin had not been prompted by ideology or love of country. His real motive had been simple and chilling: to track down a man and kill him.

A former KGB officer.

An Alexandr Zaitsev.

Rakowski remembered the name. Zaitsev had featured in one of the most damaging defections to hit the KGB in the eighties. He'd belonged, unusually for a defector, to the Second Chief Directorate (Internal Security), an arm of the KGB in which CIA interest wasn't, normally, much more than tepid. And since CIA interest in defectors expressed itself, normally, in terms of dollars, Zaitsev had attempted to jack up his value by acquiring, in exchange for a shipment of Japanese tape decks, a slew of secrets belonging to the First Chief Directorate (Foreign Intelligence). At his trial in Moscow, which was held necessarily in absentia—Zaitsev being busy at the time spilling his guts in a safe house in Virginia—it emerged that the tape decks themselves had been looted, in a kind of involuntary golden handshake, from a black market operation in which he was also involved. Convicted of racketeering as well as espionage and treason, he'd been sentenced to death on each of the charges. So far as Rakowski could recall, however, the sentence had not been carried out.

He wondered why.

There were obvious reasons, of course, why the CIA would protect its KGB defectors, just as there were obvious reasons why the KGB would kill them. But killing people was easier than protecting them, and Zaitsev could hardly have seemed to merit special care. It appeared odd that the KGB's Death to Defectors unit, which was staffed by skilled and determined assassins, had in almost eight years had no luck with Zaitsev.

He wondered if they'd really been trying.

The facts had taken some unearthing, but by then Rakowski had been sufficiently intrigued, or disturbed, to consider the effort worthwhile. And in the end, the effort had paid off. The facts, unearthed, had been revealing.

The CIA had done more or less what the circumstances had seemed to warrant. They had squeezed Zaitsev dry, then paid him off and ditched him. The Death to Defectors unit, for its part, had taken less than six months to track him down and had kept a close watch on him since. At present he was living in Geneva and working for an "import-export company" whose clents were principally Arab and whose exports, though listed on the manifests as "machinery," were principally arms and explosives. The inference to be drawn from this was clear: Zaitsev was still alive because the KGB wanted him that way.

Though all he had to go on were some comments in the personnel file and a rough coincidence of dates, Rakowski felt he could hazard a guess at the reason. Zaitsev had defected in August 1982. By late May 1983, his new identity and whereabouts were known to the KGB. On June 24, or barely one month later, the KGB had learned of Kalugin's desire to kill him. On July 4, Kalugin had been permitted to graduate from the Sleeper School together with the rest of his class. But then, for three months, he had dropped out of sight. It was not until mid-October that, enrolling in Warsaw University as a graduate exchange student, he had taken his first step down the road that would lead him eventually to exile in London.

In answer to the obvious question of what he had been doing those three months, the personnel file had little to offer. It confined itself to stating that, as of July 5, Lieutentant Kalugin had been granted an indefinite leave of absence. But the KGB, Rakowski knew, was never *that* generous with leave, especially not with newly commissioned lieutentants. On the transcript of Kalugin's last question-and-answer session there occurred, however, an interesting comment. The same Major Volkhov who'd earlier condensed the psychologist's findings into vivid metaphor had written:

"A specialized employment suggests itself here. It would deal with the problem of motivation."

This comment, read in the light of Kalugin's aptitude for violence and Zaitsev's continued presence in the land of the living, suggested, to one as familiar as Rakowski with the workings of the KGB mind, an explanation of the gap in Kalugin's official history. He'd been receiving further training, training for a mission so secret it couldn't be mentioned, even in the Sleeper School's highly secret files. There was only one kind of KGB mission *that* secret . . .

In a way, Rakowski thought, the whole thing made a lot of sense. Since the qualities demanded for success as an illegal coincided rather seldom with a willingness to live that dangerous and isolated life, one couldn't, when one found the combination, afford to be picky about motive. One controlled an illegal with whatever came to hand: by waving a stick or dangling a carrot. In Kalugin's case it clearly had been the carrot. He'd been given the mission of executing Zaitsev. Or rather—since a carrot, once eaten, can no longer function properly as a carrot—he had been *promised* that mission.

If this was true—and Rakowski would have bet his general's stars it was—Kalugin was serving two masters. His private agenda, moreover, would always take priority over anything Rakowski might want. He was, in other words, about the last person one should think of placing in a key role in *any* operation, let alone one where so much was at stake.

The problem was, one didn't have a choice.

"Don't dive off a cliff into three feet of water." The worst kind of fool, in Rakowski's view, was the one who ignored his own sensible advice. The fact that one didn't have a choice didn't mean, did it?, that one couldn't minimize the risk. If Kalugin was both indispensable and undependable, what one had to do was limit the consequence of failure. Make the water deeper. Muddier at least.

But in practical terms, what did this mean?

What it meant, for a start, was putting a wall between oneself and trouble. When the Knights of Vladimir started their terrorist campaign, there must be no evidence on file that the KGB or General Rakowski had known it was planned and could have stopped it. In the short run this Kalugin must therefore be isolated, detached from the KGB establishment in London. He must continue to observe the activities of the Knights of Vladimir, but his reports must be kept from general circulation. Above all, there must be no traceable connection between him and General Rakowski.

And in the long run?

In the long run, Rakowski thought, since only principals could be permitted to know the scope and purpose of this operation, it meant that one had to concur, regretfully, with that Colonel Primakov, whose neatly handwritten comment had closed out Kalugin's Sleeper School file:

"A useful weapon, but of limited life."

BOOK II
(July 9 to July 23, 1990)

CHAPTER SIX

(London. July 9, 1990)

KALUGIN LEFT HAMPSTEAD AT NINE-THIRTY. BY TEN HE WAS IN Highgate. There, after making some calls from a box outside Highgate Station and extracting, from between the pages of the A to M directory, a slip of paper someone had left for him there, he took a bus for Swiss Cottage and then changed to another for Notting Hill. At Notting Hill he paused to eat breakfast in a Cypriot café whose owner, Costakis, was friendly, or indifferent, at least, to Kalugin's odd comings and goings. For fifteen minutes or so Kalugin sat at a table by the window, consuming part of a stale filo pastry and pretending to read the morning paper while in actuality watching the street. Then he exited, by way of the kitchen, through the service entrance to an alley at the rear. Continuing his journey by Underground, he reached Aldgate at eleven thirty-seven. The contact was set for eleven fifty-five, the morning was pleasant, and the distance not very great. By now he'd had enough of public transportation. He would walk.

Making his way down Aldgate to Tower Hill, he employed the standard maneuvers for detecting surveillance. It was not that he expected to find it, simply that checking, like so much else in his life, was a habit. And habits, *good* habits, as his teachers at the Sleeper School had stressed, could save your life. So he varied his pace, crossed and recrossed the street, entered shops to browse for a moment, paused to check reflections in windows, seldom seeming to look around and never behind, but scanning, always, for irregularities in the flow of traffic, for dawdling vehicles or recurring faces, anything whose course was leisurely, erratic, or suspiciously parallel to his own. He found nothing. He had never found anything. He was more or less convinced he never would. Events in Prague had seen to that, in Prague, Warsaw, Budapest, Berlin. The Cold War, it was starting to be clear, was over. History had spoken and pronounced him redundant. And all his good habits, painfully cultivated instincts for survival, were nothing more than post mortem reflex; like the twitchings of a snake—it said something about his attitude to his work, perhaps, that his mind should turn up exactly *this* image—after the head has been cut off.

He wondered what Zebo could want with this contact.

He got to the Tower eight minutes early. The weather, low clouds threatening to turn into drizzle, had discouraged most of the tourists. The courtyards and quadrangles were almost empty. No line, today, for admission to the Armory, not much of one for the crown jewels. Beefeaters, wrapped in their cloaks, shivered in arches and doorways. Even the ravens looked damp and discouraged.

Zebo would be late. It was part of the procedure. Since he ran the greater risk of attracting hostile attention, it had to be his option to abort. But Kalugin was tired of always waiting, bored with always looking at his watch. He resented, too, the need to be always pretending, the pantomime he was forced to put on for spectators whose existence was probably imaginary. He spent too much time, it often struck him, watching his life through someone else's eyes.

So afterward, when he asked himself why this time he'd varied the pattern, the only answer he could find was impulse; it just came to him that this time *Zebo* could wait. He knew it was a breach of procedure, also, in theory, a serious risk. Zebo had diplomatic cover, was known to British and American security. He was therefore suspected, as were all Soviet diplomats, of actually belonging to the KGB. If he happened to be under surveillance at the time the contact was made, then he, Kalugin, would be noticed, maybe blown. But the fact was that Zebo *wouldn't* be under surveillance. For one thing, surveillance was labor intensive; it took a minimum of four vehicles, eight people, to keep track of even one errant diplomat in the labyrinth of Central London. Besides, Kalugin thought, the Cold War was over. Nobody cared anymore.

His watch now showed eleven-fifty. That gave him five, at most ten, minutes. He made his way to the Armory. Inside, ignoring the displays of weaponry, he climbed the spiral stairway to St. Stephen's Chapel whose embrasures, commanding a view to the southwest, looked down on the redbrick Tudor building. It was there, according to Zebo, that Sir Walter Raleigh had spent eighteen years in prison.

And it was there, according to the instructions left between the pages of the A to M directory in the phone box near Highgate Station, that the contact was scheduled to take place. Shortly after twelve Zebo would show up. Failing to find Kalugin, he'd wait exactly five minutes. What he'd do afterward was anyone's guess. He'd be trapped, Kalugin thought, in a difficult conflict of instincts. Procedure demanded orderly and speedy withdrawal, but Zebo, though a stickler for procedure, was more than anything a mother hen. It would be interesting to see what he'd do here, with his agent, Cobalt, missing, maybe taken. Kalugin guessed he'd hang around for a while, make an anxious reconnaisance of the neighborhood perhaps, then post himself discreetly near the exit. One would leave him to sweat a bit, first, then find some way of discreetly making contact: bump into him as if by accident, perhaps, or plant oneself on a bench along his way. He'd be angry, but not for long.

Zebo, thank God, had a sense of humor.

Zebo showed up three minutes after twelve. The stooped, Burberry-clad figure, hands in pockets, shoulders hunched against the damp, emerged from the archway at the quadrangle's southwest corner, paused for a moment to survey the surroundings, then continued, with a distinctive loping walk, in the direction of the Raleigh Apartments.

Kalugin watched him enter. He hadn't hesitated before proceeding, so presumably he felt that he wasn't being tailed. Still, it was always best to make sure. Kalugin lingered for a while at the embrasure, watched the archway for another half minute before making his way down through the main exhibit, past the suits of armor in their glass cases, to the exit on the north side of the tower. Outside, half circling the building, he stationed himself on a bench at the southeast corner. From here he could watch both the archway and the apartments. To get here from the embrasure, he figured, had taken him slightly longer than two minutes. In somewhat less than three minutes, therefore, Zebo would reappear.

A minute passed.

Nobody came through the archway. Nobody entered or left the Apartments. This didn't surprise Kalugin much. The Apartments were darkly furnished, poorly lit, even on fine days not much of a tourist attraction. Zebo, of course, had chosen them for this reason. Right now he seemed to be their only visitor. It was easy to imagine him, tense and impatient (his lips pursed in a line of disapproval, eyebrows doing their dance of irritation), simulating, for the benefit of spectators, an interest in Jacobean antiques. The thought of it made Kalugin grin. He hoped Zebo was enjoying his wait.

Kalugin killed time, himself, trying not to seem to be waiting, though on reflection he wasn't sure why. Another conditioned reflex perhaps? It was testament to the effectiveness of his training, at least, that having broken a major rule, he continued to observe the minor ones: to watch the exits, moving only his eyes in a series of quick sidelong glances, and refrain, meanwhile, from looking at his watch. When he did, at last, permit himself to check, he found that eight minutes had gone by.

Eight minutes?

What the hell was Zebo *doing* in there?

And what should *he* do? Follow procedure. But here procedure offered no help. Procedure, not surprisingly, had nothing to say about what to do if you *breached* procedure. Instinct suggested leaving, and at once; if Zebo was in trouble, it was Zebo's problem; getting involved would probably not help. On the other hand, Zebo was a friend and a colleague; loyalty prohibited walking away. And what if Zebo was *not* in trouble? It would be embarrassing to have to tell him he'd wasted the better part of a morning because he, Kalugin, had felt like playing games. His sense of humor was not *that* good.

Kalugin let another minute pass. Maybe Zebo, spotting him somehow, was playing some kind of game of his own. He'd exited, perhaps, while Kalugin was moving from the Armory, and was watching him from somewhere, letting *him* do the sweating. Or maybe . . . Or maybe nothing, Kalugin told himself sternly. One could sit here or-maybeing all day. There was one sure-fire way to find out what had happened: go in and see for oneself.

Having checked to make sure there was no one behind him, he crossed the courtyard, ducked into the arched doorway.

A staircase led to the Apartments; two rooms connected by a narrow double doorway. In the first, Sir Walter had spent his waking hours. A large open fireplace was flanked by stools and benches. Against one wall stood a wooden dresser. Opposite was a heavy oak table, laid for a meal with dishes and goblets.

There was nobody in it. No sign of Zebo.

Kalugin paused. Perhaps because he was listening so intently, the place now struck him as unnaturally still. No movement from the adjoining room, no sound but the faint hiss and sigh of his breathing. He held his breath. Still nothing. But maybe Zebo was listening, too, hiding in there, holding *his* breath. He had heard Kalugin enter, perhaps, and was waiting to see who it was.

If so, he was keeping amazingly quiet.

Kalugin wasn't ever sure exactly what it was told him something was wrong. Several things, probably—anxiety, silence, guilt at having broken, for no good reason, rules established for his and Zebo's safety—and none of them entailed, by any normal logic, the alarming conclusions instinct now urged. But though reason might tell itself anxiety was groundless, anxiety spoke to something deeper. Something, some animal sense kept warning him, *had* happened to Zebo. Someone might be in the next room right now, waiting to see who Zebo had been waiting for.

He needed to get out of here.

Now.

He resisted the impulse to bolt, however. He resisted, too, a temptation to forget the other room, simply retreat the same way he'd come in. If anyone was watching, it would look suspicious. And looking suspicious, now more than ever, ranked high on his list of things to avoid. Besides, he thought, retreating would be giving in to fear. Once you started that, it was difficult to stop. He had come to check for Zebo, and check he would.

But first he must take stock of the situation. He had no assets, no weapons but his hands. And surprise, he thought. Surprise to pre-empt the surprise that might well be waiting beyond the doorway. He must make the trap, if there was a trap, spring itself prematurely. If by doing so he won half a second's edge, his hands could take care of the rest.

Where, he asked himself, would *he* lie in wait?

Behind the door. The outer wall was to the left; danger would have to come from the right. Steadying himself for a moment, he marched heavily up to the double doorway, footsteps thudding on the floorboards.

Between the two sets of doors was a space of roughly two feet. When he reached it he paused for a beat, hoping the sudden break in rhythm would throw off the timing of an attacker. Then he sprang forward and to the left, twisting in midair so he landed with his back to the wall. His momentum carried him well into the room, perfectly in balance and poised for action, eyes scanning swiftly from right to left.

There was no movement, no sound.

Nobody was there.

So much for instinct. Embarrassed now, grateful nobody had witnessed his abortive Kung Fu imitation, he took a more leisurely look around. To the left, under the window, was a writing table, and next to it a chair. On the far wall, a wooden crucifix. Beneath it, a prayer desk, Bible open on the lectern. Against the right-hand wall was a canopied four-poster, the curtains surrounding it half open.

It was then he saw that there *was* someone here. On the bed, or *half* on it, was a body. It was sprawled across the bed from the far side, partly kneeling, partly lying, arms thrown forward in a posture of supplication. At first glance it could almost have seemed to be praying, but Kalugin, coming closer, could see enough to recognize the face. He could see also, above and a little forward from the ear, bluish round the edges and leaking blood in a thin dark trickle, what he recognized at once as the entry wound of a bullet.

For a moment he was too shocked to feel. Then he was seized by a surge of anger. This was murder, plain and ugly; and not just vicious, utterly senseless, a flagrant breach of all accepted rules. Zebo was a diplomat, off limits to violence. If you wanted rid of him, you didn't kill him, you sent his embassy a politely worded note giving him forty-eight hours to pack and get out of the country. Killing, even on those very rare occasions when diplomatic courtesies broke down, was reserved for people like himself, illegals. And nowadays not even for them. The Cold War was over, wasn't it?

What was there left worth killing for?

But he didn't have time to think about that. The next few minutes could be crucial. What he did now could determine his future. He needed to act fast and act correctly.

Zebo had clearly been murdered. Presumably for some reason connected with his job, and presumably by a rival intelligence service, probably the Americans or British. Someone must have tailed him then. While he, Kalugin, had been leaving the Armory, someone must have come here, shot Zebo, and left. There were other possible scenarios, granted, but none that seemed to make as much sense. It was therefore possible, and even likely, that the killer was still hanging around. Since he'd managed to tail Zebo to the Tower, he'd no doubt deduced, from Zebo's efforts to avoid being tailed, that Zebo was planning a contact. Probably he was lurking somewhere now, hoping to identify that contact.

The important thing was not to let him.

With more time to think Kalugin might have questioned the assumptions that guided his actions. Unfortunately, there wasn't more time. Someone might come in at any moment. In any case, he'd been here too long already. He had to do something. He had to do it now.

Roland Meigs had obtained his position as a Beefeater at the Tower of London in reward for long and undistinguished service as a sergeant in the Grenadier Guards. His assets were: a) an imposing physical presence, and b) the kind of face people tended to trust. His liability was a certain rigidity of mind. No one had ever accused him of being quick. His superior officers, searching to convey the exact combination of soldierly qualities he offered, usually hit on some such word as "solid," the less charitable adding t before the o. When told of Meigs's actions on discovering the body, Vance Ackerman, the CIA's station chief in London, was considerably less charitable still. It was typical of his dumbass luck, he fumed, that the first representative of authority on the scene should be "some bozo in fancy dress who can't walk and chew gum at the same time."

Ackerman was overreacting. In fact, Meigs's account was concise and accurate, and his description of the man who'd reported a corpse in the Apartments was definite and reasonably detailed, albeit not very useful, since as Meigs himself conceded, he might not recognize him if he saw him again. The man was of medium height and stocky build, with medium-length light-brown hair, a square face, and rather high cheekbones. He'd been wearing a tan raincoat, and surprisingly —in view of the rain, Meigs acknowledged, it had struck *him* as odd at the time—very dark sunglasses, aviator-style. This man, Meigs said, had emerged from the Apartments, "looking worried," and made his way "hastily" to the quadrangle's southwest corner where Meigs himself had been sheltering in the archway. There seemed to be an emergency, he'd said. Someone had passed out in the Raleigh Apartments, possibly from a heart attack or stroke. Meigs should go and investigate, he'd said; *he* would phone for a doctor.

Meigs had therefore gone to investigate.

Police and security officers to whom this story was told had tended, at this point, to roll their eyes. Didn't Meigs know, they'd demanded, that in any murder investigation, the person discovering the body was always high on the list of suspects? To this Meigs had replied, with some justice, that he hadn't known it *was* a murder investigation. It was only after he'd arrived at the Apartments and, examining the body, seen the bullet wound that he'd been in a position to draw conclusions. But by then, of course, it had been too late. No one, it turned out, had called a doctor. And the man in the raincoat and sunglasses had vanished.

CHAPTER SEVEN

(London. July 10, 1990)

"GRYAZIN, ANATOLI . . ." ACKERMAN SHOWED PICKETT HIS COPY OF the *Times,* folded to display the front-page headline. "What can you tell me, just off the top of your head, about this Comrade Gryazin, Anatoli?"

In answer Pickett offered him the file. RUSSIAN DIPLOMAT MURDERED, the placard displayed at the newsstand near the Green Park Underground had announced in large black letters, prompting him to buy a morning paper. When he'd learned on entering the embassy, therefore, that the chief of station wanted to see him "on arrival" he'd known immediately why. His response to Ackerman's summons, therefore, had been delayed by a trip to the Registry, ten minutes to scan the file, and fifteen more on the phone to various colleagues. "Off the top of your head" was a figure of speech. Ackerman expected you to have done your homework.

"He was KGB," Pickett said. "We don't have absolute confirmation, but the career pattern fits. For one thing he switched tracks too often. In Brussels, where he was posted from '80 to '84, he was listed as 'second secretary, political.' In Bern it was 'cultural attaché.' Here he was part of Trade Delegation. Not very active promoting trade, however. Usually he was out of the office somewhere. Sightseeing."

Ackerman, ignoring the proffered file, eyed him for a moment without speaking. Pickett returned the stare. Ackerman, MIT and Stanford, was reputed to be brilliant, passing through London on his way to the top. To Pickett's taste, however, the brilliance was a tad self-conscious. In the Navy, where his own intelligence career had started, MIT and Stanford hadn't cut a whole lot of ice.

"Passing lightly over the obvious," Ackerman said, "what can you offer on the rather more interesting questions of who'd want to hit this Comrade Gryazin and why?"

Pickett shrugged. "I can tell you who it *wasn't*. It wasn't a mugger and it wasn't a jealous husband. The wallet was found on the body intact, and Gryazin was shot at very close range with a silenced .22 automatic. That would suggest a professional hit."

"I know that," Ackerman said. "The question is *which* professionals?"

"There are several possibilities. For a start . . ." Pickett hesitated. "I'm assuming, naturally, that it wasn't us?"

Ackerman took a puff at his corona, grimaced, flapped his hand to wave away the smoke. He smoked six to eight of them a day—Romeo y Julietas, Havanas, purchased each morning from the humidor at Dunhill's—and always acted as if they made him sick. Since they sold for several dollars apiece, Ackerman's smoking habit, Pickett had often thought, looked like one hellishly expensive affectation.

"Assuming because I'm asking?"

"Passing lightly over the obvious." Pickett nodded. "Though that could be what you *wanted* me to assume."

Ackerman regarded him without expression. He had heavy features, a permanent five o'clock shadow, and, apart from a certain fastidiousness in speech, the manners and demeanor of a pit bull. But the belligerence, Pickett thought, was almost certainly assumed for effect. Ackerman might behave like a pit bull; he thought like a fox.

"The Cold War is over," Ackerman said.

Pickett shrugged. "So we're always being asked to believe."

"Well, in this instance, believe it. If by 'us' you mean personnel controlled by this station, it wasn't." Ackerman frowned. "Could it have been the Brits?"

"I doubt it." Pickett shook his head. "For one thing, it's not their style. For another, they'd have dropped us a hint. When I talked with our counterparts across the river, they seemed baffled. Almost as baffled as us."

"Almost?"

"Well they had the autopsy and ballistics reports, and a deposition from that Beefeater guy who found the body. They could offer theories, but as to support . . ." Pickett smiled faintly. "Their Theory Number One was it could have been us."

"Which of course you denied."

"Of course," Pickett said. "Citing our obvious lack of motive."

"Or our lack of obvious motive."

"That, too," Pickett said. "And our long-established policy of not making hits on the turf of a friendly service without first clearing said hits with the friendly service in question. And of course they believed me. I mean, why would I ask if I already knew? As by the same reasoning, why would they?"

"As by the same reasoning, perhaps, why would I?"

"Correct." Pickett's voice was dry as chalk. "If you can't trust your own side, who *can* you trust?"

"There's a difference." Suddenly and surprisingly, Ackerman grinned. "*I'm* on your side, they're just allies. What was their Theory Number Two?"

"The emigré mafia. Some of those exiled Ukrainians or Balts. Wannabe freedom fighters getting in a bit of practice. The Knights of Vladimir, for instance."

"The Knights of Vladimir?" Ackerman stared. "Those idiots who asked us for half a million dollars to help them start a war in the Ukraine?"

"Those idiots." Pickett nodded.

"But those guys are amateurs. This was professional work."

"The Brits didn't mention them specifically. I was using them mostly as an example. As to professional . . ." Pickett shrugged. "Anyone can hire help."

"I don't buy it," Ackerman said. "For one thing, where's the motive?"

"I don't buy it, either. But where's *anyone's* motive? It's the sixty-four-dollar question, isn't it? If we knew why, we'd know who." Pickett paused. "The Brits' other theory was the KGB did it."

"The KGB? Why would they want to hit one of their own?"

"You tell me." Pickett shrugged. "Maybe they thought he was fixing to defect. The reasoning rests on circumstances mostly: What was a member of the Soviet Trade Delegation *doing* at the Tower at a time when he should have been working? Sightseeing? The Brits don't think so. They think he *was* working. They think he was making contact with an agent. And if so, they figure, who more likely to have killed him than the agent he was making contact with?"

"This guy in the raincoat and shades, in fact."

"Maybe. Though *his* behavior seems to cut both ways. If he did it, why report it? If he didn't do it, why disappear? The cops have broadcast the usual appeal, asking Mr. Raincoat and Shades to come forward, but I don't think they're holding their breath."

"Intelligent of them." Ackerman thought for a moment. "I'll lay you odds Raincoat and Shades didn't do it."

"Because he reported it?" Pickett looked skeptical. "He could have been hoping to divert police suspicion."

"Only if he was totally moronic." Ackerman rolled his eyes. "If you want to divert police suspicion, you don't draw their attention by reporting the body, then ensure you keep it by promptly disappearing. I think he was trying to divert suspicion all right, but not the suspicion of the police."

"If not theirs, then whose?"

"Think for a moment," Ackerman said. "Suppose, for example, you're one of Gryazin's assets. You show up at a contact to find Gryazin shot. You have to figure that whoever shot him must have known who he was and what he was up to. This killer, therefore, may be monitoring the scene, hoping to identify Gryazin's contact. And that contact is, of course, you. It's a formula for instant paranoia: how the fuck do you protect your cover? If you go to the cops, you invite their unwelcome attentions. If you *don't,* on the other hand, you can only have one motive; you might as well declare yourself to the killer." He paused. "So what do you do?"

"You attempt to avert the killer's suspicions by noisily raising the alarm, then you quietly disappear so the cops can't ask awkward questions? It's a theory." Pickett paused. "But open to obvious objections, I'd have thought. If the killer's suspicions *were* averted, they wouldn't have been averted very long. The moment he opens his morning paper, he knows Raincoat and Shades is Gryazin's contact."

"Granted. But by that time, unfortunately, Raincoat and Shades has vanished into the woodwork. I'm not claiming it's foolproof," Ackerman said. "I'm proposing it as the kind of scheme a desperate man might improvise on the spur of the moment."

Only a *very* desperate man, Pickett thought.

"Not that it helps at all," Ackerman continued. "It maybe suggests who didn't do it; we want to know who *did."* He paused. "What about the Soviets? How are they reacting?"

"About as you'd expect. Their ambassador stormed over to Downing Street to lodge an outraged protest. The Soviet press, on the other hand, is treating the hit as a garden variety mugging. An indication of the lawlessness to be found in this stronghold of imperialism, etc., etc., that a diplomat can be murdered with impunity within a stone's throw of the ultimate symbol of the British state's authority, etc., etc."

Ackerman sighed.

"Anything else to go on?"

Pickett shook his head. "The bottom line is that, so far, none of it makes any sense."

Ackerman frowned. "I don't like things that don't make sense."

"Me, neither." Pickett shrugged.

"So get on it," Ackerman snapped. "Stay close to the Brits. Keep your ear to the ground. And check out the emigré groups. See who's been hiring professional help."

"I will." Pickett nodded. "But it may not do any good. After all, ignorance is a condition of life."

"Fuck ignorance," Ackerman said. "A Russian got murdered on my turf. Langley's going to be asking questions. I want to know what's going on."

CHAPTER EIGHT

(London. July 15, 1990)

ACCORDING TO THE TWIN OBSERVATORY CLOCKS, WHEN BENKO AND Kalugin reached the observatory entrance it was three seconds short of noon, Greenwich Mean Time. It occurred to Kalugin that he had never been quite so unarguably on time. These observatory clocks were master clocks, the clocks by which the other clocks were set. Or they had been at one time, at least. He seemed to recall reading somewhere that for time as for so much else authority had moved across the ocean. These Greenwich clocks had been forced to abdicate, cede their power to some gadget in America, which in some way linked time to radioactive decay. If so, this was only as it should be, he thought. The master clock should be in America. Time should be linked to radioactive decay.

He wondered whether there was any other profession in which people watched time so closely and wasted it so much.

Benko said, "That's him over there."

Kalugin turned. A man was walking toward them. Half a head taller than Kalugin, but slighter, he had short blond hair, a smooth, sharp-featured face, and the kind of suntan that here in England had to have come out of a bottle. The suit was diplomatic gray, the shoes loafers, the shirt a button-down white oxford cotton, the tie paisley. The eyes, an indeterminate blue-green, were busy looking him, Kalugin, over.

"Randall Pickett." The man held out a hand. "And you would be . . . ?"

"Kalugin. Adam Kalugin from Kiev." Benko preempted Kalugin's response. *"Originally* from Kiev, that is. He came over in '81 from Warsaw. Got too active in support of Solidarity and attracted the attention of the KGB."

"Too active?" Pickett queried. "Too active how?"

"I threw things." Kalugin grasped the proffered hand, shook it perfunctorily, released. He felt a spasm of irritation, wished once again that Benko hadn't insisted on his coming to this meeting. Introduce me by all means, he thought; you don't have to give him my life history.

"What kinds of things? Bottles? Rocks? Bombs?"

"Not bombs." Kalugin shook his head. "No one in Warsaw at the time was throwing bombs."

"How did you happen to be in Warsaw?"

Pickett was regarding him with grave attention. His questions could have been harmless, the product of that casual personal curiosity which sometimes passed, among Americans newly met, for good manners. With CIA men, on the other hand, curiosity was never casual, seldom harmless.

"I was at the university. An exchange student."

"That's interesting. That you got into the exchange program, I mean. I'd have thought that studies abroad, even in Poland, were reserved for the politically reliable."

"I *was* reliable so far as they knew. One learns to conceal one's convictions." Kalugin paused. This conversation was starting to sound like a grilling. His answers struck him as grudging, defensive. It might be good to seem more forthcoming. "I wasn't planning to get involved. The excitement was catching. I got swept up."

"Completely swept up, by the sound." Pickett lifted an eyebrow. "A Ukrainian throwing rocks for *Poland?*"

"My father was half Polish." Kalugin shrugged. "And wasn't it you Americans who used to say that freedom is indivisible?"

"Did we?" Pickett grinned. "Sounds like a Cold War slogan to me. It must have been before my time."

Silence.

Benko said, "It's amazing, isn't it?"

"What is?" Pickett turned to him.

"These English . . ." Benko's sweeping gesture embraced the Observatory, the park below, the classical facade of Queen Anne's Hospital, the distant symmetry of the Naval College. "Did you know the meridian runs through here? The line that separates east from west on every working map in the world runs right through the middle of this building."

"I think I did." Pickett nodded. "I guess I must have learned it in the Navy. But it's got to run through somewhere, why not here? I'll be frank," he added. "I don't find the Observatory so amazing. I'd expected something bigger."

"But that's my point," Benko insisted. "This modest brick building, the miniature telescope, the clocks, the little white line . . . they assert not only the English passion for order, but English authority over order's very foundations, time and space. What amazes me is that they say these things without ever raising their voices. In America," he smiled nastily, "this would be Disneyland."

"You figure you know America that well?" Pickett's voice acquired an edge.

"I've been there." Benko shrugged.

"Yeah? Well then, what you *don't* know are the English. They're not modest. If they don't raise their voices, it's because they think they don't have to."

Benko smiled. "Why don't we sit? Over there on the grass. We can look at the view, enjoy the sunshine, watch the English not raising their voices."

He walked away. Pickett and Kalugin followed. They flopped down at a spot on the brow of the hill just above where the slope was steepest. As it had been for several days, the weather today was magnificent. No trace of the drizzle that had shrouded London, or so it seemed to Kalugin, for most of the month of June. The sky was hazy, shimmering with heat. The air smelled faintly of roses and strongly of freshly cut grass. Below, beyond the slope, the park was dotted with the English making the most of a rare opportunity. Delicate-skinned girls in skimpy bikinis recklessly courted second-degree sunburns. Kids with dogs chased balls or Frisbees. Half-clothed lovers, tangles of arms and legs, wrestled on blankets in none too secluded spots. Women pushed strollers along the graveled paths, pausing to chat and compare offspring. Farther down, on a stretch of level ground, a handful of men with bare white chests, their trousers rolled up and handkerchiefs knotted round their heads, were playing some game with a bat and ball which, to judge from its indolent, aimless character, was almost certainly cricket. There was no one in earshot, but to the left a boy and a girl, stretched out on the grass with their arms above their heads, were rolling themselves like logs down the slope. At the foot they tried to stand. They staggered about drunkenly for a moment, then collapsed and lay on their backs, giggling. Perhaps it was the smell of hay, perhaps the wholehearted enjoyment of the rollers, but something in the scene reminded Kalugin of home, of picnics in the country outside Kiev: Katya reading Malory to him in English, switching occasionally into Russian to comment on the characters and action; he lying on his back in the grass, staring up into blue eternity, half listening to Katya and half dreaming. He felt a wave of homesickness, mingled with self-disgust. What was he doing here? he wondered. What did he have in common with these clowns?

Then he remembered Zebo and he knew what he had in common. Everything.

"I'll tell you something else," Pickett said. "The English talk softly, but who's listening any more? Our maps still use their meridian, but they don't show a whole lot of red. Two world wars took care of that. Pax Britannica is ancient history."

"We know." Benko nodded. "The time for speaking softly is over. Which brings us the purpose of this meeting. Are you willing to help us raise our voices?"

Kalugin glanced at Pickett. To anyone except Benko, it was obvious what the answer must be. He expected some show of awkwardness, however, an attempt perhaps to soften the blow. But Pickett didn't beat about the bush.

"If you mean will we give you half a million dollars, help you murder a bunch of people, the answer is what I told you it would be . . . No."

"I see," Benko said stiffly.

"Look," Pickett said. "Your plan makes no kind of sense. You'd be asking to to be killed."

"We are willing to be killed."

"Maybe so." Pickett paused. "I'm going to be frank. Helping you destabilize the Ukraine is inconsistent with any current, or currently conceivable, goal of United States foreign policy."

"Inconsistent?" Benko stared in disbelief. "The establishment of an independent, non-Communist Ukraine republic is inconsistent with any currently conceivable aim of US foreign policy?"

"Let's be real," Pickett sighed. "You're not *going* to establish an independent Ukraine. The most you'll achieve is a few dead bodies. Where does that get you?"

"It gets us in the headlines," Benko said. "It gets us on the TV nightly news. Take the Palestinians, for example. When they spoke softly, nobody listened. People made sympathetic noises, did nothing. Then the Palestinians raised their voices. There were kidnappings, killings, jetliners exploding in midair. And suddenly Arafat was invited to Geneva. And one of these days—in five years or ten or however long it takes—one of these days Palestine will be liberated. Just as one of these days the Ukraine will be free."

Silence.

"And what about you?" Pickett asked Kalugin. "What do *you* think?"

Kalugin shrugged. "I think it doesn't matter what I think. History will happen, with or without my permission . . ." He paused. Maybe he was being too detached. His mission, after all, was to get close to Benko; it might be wise to offer him support. But six days had gone by now since Zebo's murder and still no word from his KGB masters. It wasn't clear that the mission was still on. He looked over at Benko, tossed him a bone of consolation. "One of these days the Ukraine will be free."

"But why not by peaceful methods?" Pickett asked. "Negotiated secession. Reform of the system from within. The Russian empire seems about to break up on its own. I doubt it needs any help from you."

"Negotiations," Benko sneered. "Cutting some kind of phony deal with Moscow. Limited autonomy in economic matters, the freedom to fly our own flag. But limited freedom is not freedom. You do not *bargain* for your right to exist, you seize it." He paused. "We intend to seize it. If we have to, we will die in the process. If we have to, we will kill."

Silence.

"And *have* you ever?" Pickett asked softly. "Killed anyone, that is."

Benko, avoiding Pickett's gaze, glanced uneasily at Kalugin. "Not personally."

"Not *personally?* What does that mean? That you've given the order but never actually pulled the trigger? Or do you *know* someone who's done it? Maybe you think you can *imagine* what it's like?"

Benko shrugged. "I think we can all imagine."

"Can we?" Pickett's sarcasm was icy. He shook his head. "If you *could,* you wouldn't be so eager."

He turned abruptly to Kalugin.

"And you, Mister Freedom-is-Indivisible, can *you* imagine it?"

He seemed angry. This surprised Kalugin. True, Benko's scheme was criminally frivolous, but the CIA, surely, had never objected to that.

"If you're going to do it, you don't need to imagine. Likewise if you're not going to do it. Imagining just confuses what needs to be kept clear." Kalugin paused. "We're speaking of trash . . . Communist parasites, KGB torturers, thugs. People who've forfeited their right to live. Why waste sympathy on such people?"

It was the right note to strike, he thought—ruthlessness of the armchair terrorist, callousness of the theorist who has never drawn blood—but he had the impression, briefly, of having startled Pickett. It was nothing pronounced, just a momentary blankness of expression, a flick of the eyes in Benko's direction, a hesitation in which, perhaps, information was registered and processed.

Pickett shrugged. "This is all academic. The decision has been made, and not by me. No point arguing about it." He paused for a moment, turned to Benko. "Speaking of murders and KGB trash, can you guys shed light on this Gryazin?"

"Gryazin?"

"The Russian murdered at the Tower of London. You must have read about it. The newspapers called him a diplomat"—Pickett turned his gaze on Kalugin—"but obviously he was KGB."

"Obviously?" Kalugin queried.

"Well, he must have done something to get himself murdered. Presumably it wasn't diplomacy." Pickett smiled faintly. "It occurred to us that you guys—the Knights of Vladimir, that is—might have some suggestions to offer."

"Why us?" Benko demanded.

"No special reason. Unless"—Pickett shrugged—"you claim to be willing to kill. You could have been getting in some practice."

"We *are* willing to kill," Benko said coldly. "We are not willing to kill *senselessly.*"

Pickett met the stare without blinking. "There's room for two opinions about that."

Silence. It was time to change the subject, Kalugin thought.

"With regard to the matter of assistance," he asked. "The decision is final? There's no chance of review? In Washington, maybe, or Langley?"

"No chance." Pickett shook his head. "This is *Washington's* policy. Also Langley's."

"Then, as you say, discussion is pointless." Kalugin got to his feet. He turned to Benko. "They will not help us. We must help ourselves."

CHAPTER NINE

(London. July 16, 1990)

"KALUGIN?" ACKERMAN ASKED. "UKRAINIAN?"

"Considers himself." Pickett nodded. "His mother was Ukrainian. The father, apparently, was half Polish. He was studying in Warsaw in '81, defected from there. Had to, he claims. Got too active on behalf of Solidarity."

"Claims?" Ackerman raised an eyebrow. "Meaning you don't believe him?"

"Meaning I suspend judgment," Pickett said. "He seemed to be giving off odd vibes is all."

"Odd vibes? Explain."

Pickett hesitated. "It's intuition mostly."

"Nothing the matter with intuition," Ackerman grunted. "It's not black magic, at any rate. Concealed induction, more like. Reasoning based on observation recorded unconsciously, therefore not subject to conscious analysis. Like all reasoning subject to error, of course. What kind of odd vibes?"

"It's hard to pin down." Pickett considered. "Normally, people like to talk about themselves. I got the impression he didn't. He answered my questions, but without volunteering much . . . as if he found them intrusive."

"Could be he did." Ackerman shrugged. "Europeans are more private than we are. If they think you're interrogating, they tend to clam up. What else?"

Pickett suppressed a sigh. This was Ackerman at his worst: admitting that intuition was essentially nonrational, but pissing all over yours for not being grounded in evidence and logic. In the process, moreover, managing to imply that you'd screwed up.

"There was something about his attitude. Not indifferent, exactly, but detached. As if the conversation didn't really concern him."

"Acted superior, then? Above it all?"

"Kind of . . . like a competent actor"—Pickett surprised himself with the image—"reading for a part he didn't really want."

"A competent actor . . ." Ackerman thought about this. "But if he was competent he'd hardly have conveyed that impression, would he?"

Pickett shrugged. "Maybe not. But you know how it is with actors sometimes; they get everything right except the eyes. This Kalugin's performance—if it was a performance—hung together fine; it just seemed to lack that last ounce of conviction."

Ackerman considered. "Intelligent, would you say?"

"I would say very." Pickett nodded. "Maybe *that* was what bothered me. I had the feeling he was *too* intelligent to be hanging out with Benko and those clowns."

Ackerman didn't respond immediately. Instead he reached for one of the half dozen aluminum tubes that he'd lined up like missiles on the desk in front of him. There followed what his secretary, a woman of wit who'd spent time in Japan, referred to as "the tobacco ceremony," a ritual of sniffing, twiddling, listening, clipping, and lighting which occupied the best part of five minutes, and which nothing—least of all a discussion with Pickett—could be allowed to interrupt.

"But if not with them, then with whom?" Ackerman puffed, grimaced, puffed again. "Dzerzhinski Street? First Chief Directorate, perhaps?"

"Could be." Pickett paused. "He certainly fitted the description."

"Description?" Ackerman looked blank.

"Raincoat and Shades," Pickett said. "The guy who reported finding Gryazin in the Tower and who disappeared immediately thereafter. Medium height, stocky, short brown hair, high cheekbones. Characteristics he shares, of course"—he forestalled the predictable zinger—"with at least a quarter of the male population of London. But a coincidence worth noting, isn't it? Gryazin gets hit, perhaps by one of his own agents. You tell me to ask round the emigré groups, and what do I find? A newly inducted Knight of Vladimir noticeably resistant to personal questions and not quite presenting the Wannabe terrorist profile."

And this was *your* idea, Mister Ackerman, he thought; so piss on it all you want.

Ackerman inspected the tip of his cigar. "Overstating, aren't you?"

Pickett nodded. "That's the trouble with intuition. To make it sound reasonable you have to overstate it."

"Point taken." Surprisingly, Ackerman smiled. "Kalugin . . ." he mused. "Sounds Russian, doesn't it?"

"Russian or Polish. It's hard to tell the difference. Dzerzhinski himself was Polish, you'll recall. East Poland's changed hands so damned many times, it's hard for *them* to tell the difference. If he *were* KGB . . ." Pickett paused, "with a mission to infiltrate the Ukrainian emigré groups, wouldn't they have given him a Ukrainian-sounding name?"

"You'd expect them to. But then they'd expect us to expect them to, so they might not, etc., etc. Regression leading to infinity. Stargazing . . ." Ackerman shrugged. "What you seem to be suggesting, to get back to the issue at hand, is that this Kalugin *might* be KGB. Or he *might* be the bozo who hit Gryazin. Or, just conceivably, he might be both. Am I reading you correctly?"

"Correctly." Pickett nodded. "Emphasis on the 'might.' "

"A Ukrainian-Polack hitter with a Russian-sounding name? If true, an intriguing combination. So you'd better find out how much *is* true. I may want to talk to him, ask him why the Russians are hitting their own side." Ackerman grinned wolfishly. "Who knows? I may even want to recruit him."

CHAPTER TEN

(London. July 20, 1990)

THERE WERE DAYS, KALUGIN THOUGHT, WHEN YOU COULD FEEL IN-vincible. Everything seemed larger and clearer than usual. You seemed to have all the time in the world. There were days when your hand took orders direct from your eye, when instinct shook off thought's restraints, when purpose was identical with act. And today, watching Benko scheme to set up an attack, he felt that he could read him like a book, hit him whenever and wherever he chose. There were days when you could feel invincible. Today was one of them.

Benko seemed to sense it, too. He had started out wilder than usual, losing three touches with hasty, off-balance attacks. Now he was practicing discretion, slowing the tempo to a crawl, hoping to make one lose patience, overcommit. His breath rasped through the face piece of his mask, and his foil tip flickered, sketching intentions. Between breaths he muttered to himself in Ukrainian, strings of cheerful, elaborate profanity, aimed at his opponent or perhaps at himself, whose purpose was mostly to distract: "Cocksucker . . . Statutory rapist . . . Molester of innocent farmyard animals." Kalugin blocked it out. It was one of his days, too, for being undis-tractable. He focused on the bell of Benko's foil, alert for any signal of commitment, but registering, too, with perfect clarity and detach-ment, the stain at the elbow of Benko's jacket, the habit Benko seemed to have developed of tugging with his free hand at the bib of his mask, and the fact that his back foot (whose shoelace was coming undone) was now within an inch of the meter warning line. He feinted, hoping to provoke a hasty counter. Benko gave ground but otherwise didn't respond. His back foot, however, crossed the line.

"Meter warning," Kalugin said.

"Cocksucker," Benko said, this time in English.

"This won't make any difference." Kalugin lowered his foil. "But I don't want to listen to excuses. One of your shoelaces is undone."

Benko knelt to attend to the lace. Kalugin watched him. In the months spent getting close to Benko, he had come to rather like him. Politically the man was an idiot, of course, or, what amounted to the same thing, a dreamer, but he was good company. Though his view of the world and the way it worked belonged in the playground, if not the nursery, there was still something about him—an appetite for enjoyment, a cheerful transparency of motive—that was hard not to like. In other circumstances one might have had to take care not to like him too much. Now, probably, it no longer mattered. As the meeting with Pickett had once and for all made clear, Benko and his friends no longer merited, if they ever had, the serious attentions of the First Chief Directorate. The Knights of Vladimir were harmless, talkers not doers, not worth spying on, certainly not worth destroying.

It was only when they moved back up the strip that Kalugin noticed they now had an audience. She was standing in the doorway behind Benko, had presumably come from the exercise room. Perhaps because the leotard she wore showed them off to advantage, her legs were what he immediately noticed. They were athlete's legs, thighs solidly muscled, calves tapering to slender, well-shaped ankles. The rest of her, he noted, lived up to the high standard set by the legs.

"Don't look now," he told Benko, "but we've got an audience. It's a woman, so watch your language." Sighing theatrically, he switched to Ukrainian. "I only wish you could see her, Pavel. The face of an angel, the body of Venus. A woman *created* for the purposes of love."

"Switch sides with me then," Benko demanded. "Let *me* look at this goddess. I need some inspiration at this point."

Kalugin shook his head. "For you she'd simply be a distraction. You're distracted enough as it is."

Benko glanced, none too subtly, over his shoulder. He gave a low appreciative whistle.

"It's me she's watching," he told Kalugin. "All she can see of me is my back, but she senses something. An electricity. An aura."

"A negative charge." Kalugin grinned. "An aura of defeat."

Benko picked up his foil.

"For that I shall teach you a lesson." He took position on the strip. "I've been toying with you so far, but no more Mister Niceguy."

Kalugin shrugged.

"I wonder why I waste my time on you. You're not even exercise. You haven't won a touch." He paused. "And you're not going to."

"Want to bet?"

"Bet?" Kalugin shrugged. "Sure . . . What?"

Benko considered.

"Her." He nodded at the woman. "The winner gets to try his luck. The loser, you, withdraws to lick his wounds." He raised his foil, cut the air in salute. *"En garde.* Prepare to die."

Kalugin beat with his point on Benko's blade, not to attack but to gauge his opponent's intentions. Benko countered, but without real conviction. In spite of his talk he still seemed on the defensive. But maybe, Kalugin thought, he'd taken the meter warning on purpose. He fenced best with his back to the wall, and here, where another retreat could cost him the touch by default, you had to avoid getting overeager. It might be best to back off a little.

He gave ground, beckoned Benko forward.

"Chickenshit," Benko said. "Technically, I could call you for stalling."

"Stalling. Me?" Kalugin queried. *"You've* been going backward all your life. Anyone would think you'd got stuck in reverse . . ."

As he spoke, Benko stamped. Instinctively Kalugin straightened his arm. Stamping was another of Benko's tricks. The first time you'd jump back, avoiding the lunge. Nothing would happen. Benko wouldn't follow. *You'd* end up halfway down the strip, yards from danger, looking stupid. Presently he'd do it again, almost certainly with the same result. The third or fourth time, just when you'd convinced yourself to stay put, he'd nail you in the chest with a sudden lunge. The best response was to stick your foil in his face. It gave you the right of way, *him* something to deal with if he went for the lunge.

Benko stamped again.

Kalugin kept his foil where it was. Actually this stamping was a little insulting. It could work with beginners and people who were jumpy, but he, as Benko well knew, was neither. The temptation was to try and make him pay, but this, no doubt, was what he had in mind. Anything to put you off balance. People called fencing "physical chess." With Benko it was more like physical poker.

And maybe it was time to call his bluff.

Later, he would be able to reconstruct, almost step by step, what must have happened. At the exact moment when Benko, looking more than usually wooden, stamped again, he, Kalugin, had launched his attack. What he'd had in mind, though action in this case had largely anticipated thought, was beat-attack, parry, riposte, parry, lunge; the lunge at full stretch, his point hitting Benko a thoroughly satisfying thump somewhere below the right armpit. Included, too, but at another level of awareness entirely, had been the notion that this decisive response to Benko's stamping was emotionally and aesthetically apt. And then, of course, he was grandstanding a little, showing off to this woman whose charms had become, in fantasy at least, the issue in this contest. And perhaps it was that, the tiny lapse in attention caused by his having, at the critical instant, a divided focus, that made him a split second late in noticing that the third time Benko stamped, the bell of his foil started forward.

But even played over in slow motion, parts of the sequence remained unclear. At the time it seemed to take place, not as a series of separate events, but as a single blur of sensation: a clash of blades, a jolt in his wrist as his point found its target, a blow to his chest as Benko's point did the same, a sound of metal snapping, a pain slicing into his shoulder, the clatter of a foil on the floor.

Then they were standing there, a tableau of consternation, frozen into attitudes of shock. A foil, Benko's, was lying at their feet, the blade broken off some inches from the tip, the point jagged and painted with blood.

"Jesus . . ." Benko's voice was shaky. "I tried to let go, but everything happened too fast." He paused. "Jesus, Adam, you're bleeding like a pig."

Kalugin took off his mask, laid it and his foil on the floor. Gingerly, he examined his shoulder. There was no pain yet, but his fingers, probing the tear in his jacket, encountered wetness and a gash, perhaps two inches long, between raised welts. It felt like a small sticky mouth.

"Can I be of help?"

In the shock of the moment they'd both forgotten the woman. At the sound of her voice Benko turned and removed his mask, ran an arranging hand through his hair. Kalugin just stared. He'd described her as having the face of an angel, but in fact the analogy was more than usually inept. Her hair was almost jet, straight and chopped off at the shoulder. Her looks were of the kind that were apt to be called "interesting." The features, perhaps, were less than ideal—the nose a shade long, the face too narrow, the mouth a little wide—but they achieved, collectively, an appeal which, individually, they might have seemed to lack. What really struck him was the way her eyes, sea-green and flecked with hazel, returned his inspection with a steady curiosity, an appraisal, like his, that was candidly physical. And this, he thought, was where the "angel" analogy really fell on its face. Angels were supposed to be sexless; she, quite obviously, wasn't.

"May I see?" She indicated his shoulder. Her voice went well with her eyes, he thought. It was clear, level, confident but not pushy. The accent, surprisingly, was American.

"Are you a doctor?" he asked.

She shook her head. "But I have some first aid training." Her eyes rested on him a moment. "I can tell you, at least, if you'll live."

"I'll live." He offered her the shoulder. "It can't be much more than a scratch."

"It *looked* worse." She paused. "I can't see much through that jacket."

He hesitated. "I'm not wearing a vest."

"So I get to see your manly chest." She shrugged, smiled faintly. "I think I can manage to restrain myself. Just."

He took off the jacket. Her touch, cool and impersonal, produced in him, nonetheless, an electric shiver. If she felt anything of the kind, it didn't show, but he noticed that she avoided his eyes, keeping her own on his shoulder, as if, now that she'd made her appraisal, she was anxious to keep her distance. Benko, standing behind her, grinned ruefully. Some people, he conveyed, had all the luck.

"It's quite deep," she announced. "There's going to be junk in there. Jacket fibers, dirt from the blade. . . . You need cleaning up and stitches. A tetanus shot, if you haven't had one lately." She paused. The green eyes looked at him sideways. "I used to think of fencing as a *civilized* sport. Until I watched you two, that is. All that stamping and leaping around. That blade could have gone right through your mask. You could have been killed."

"It happens sometimes. Not often." Kalugin shrugged.

"It could have happened to you."

"It could have. It didn't. Too late to worry about it."

She smiled. "A fatalist, I see."

"One takes what life offers." He smiled back, showing his teeth. "If I hadn't got jabbed in the shoulder, I wouldn't be standing here talking to you now."

"We're certainly grateful." This contribution was from Benko, who seemed to be feeling left out. "The least we can do is offer you lunch."

She shook her head. "Thanks, but I have to get back to work. And you," she told Kalugin, "need to get that shoulder to a doctor."

Kalugin nodded.

"You work out here?" Benko wasn't easily discouraged.

She nodded.

"Often?"

She shrugged. "As often as I can."

"Then if not lunch today, another time perhaps?"

"Perhaps." She sounded doubtful. For a moment she hesitated, then, suddenly brisk, speaking, it seemed to Kalugin, mostly to him: "I enjoyed the swordplay, now I have to leave."

She turned, started for the exit.

"Wait . . ." Kalugin said. "We don't even know your name."

She looked back over her shoulder, smiling but not stopping.

"That's right. You don't, do you?"

And then, not waiting for his answer, still not stopping and in flawless Ukrainian:

"Which of you was it won me, anyway?"

CHAPTER ELEVEN
(London. July 22, 1990)

HE HADN'T EXPECTED TO SEE HER AGAIN. BUT HE SAW HER TWO DAYS later, at a cocktail party.

She was talking to Randall Pickett.

Kalugin didn't like cocktail parties, didn't normally attend them, but since legend ascribed to him a half-Polish father and a history of militant support for Solidarity, it had seemed only sensible to accept the invitation to the annual reception of the Anglo-Polish Alliance. The Alliance had been formed in the forties to further the Government in Exile's campaign against British recognition of the Communist regime in Warsaw. Later, after what members termed "the Betrayal," the Alliance became purely social, an expression of nostalgia for a vanished society and the wartime partnership against the Germans. Now, almost fifty years later, its membership suggested, even to a sympathetic eye, the remnant of some very lost crusade. Elderly Poles rubbed shoulders with elderly Hungarians and Czechs. To these were added elderly Anglo-Saxons (here, no doubt, to fill an empty evening, or themselves, at least, with someone else's gin) a few retired soldiers of various stripes, and a handful of diplomats, also elderly. Since the average age was well on the wrong side of sixty, it surprised Kalugin to find her here. But it was her all right, on the far side of the room, deep in conversation with Pickett and just as attractive as he remembered . . . How did she come to be here? he wondered. And how did she come to know Pickett?

It might be interesting to find out, he decided.

If he could escape from his current predicament.

His current predicament was large, predatory-looking woman in a shiny magenta dress, a great-niece or some such of General Pilsudski. From the moment some acquaintance had introduced them, then

slipped treacherously away, she'd been lecturing Kalugin, whom she
seemed to suspect of being American, on the short-sightedness and
iniquity of postwar Allied policy toward Poland. Now, noticing perhaps that her audience's attention had wandered, she paused in mid-
sentence to recall it to duty.

"You look far away. Your thoughts shy away from unwelcome
truths, perhaps?"

"Perhaps . . ." Kalugin smiled. It was time, he told himself, to get
rid of this pest. "But not into regions of total irrelevance, I think.
What you were saying reminded me of Cyprus."

"Cyprus?" She looked puzzled. "The Mediterranean island? But
Cyprus was not invaded by the Russians. Cyprus was not cruelly
abandoned by its allies. How does Cyprus fit into the conversation?"

"Perhaps not obviously." He smiled. "Only when I was on vacation
there once, there was something I noticed about their maps. They all
put Cyprus at the center of the universe."

"But how is that relevant to our discussion?"

"Perhaps like this . . ." *Christ,* he thought, how obtuse could you
get? "Though we're always at the center of *our* maps, we're usually
on the margins of other people's." He paused, bestowed on her his
blandest smile. "I've enjoyed our talk, but I mustn't monopolize you.
I've just seen someone I should say hello to."

"So, Adam Kalugin . . . How's your shoulder?"

She was even more attractive than he had remembered, and eye-
ing him now with that mixture of amusement and appraisal he remembered from their earlier encounter. Her name, he'd discovered,
was Chance.

Chance Davenport.

"My shoulder?" For a moment he'd forgotten. "Oh . . . *that*
shoulder. I took your advice and had it stitched. It'll be OK, I imagine."

It had taken some maneuvering to get her on her own. Pickett had
been supplanted by someone, and then by someone else. Kalugin
had stalked her from group to group, edging closer and awaiting his
opportunity. It had come when she was talking to the Vellistes, a
professor of history and his wife, with whom Kalugin was slightly
acquainted. Their previous encounter had not been altogether
friendly—he'd called the Government in Exile a "farce," only to
learn that Frieda Velliste's father had been a junior minister in it—
but this wasn't altogether a drawback. Frieda Velliste, greeting him

with reserve, had introduced him frostily as "Your name, I'm afraid, escapes me," adding as a gloss (when he refreshed her memory) that he was "some kind of militant, I recall, someone who thinks the solution to any kind of problem is to *throw* something, preferably something that explodes." It had not been long before the Vellistes had left him alone with Chance.

"It wasn't your *throwing* arm, one hopes?"

He acknowledged the hit with a lopsided grin. "I seem to have offended the Madame Professor. I should learn to limit myself to small talk, give up expressing my political opinions."

"But any opinion can get you into trouble, don't you find?" Switching into Ukrainian, she quoted, " 'The face of an Angel, the body of a Venus. A woman designed for purposes of love.' "

He winced. He'd been expecting something like this.

"Well clearly I was wrong about the angel." He paused. "How much trouble am I in?"

"I'll need to think." She knotted her brow, went through the motions of inner debate. A smile gathered at the corners of her mouth.

"We never *dreamed* you would understand." An apology might not come amiss, he thought. "So few people here speak Russian, you see, far less Ukrainian. It was one of those male things. Locker room talk. The sort of thing men say without meaning it much, mostly to impress one another. Please believe me that we didn't mean to offend."

"I wasn't that offended. Clearly you didn't expect me to understand. And what you said wasn't *too* crudely expressed nor in essence unflattering, I think." She paused. "Except that, as I now understand, you didn't mean it."

"I leave it to you to decide what I meant."

"It's my invariable policy in these cases"—she was smiling openly now—"to accept the compliments and ignore the rest."

"Accept my apologies, too. It was stupid." He paused. "I wouldn't want you to think of me as some kind of chauvinist pig."

She looked surprised. "Why would I?"

He shrugged. "I guess you could interpret what I said as expressing an interest in you that was purely physical."

"But that wasn't odd in the circumstances, was it? All you knew of me was what you saw. It would certainly make you a sexist pig if your interest in me *stayed* that way."

Another pause.

It struck him that this last remark could be interpreted as a gambit. Her look, on the other hand, provided no clue to her intention.

Her eyes were not expressionless so much as enigmatic, and as always a suspicion of mockery seemed to be lurking behind them. But whatever she had meant, the ball was in his court. It was up to him to return it.

He was saved the trouble of deciding how by the sudden reappearance of Pickett.

Pickett didn't seem pleased to see him. He cut short with a curt "We're acquainted" Chance's effort to introduce them, and followed this up by abruptly, almost peremptorily, asking her to dinner. In the circumstances, Kalugin thought, it wasn't surprising she declined. What was surprising—startling in fact—was the reason she offered for declining.

"I'm sorry, Randall. Another time I should love to. But tonight I'm having dinner with Adam."

CHAPTER TWELVE

(London. July 22, 1990)

"If I startled you, I'm sorry."

In fact Chance's announcement had nonplused *both* her companions. Pickett had stared at her briefly, collected himself, shrugged, muttered something almost gracious about another time being fine of course, and departed. Kalugin had said nothing. He felt, if he'd succeeded in hiding his astonishment, that nothing more was called for, at least for the moment. In spite of her last statement, he noted, Chance herself looked neither sorry nor embarrassed.

"I didn't want to have dinner with Pickett, but he took me off guard. I improvised . . ." She shrugged as if to imply that the decision had been self-evident. "You must think I'm very bold."

"Not bold." Kalugin hesitated. "A risk taker perhaps."

"Of course." She nodded. "Always. That's my name . . . Chance. Given me by my father, a professional gambler, whose temperament I seem to have inherited. Though that just now wasn't much of a risk. I counted on your quick-wittedness, also your good manners." She paused. Though her gaze was as steady as ever, he thought that for the first time he could detect in it a trace of awkwardness, as if maintaining this unusual level of candor was getting to be something of an effort. "Just as I count on your having the good sense to tell me if having dinner with me tonight is inconvenient, or . . ."—fractional hesitation—"unappealing."

"It's not inconvenient." He shook his head. "Nor unappealing. If Pickett hadn't got in first I'd have asked you myself. I was just about to."

"Good, *that's* settled then." Her smile conveyed relief, but also the conviction that the issue hadn't, really, ever been in doubt. "Where shall we go to dinner?"

* * *

They went to a bistro on Fulham Road. In a conversation that lasted till after midnight, he learned a number of things about her; more, he was able to assure himself later, than she managed to learn about him. She liked food, Italian opera, blackjack but not roulette, being read to, Chagall, the poetry of Pushkin, sapphires. She disliked leeks, cigars, men who wore hairpieces, golf. She was in her early thirties and divorced. She spoke, apart from English, five languages, three of them Slavic. She had an MA from Stanford and a PhD in history from Oxford. She had written her dissertation, hence her interest in the Anglo-Polish Alliance, on the Polish Government in Exile and its role in the Warsaw Uprising. On receiving her doctorate she'd had offers from several universities, but had gone to work— more money, she told him, less bullshit—for her current employer, a London-based political research organization, the Foundation for Freedom.

"I've heard of it somewhere." He affected to consider. Actually he'd heard of it from Zebo. The Foundation for Freedom, headed by Martin Rosenthal, was some kind of front for the CIA. No wonder she knew Randall Pickett. "Isn't it some kind of think tank?"

"I suppose you could call it that." She nodded. "Though an image of eggheads in windowless cells, thinking deep thoughts with furrowed brows and wet towels round their heads, would be misleading. Most of my day is spent reading, making notes, filling out file index cards, the usual academic drudgery."

"But presumably it involves some thinking."

"A lot, actually. I sort, I assess, I decide what to feed the computer. Quite a bit of my time is spent in the actual gaming."

"Gaming?"

"We play war games"—she nodded—"on this giant computer. It's capable of zillions of transactions per second and programmed to simulate the current world scene. We feed it hypothetical scenarios— the Soviet wheat harvest fails, for instance—and ask it to predict a range of outcomes." She paused. "You could think of it, I guess, as geo-political Dungeons and Dragons."

"Dungeons and Dragons?" He thought about this. "A lot of fun, you mean, but not having much relation to reality?"

"It's certainly fun." She nodded. "At least *I* enjoy it. It involves a lot of what drew me to history in the first place: problems of weighing and testing evidence, determining the relative importance of factors, finding out what makes things happen. As to its relation to reality . . . I don't think it's totally divorced. We attempt to consider at leisure and systematically the kinds of questions policymakers get faced with all the time. And using the computer lets us handle more data than we could dream of dealing with otherwise. I *think* what we're doing is useful, at least as long as we don't start assuming, because its predictions seem so precise, that the computer is infallible. And it's precisely to stop us doing it that there's something built into the system to remind us not to."

"A reminder not to take the whole exercise too seriously?"

"Or not to rely on it too much. We call it the Doomsday Factor."

"It sounds ominous."

"It does." She nodded. "More ominous than it actually is. It's really an error factor, an attempt to quantify the fuzziness inherent in this kind of thinking. When we feed a scenario into the computer, it responds with a range of predicted outcomes, each with a probability estimate attached. It also comes up with an estimate of the likelihood that the real-life outcome would be *none* of the ones predicted."

He thought about this.

"But presumably, if I remember my mathematics, that should be simply a hundred percent minus the sum of the probabilities of outcomes that *were* predicted."

"You'd think so," she nodded, "but it's a little more complex than that. What the Doomsday Factor really measures is the instability, or uncontrollability, of the scenario being gamed."

"Uncontrollability?" he queried. "Do you mean that the scenarios you game are not only events that might randomly happen, like failure of the Soviet wheat harvest, but also those that might be *caused* to happen—the assassination of an Austrian archduke, perhaps?"

"Sharp, aren't you?" She eyed him thoughtfully for a moment, nodded. "That's why we call it the Doomsday Factor. In scenarios having serious military implications, you could see it as measuring the possibility that things could spin out of control, setting off, in an extreme case, World War Three. Of course," she went on, "that particular risk may no longer be what it was, now that the Cold War seems to be over."

"Seems?" he queried. "Do you mean you think it may not be?"

"It *should* be." She shrugged. "In theory there should be nothing to fight *about*, if indeed there ever was. But the Cold War was largely a product of paranoia, much of it whipped up by leaders on both sides, for motives that don't bear close scrutiny. Joe McCarthy was the most notorious, but others were not much better." She paused. "And that's what makes me reserve judgment . . . the human element. People don't change that fast. Politicians still have the normal motives, they still pander to the normal fears, they still cling to a mindset that belongs in a preschool playground. And they still control the same huge arsenals, the same mind-numbing quantities of missiles."

She paused.

"And that's what bothers me most, I guess. Did you know that in the early eighties, when the B-feature actor we'd elected President was mouthing off with that Evil Empire bullshit, the Russians thought there really was a chance the US would launch a first strike attack? Did you know that KGB residencies were instructed, as a matter of top priority, to watch for the signs of such an attack."

He felt as if he'd been suddenly sandbagged. Her question reminded him, suddenly and forcibly, of something he'd more or less managed to forget: just how awkward a relationship with her would be. For one thing, since her employers were people his employers would like to know more about, duty would require him to exploit the acquaintance. There had to be a serious question, moreover, about what duty might require *her* to do. The Foundation for Freedom, after all, was some sort of front for the CIA. And though this didn't mean, necessarily, that all its employees were CIA agents, it was almost inevitable some of them were. So why not this alluring Chance, who spoke flawless Russian and Ukrainian, who was clearly an acquaintance, if not more, of a man who *was* a CIA agent, and whose actions this evening could hardly be seen as other than an effort to pick him, Kalugin, up? Wasn't it very possible, indeed, that Pickett, wanting to know more about him and not knowing how to inquire himself without arousing suspicion, had done the obvious and delegated? It was very possible. It was more than possible. It was a thought he resisted, it struck Kalugin, only because, having spent these few hours with her, he no longer *wanted* to believe it. But what one wanted was irrelevant. Training taught one to suspect attractive women, especially those who seemed to be making the advances. The profession had a term for them.

Honeytraps.

"I seem to have lost you," Chance said.

"Lost me?"

"Your attention, at any rate. You were with me until a few moments ago, then you went away."

Her eyes, it struck him once again, were almost unbelievably direct. He wondered if it was possible for anyone to be as candid as her eyes said she was. Probably not, he thought sadly. Almost certainly not.

"My attention did wander for a moment. I'm sorry . . . What were we talking about?"

"The Cold War." She shrugged. "Not that it matters. Where *were* you?"

"Actually, I was thinking about your eyes."

"My eyes?" She rolled them. "That sounds like a ploy to distract me. An obvious ploy and therefore condescending. I'll do you a favor and ignore it." She paused. "Where did you learn your English? It's amazingly good."

"Amazingly?" He raised an eyebrow. "Mightn't one regard *that* as condescending?"

"I guess what I meant"—she grinned, acknowledging the hit—"was amazingly British. Not only the accent but the idiom. So good it sounds as if you'd learned it here, starting in your cradle."

"Actually I did . . . learn it as a child. Not here of course. Kiev."

"As a child in Kiev?" She was openly skeptical. "Now you sound like one of those privileged exiles, Nabokov or someone. Are you telling me you had the only English governess to survive the Revolution, integrity and spinsterhood intact?"

He shook his head. "My sister taught me. She learned it from an Englishwoman, spoke it perfectly. She used to teach English, language and literature, at the university. At home there were times when we spoke nothing else. When she read to me at bedtime, it was always the English classics. Her favorite was Malory. *Le Morte d'Arthur.* She was translating it into Russian."

"You must have been very close to her."

"I was. My mother died when I was still a boy. My sister raised me." He paused, remembering. "In some ways my sister was very old-fashioned. Entranced by a notion of England and the English she'd gotten entirely out of books. She had this ideal of a life conducted with honor. I guess you could say she was in love with it."

"Was?" Chance asked gently.

"She's dead." Kalugin nodded. It was a long time since he'd told anyone this much about himself. For a panicky moment he thought he'd told her too much. Then he remembered. When his masters, making his legend, had woven their falsehood from threads of truth, their purpose had been to guard against such lapses. Pickett, if he checked, would find nothing amiss.

"She died in Russia? Before you came away?"

He nodded. "It was 1975, the height of the Brezhnev era. She had a run-in with the authorities, didn't survive the encounter."

"I'm sorry." Chance frowned. "I shouldn't have probed."

"It's OK. A painful memory . . ." He shrugged. "I suppose that's where I'd gone when you lost me. When you mentioned the KGB, it reminded me of Katya."

Another lie that made use of truth. He felt a wave of self-contempt. At times like this it was more than he could bear that even what was honest in his life got pressed into service by its central falsehood. He'd become, he thought, completely hollow. The shell that called itself Adam Kalugin no longer housed anything of substance. Somewhere in the ten-year imposture that had brought him from the Sleeper School to here, Vadim Stolypin had quietly died.

"I've made you sad," Chance said. "I'm really sorry."

"Not you." He shook his head. "Things."

"So let's get out of here, go somewhere else. Change of scene to induce change of mood." She paused. "Let's go to my place."

They made love first on Chance's couch. Later they made it in her bed, but that first time hunger preempted thought for comfort. There were no preliminaries. No one even turned on the light. Instead they were hardly in the door before they attacked each other, mouth seeking avidly for mouth, hands fumbling at buttons and zippers, both of them tearing, in their urgency of need, at the barriers of clothing between them. He carried her to the couch and, as she raised herself to receive him, crying out and shuddering with pleasure, entered her. Her orgasm started almost at once, his only moments later; a frenzy of mutual release so total it seemed to take them to the edge of extinction. It was only afterward that anything was said. It was Chance who said it, murmured it rather, so quietly he hardly heard it, and ruefully, as if to herself:

"I guess I could tell myself I didn't have a choice."

CHAPTER THIRTEEN

(London. July 23, 1990)

"ADAM . . . ADAM KALUGIN. WAKE UP."

Kalugin came awake with a jerk. For a moment he didn't remember where he was. He was instantly conscious, however, that the bed was not his and that he was lying on top of the covers, naked. Then he sat up and saw Chance. She was lying beside him, propped on one elbow, watching him. She looked, in the faint light that filtered through the weave of the curtains, like the marble statue of some goddess.

"What time is it?"

"About four. You were having a dream. A nightmare, by the way you were carrying on. I let you be for a while, but then it seemed better to wake you." She paused. "You were also talking in your sleep. To a woman. Someone called Katya. You were telling her, over and over, you were sorry."

"My sister. I dream about her often. I'm sorry if I woke you."

"*Dream* about her? Do you mean have nightmares?

"Yes."

"The same nightmare?"

"The same one." He nodded. "The same one always."

He'd had it so often now that even while it happened he knew it *was* a dream, but this never made any difference. He was never able to wake himself up. He'd long ago concluded it was part of the price he paid for being who he was; something he had to submit to, suffer through, until it had run its course. Like some recurring but nonfatal fever, it would rage in him for a time, then depart, leaving him alive but ravaged and depleted.

He was thirteen. In the country outside Kiev. A summer evening, the sun low on the horizon, everything bathed in a fierce copper light. The Tribunal, posed in three rows as if for a portrait, stood like a wall between him and the sun. He was never able to see their faces.

Nor was anything ever said. There was no handing down of the sentence. He would stand there, facing them, till the silence grew overwhelming and someone—it was always the man on the left of the row seated—walked over and handed him the rope. It was white and stiff, like new laundry line, the ends secured by a lashing of twine. And it was always then, when the man turned away to resume his place with the others, that the sun caught and illuminated his features: the hatchet face, the high, beaked nose, the deep-set eyes, the thin unhumorous smile.

Zaitsev.

Then he and Katya were walking in the trees, not looking at each other, not speaking, both numb with the knowledge of what he had to do. And though at the time it seemed merciful that he'd lost the capacity for feeling, it was this not-feeling, precisely, that afterward troubled him most, compounding his grief with the acid of guilt. It was as if the Tribunal had sucked out his soul, indentured him to an evil beyond his capacity to imagine; as if, like some bureaucrat of the death camps (for whom virtue consisted of meeting production quotas), he never thought to question his orders. Instead, reducing horror to a problem in logistics, he scouted the trees for suitable branches, estimated breaking strains and drops. But even so, there was always part of him, some small despairing pocket of dissent, which, though incapable of active rebellion, searched frantically for an avenue of escape.

He was never conscious of time passing. The sun stayed fixed just above the horizon, but it seemed to him that they walked like this for hours. And always close to the fringes of the wood, so that not far off, through a lattice of trunks and branches, he could see the open fields. And though he knew he was miles from the Tribunal, he continued to feel the pressure of its scrutiny, so that when they reached the place—he never knew *how* they chose it, only, by some tacit process of consent, that they had—he gestured with the rope and spoke to Katya, loudly, almost shouting, as if to be sure he'd be heard in the proper quarter: "I can't manage this if I have to guard you, too. I'm going to put you on your honor. When I look for you next, don't let me find you not there."

And for just a moment it would seem that easy. When he'd set the rope she was gone and a shadow had been lifted from his life. He could say she'd run off, that they should have sent someone to help him, that he hadn't been able to manage the whole thing by himself. But just as he was starting back, mentally rehearsing his story, he saw her. She was handcuffed, frogmarched between men in hats and trenchcoats. When she saw him she shrugged and smiled.

Her smile was always what tormented him most. Asleep or awake, whenever he recaptured her features, that half-smile was what they were always wearing. It expressed resignation, also a kind of entreaty, as if she were asking *his* forgiveness, apologizing for getting caught.

And that was where it always it ended. He would wake up, sweating and trembling, often to find the pillow damp with tears. Of what came afterward there was never anything. It, by some merciful process of editing, was always permitted to happen offscreen. This puzzled him because the images existed. They were in him somewhere, some corner of his mind. They *had* to be, he knew, because the mind erases nothing. Even the faintest brushstroke of experience stays forever on the canvas of memory. It was he, after all, who had found her that day in the stairwell.

He who had had to get her down.

"You want to tell me about it?" Chance asked.

"Tell you about what?"

"Well . . ." She considered. "You kept saying you were sorry. Maybe what you were sorry about."

He shrugged. "What *are* nightmares? . . . Imaginary terrors. Guilt or anxiety, surfacing in sleep. Compelling to the dreamer, boring to anyone else."

"In other words, you don't want to tell me."

"I guess not." He shook his head.

She was silent for a moment.

"How come you know Randall Pickett?"

"I met him somewhere. I can't remember where exactly. Why?"

"He called you a young thug." She leaned over, brushed his cheek with her lips, as if to distance herself from the judgment. "It doesn't seem to fit you very well. I was wondering why he said it."

So Pickett had discussed him with her. The warning sounded again in his head. Beware attractive women who ask too many questions.

"Why?" Chance repeated.

"It must be my past." He shrugged. "Pickett must be like that woman at the party. A single lapse and you're labeled for life. 'That

young man who throws things.' " He paused. "I could write the defin-
itive history of the world, devote the rest of my life to good works,
but to people like her I would always be 'that young man who throws
things.' "

"You sound bitter."

"Not bitter, tired of being labeled."

She was silent again. When he looked over, she was smiling.

"Did I say something funny?"

"Not you. Frieda. I was thinking of your exchange at the party.
You asked her if she'd ever tried arguing with Russian tanks. And *she*
said . . ."—Chance achieved briefly a startlingly accurate imitation
of the frosty contralto of Frieda Velliste—'No, but it could hardly be
less effective, I should think, than throwing cobblestones at them.' "

"Bitch." Kalugin grinned.

"But you didn't throw cobblestones at tanks, did you?"

Was this some kind of trap? He was reminded, by some sideways
skip memory, that Pickett had asked him a roughly similar question.
If it *was* a trap, on the other hand, it was incredibly clumsy.

He shook his head. "I'm not that stupid. Mention of tanks, in any
case, was exaggeration on my part. As you must know"—he placed
the emphasis on "must"—"there *were* no tanks in Warsaw in '81."

"I do know." She nodded. "It occurred to me your career as a
dissident might have been more extensive than you've admitted.
Frieda Velliste mentioned bombs. Did you ever throw bombs at anything?"

He shook his head wearily. "Just cobblestones. Just once."

She thought about this. "It would take more than cobblestones
hurled in anger, I'd have thought, to make Randall Pickett sound so
disapproving. He's not normally given to moral judgments."

Kalugin shrugged.

"Then Randall Pickett is misinformed. Or an idiot."

"Actually Randall Pickett is a spook. In some respects very well
informed, and in most respects not at all an idiot." She watched him
carefully. "Are you a spook?"

Though he was careful not to show it, the question startled him.
She certainly was *direct.* It was hard to gauge, however, whether the
directness was real or seeming.

"I told you." He returned her gaze steadily. "I do translations.
English to Ukrainian, English to Russian, and sometimes the other
way around. Why are we talking about this? Are *you* a spook?"

She shook her head. "My work at the Foundation is funded by a

branch of the Government, quote unquote, and I have my dark suspicions as to which, but I'm not a spook myself." She paused. "If
Randall Pickett calls you a thug, you must be some kind of bad boy."

"Would it make me more attractive?" He cocked his head to one
side. "This would raise interesting questions about *you*. Are you one
of those women, perhaps, who get turned on by bad boys?"

She considered the question, smiled. "One can't discount that possibility, I guess. *Are* you a bad boy?"

He shook his head. "I'm a translator. I was a bad boy once. For
two days in Warsaw. Now I just have bad dreams." He paused. "After we made love, the first time, you said something. Something
about not having a choice. . . . What did you mean?"

She was silent, this time, for several seconds.

"It's hard to explain." She shrugged. "I'm a PhD. I'm supposed to
be this logical, analytical person, and yet sometimes I find my body
taking decisions for me. When I saw you at that party I think I
already knew what decision it would make about you. But then, *after*
we made love, about five minutes too late to make any difference, my
logical side started entering objections: Who *is* this guy? What are
you *doing* hopping into bed with someone you don't even know? I
guess what I said was my way of telling my logical side to shut up.
'The step has been taken,' I think I was saying. 'All we can do now is
see where it leads.' " She paused. "Does that make any sense?"

He nodded. It made sense. And maybe it was true. Even if it
wasn't, he reminded himself, he was hardly in a position to object. In
any case, part of what she'd said was true: all they could do now was
see where it led.

"Is it *going* to lead somewhere?"

She considered him gravely. "I'd like to think so. Would you?"

He nodded.

"Then it all depends, don't you think?"

"Depends on what?"

"On who we turn out to be. You could say we've done this thing
backward, started it from the wrong end. Now we have to go back
and fill in the blanks." She paused. "So tell me, Young Man Who
Throws Things, who are you, really?"

"Ukrainian emigré. Single. Twenty-eight. Speaks four languages,
three of them well. Fences. . . . Actually"—he shrugged—"though
it may be disappointing, what you see is in my case more or less what
you get."

"More or less." She eyed him speculatively. "As my daddy the

gambler used to say: when considering any proposition, be sure to read the fine print. Oh, well." She gave him a sudden, wicked grin. "At least we got part of it right."

"Part of it? Which?"

"Are you being *deliberately* dense?" Pulling him down beside her, she leaned over him and kissed him, pressing against him the heat and fullness of her body. She ran her hand up his thigh till it came to rest on his penis. "This part."

"You're right." He rolled on to her, felt, like a wind kicking up, the renewal of desire. "Enough questions. We can fill in the blanks later. For now it doesn't matter who we are."

CHAPTER FOURTEEN
(London. July 24, 1990)

IT WAS NOT UNTIL HE WAS ALMOST HOME THAT KALUGIN KNEW HE WAS being tailed. To that point he'd been merely suspicious; and in his profession suspicion was such a normal state of mind that, to fend off the paranoia which, if permitted, could easily become a threat to sanity, he'd trained himself to view his anxieties calmly, as if they belonged to someone else. When the man in the olive-green corduroy jacket, whom he'd noticed first at the ticket counter in the Leicester Square Underground station, got off the train behind him at Belsize Park, he didn't think much about it. Since the man had bought a ticket to Belsize Park, it was hardly a very sinister coincidence that he'd used it for travel to that destination. Nor was it cause for alarm, necessarily, that he'd happened to be next in line when Kalugin bought *his* ticket. What did seem to stretch coincidence a little was the fact that this man in the corduroy jacket, who had exited at Belsize Park station just a few steps behind Kalugin, appeared to live in Kalugin's neighborhood and to share with him a fondness for walking. For why otherwise would he exit at Belsize Park when his real destination, as was evidenced by the fact that twenty minutes later he was still behind Kalugin (albeit on the other side of the street), was Hampstead?

Suspicion hardened into actual certainty when Kalugin turned left off Hampstead High Street and the footsteps that had sounded behind him for the past twenty minutes persisted. Coincidence had now multiplied beyond the point of plausibility.

The man was definitely tailing him.

Why?

To mug him? . . . Unlikely. What mugger, after all, would stalk his intended victim, and none too discreetly at that, halfway across

North London? M15 then? . . . Doubtful, too. M15 were professionals. An M15 tail would consist of a team, none of whose members would conduct himself with the lack of subtlety displayed by the
man in the corduroy jacket—a lack, it struck Kalugin, that was almost conspicuous enough to be deliberate. Whatever might be happening here, surveillance, he thought, was *not* the name for it. The
police then? They'd connected him somehow with the death of Zebo
and were trying to spook him into compromising himself? But this
theory was implausible, too, except perhaps to an inherited consciousness formed by exposure to a secret police whose acronym
might have changed over time but whose methods had varied hardly
at all. Russian cops might have acted that way, but their London
counterparts were straightforward; if *they* suspected you, they hauled
you in. In any case, he told himself, they had no grounds for suspecting him of anything, and only paranoia could suggest otherwise.

Then who *was* this nuisance in the corduroy jacket?

The way to find out was to ask. The correct procedure here, the
natural reaction for an ordinary Englishman, was to wheel right
around, confront this corduroy-jacketed leech, and demand, in that
tone of justified belligerence the English have made peculiarly theirs,
just what the hell he thought he was doing, dogging one's footsteps
like this.

The thought, however, was preempted by events.

"Excuse me, please . . ."

The voice from behind him was soft, even hesitant. The accent was
not very marked, but its foreignness was revealed, nonetheless, by
too great an emphasis on the l and an almost caressing lingering on
the sibilants.

Kalugin turned.

Corduroy Jacket was advancing on him, waving an unlit cigarette
and wearing a diffident, ingratiating smile.

"Can you spare me, perhaps, a match?"

Eccentric word order, outdated idiom. Language school English,
East European variety. The native tongue, Kalugin guessed, would
be Russian or maybe Polish. Seen closer, by the less than flattering
light of a street lamp, Corduroy Jacket revealed pudgy features,
brown eyes that blinked myopically through thick-lensed, wire-
rimmed glasses, and a serious case of five o'clock shadow. The head,
slightly too large for the body, was topped by a mass of wiry hair that
seemed to spring straight up from the scalp. But the body, Kalugin
noticed, belonged to a wrestler: not fat but burly, the center of grav-

ity low, thick in the trunk and limbs, extremely powerful. The walk was a sailor's, rolling but balanced.

"I don't have a match." Kalugin watched carefully for signs of aggression. He added coldly, "And you haven't been following me for the last half hour simply in order to cadge a light. Who the hell are you and what do you want?"

"Speak softly, please, and act naturally." Corduroy Jacket, glancing around as if to assure himself the street was still deserted and lowering his own voice to a whisper, switched to Russian. "You may call me Atlas. I'm your new control."

Your new control. Kalugin's mind raced. He should have been expecting this. He *had* been expecting it, he thought, had until the days following Zebo's murder had lengthened into weeks and expectation had turned into disappointment. But was this man who he claimed to be? He was almost certainly Russian; his command of the language was perfect, at any rate. But caution was still in order. This could be an M15 trap. Decision number one was whether to admit knowing Russian. An instant's reflection persuaded Kalugin he had to. His work, after all, was translating the language, and M15 would presumably know it. He might do best, however, though acknowledging that he understood, to give the impression he preferred English.

"I've no idea what you're talking about." The right note of chilly reproof, he thought. No Englishman could have done better.

"You want proof of my identity? Very sensible . . ." Corduroy Jacket shrugged, continued in Russian. "Very well. Your name is Vadim Stolypin. You work for Section S of the First Chief Directorate of the KGB, holding the rank of first lieutenant. Your former control, Anatoli Gryazin, code name Zebo, was recently murdered at the Tower of London—"

"I *still* don't know what you're talking about." Kalugin cut him off. "My name is Adam Kalugin. I work as a translator, mostly freelance, sometimes for the Overseas Service of the BBC. You're either confusing me with someone, or constructing a fantasy of which I want no part." He paused and smiled coldly. "I think we should stop this conversation before you embarrass yourself more than you already have."

Corduroy Jacket ignored the interruption.

"In 1976 you graduated from the Sleeper School in Kiev . . . Fifth overall in a class of fifty-three, first in languages and unarmed combat, third in communications techniques, forty-ninth in Marxist theory. Your psychological profile showed unusual features. It spoke of misplaced idealism, low ideological commitment. I hope"—he peered over the tops of his glasses, his gaze reproachful but also slightly mocking—"that the latter is no longer the case?"

"If you'll excuse me . . ." Kalugin, shrugging, began to turn away. "Another time I might have been entertained by this nonsense. But now it's too late at night."

"One moment, Lieutenant." Without being raised at all, the soft voice acquired a sudden authority. It came to Kalugin that, whatever else, this was a rather formidable man.

He halted.

"Of course I understand your hesitation." Corduroy Jacket spoke again. "You worry that someone has defected; that your Sleeper School records have fallen into enemy hands; that actually I work for British security and am using details obtained from your biography to trap you into self-incriminating statements. Such caution is commendable and, in the present circumstances, not inappropriate. On the other hand, it ought to be obvious that if I *am* working for the British, I know too much about you already for denials to do you any good. Still, if it will help to reassure you, I will tell you something else about yourself. A detail *not* included in your Sleeper School file."

He paused, regarded Kalugin sternly.

"Shortly after leaving the Sleeper School you received special training from a branch of the Second Chief Directorate for an unusual and highly secret mission, to be undertaken in addition to your regular duties. This mission was to carry out, as soon as his current identity and whereabouts were discovered, the death sentence passed by a Soviet court on the KGB defector Alexandr Zaitsev. You received this mission at your own request."

Another pause. Though a reaction was clearly expected, Kalugin gave none. Corduroy Jacket continued:

"In view of this, you will no doubt be happy to learn that after years of fruitless inquiry, the Second Chief Directorate has recently obtained several promising leads as to Zaitsev's current identity and whereabouts. We expect, in the near future, to provide information enabling you to carry out your mission. In the meantime, however, we have other work for you."

In the meantime, other work. It was typical, Kalugin thought. Though his knowledge of Zaitsev was evidence enough that Corduroy Jacket *was* what he claimed to be—it being a good deal more than improbable that two separate defectors had stolen files on Vadim Stolypin from two separate KGB departments—nothing that

Corduroy Jacket had so far said was quite as indicative of KGB membership as this proof of his possession of the KGB mentality. Every human transaction, to the KGB, reduced in the end to buying and selling, and they always made sure to get more than they gave. They discovered your need, whatever it was—friendship, money, sex, or revenge—and they used it to control you. But he'd always known this, of course, always accepted the unequal bargain. And he'd continue to, he thought, because he knew that *eventually* they would pay. Sooner or later they would give him Zaitsev.

And sooner, it was now beginning to seem, than later.

"Tell me . . ." Now for the first time he switched to Russian. "Since you know so much, who murdered Zebo?"

CHAPTER FIFTEEN

(London, July 24, 1990)

"IT WAS THE AMERICANS," ATLAS SAID.

Kalugin stared. "You know this for a fact?"

They were in a restaurant-cum-nightclub off the Edgware Road. Bad Chinese food, outrageously priced, the kitchen's larceny not really mitigated by a floor show of overweight, middle-aged women, revealing far too much of themselves to a mostly uninterested public. But as Atlas, whose choice it was, had pointed out, the perfect location for their purpose: dark and noisy, waiters inattentive to the point of rudeness, the kind of place it was hard to keep under surveillance, virtually impossible to bug.

"For a fact." Atlas nodded.

"How do you know? . . . Did someone see them?"

"Of course not. We deduce. Given the circumstances, the timing, other information available to us, the inference is inescapable."

The inference is inescapable . . . And yet, Kalugin thought, *Pickett* hadn't known. Or hadn't *seemed* to know, at least at the time of his meeting with Benko. Why otherwise had he *asked* about it? Why would someone who worked for the CIA (and presumably would have heard if they'd taken to murdering Soviet diplomats) go to the trouble of *raising* a subject, simply in order to feign ignorance about it? To mislead people, perhaps? To make them think the CIA hadn't murdered Zebo when actually it had. That might make sense, Kalugin thought, except for Pickett's perfect indifference to what Benko believed on any subject. So the truly inescapable inference here, unless you were willing to believe that Atlas knew more about the CIA's activities than a senior officer in its London station, was that Atlas was misinformed.

Or lying.

"What other information?" Kalugin asked.

"The girls in this place are certainly well upholstered . . ." Atlas's attention had evidently wandered. He nodded at the stage, where the latest in a series of "artistic impressions" was grinding to its predictable conclusion. "That woman has breasts like pumpkins. I wonder if they're for sale."

Kalugin shrugged. In this place everything would be for sale. Erotic suggestion reminded him of Chance, whose breasts were not like pumpkins, but whose powers of physical attraction beggared those of this vegetable seller. He wondered why Chance appealed to him so much. Was it the danger? The possibility she worked for Pickett? In view of his still lingering suspicions about her, it occurred to him that he ought to report their relationship. It also occurred to him that he wouldn't.

"*What* information?" he repeated.

"Sensitive information." Atlas's smile was bland. "Information you don't need to know. But since your position is to some extent affected, there *are* certain facts I think you're entitled to . . . We've had a defection to the Americans recently. A Line N officer in the Residency here. Since we don't know yet exactly what he took, we have to assume that it was everything: identities of officers, contact lists, targets, drops, a complete profile of the London operation. It was two days after the defection . . ." Atlas paused, "that, on his way to a contact apparently, Zebo met his death."

On his way to a contact *apparently?* Atlas didn't *know* who Zebo had been going to meet? But perhaps this wasn't altogether surprising. In fact, Kalugin thought, it was rather the reverse. Case officers weren't apt to advertise their impending contacts, especially with illegals. What was surprising, given that he'd have known about the defection, was that Zebo hadn't aborted the contact. Maybe he'd thought it was too soon for the defector to have been debriefed and had simply taken a chance. But if so, it was out of character.

Zebo never took a chance.

"And this is your basis for accusing the CIA?" Kalugin let skepticism show in his voice. "A simple coincidence of timing?"

"Not at all." Atlas frowned. "We're not idiots. We can reason. I tell you this to help you understand the instructions I'm about to give you. Our conclusions about Zebo are based not on timing, but on facts which, as I've mentioned before, your lack of a need to know precludes my sharing with you."

"But at least these conclusions are certain?"

"More or less." Atlas's eyes narrowed. "In any case, why does it matter? Zebo is dead. I am here to replace him. Why do you care about who killed him?"

Because I'm not sure I believe your information. Or indeed your conclusions. Kalugin was tempted to say it. He restrained himself, however. Mistrust, articulated, would become mutual. If Atlas *was* lying, one would find out more by pretending to believe him than by casting one's suspicions in his teeth.

"He was my case officer." Kalugin shrugged. "My friend. And if the CIA has taken to killing, I would seem to be in an environment hazardous to my health."

"I don't think so." Atlas shook his head. "Not more than normally hazardous, that is. It's precisely to guard against this that, as you know, information about illegals is never kept on file with the local residencies. Apart from myself, and one or two people in Section S in Yasenevo, no one knows your identity or is even aware of your existence." He paused. "Our major concern now must be to keep it that way."

"No argument there." Kalugin smiled faintly. "It's always been *my* major concern."

There was no answering smile. *Zebo* would have smiled, Kalugin thought, or in some way acknowledged that a joke had been made. From courtesy, if for no other reason. Zebo would have realized that jokes on this subject were made mostly to keep anxiety in check. And that was the difference between him and this Atlas; the reason— quite apart from gathering mistrust—that he didn't find himself warming to his new case officer. Atlas might be concerned for his safety, but only because Atlas had work for him to do. To Zebo, agents had been people also. Zebo had cared about one's anxieties.

"So no contact with the Residency." Atlas fixed him with a stare. "From now on no contact whatever, at any time, for any reason."

"You mean, of course"—Kalugin was a little offended by the tone —"any Residency officer but *you.*"

"I mean any officer." Atlas shook his head. "I'm not attached to the Residency. I was sent from Moscow. I report to Moscow directly. That's why it took us so long to get back in contact with you. I had to be provided with cover. As I tried to make clear to you before, we're regarding the Residency as thoroughly compromised. Pending a full investigation, every officer from the Resident on down has to be regarded as suspect."

Kalugin considered. This at least was normal. Any defection from a station abroad brought the wrath of Moscow down on the whole station. It was one reason KGB officers watched each other so closely. Full-scale security investigations—special inquisitors from Section K with their polygraphs, their dossiers, their awkward personal questions, trampling through people's secret gardens like a herd of buffaloes—had wrecked more than one promising career.

"What about emergencies?" he queried. "If I think I've been blown and need to get out in a hurry, am I free to contact the Residency then?"

"Not for any reason, ever." Atlas reiterated. "In due course we'll provide an alternative. For now, you'll have to do without."

"In other words, you're my only contact?"

Atlas nodded. "That disturbs you?"

Kalugin thought. Actually it disturbed him a lot. He was isolated, deprived of a bolt hole, totally dependent on this Atlas, whom he didn't trust and knew nothing about. Except, he thought, for the uncomfortable fact that this Atlas knew all about *him.* And this was uncomfortable, it struck him, for precisely the reason it ought to have been reassuring. Atlas, as his mastery of one's biography proved, obviously had been sent from Moscow. If what he'd said about a defection was true, he was here for the safety of Moscow's agents, specifically of its agent Cobalt, cover name Adam Kalugin. But if what he'd said *wasn't* true, then he was here for some other purpose entirely. This wasn't sinister, necessarily, but there was too much here to be taken on trust, Kalugin thought, too much left unexplained and, among the explanations that had actually been offered, too much improbability, too many small disharmonies with fact: the Americans acting out of character, for instance; Zebo acting out of character, too; Pickett dissimulating for no reason that made any kind of sense. Now more than ever, Kalugin found himself missing Zebo. Zebo had been family, he thought. With this Atlas he felt like an orphan.

An orphan in the custody of lawyers.

"It disturbs me a little." He shrugged. "I'm on a tightrope, and now you just took away the net. Naturally that disturbs me a little."

Atlas smiled. "An overdrawn analogy, at least as to risk. But conveying useful suggestions, perhaps, as to conduct. Step carefully. Keep your eye always on the objective."

"The objective? What *is* the objective?"

"The objective hasn't changed. The penetration of emigré organizations in London hostile to the interests of the Soviet Union." Atlas paused. "Did the meeting of the CIA and the Knights of Vladimir take place?"

"It took place." Kalugin nodded. "It turned out as predicted."

"What happened? Specifically."

"The Americans turned them down." Kalugin shrugged. "Not only refused to help them, but ordered them not to proceed. According to the CIA's representative, Pickett, the US is totally committed to détente. The operation proposed by the Knights—I quote—is 'contrary to any current, or currently conceivable, interest of either the US or its allies.' "

Atlas thought for a moment.

"And the Knights? How did they react to this rejection?"

"With the usual all-night debate. The usual arguments repeated ad nauseam, the usual people losing their tempers. Benko and Raina were for going on, with or without CIA help . . ."

Atlas held up a hand to stop him.

"With or without CIA help? But you just said CIA help was refused."

"It was. But Benko thinks they will change their decision. Or rather that they haven't yet decided. Their refusal, he claims, was purely for the record. Like a woman confronting an intriguing proposition, they assert their virtue, buy time to make up their minds."

Atlas smiled. "An expert in female psychology, this Benko."

"Benko . . ." Kalugin dismissed him. "Benko lives in his dreams."

"Not a bad place to live." Atlas's eyes strayed in the direction of the stage, where the vegetable seller was down to G-string and pasties. "Some of the happiest people live in their dreams."

"Also some of the unhappiest. It depends upon the dreams."

"True . . ." Atlas shrugged. "What did the others argue?"

"That the time was not ripe. At four in the morning, when the whiskey ran out, the issue was put to a vote. 'Objective conditions'— this was the motion that was made and carried—'precluded moving to the armed phase of the struggle.' "

" 'Objective conditions . . .' " Atlas raised an eyebrow. "Lenin would have been flattered. They reject his revolution but employ his language. You speak as if you'd been present."

"I was." Kalugin nodded.

"Good," Atlas said. "So what will they do now?"

Kalugin considered. "Continue to live in their dreams. Debate, distribute leaflets, preach to the converted."

"What is your assessment of their potential?"

Kalugin stared. "Their potential for what?"

"Their potential for carrying out their plans."

"I thought I'd already made that clear. Without the Americans they have no potential."

"And with the Americans?"

"A hypothesis contrary to fact and therefore not worth considering." Kalugin shrugged. "They have no potential for obtaining American help. Why waste time worrying about it?"

"I was instructed to ask."

Kalugin stared. "Specifically instructed?"

"Specifically." Atlas nodded. "You should know that, in the light of facts obtained from other sources, Moscow doesn't entirely share your assessment of CIA intentions. There's a feeling there that Benko may be right. If so, the situation can be turned to our advantage."

"Turned? How?"

"Propaganda," Atlas said. "It's obvious, isn't it? A CIA-sponsored plot to assassinate Ukrainian Party leaders is foiled in the very nick of time. When plastered all over the world's front pages, this becomes concrete proof of American duplicity, of the CIA's unwavering hostility to the Soviet state and progressive elements in Soviet society." He paused. The spaniel eyes rested mournfully on Kalugin. "I therefore repeat my earlier question. With CIA support, what is the potential of the Knights of Vladimir for mounting a credible terrorist campaign?"

Propaganda? Proof of American duplicity? The situation turned to our advantage? In a way it *was* obvious, Kalugin thought, obvious to a logic driven by old assumptions, to minds still traveling in Cold War ruts. There was one thing, however, not quite so obvious: Who would profit from all this maneuvering. To *whose* advantage could the situation be turned?

"I think it would be credible to this extent . . ." He smiled faintly. "People would be certain to get killed. With CIA support, this becomes of course a CIA operation. In effect, a sort of lesser Bay of Pigs: CIA planning and training, CIA financing and logistics, the Knights supplying cannon fodder, sacrificial victims, martyrs to the cause."

"You sound skeptical." Atlas eyed him. "Is there something you don't agree with, something you don't understand?"

Kalugin shook his head. "I understand my mission well enough.

What I don't understand is what it achieves. The Cold War is over, why are we still fighting?"

Atlas's expression was difficult to read.

"The Cold War is over. Who *told* you it was over?"

BOOK III
(July 27 to August 28, 1990)

CHAPTER SIXTEEN

(London. July 27, 1990)

"THIS KALUGIN, HOW DID HE COME TO YOUR ATTENTION?"
The question was put to Pickett not by Ackerman, but by the man who up to now had sat silently in an armchair slightly to one side of Ackerman's desk. Ackerman had introduced him simply as Meredith. But the reticence, Pickett thought, was misplaced. Everyone knew who Meredith was. The mystery was why he was in London, inquiring about a Soviet defector whose only claim on anyone's interest was his link with a Ukrainian emigré group, whose only claim on anyone's interest, in turn, was the ludicrous nature of its ambitions, the disproportion between reach and grasp. Presumably Meredith had heard of Kalugin from Ackerman. But why on earth was he interested in him?

"He runs around with that Benko group. Wannabe terrorists, call themselves the Knights of Vladimir."

"I've heard of them." Meredith nodded. "Please go on."

"I met him first with Benko, when I gave them the turn-down on their terrorism proposal. I thought that maybe he was babysitting Benko, though what Benko needs babysitting *from* eludes me." Pickett shrugged. "Himself, mostly. Then later I ran into him again, at a cocktail party given by the Anglo-Polish Alliance. He was hanging out with Chance Davenport."

"Davenport?" Ackerman queried. "The one who works for Rosenthal's foundation? PhD in history or something? Hot little number?"

"Affirmative." Pickett grinned. "To all of the above."

"And Kalugin was cosying up to her?"

Pickett considered. "I'd have to say it was the other way round."

"If true, lucky bastard." Ackerman grinned. He turned to Meredith. "You ought to see this Davenport, Turner. She's a piece of work."

Meredith smiled, but perfunctorily. He looked, Pickett thought, like the type who didn't go in much for locker-room talk. Not, at least, in the course of business.

"Does she have access?"

"She works on that computer simulation they run over there, the one they sometimes call The Game. Heads up the Soviet and East European Section. Since they frequently run scenarios for us, she's cleared for Agency classified up to Secret. Above that level, only if authorized."

"Authorized by whom?"

"Her boss. Who I guess would be Rosenthal."

"Who drools," Ackerman put in, "whenever he's around her."

"To get back to Kalugin . . ."—Meredith ignored the interruption —"you said he *claimed* to have had to defect. Does that mean there's some doubt about that?"

Pickett considered. "I guess it depends how you read the security file."

"The file? You mean *we* have a file on him?"

"Not we, the Brits. It occurred to us that since he'd defected to them, they'd certainly have done a background check."

"So you asked. And they had."

Pickett nodded.

What M15 had come up with, he said, was in itself not all that revealing. Kalugin, whose father had been Polish, had been granted a scholarship to study in Warsaw. He'd arrived in time to take part in the pro-Solidarity demonstrations of the early eighties, and following a brief career of what he'd described to the debriefer as "militantly anti-Soviet activity," had left Poland in a hurry with the KGB hot on his heels. He'd been granted political asylum in England. He spoke Polish, Ukrainian, Russian, and English fluently and worked as a translator, sometimes freelance, sometimes under contract to the Overseas Service of the BBC. To the extent that confirmation was possible, the report had added, Kalugin's claims about his activities in Poland had been confirmed by "independent sources." It had all seemed more or less innocuous. The only things capable of arousing misgivings were relatively minor. Both required one to read between the lines.

"The scholarship is one." This from Meredith, not a question.

Pickett nodded. "It struck *me* as odd. I mean, here's a guy who the moment he gets to Warsaw engages in militant anti-Soviet activity. He told me he got 'swept up,' that he had no previous record. But Soviet citizens who get sent abroad on scholarships also get heavily vetted. They sure as hell did in 1981. So what happened with him? Did the KGB vetters screw up?"

"It's at least conceivable." Meredith smiled faintly. *"Ours* do all the time; theirs must sometimes. What was the other thing?"

"It was what M15 *didn't* say. What I think they *should.* "

Meredith leaned forward. He was paying a lot of attention. More attention Pickett thought, than the subject seemed to warrant. "What should they have said?"

"Whether they tried to recruit him and what happened. It had to have *occurred* to them," Pickett insisted. "The guy is a natural, isn't he? Has the motivation, the languages, the background. You fix him up with papers, a reasonable-sounding legend, minor alterations to his appearance, and you send him back in. Not to Kiev, perhaps— even after an eight-year absence that might have been a little risky— but Lvov or Odessa or some other town." He paused. "The Brits aren't blessed with so many Soviet assets that they can afford to pass up that kind of talent."

"So maybe they didn't?" This from Ackerman. "Maybe they recruited him, or are *trying* to recruit him, and they just aren't telling."

"Doubtful." Meredith shook his head. "Appearances to the contrary notwithstanding, the Brits aren't completely stupid. It's bound to have occurred to them that if we're asking, we're thinking of recruiting him ourselves. If *they* were trying to recruit him, too, or had, presumably they'd want to warn us off."

"So what's your theory?" Ackerman turned to Pickett.

"That they *thought* about recruiting him and for some reason decided not to." Pickett shrugged. "And *that's* what they're not telling us."

"Why wouldn't they?"

"Well, my inquiry was made to Five. They would have done the original background check. But a move to recruit him would have come from Six. Maybe Five didn't wish to divulge info relating to the doings of a sister service." Pickett made a face. "You know how much they despise one another."

Pause for digestion. Nobody present, Pickett knew, could fail to understand him. The Secret Intelligence Service (SIS), formerly

M16, was fiercely hostile toward M15. As was the Agency toward the FBI. Bureaucrats everywhere were insane about turf.

"Let's assume for the moment you're right," Meredith said, "and the Brits do have reservations about this Kalugin. How do *we* find out about him?"

"Go back to the Brits?" Pickett suggested. "Only this time to the horse's mouth. I have good rapport with Faraday, Six's liaison."

"That would certainly be a start." Meredith looked doubtful. "It may not get us very far."

Another pause for meditation, broken this time by Ackerman.

"Why not a Honeytrap?" he said. "Using the Davenport as bait."

"Using Chance?" Pickett stared. "She doesn't even work for us."

"So what?" Ackerman shrugged. "She'd only be doing what, by your report, she's probably doing already. So it's mostly a question of alerting her to possibilities she ought, given her access, to be alerted to anyway. And asking her, of course, to keep her ears open. Who knows?" Ackerman grinned. "Maybe this guy talks in his sleep."

"And who's going to ask her?"

Stupid question. Pickett's heart sank.

"You are. Appeal to her patriotism," Ackerman said. "You could tell her to look at it this way perhaps. It's an opportunity to screw for her country."

An opportunity to screw for her country. One could look at it that way, Pickett thought later, but he doubted Chance Davenport would. Chance, he'd gathered, wasn't much of an admirer of the CIA. She'd almost certainly, if her patriotism were thus appealed to, tell the CIA to go straight to hell. She might tell *him* to go straight to hell, too, and that wasn't a prospect he welcomed. He liked Chance. He en-joyed her company, enjoyed what he hoped he could call their friendship. He'd nursed a hope, too, that friendship might in time turn into something closer. And this hope, though temporarily on hold, might be revived when her affair with Kalugin—if indeed she was having an affair with Kalugin—had run its inevitable course. So he, Pickett, though not normally insubordinate, was not about to do anything so crass as approach her head-on to suggest that she screw for her country. What he *might* do—done right it could even further his own interests—was to slightly reinterpret Ackerman's instruc-tions and warn her, in a roundabout way, of the risks inherent in her current relationship. If she then volunteered to place that relationship at the service of her country, this was a different matter entirely. But before he even approached her this way, he would need to be more certain of the facts about Kalugin. He would go first, he decided, to Faraday at M16, and only afterward, possibly, to Chance.

CHAPTER SEVENTEEN
(London. July 30, 1990)

WHEN THEY MADE HIM WAIT IN THE DOWNSTAIRS CONFERENCE ROOM, Pickett knew at once that the Brits were going to be unhelpful. Had they been planning to confide, they'd have taken him upstairs, to the grubby, ill-lit maze of passages and cubicles where Faraday, their liaison, had his office, an environment, Pickett had often thought, very appropriate to the trading of confidences, especially the kind Faraday and he were in the habit of trading. This conference room, by contrast, looked about as confidential as Union Station: twenty-foot ceiling, enormous fireplace, huge gilt mirror above the marble mantel, crystal chandeliers that must each have weighed more than a ton; and beneath them, taking up most of the floor space, half an acre of polished mahogany table and two or three dozen straight-backed mahogany chairs. It was the ideal setting, he thought, for British Diplomacy with a capital D, with its bland evasions, cagey silences, the kind of chilly magnificence the Brits always wrapped themselves in whenever they planned to be unhelpful. It reminded them, no doubt, of who they used to be, gave them the courage to be snots.

To kill time while he waited, he inspected the portraits that lined the walls. Viscount Palmerston, languid pose suggesting the confidence with which, for more than two decades, he had lorded it over the nations of Europe, stared coolly back from a frame above the fireplace. From the wall opposite, Lord Castlereagh looked down his nose. Beside him, and displaying the same serene conviction of their own perfect fitness to manage the affairs of the planet, were Curzon and Pitt the Younger and, beyond them, others: ministers, viceroys, secretaries of state, the founders and preservers of empire. Indeed, it struck Pickett, the place was less conference room than pictorial history lesson, a shrine to the memory of Pax Britannica, the portraits flanking and dominating the table so that those who sat there must always be conscious of eyes looking over their shoulders, the bleak, censorious gaze of the past.

"Ah . . . Brother Pickett. *There* you are."

Faraday, entering, gave his usual impression of having slept in his clothes. He was coatless, and his shirt, which was coming untucked at the back, lacked a button and had damp patches at the armpits. A lick of hair had fallen into his eyes. The thick horn-rimmed glasses perched on the end of his nose were held together with what looked to be Band-aids. He seemed, at first glance, an odd choice for liaison, the scruffy antithesis of the chilly nobleman whose portraits lined the walls. But acquaintance revealed him as their lineal descendant. He had their brazen, amiable rudeness, and beneath a seemingly distracted manner, a heart like an adding machine. His smile was affable enough, but his greeting conveyed a hint of reproach, the suggestion it was Pickett, and not he, who was late.

"Didn't keep you, did I?" Faraday made a show of consulting his watch. "We did say ten-fifteen?"

"Actually, we said ten." Actually they'd said ten-fifteen, but it was now closer to ten-thirty. "I've been in good company, however. Surrounded by the heroes of your glorious past."

"Heroes?" Faraday looked blank.

Pickett indicated the paintings.

"Oh, those." Faraday shrugged. "Ancestor worship. In that respect, I'm afraid, we're as bad as the bloody Chinese." He cast a disparaging glance at Pitt and Castlereagh. "Old farts."

He turned back to Pickett. "Bit of a hectic day, I'm afraid. Some flap or other in the Middle East. I would have suggested lunch at my club, but I shan't be able to get away. Some other time, perhaps." He paused. "You won't mind if we take the civilities as read, get right down to the nitty gritty?"

He directed a look of inquiry at Pickett, as if waiting for him to state his business. Given that his business had already been stated, this struck Pickett as another discouraging sign.

"Kalugin," he said. "Ukrainian refugee, first name Adam. I called yesterday, remember, asked you to dig out what you had."

"Kalugin . . . Ah, yes, Kalugin." Faraday inspected one of the chandeliers. "Might one ask *why* the so urgent interest in Brother Kalugin?"

"It's not urgent. I happened to run into him at a party. He struck me as interesting." Pickett paused. "The type you guys might have thought of recruiting."

Silence. Faraday peered over the tops of his glasses.

"Also, perhaps, the type *you* guys might have thought of recruiting?"

Pickett shrugged. "It occurred to us, since great minds think alike, that you might know something we ought to know."

"I see." Faraday paused. "Well I'm authorized to tell you that we did, at one point, regard him as a prospect. Also that at a fairly early stage, his file was marked 'No further action.' "

"No further action?" Pickett's impulse to applaud himself on an accurate reading of the M15 report was checked by a twinge of anxiety; he didn't *want* to have read it right. "Are you authorized to say why?"

"Actually not." Faraday's look was opaque. "Not in any detail, I'm afraid."

It was what Pickett had been afraid of. The family tie that in theory existed between the Agency and its British counterpart, SIS, was in practice a bitter sibling rivalry, a closeness bedeviled by fierce competition and a more or less habitual distrust. The Brits, resenting their role as junior partner, had more than once been heard to complain that the "special relationship" was a one-way street, that while they were invariably forthcoming, the Agency was not. Now, it seemed, they were going to play tit for tat.

"Can you tell me, at least, if it had to do with security?"

"I can tell you this much . . ." Faraday, his unblinking watchfulness, reminded Pickett suddenly of a lizard. "If you guys *did* happen to be thinking of trying to recruit him, our recommendation would be that you didn't."

More silence. Pickett was struck by an odd, irrelevant perception about patterns of upper-class English speech. It was the verbs, he thought; there were always either too few or too many.

"That help at all?"

Pickett considered. In one respect it helped a lot. If the Brits, for whatever reason, thought Kalugin unreliable, it wasn't likely that Ackerman would want to recruit him. But recruitment wasn't the only issue. There remained a more pressing and delicate one.

Chance.

Chance and Kalugin. He could see them now, leaving the reception, still almost strangers yet somehow already lovers, connected even then in the subtle alliance lovers always form against the world.

They hadn't touched. And that, of course, had been the giveaway. They hadn't, in the whole time he'd been with them, ever touched. It was almost as if, for fear of too nakedly revealing their need, they hadn't trusted themselves to. Not, of course, that they hadn't revealed their need. Sexual tension had surrounded them like static.

"You all right?" Faraday queried. "You look as if you'd swallowed a toad. This Kalugin bothering you that much?"

"He's not bothering me." Pickett shrugged. "He's just not a problem I feel able to solve, as you guys apparently did, by closing the file. So advising us not to recruit him doesn't help us very much. In fact, if anything, just the opposite."

"I see . . ." You could almost hear the wheels turning in Faraday's head. "I take it, then, that your problem may be not so much with Brother Kalugin as with—could it be?—one of your own."

One of your own. . . . Faraday was a pain, Pickett thought, but not stupid. Though Chance wasn't, strictly speaking, CIA, she *was* a trusted employee of the Foundation for Freedom and an assistant, apparently, to its director. And Martin Rosenthal, though no longer Secretary of State, was a man still consulted by the President and still regularly wined and dined at Langley. He knew more of the nation's secrets, more of what was really going on in the upper reaches of the US government than did most cabinet members. Employees of the Foundation, therefore, and especially employees close to Rosenthal, were subject to regular security checks. Files were kept at Langley. Details of private lives were recorded and acted upon. Occasionally someone who worked for the Foundation would be told that the facts of his private life had been found incompatible with his choice of career. To Pickett, this was entirely reasonable. If you wanted access to Agency secrets, you had to live by Agency rules. A liaison, actual or potential, between an employee of the Foundation and a man whom the Agency might hesitate to recruit was something the Agency was not so much entitled as obliged to look into.

The problem was that "might." There were various reasons why the Agency *might* hesitate to recruit Kalugin, or why the Brits might advise them against it, and not all of them were sinister. It might be Kalugin's character, not his loyalties, that were suspect. In any case, the Brits might be wrong. But one possibility was distinctly troubling: if the Brits thought Kalugin was, or might be, a KGB agent, then Kalugin was strictly off limits to Chance. Anything between them would have to be nipped in the bud. Or rather, since matters between them had obviously passed beyond the budding stage, not nipped but reported to Langley.

But he didn't want to report to Langley. Not, at least, until he knew more about Kalugin.

"You do see *our* problem, of course . . ." The silence had lengthened. Faraday, it seemed, was construing it as an admission. "Whatever he once was, this Kalugin is now a British subject with a constitutional right to privacy. Entitled to expect, in other words, that information obtained by Her Majesty's Government in the course of a confidential security search will be kept confidential, not handed over, no questions asked, to anyone who happens to walk in off the street." Faraday paused, continued blandly. "Unless, of course, the national interest is thought to demand otherwise."

A constitutional right to privacy *unless*. . . . It was, Pickett thought, typical. Pompous British double-talk, meaning in practice no right at all, because the national interest was always whatever Faraday and his ilk—shysters to a man and unhampered by the possession of principles or policy—*wanted* it to be. And it was dollars to doughnuts that what the national interest in this instance was thought to demand was that hayseed allies from across the ocean— that "anyone who happens to walk in off the street" was the giveaway here, of course—should receive a sharp and timely reminder that, special relationship or no, Her Majesty's Government (or at least the shady subbasement division for which Faraday was the official mouthpiece) was not to be taken for granted.

"A constitutional right?" He stared. "You guys actually have a constitution? I thought you made it up as you went along."

"We have one all right. We just don't happen to have it written down. But we can always remember it"—Faraday had the grace to grin—"when we have to."

"And it guarantees privacy to all?" Pickett didn't return the grin. "Exemption from the vulgar curiosity even of long-standing allies guaranteed to all British citizens regardless? Even," he paused, "to former Russians of dubious origin who may or may not work for the KGB?"

Faraday didn't blink. "No one said anything about the KGB."

"True." Pickett nodded. "A significant omission, perhaps?"

"Look," Faraday said. "I've said all I'm authorized to say." He paused. Looking innocent, he added, "If I knew what your problem was, it might help."

"My problem is, I don't know if I have a problem."

"I see," Faraday said. "That makes things difficult, doesn't it?"

"It certainly seems to," Pickett said. "Well, I mustn't take up more of your time. You had some flap going. In the Far East, I recall."

"Middle, actually." Faraday thought for a moment. "Look, I don't want to seem disobliging. What I'm gathering from all this is that someone on your side may have developed a vulnerability to this Kalugin." He paused. "A fair statement?"

A vulnerability. Faraday's knack for hitting the sore spot was uncanny. A vulnerability, Pickett thought, was exactly right.

He nodded. "Close enough."

"Then let me see what I can do." Faraday smiled winningly. "First chance I get, I'll put your predicament to my lords and masters. See if I can get them to unbend a little."

CHAPTER EIGHTEEN

(London. July 31, 1990)

THE LONDON HEADQUARTERS OF THE KNIGHTS OF VLADIMIR, A RENTED one-bedroom apartment above a Tandoori restaurant in a terrace in Westbourne Grove, presented, with respect to the organization it housed, a less than encouraging first impression. The apartment served also as living quarters for Benko and was, in addition to being small, very cramped. The kitchen-cum-dining area, by virtue of the copy machine that took up most of the available space, functioned part-time as what Benko insisted on calling a Publications Room. The bedroom, one corner of which was occupied by short-wave radio equipment and another by a workstation complete with a word processor and printer, did occasional duty as what Benko called a Communications Center. The living room, which was only fifteen feet by twelve and used for meetings of the Knights' Executive Committee, was not quite as cluttered as the others; it contained only a TV set, a large padlocked cupboard, and a couple of beanbags to sit on. Known most of the time as the Operations Room, it was sometimes referred to, presumably on the strength of an ancient Kalashnikov rifle and World War II Mauser that were stored in the padlocked cupboard (there was no ammunition for either), as the Armory.

Kalugin had never been able to quantify precisely the membership of the Knights. He had heard Benko, in his more expansive moments, refer to "chapters" in other English cities and even to "networks of supporters" abroad. He knew that when the short-wave radio was working, Benko was in contact with groups of Ukrainian emigrés elsewhere, though who they were was still a mystery. He had also been told that the Knights' monthly newsletter, *The Flagship,* had a circulation of roughly fifteen hundred; but since a good part of this resulted from Benko's simply depositing copies, unsolicited and in batches of fifteen or twenty, in local restaurants and bars, the figure couldn't be taken, perhaps, as any kind of index of support. Probably Pickett's unflattering estimate of the Knights' constituency ("One half of one percent of the Ukrainian population of West London. Tops.") came a lot closer to the mark. Indeed, it was only by defining the word very loosely that the "membership" could be stretched, it seemed to Kalugin, beyond the half dozen currently assembled. In his *less* expansive moments, even Benko displayed some awareness of this. He was apt to point out, in a somewhat defensive tone, that Lenin himself had started out this way—with a handful of trusted comrades and a printing press in a garret—that to make a splash, moreover, one didn't need large numbers; the world could be, indeed *had* been, altered by a couple of fanatics and a bomb. Such statements, though incontestable, had seemed to Kalugin to offer no grounds for optimism here. Benko, for one thing, was no Lenin. His handful of trusted comrades, for another, appeared to have close to zero potential as bombers: no expertise, no access to explosives, no network of contacts inside the Ukraine, no transportation, no weapons (unless you were willing to count the Kalashnikov and the Mauser), no money to buy the things they lacked and no reasonable prospect of acquiring it. Their only assets were a modest command of the rhetoric of violence and an almost unlimited capacity for wishful thinking. It had therefore seemed, at least until now, that Moscow's instructions regarding these aspiring terrorists were absurdly misconceived. They could order him till doomsday to penetrate the Knights, but compliance would always be frustrated by the fact that there was nothing substantial here to penetrate; the Knights of Vladimir were perpetual adolescents, playing at soldiers on the fringes of history. Or so, at least, he'd firmly believed.

It now appeared he'd been wrong.

"It was around noon," Benko said. "I noticed him first when I came out of Goodge Street Station. I walked him around for a while to make sure he was what he seemed, then I ducked into one of those sandwich counters. You know the kind, they're all over Tottenham Court Road, people packed in shoulder to shoulder, grabbing a bite of lunch on the run. I let him know I knew he was there, gave him chance to make his move."

He paused, looked around the room, his air of laid-back expertise and understated narrative style imperfectly masking real excitement.

Having captured, for once, his membership's attention, he was going to milk it for all it was worth.

"And did he?" somebody asked. "Make his move, I mean."

"Of course. He wasn't that discreet about it, either. Spooks . . ." Benko rolled his eyes. "They're supposed to have all these subtle contact procedures. He stood right next to me at the counter, hardly bothering with his ham and swiss cheese, made a couple of trite remarks about the weather, then started straight in with his pitch." Benko looked over at Kalugin, lounging in one of the bean bags. "You remember Pickett?"

Kalugin nodded. "I remember him. What about him?"

"This guy could have been his clone. He was dressed in that uniform they wear: business suit, wingtips, button-down shirt. He claimed to represent 'important interests.' *Whose* interests he didn't say, but it stuck out a mile he was CIA."

Kalugin refrained from comment. CIA agents, to his certain knowledge, came in a variety of shapes and sizes. No uniforms. No types. Benko's notion of the CIA must have been drawn from books or movies. Likewise his notions of contact procedures. What had actually happened, Kalugin guessed, was that Benko's spook—if he was a spook—had followed him *undetected* for half the morning, establishing thereby that no subtlety was needed.

"What *was* his pitch?"

The question was asked by Raina, Benko's only rival for leadership of the Knights. When not engaged in what he referred to as "the struggle," Raina worked in the post office as a sorter. A surly-looking type with a sallow complexion and straggly beard, he bore some resemblance to Fidel Castro, a notion he encouraged, when not sorting mail, by habitually dressing in camouflage fatigues. When Kalugin had come up for election to the Knights' executive committee, Raina had cast the only negative vote. On the grounds, or so he'd claimed, that Kalugin's background had been insufficiently checked. For all they knew, he'd asserted, this fencing buddy of Benko's could be a KGB spy. At the time this statement had bothered Kalugin. Did Raina, he'd wondered, have extraordinary intuition? Or had he, Kalugin, made some kind of slip? On reflection, however, a less troubling explanation seemed more plausible. He, Kalugin, had been sponsored by Benko, and anything Benko favored Raina on principle opposed.

"He said his people had heard about us." Though responding to Raina's question, Benko didn't address him directly, speaking instead to the rest of the group. "He said they might be willing, under certain conditions, to sponsor certain of our activities. He wrote a number on the back of a napkin, told me if I was interested to call it." Benko paused. "So naturally I went ahead and called."

"You took this action on your own initiative?" Raina again. "Without consulting the Committee?"

This time Benko did look at him. Wearily.

"I'm consulting you now." He spoke without heat. "Now that there's something to consult you *about.* The process would be easier, I might add, if you'd shut up for a moment and listen."

"What about security?" Raina persisted. "This so-called CIA man could easily have been some KGB provocateur. Did you ask him for any identification."

"But *of course.*" Benko sighed. "I got him to show me his Agency ID. Demanded it right there at the luncheon counter. And of course he showed it to me. It displayed his photograph, passport size, identified him as Agent X, currently employed by the CIA and operating under deep, deep cover." He conferred on Raina the kind of look normally reserved for idiots and tiresome children. "His identification, the only one he needed, as you'd realize if you'd *think* for half a second, was the fact that he *knew* about our activities, especially our approach to the CIA. Who else, beside us and the CIA, has access to this information?"

"Who knows who has access to it?" Raina gave a theatrical shrug, glanced significantly at Kalugin. "Your fencing partner did. And *before* we elected him to this committee. An action which, as I'm sure you'll recall, I was adamant in opposing."

"I recall perfectly." Benko nodded. "You were adamant and without support. An adamant minority of one. Now"—turning smoothly to the others—"should I continue with my report? Or shall we reopen already decided questions?"

"I'm reopening nothing," Raina said. "I'm pointing out, merely, that your previous carelessness in matters of security renders your conclusions about this man's identity open, at least, to serious question. You should have proceeded with more caution."

"Well, he didn't," somebody cut in. "Maybe he should have, but he didn't. Why don't you let him get on with the report."

Raina ignored this. "As a point of procedure"—mulishly—"I move that my reservations about the director's actions be entered in the record."

"Is there a second?" Benko queried, blandly.

It appeared there wasn't.

"Motion denied." Benko shrugged.

Kalugin resisted an impulse to sigh. The exchange was typical of these meetings, which were governed always by some bastardized version of Roberts' Rules of Order. There actually was someone taking minutes, solemnly recording in a leatherbound notebook not only the interminable points of order, every sophomoric motion or interjection, but also full details of the Knights' terrorist plans. What happened to these minutes between meetings wasn't clear. Probably Benko hid them under his mattress.

"As a point of procedure . . ." Some impulse of mischief prompted him to break his normal habit of silence. "I move that Committee member Raina be instructed to defer his reservations until the director has completed his report." He paused. "I also move that Committee member Vottichenko be requested to stop hogging the whiskey."

General laughter.

"Second both motions," somebody said.

It took them a while to get back on track. Someone wondered, at considerable length, whether Roberts' Rules permitted their considering two separate motions at once. Raina made a speech, interrupted by jeers and whistles, denouncing tyrannical majorities. Vottichenko denied hogging the whiskey, but when the bottle was discovered to be empty, volunteered to go out for more. Contributions were solicited. Someone suggested sending out for food, but a motion to this effect, though seconded, failed to carry. Benko patiently sat through all this, glancing at Kalugin and rolling his eyes, but otherwise not objecting.

And this patience was out of character for him, Kalugin thought; he clearly had something momentous to report. Had the CIA *really* changed its mind? This seemed to be the conclusion to which the narrative was tending, but it was inconceivable, wasn't it? Whatever else they might be, the senior officers of the CIA weren't irresponsible fools. They wouldn't, surely, do anything so irrational as to encourage, even *sub rosa,* the terrorist ambitions of these clowns. But Atlas, on the other hand, had predicted this outcome. Or rather he'd said that *Moscow* predicted it. Did Moscow have some extraordinary gift of foresight? Or did someone in Moscow know something that he, Kalugin, didn't?

It seemed, when Benko continued, that one of these alternatives had to be correct. Benko's phone call to the number on the napkin had led, at any rate, to a meeting in the Park Lane Hotel. He'd been instructed, he told them, to present himself there as an applicant for employment with the Seagrave Electronics Corporation. Though Seagrave Electronics, as it turned out, was indeed registered as conducting job interviews in Suite 294, Benko had had the notion, prior to going to the meeting, to look into the background of his putative employer, mostly, he'd confessed, from pure curiosity. A quick phone call to the Registrar of Companies had revealed that no Seagrave Electronics was licensed to do business in the United Kingdom. He'd felt safe in concluding, therefore, that the identity of the Robert Seagrave who'd conducted his interview had been as fictitious as the corporation.

Encountered in person, moreover, Robert Seagrave had shown little interest in maintaining fictions, at least about himself and Seagrave Electronics. The interests he represented, he'd told Benko, had learned "on the proverbial grapevine" something of the activities of Benko's group, in particular of a request they had recently made to the London branch of "a multinational company" for help in expanding their operations into markets opened up by the recent relaxation of Cold War tensions. Technicalities connected with its charter unfortunately prevented the multinational in question from complying with the request. The interests he, Seagrave, represented were subject, however, to no such restrictions. They saw in Benko's suggestions "an opportunity for profit" and accordingly wished to propose a joint venture. Their contribution would be money, such special resources as the project might require, and a "management and planning capability," Benko's group would furnish, simply, manpower.

"You see," Benko said. "I was right. They shut the front door in our faces, but now they're inviting us in through the back." He surveyed them for a moment, relishing his triumph. "I *told* you."

They were silent for a moment.

"What did you tell *him?*" Raina asked.

"I told him"—Benko spoke with quiet dignity, also, Kalugin thought, with a certain dry satisfaction—"I told him I'd have to consult the executive committee. I also told him that I felt confident the Committee would accept what was, after all, *our* proposal."

He paused.

"This is our chance," he said. "For years we've screwed around here in London, distributing newsletters and holding meetings, squabbling about policy, disputing points of order, voting whether to send out for food. This is our chance to actually do something. This is our chance to step off the sidelines, to act instead of perpetually talking, to offer a sacrifice to our country. I think it will be our *only* chance. We do it now, or we don't do it. We do it now, or admit to ourselves, once and for all, that all we've been doing is playing games, that our patriotism is nothing but noise."

He paused again, looking at each of them in turn, subjecting his cohort to grave scrutiny. He really meant it—somehow this had never struck Kalugin before—Benko actually *believed* what he said. And because of it, because he was willing to offer what he asked, he achieved, at this moment of borderline lunacy, dignity and even a kind of charisma. His aspirations might be ludicrous, his efforts to attain them, as he'd more or less acknowledged, might at times include most of the elements of farce, but at least he'd stayed faithful to his cockeyed ambition. It was easy to ridicule his innocence, his earnestness, the yawning gulf between his reach and his grasp, but he'd kept, in spite of everything, his honor. It was more than could be said about most people. More, Kalugin thought, than could be said about himself.

"Personally," Benko continued, "I don't think there's anything to debate. The risks are obvious, both political and otherwise, but it's obvious also we have to take them. Where else are we going to get what we need: weapons, training, transportation? What do we have to offer in exchange, except our lives. Is there anyone here"—he looked at Raina—"who disagrees?"

Raina said nothing. He and the rest were looking nonplused, like terriers that had chased a bear and unexpectedly caught it. It was always awkward, Kalugin thought, to have your rhetoric taken at face value.

"It'd be nice . . ." someone offered hesitantly. "I personally would feel more comfortable, that is, if we knew for certain who we were dealing with."

"We can't know that," Benko said crisply. "Not for certain, at any rate. It's an elementary security principle. Since what they're doing is officially prohibited, they have to operate through a front. It's exactly what they did with the Contras. We're what's known in the business as disavowable."

Disavowable? That, Kalugin thought, was what it was known as in the newspapers, by wheelers and dealers in the back rooms of power who in general preferred to avoid the unpleasantness of actually calling a spade a spade. In the business it was known more honestly:

"covering your ass," "letting the other guy sign the papers," "putting some other sucker's head on the block." And there would be heads on the block, he thought, most of them heads right here in this room. That reference to the Contras—surprising no one else had picked up on it—ought, in context, to have struck them as ominous.

"Then how do we know they're dealing in good faith?" The question was put by Leonid Vasa, an occasional ally of Raina, a small, spare man whose ash-blond hair and bleached subterranean pallor seemed to indicate Estonian ancestry. Vasa spoke seldom, seemed to think more than most. His question struck Kalugin as a good one.

"That will be answered in due course. We'll know, eventually, by how they act, whether they deliver what they promise. For now, we have at least this to go on . . ." Benko paused, looked around, addressed himself to the meeting at large. "People like that don't screw around. They've better uses for their time and money. If they *aren't* dealing in good faith, why bother?"

Vasa nodded, apparently satisfied. The others, too, seemed to find this logic compelling. Kalugin didn't. Looked at another way, he thought, what Benko had asked raised doubts more disturbing than any it was meant to lay to rest. Why would people like that, people averse to wasting time and money, bother with screwballs like the Knights of Vladimir? It was only blindness to reality, *purblindness* in respect of their own abilities, that prevented Benko, Vasa, and the rest from seeing, as he did, something mysterious and sinister here. Either some high-up in the CIA had taken absolute leave of his senses, or more was going on here than met the eye. And either way the Knights of Vladimir were in over their heads, were pawns in a chess game whose outlines and purpose one couldn't at the moment begin to guess. Benko, earlier, had mentioned sacrifice. That word, Kalugin thought, was likely to prove apt.

And he was to be the Judasgoat. His role, as Atlas had made clear, was to lead these lambs to slaughter. Until now he'd managed, more or less, to keep from owning that knowledge. So long as the Knights had confined themselves to playing, he'd been able to persuade himself that so was he. What guilt he'd felt at exploiting his friendship with Benko was mitigated by the conviction that this exploitation was essentially harmless. His reports to Moscow, he'd thought, would be filed and quickly forgotten. In the last half hour all that had changed. What faced him now were the full, ugly consequences of what he had chosen to be. What he was was a spy, a KGB illegal. His business was deceit and betrayal, in this case the betrayal of a friend. He was ambushed, suddenly, by self-contempt.

"They propose a team of four." Benko, having cleared his major hurdle, galloped briskly to the finish. "Plus two reserves for accidents or injuries in training. Preparations and training will take place at a facility in the country. Transportation, to and from, will be provided. Training is expected to take about a month. When a final determination of targets and dates has been made, the team, for obvious security reasons, will be quarantined until after the mission. Since training and planning will be full-time, those involved will quit their jobs. Compensation will be provided." He paused. His succinct presentation of these details, Kalugin thought, suggested his response to Seagrave's proposal had been rather more forthcoming than he'd previously let on. No one else seemed to have noticed, however.

"I myself, obviously, will lead the team. We need volunteers for the other positions."

"I volunteer." Raina's hand shot up. It was instantly followed by others, Kalugin's among them. It was obvious he *had* to volunteer, not only in order to pursue his mission, but to retain Benko's trust, to preempt Raina's insinuations. If chosen, of course, he would need to wriggle out later. *How* he didn't have any idea, but this was a bridge he could cross when he came to it. He looked round at the others. Everyone of them had raised their hands.

"I expected this," Benko said simply.

He seemed genuinely moved. So, suddenly, did the others. Something important, their flushed faces and shining eyes told Kalugin, had happened to them in the last few moments. As the hands had gone up, a bond had been forged between them. After all the years of tedium and futility, destiny, they thought, had summoned them to glory. And the *feeling* at least was genuine. Though destiny, as they'd soon enough find out, had summoned them to nothing but disaster, the promptness with which they'd answered that call was something in which they could take pride. And watching them, pretending to be one of them, knowing that this time *he* was playacting and *they* were not, he could only feel diminished.

"So many volunteers." Benko was grinning delightedly. "We need some method of selection. How?"

This, the kind of question they relished, prompted a return, temporarily, to earlier habits of discussion. The debate that followed was punctuated, as usual, by points of order, elaborately argued. Most of the speakers, ignoring the topic of method, urged with varying degrees of immodesty their own qualifications for inclusion in the team. In the end, a proposal to let Benko choose was defeated by a motion offered by Raina: each member to list his three choices, the lists to be then collated and the three names occurring most frequently to be selected, the two runners-up to be reserves, ties to be decided by run-off election. This process—a number of run-offs proved necessary—took up most of another hour. It was close to midnight when the team was announced.

Kalugin was named one of the reserves.

CHAPTER NINETEEN

(London. August 2, 1990)

"AHA . . ." ATLAS SAID. "I SEE YOUR LITTLE PLAN. FOR YOUR NEXT move you contemplate bishop takes pawn. If I then take the bishop, you play knight to knight five, discovered check, and capture my queen. End of story." Atlas paused, peered at Kalugin over the tops of his glasses. "But if I *don't* take the bishop, what then?"

Kalugin shrugged. Failure to take the bishop would lead at once to the loss of another pawn and the destruction of Atlas's inadequately defended center, ultimately to an irresistible attack on the square at his king's bishop two. He wasn't about to explain this, however. In due course Atlas would discover it for himself.

"So . . . You like this Benko, some of those other Knights?" Atlas, moving his queen to avoid the threat from Kalugin's knight, took up the thread of their previous conversation as smoothly as if it had never been broken. "Explain to me, please, the relevance of that."

He subjected Kalugin to momentary scrutiny. He had, Kalugin thought, a talent for keeping you off balance, an ability not only to keep track perfectly of several thought processes at once, but to do the same with his feelings, to alternate with seeming conviction and no apparent effort between genial chess partner and frowning superior. It was hard to decide which, if any, of his seeming emotions was real.

"Liking is liking," Kalugin said. "Does it have to be relevant to something?"

He glanced at the board. The tactical threat that Atlas was no doubt pleased with himself for spotting had served its deeper strategic purpose. Atlas's countermove, though removing his queen from danger, had removed it also from the defense of his king. The assault on black's bishop two square could now begin with the capture of the pawn on queen five.

Kalugin took the pawn.

Atlas, looking startled, studied the board intently. Presently, having moved (without, Kalugin saw, noticeably improving his position), he spoke again: "We were speaking of your mission to entrap these so-called Knights. Presumably when you mentioned *liking* these would-be killers, you intended the statement to bear in some way on that mission. My problem is in understanding how."

He broke off, hearing footsteps. Kalugin glanced up. The kibitzer was a boy this time: around twelve years old at a guess, pale skin, freckles, carroty hair, thick-lensed spectacles—the kind of kid, by the look of him, who spent every evening at his local chess club, most of his spare time studying opening theory. It hadn't been much of an idea, Kalugin thought, Atlas's notion for disguising this contact. Though intended to make them less conspicuous (on the dubious assumption that meeting on Wimbledon Common to play chess was inherently less likely to attract hostile attention than meeting on Wimbledon Common to just talk), it was actually accomplishing just the reverse. This kibitzer was their fourth in forty minutes. Another drawback was that Atlas played lousy chess.

The newcomer stood over them, subjected their game to a brief, condescending inspection.

"Black is *kaput,*" he announced. "Up shit creek without a paddle."

Atlas gave him an affronted stare.

"What the hell would you know about it? And who asked you, anyway?"

"My rating is over two thousand. What's yours?" The boy seemed not to mind, indeed to actually welcome, the display of hostility from Atlas. "I can tell you this much for free . . . If you quit right now, you wouldn't be hurting your chances." He turned in appeal to Kalugin. "Am I right?"

Kalugin grinned and nodded.

"His throat is cut, he just doesn't know it."

"Why don't you bug off?" Atlas was staring at the board, presumably in an effort to discover just where and how his throat had been cut. "Go play with yourself in the bushes or something."

The boy affected to consider this suggestion.

"Be a lot more fun than chess with a hacker like you."

As he walked away he paused to look back for a second, delivered himself of the ultimate insult. "Woodpusher."

Atlas ignored, turned back to Kalugin.

"I read somewhere," he said, "in some psychiatric journal or other, that chess players, habitual, dedicated chess players—like you and presumably that child—are actually sublimating an impulse to parricide. The urge to kill the father, guiltily repressed, is symbolically expressed in the quest to kill the king." He paused. "What is your opinion of this theory."

"What's my opinion?" Kalugin considered. "I ask myself what relevance this has to the previous subject. Which was, if you recall, my mission."

Atlas looked at him sideways. "Did you ever read Kafka?"

"In college." Kalugin shrugged. "In translation."

"You'll remember then that in Kafka, the father, like the king, is almost always a symbol of authority." He paused to scrutinize Kalugin for a moment. "A control could, I suppose, be considered a substitute father. Authority, after all, is implicit in the word."

Kalugin thought about this.

"I don't think your theory can apply in my case. My father was hardly ever home. My mother died giving birth to me. I was mostly raised by my sister." He paused. "The authority figures you cite are all male. Mine were, or ought to have been, female."

But I did kill her, he thought. At least I permitted her to die. By doing nothing to help her, I assented to her death. The self-accusations stabbed him suddenly, without warning, like knives. But they made no sense, he told himself, no logical sense. Katya had killed Katya. His only role had been reluctant witness.

"I find such theories tedious," he continued, "persuasive only if you ignore the details. If you want to believe that in beating you at chess I express resentment of your authority, I can only point out that the chess was your idea."

"But you can't deny that you don't like me?" Atlas's gaze was quizzical, even amused. "That you take great pleasure from beating me so easily?"

"The pleasure would actually be greater if the process weren't so easy. As for my disliking you . . ." Kalugin shrugged. "We were speaking earlier of relevance. *That,* truly, is irrelevant."

"I don't think so. I concede that the theory about chess may well be nonsense. But I think your evident dislike of me, your admitted liking for this Benko, are expressions of a basic disaffection. You dislike your mission," Atlas said. "Subconsciously you resist it. As your control, I need to be concerned about this."

He paused, waiting for some response. Kalugin said nothing.

"I think it would help both of us." Atlas's tone was almost gentle. "If you'd explain what is bothering you here."

What to tell him? For a moment Kalugin was tempted from sheer weariness with his own isolation to believe that the act of conferring his trust could somehow make Atlas worthy of it. But he knew that the feeling was one interrogators routinely made use of, exploiting in their subjects the need to give trust, the urge to break down walls of isolation. And he remembered that Atlas had lied to him, had *started* their relationship by lying. Atlas was not to be trusted. No more to be trusted, though he hadn't yet caught her in a lie, than Chance Davenport was. No more, since the ultimate agendum of this conversation was his own betrayal of the Knights of Vladimir, than he himself was. His profession—its essential nature was now for the first time becoming really clear to him—was deception piled on deception; its methods were lies and betrayal; its purpose was survival; and its first commandment was, "Trust no one, least of all your friends."

In the meantime, however, he had to respond plausibly to this overture of friendship from Atlas.

"If I've been hostile, I'm sorry," he said. "But as you say, a control can come to seem like a father. The man who was my control for five years is dead. Perhaps the cause of my coldness to you was simply this: that you are not Zebo."

Atlas considered this for a moment, nodded.

"That makes sense," he said. "I sincerely hope that in time we can come to be friends, that eventually you'll feel as comfortable with me as you clearly felt with your former control. However . . ."—he paused, looked at Kalugin squarely—"that is only desirable, it is not vital. What is vital is that we function effectively together, and this brings me back to the crucial issue. What is it you so dislike about your mission?"

Kalugin thought for a moment.

"You were speaking earlier," he said, "about the significance of chess. To you, it's essentially displacement activity; it permits the harmless release of what might otherwise be lethal aggression. To me, it's much simpler; it's a game, an end in itself." He paused. "I think that what bothers me about this mission is its similarity to chess. The process seems to have become the purpose. We exploit an opportunity that seems to be offered, simply because it *is* offered. And whatever their specific objective may be, the Americans essentially are doing the same. As for these Knights of Vladimir, they're clowns, but the question is: who empowers them? I think the answer is that we all do: the Americans by handing a loaded revolver to people who, politically, are hardly more than backward children, and we by permitting this farce to go forward when we stop it right now without bloodshed." Kalugin shrugged. "A phone call from Moscow to Washington would do it."

And actually, he thought, *I* could do it.

He noticed that Atlas was looking at him oddly.

He had said too much, he thought. Far too much. Though he hadn't actually acknowledged his distrust, what he *had* acknowledged was perhaps even worse. It came close, in the twisted theology he lived by, to the mortal sin of despair. Like a novice confessing doubt as to his hope of eventual salvation, he'd admitted to Atlas (who'd be less understanding than any confessor) doubt as to the point of their professional existence. What he'd really told him, in almost so many words, was that he, Kalugin, wasn't to be trusted.

"Of course, as they say, the soldier in the trenches always knows least about the progress of the battle . . ." What he had to do now, and at once, was repair as much as he could of the damage without revealing his knowledge that damage had been done. "I'm sure there are purposes here I'm unaware of. And it's important to me to feel that there are such purposes, because otherwise my deception of Pavel Benko is, in my eyes at least, merely dishonorable."

Merely dishonorable . . . He was inclined to congratulate himself on that "merely." He could almost see, behind the impenetrable stare, Atlas turning the word over, examining it from different angles. Since honor wasn't a word encountered very often in their profession, his joining it to that interesting "merely" would suggest, he hoped, conflicting motives held in precarious balance: idealism tempered by respect for the pragmatic, the desire to think "well" of himself joined sensibly to the recognition that other considerations must at times be allowed to prevail.

The question was, would Atlas buy it?

"I understand your concern." Eventually Atlas nodded. "I can personally assure you, moreover, that there *are* serious purposes here which require that this 'farce' be permitted to go forward and that you play the role allotted to you in it. I may add that you've done well so far and that this fact has been duly noted. Your orders now are to build on your success. We need details." Atlas was suddenly peremptory. "Details on everything. Dates, targets, methods, means of transportation, intended points of entry, location of the training facility, identities or descriptions of the people engaged in the training." He paused. "Do you have a camera? A miniature? For photographing the training facility."

"Not wise." Kalugin shook his head. "The people who made the approach to Benko have been careful so far to conceal their identities. I don't see them getting careless now. Before they admit us to the training facility they may well search. If they found me smuggling in a Minox, I don't think I'd last very long."

"A good point." Atlas nodded.

"On the subject of lasting . . ." Kalugin hesitated. "Several issues occur to me."

"Issues?" Atlas stared.

"Contacts for one. If the CIA hopes to conceal its role in this business, I think we can expect them, once they know the makeup of the team, to take a close interest in its members. That means, for one thing, background checks." Kalugin paused. "Those I should be able to survive. Or I should, at least"—he shot a sideways glance at Atlas —"if the makers of my legend knew their business."

"I'm confident of that." Atlas frowned. "Please make your point about contacts."

"I think we can expect surveillance. Or I think *I* can. As anyone checking my background will discover, I'm a refugee from the Soviet Union. If I were CIA security, worried about KGB penetration, the object of my deepest suspicion, my closest scrutiny, would be Adam Kalugin."

"So?"

"I think we need to limit our contacts, because now they're my point of maximum exposure. The less we meet, the safer I'll be."

Atlas thought about this.

"That makes sense, I suppose, on general principles. But why, if you were CIA security, would you worry particularly about penetration?"

"On general principles," Kalugin said. "Since I'm involved in something completely unauthorized, I'd worry about getting caught. I'd worry that perhaps I was being sucked into some kind of KGB provocation."

"Would you?" Atlas looked at him sharply. "Then perhaps it's just as well for us you're not CIA security. You might worry out the truth of this operation." He gave Kalugin a sudden grin and just as suddenly went back to frowning. "You worry a lot. Perhaps too much. Tell me what else you worry about?"

"Surviving," Kalugin said. "I'm ordered to obtain intelligence on an ultrasensitive operation whose authors will therefore be ultravigilant and focusing their vigilance, most probably, on me. I worry about the things I've mentioned, but I worry even more that, in this environment of heightened risk, I don't any longer have anywhere to run to." He paused, stated his conclusion bluntly. "I need a Residency contact number."

"No." Atlas shook his head. "I've told you already. The Residency may not be secure. If you used it as an emergency contact, you'd be adding to your personal risk and might also jeopardize the operation."

He paused.

"As I said before, you worry too much. The guarantee of your safety here is the fact that we need you. You can be sure we'll do all in our power to protect you. My advice to you is to stop worrying and focus on your mission. Leave the worrying"—Atlas smiled—"to us."

We'll protect you because we need you. One ought, Kalugin thought, to be reassured by such candor. He found himself, however, failing to be. For one thing, he seemed to be involved—a fact that would make anyone uneasy—in a situation that didn't make sense. But there were other imponderables, too: Why, for instance, had Zebo been killed? And why had Atlas lied about who did it? Why had Chance Davenport pursued him, practically dragged him into bed? And what was her real relationship with Pickett? There was, in short, even if one conceded the will, serious reason to doubt his masters' *ability* to protect him. And should he necessarily concede the will? How much, really, did they need him? And even if they needed him now, what about later? Atlas's assurances notwithstanding, the best guarantee of his safety, he decided, was and always would be his own vigilance, his obedience to his calling's first commandment:

Trust no one, least of all your friends.

CHAPTER TWENTY

(Sussex, England. August 4, 1990)

"C'MON THEN, LET'S 'AVE YER."

This one at least seemed to know his business. He faced Kalugin in a loose half-sideways crouch, circling always to the left, hands open and held low, weight balanced lightly on the balls of his feet. A big man, probably in his early fifties, with tree-trunk legs and simian arms, he'd be strong as a bear and, in spite of a heavy build and the spare tire of flesh round his middle, fast. He was wearing Levi's, rope-soled sneakers, and a dirty white T-shirt with the sardonic instruction, "Visualize Whirled Peas," stenciled in green on the front. An ex-serviceman, probably, with a talent for violence and a taste for inflicting it on the unwary, he reminded Kalugin of instructors he'd encountered in Kiev.

Thugs were thugs, it seemed, the world over.

"C'mon." Whirled Peas leered and beckoned. "You're the one that's got the knife. Take a cut at me. Kill me."

It was tempting to take him at his word. A quick feint from the right, the attack coming in low and fast, the knife switching hands at the very last instant, and Mr. Whirled Peas ("If you 'ave to call me anything, you may call me Sir") would find himself breathing through a hole in his gut. Commitment was what it took. Speed helped, of course, as did a little technique, but mostly what you needed was a disregard of cost. Most people lacked this of course. Since the notion of inflicting pain was as hard for them to bear as the thought of receiving it, their aggressions were not only unskillful, but half-hearted. Which was why a thug like Whirled Peas could feel confident with only his bare hands against a knife. It helped, too, of course, when the knife, as it was in this instance, was rubber.

"C'mon, laddie . . . Whadd'ya waitin' for, Christmas? Mebbe

you 'ope if you stall long enough, I'll fall down an' die of old age."
Whirled Peas grinned at his own refulgent wit. "Come on then, let's
'ave yer."

It was tempting, but Kalugin knew he mustn't. He was meant to be
an amateur, not meant to know about these things. It wouldn't do
anything at all for his cover, which so far seemed to have survived
whatever scrutiny had been leveled at it, to display here anything of
the expertise that, in the Unarmed Combat course in Kiev, had
placed him first in a class of forty. The trick here, difficult to pull off,
was to seem convincingly clumsy without, in the process, exposing
himself too much. The pleasure Whirled Peas took in his work bordered, it was clear, on the unhealthy.

For those on the receiving end, at least.

But here again the issue was commitment. Commitment meant
not thinking about pain. Though Whirled Peas might hurt him, he
wasn't going to kill him. Kalugin came in suddenly with kamikaze
abandon, left shoulder leading, the knife thrust delayed then slicing
upward at the solar plexus, more blow than thrust and delivered with
all the force he could muster. He met no resistance. His right wrist
was grasped and twisted, the thrust deflected past its target, momentum hurling his upper body forward at the same time as his feet,
encountering a firmly planted leg, went out from under him. He
pitched face-forward onto the turf and suffered, almost in the same
split second, a bone-jarring shock as a hefty knee, driven by Whirled
Peas' fifteen stone, came slamming into the small of his back. A
handful of his hair was seized, his head was peremptorily yanked
back, and the edge of his own (rubber) knife drawn deliberately,
derisively, across his Adam's apple.

"Consider yer throat cut," Whirled Peas said. "If I were a Russkie
Border Guard, *you* would not be getting up again, ever."

Kalugin said nothing. His throat was cut. In any case, he was dazed
and winded. A trickle of blood, descending from his nose via his chin
to his neck, lent a touch of lurid color to the fiction.

Whirled Peas made no move to release him, and instead addressed
himself to Benko and the others.

"Let us now," he said, "as teachers always should, focus first on
the positive aspects, defer until later our criticisms. 'E may be lying
'ere, flat on 'is face, drownin' in pools of 'is own life's blood, but at
least 'e got some things right . . .

"Item one." Theatrical pause. The voice took on a hectoring, di-
dactic quality, as if quoting, as it probably was, from some manual of

instruction. The cockney accent, Kalugin had noted, was intermittent. It alternated with intonations whose origins were obscure and conceivably not even English. "The knife was gripped correctly, palm up, the blade directed by the forefinger and thumb, the thrust delivered from below with the ascending motion needed to carry the point up under the ribs, invading the vital organs. The lungs are always the target of choice." Pause here to release Kalugin's head. "Very painful, that is, suckin' air through the gut. Takes the fight out of almost anyone."

Removing his knee from the small of Kalugin's back, Whirled Peas stood up. Almost gently, he helped Kalugin to his feet. He inspected him briefly, as if to satisfy himself no permanent harm had been done. Then, surprisingly, he reached into his pants' pocket and, extracting a dirty white handkerchief, handed it to Kalugin.

Kalugin, feeling foolish, wiped what he could of the blood from his face. Whirled Peas turned back to the others.

"Item two. 'E did it like 'e meant it. If that knife'd found its intended target, my guts'd be pinned to the back of my 'ead . . ." Kalugin received a nod of approbation. Whirled Peas turned back to the others. "And that's the foundation for everything really. If you're gonna stick someone, do it. Don't pussyfoot around. Fuckin' well do it or someone'll stick you."

A moment was allowed for this point to sink in.

"Now." The lesson continued. "We come to the sixty-four-dollar question. If he did so much right, 'ow come he ended up dead?"

There followed a disquisition on balance to which Kalugin, who knew very well where he'd gone wrong, paid little attention. To him the vital question was different: What was the *point* of this charade? That it was a charade had been more than once proved, in the five days of training they been given so far, not only by some startling inaccuracies of detail, but by the whole program's inaptness to its stated purpose. Whirled Peas' reference to Border Guards, for instance, was a striking illustration of both deficiencies. If you tried to cross the border illegally and got unlucky enough to bump into a Soviet Border Guard, unarmed combat or for that matter knife-fighting skills weren't going to do you any good. For the Border Guards, who constituted a separate directorate of the KGB, were armed with automatic weapons and the very latest in night-vision equipment. A Border Guard wouldn't cut your throat, he'd blow the back of your silly head off. But this information, though important to have if you did happen to be planning an illegal border crossing, was here completely beside the point. There was simply no *need* to cross illegally. The way things were in the Soviet Union now, getting in was a simple matter of applying for a tourist visa. The documents necessary for the subsequent operation could sent in by diplomatic bag—presumably these people, whoever they were, had *that* much access at least —to await collection at one of the US consulates in the Ukraine. Some such procedure, at any rate, was not only ten times less risky than border-jumping but also much better suited to the mission. If you planned to assassinate officials in Kiev, your only hope of success was through stealth. Violence at the border, of whatever variety, would doom the enterprise from the start. The Knights' team would need to melt into the background, seem like ordinary Soviet citizens going about their lawful business. Roughhousing with Border Guards, creeping thereafter through the countryside, armed to the teeth, subsisting on emergency rations and communicating by (out of date) shortwave radios like so many World War II freedom fighters, was a scenario for nothing but disaster. It was theatricals, pure and simple. Amateur theatricals, at that.

But this, the amateur quality of the training, didn't extend to the security arrangements. Or not those arrangements pertaining to the security of the *hosts*. At five o'clock each morning the Knights' team would assemble at a house in Putney and submit to a careful body search. (Thank God, he thought, that he'd refused to carry a Minox!). Then, having loaded themselves into an entirely windowless compartment in the back of a passenger van, they'd be driven an indeterminate distance—the drive was never less than one hour or more than two—to arrive at a sprawling Victorian mansion whose spacious park was enclosed by a fifteen-foot-wall and patrolled by men with shotguns. Presumably it was somewhere in the country. Presumably also, though Kalugin, from inside, wasn't able to verify this, the van was escorted on its daily odyssey by the normal complement of sweepers. These travel arrangements, and the fact that certain areas of the grounds, notably those close to the walls and around the gatehouse, had been declared off-limits to the Knights, were allegedly for their protection. To Kalugin, however, the real purpose was obvious. The anonymous sponsors of this project, whatever guesses as to their identity Benko and his cohorts might care to make, fully intended to remain anonymous.

Benko, though aware of this, saw nothing sinister in it. It was understandable, he told Kalugin, that the CIA, while providing vital support, should insist on avoiding the risk of exposure. It was not *their* homeland whose freedom was contemplated here, nor would anything useful be achieved by an open acknowledgment of involvement. Had he been able to share Benko's conviction that the source of the support was indeed the CIA, Kalugin could have granted the reasoning some force. The problem was, he couldn't. He'd been trained to view the CIA as a serious organization, an intelligence service rationally directed and professionally run. There was nothing rational that he could see in the decision to assist the Knights' designs, and nothing professional in the assistance so far provided. What they were dealing with here—his conviction had grown with each day of training—was some maverick group whose methods were nearly as strange as its motive was inscrutable.

It was hard, moreover, not to wonder occasionally why no misgivings, at least as to the nature of their training, had occurred to Benko and the other team members. But they had thrown themselves into "Small Arms/Use and Maintenance," "Radio Communications," and "Map-reading" with all the misplaced enthusiasm they were bringing now to "Unarmed Combat" and would shortly be bringing, no doubt, to "Explosives, Detonators, and Timing Devices." And though sessions on "Internal Means of Transport," "Soviet Institutions," and "Cultural Familiarization" were scheduled, none of the trainees seemed quite to grasp that there was more involved in passing for Ukrainians than the possession of an adequate set of documents and fluency in the language. They all seemed caught up in some Hollywood B-feature dream of patriotism and machismo that had wholly overwhelmed their capacity for critical thinking. Not, Kalugin thought, that their capacity for such thinking had ever amounted to much. Indeed, given the illogic and self-deception that colored *all* of their thinking, the lack of misgivings was perhaps not surprising at all. Anyone who could swallow whole *their* cockeyed fantasy of counterrevolution would hardly choke on a few aberrant details.

But surprising or not, it was still rather sad. However this scenario was meant to work itself out, one thing was certain: if it worked itself out to the end, this dream would turn into nightmare; the Knights would find themselves littering the stage like the incidental casualties of some Jacobean drama. He'd been tempted several times to hint as much to Benko; not to declare himself, of course, but by means of the occasional pointed question ("What weapons, please, are Border Guards normally equipped with?") to steer Benko's attention to the incongruities of their training. He hadn't done so, however, and wouldn't. He was a Soviet citizen, after all, and a member of his country's defense forces. However much he might want to question the decisions and motives of his superiors here, the fact remained that they *were* his superiors. They were legally entitled to make these decisions, and probably in possession of information which, if known to him, would change his view entirely. Benko and the Knights, moreover, were not innocent. They were unsuspecting, but it was not the same thing. And whatever else might be obscure about the intentions of those who had offered them support, one thing was certain: they were deeply hostile to his country. His job here was not to feel sorry for people; it was to gather and transmit to Atlas intelligence on all aspects of this operation. Instead of standing here, with a handkerchief to his nose, indulging himself in moral misgivings, he should be taking concrete steps to get answers to the questions Atlas had asked him.

The question was, what concrete steps?

"Laddie, you look like a fart in a trance." The voice of Whirled Peas cut in on these reflections. "Are you sick? Are you stunned? Do you need to go and lie down?"

"Not stunned . . ." Kalugin shook his head. This, it occurred to him, might offer a chance to do a little snooping. The lawn they were using bordered a wing of the main house. Though not declared off-limits to the Knights, the house hadn't so far featured in their training. Maybe a quick forage through it would yield useful information. "But it seems my nose won't stop bleeding. If there's a bathroom somewhere close, maybe cold water would help."

"Cold *water?*" Whirled Peas sighed, shrugged. "I suppose . . . Go in the side entrance, then third door on your left. And look sharp. We've got work to do."

CHAPTER TWENTY-ONE

(Sussex, England. August 4, 1990)

THIRD DOOR ON YOUR LEFT . . . AND HOW MUCH LATITUDE, KALUGIN wondered, did that leave for reasonable misconstruction? Not enough, obviously, to permit reconnaissance above the ground floor, and perhaps not enough to allow him to venture beyond the green baize door at the end of the poorly lit corridor he now found himself in. Rooms *off* this corridor, however, could probably be explored without undermining, if one happened to get caught, a claim to have been looking for the bathroom. He would have to be careful, of course. As the daily body searches continued to make clear, the Knights of Vladimir were not especially trusted by their hosts. And he, the newest recruit and a Soviet defector, was probably less trusted than the rest. But the door of the bathroom was not marked, and the existence of a large open broom closet on one side of the corridor and some kind of pantry on the other left room for legitimate confusion, surely, as to what was to count as a "door" and therefore as to which one was the third. The distinction between left and right, of course, was one with which civilians notoriously had trouble. If worse came to worst, moreover, he could simply claim to have misheard.

He would start with the first door on the left.

But first he listened for a moment. No one seemed to be around. He could hear no one moving, at least, in this wing of the house, nor, so far as he could tell, on the far side of the baize-covered door. This door, he noticed, had a kind of small window let into the top. Later, circumstances permitting, he might take a quick look through that window. But first things first.

The first door on the left opened into a kind of walk-in closet that seemed to be used for storing outdoors gear. Umbrellas and walking sticks were stacked in one corner, and several pairs of rubber boots were lined up smartly on the floor. Raincoats of various colors and sizes hung from pegs on the walls, also a solitary sportcoat in a rather loud houndstooth check.

A check of the sportcoat's pockets produced nothing very revealing. A packet of Disque Bleu Gauloises, unopened, and a red, disposable butane lighter. A numbered receipt from a dry cleaning service at an address on Fulham Road, London. Ticket stubs from the Leicester Square Odeon. A black plastic pocket comb belonging to someone who suffered seriously from dandruff.

No correspondence. No wallet.

Investigating, next, the pockets of the raincoats, he drew another apparent blank. He wasn't sure, in any case, exactly what he was looking *for*—anything, he supposed, that might help him discover the location of this house. If he could learn even the name of county, he thought, it would enable Atlas to identify the owners. Large private estates behind fifteen-foot walls couldn't be all that common, after all, in the mostly urban environment to be found in every direction within an hour's drive of Putney. The pockets of the raincoats, however, contained nothing helpful on the subject of location—no copy of the local newspaper, no bill from a neighborhood tradesman— nothing at all, in fact, except a dog leash of rather formidable proportions, which caused him a moment of uneasy speculation as to whether there were Dobermans roaming the house and grounds.

He was about to move on when he remembered name tags.

The raincoats wouldn't have them, of course. And since few people nowadays had their clothes made for them, neither, most probably, would the sportcoat. Even if it did, the intelligence value would probably be minimal. Most names were shared by hundreds if not thousands of people, so a name alone wouldn't be enough to identify the sportcoat's owner. Nor, probably, even if it could actually be done, would identifying the owner help with the more important problem of discovering where he, Kalugin, was. On the other hand, as he now seemed to recall, the sportcoat had lacked any visible maker's labels; it might very well, therefore, have been custom tailored. At any rate it was worth a look.

One never got anywhere making defeatist assumptions.

He was not sure, fifteen seconds later, that he'd gotten very far *not* making defeatist assumptions. It was gratifying to find, perhaps, that the sportcoat *had* been custom-tailored, and that a tailor's label, sewn inside the interior breast pocket, specified not only the name of the purchaser but also the date of purchase. It was even interesting that the tailor was not English, but Swiss. It was interesting, Kalugin thought, but not terribly promising. Mueller, after all, was a common Swiss-German name, and so was Gerhard. And even if Gerhard Mueller had been resident in Geneva in November of 1986, there was no guarantee he was living there now. Nor that this coat still belonged to him.

Nor even that Gerhard Mueller had been his real name.

It might be something Atlas could have researched, if no more informative clue was forthcoming. In the meantime he, Kalugin, needed to move on. One could only spend so long, after all, dealing with a nosebleed.

The nose had stopped bleeding now, but he kept the handkerchief in place. He could offer no more compelling proof of innocence, he thought, than this blood-soaked symbol of injury. He tried the first door on the left. It was locked. Double locked, he noticed, a Yale-type bolt backed up by a sturdy mortise. Some kind of storeroom probably. The doorway next to it belonged to the open pantry. The one beyond that opened onto a narrow wooden staircase, uncarpeted and dusty, presumably a servants' entrance to the floors above, and clearly, for the moment, off-limits to him. The second door on the right was also locked.

He was just about to try the third on the right when he heard a noise at the far end of the corridor.

A hinge creaking.

Someone entering through the green baize door.

"You are looking for *what*, exactly?"

Kalugin whirled. The voice was calm, insinuating, soft, the syntax and accent suggesting Russian. It sounded, at first hearing, almost familiar. Almost, he thought, like Atlas's voice. But its owner was not like Atlas at all. Though his features were partly obscured by the gloom, he was hatchet-faced, tall and thin, with an upright, military bearing.

"You startled me." Kalugin accused him.

"Obviously."

The man came forward into the light. He was dressed in a polo-neck sweater, twill pants, suede boots. His features were sharp. His hair was graying and thinning on top. It looked greasy, unwashed.

"I was watching you. On this side you opened doors and on that side. You were looking for what?" the newcomer repeated.

"A bathroom, preferably." Kalugin kept the handkerchief to his nose. Stay calm, he told himself; don't act defensive. "Failing that, a source of cold water."

The man inspected him for a moment. The eyes were greenish hazel, bright and penetrating. The stare seemed skeptical, perhaps even suspicious, though Kalugin, meeting it with what he hoped was equanimity, reminded himself that to the guilty *any* stare can seem suspicious. He attempted a diversion, switched to Russian.

"Your accent sounds Russian . . . Are you Russian?"

For just a moment the man looked startled.

"I *was* Russian." He responded, however, in English. "But not anymore. And I prefer not to speak my native language, especially" —pause—"with strangers . . . You hurt your nose?"

Kalugin shrugged, reverted to English.

"Obviously."

"How?"

"An accident." If this guy wanted to be unforthcoming, so be it. "Can you direct me to a bathroom? I was told there was one here somewhere."

"*Who* told you?" Another suspicious stare.

"The instructor." Kalugin nodded in the direction of the garden. "Unarmed Combat. I don't know his name. He told us to call him sir."

"So . . ." Slight softening of the stare. "You are one of *those*?"

Kalugin nodded. The designation was vague enough, he thought, that accepting it didn't commit him to much.

"Bathroom is here." The man indicated the third door on the left. "Tell me, please, what is your name?"

"Kalugin, Adam Nicolaievich."

The man smiled, a humorless twitch of the lips. He bowed slightly.

"I will be your instructor also. . . . Explosives"—he extended his hand, offered the phrase as if introducing himself—"Detonators and Timing Devices."

CHAPTER TWENTY-TWO

(Sussex, England. August 4, 1990)

"Every action provokes a reaction," Rosenthal said. "But not, unfortunately, equal and opposite. Politics is not physics. And this is what makes our task so difficult. Situations are always two-edged, but not quantifiably so."

Quantifiably two-edged? And where, Chance wondered, had *that* mangled metaphor come from. Perhaps it was working with the computer that did it. Perhaps, like economists before them, historians were yielding to the seduction of numbers, the infinitely appealing notion that, with data accurate enough and computers adequately powerful, human behavior could be reduced to statistics, described entirely by sets of equations. Or perhaps it was just that Rosenthal (whose academic standing had never been terribly high) was aspiring now to oracle status, speaking therefore mostly in riddles. She knew she didn't have to ask, however, *which* situation was two-edged and *how*. Sooner or later he was bound to tell her.

"I'm thinking, of course, of the Soviet Union." Predictably he opted for sooner. "You've got this tension of opposing forces. Any development favoring liberals provokes a reaction from hardliners. But to any given stimulus, which will be stronger, action or reaction? That's what's always so problematic."

He paused. Clearly he expected a response, some kind of prompt to continue. And she might as well give it, she thought, because that way he'd get to the point sooner. The point of the conversation, that was. The point of this chauffeur-driven jaunt in the country she suspected she already knew. A "drive and a talk" was how he'd described it, but so far, when *not* spouting obscurities, he'd spent most of the time inspecting her legs.

"From what point of view problematic?"

"US policy," Rosenthal said. "Take, for instance, these independence movements in the non-Russian republics. Since they weaken a
former enemy and in the process promote democracy, we ought to
give them wholehearted support. If we do that, however, or do it
openly, we could be offering Soviet hardliners just the excuse they've
been praying for. In other words, the result of our efforts could well
be the opposite of what was intended."

"A coup, you mean, by the Army and the Party? A coalition of
patriotic forces, rallying to protect the Revolution and prevent the
breakup of the Soviet Empire?"

"Something like that." Rosenthal nodded. "A lurch to the right, at
any rate. We *could* be handing Stalinists a stick with which to beat
the liberals to death."

Chance thought about this for a moment.

"Then it seems to me," she said, "that our safest course might be
to butt out altogether, let the Soviets settle their internal problems in
peace. I've been convinced for some time now, indeed, that in our
policy toward them we need to *rethink* what we're trying to achieve."

"That's interesting." He inspected her gravely. "What do *you* think
we should be trying to achieve?"

She hesitated. Why was he asking? she wondered. Why should *he,*
who'd at one time had the running of US foreign policy, care what
she, a mere academic and a woman to boot, believed should be its
goals? Could his question be some kind of test, perhaps. Of her
loyalties, maybe, or her smarts?

"I think . . ." She would give him the benefit of the doubt here,
she decided. She had nothing to lose, nor, for that matter, to hide. "I
think what we *should* be trying for is a whole new level of candor.
Instead of the usual Mexican stand-off, each side with its finger on
the nuclear trigger, watching for the other side to twitch, I think we
should try for something safer. Openness, maybe, a willingness to
trust. Which again entails, with respect to the non-Russian republics,
that our best course would be to leave them alone."

"A willingness to trust . . ." He repeated the words musingly, as
if confronting a novel concept. "You know, when I taught at Harvard, I sometimes sponsored a debate among my students. The issue
was: which offers the more stable basis for international relations,
trust or mistrust?"

She thought about this for a moment, tried to imagine him in the
classroom. What course had he taught, she wondered, Machiavelli
101?

"And how did it usually turn out?"

"It was interesting," he said. "Almost always the same. Not just the outcome, the whole course of the debate. To start with, we'd hear the idealist position, moralists urging mutual trust, arguing from the analogy with personal relations. Then there'd be pragmatists who rejected the analogy, pointed out that the goals of diplomacy differed from those of friendship or marriage. The point would be debated a while. Eventually we'd hear from the poker players."

"Poker players?"

"Gamblers." Rosenthal nodded. "Habitual managers of risk. They'd point out that in any competitive game where most of the players are observing the rules, benefits accrue to the player who doesn't. And because of this, because *someone* can always gain by cheating, trust is not only inherently unstable, but in the long run actually impossible. *Mis*trust, on the other hand, tends to be relatively stable. When all the players are watching each other like hawks, attempts to cheat are unlikely to succeed and are therefore much less likely to be made."

"And the poker players persuaded the others?"

"In the end." He nodded. "Almost always."

"And you agree?"

"With human nature as presently constituted"—he smiled again—"I'm afraid I do."

"You believe, in other words, that we can't ever hope to change the way we relate to other countries. That the whole apparatus of mistrust—the armies, the missiles, the spy satellites, the CIAs and KGBs, the black operations and counteroperations—is something we're stuck with forever?"

"Unless human nature can be changed." He nodded. "And where, in all recorded history, are there any grounds for believing it can?"

She was tempted to argue. What needed to be changed, she thought, was not people's nature but their politicians' thinking, in particular that habit of mind which found in relations among sovereign states an analogy with games like chess or poker. Friendship, it seemed to her, and even marriage were safer models for foreign relations than games in which cheating was rewarded and one player's gain entailed another's loss. She didn't say so, however. She didn't see the point. She didn't think he was really interested. It was clear by now that he'd asked her opinion mostly as a pretext for expounding his own.

He seemed to take her silence for agreement, for presently he continued:

"This brings us, of course, to the two great ironies of our century's history: that an ideology so optimistic about people produced a system so brutally repressive, and that the very existence of this system, given the development of weapons of mass destruction, produced in turn an unprecedented peace."

"If the Cold War hadn't existed, in other words, we'd have been forced to invent it?"

She intended, with this quotation from his writing, an irony of her own. He didn't seem to notice, however.

"I continue to be of that opinion."

She stared. "You think we'd be better off *now* if the Cold War were still going on?"

"In some ways. I think we'd be a lot more secure."

"If that's true, I think it's tragic."

"I think so, too." He shrugged. "But I can't allow my feelings to affect my perceptions."

She was silent for a moment, gazed through the tinted window at the English countryside slipping past, tranquil and picture-book pretty, at eighty miles an hour. As the Bentley came over the crest of a rise she was treated suddenly to a view of half the county, the kind of rural panorama that couldn't have changed much in a century and always produced in her an ache of longing for an earlier, simpler era. The downs were a patchwork of hedgerows, corpses, and meadows, with occasional villages tucked into the folds. In the distance, like a sentinel guarding the peace, was the spire of what must be Chichester Cathedral, and beyond it, on the horizon, hazy and barely discernible, the sea. Why had he brought her here, she wondered? Was his motive merely sexual? To put on some kind of mating display? To whisk her off in this symbol of power and status, then tickle her libido by parading his assets, revealing, in the cushioned privacy of his limousine's passenger compartment, the hardness of his mind? Or was something more sinister afoot? She couldn't get rid of the suspicion, at any rate, that as well as maneuvering to get into her bed, he was also probing her opinions, scouting the notion of putting their work relationship also on a new and more intimate footing, of letting her in on some secret or other. She found this prospect unappealing also. It disturbed her, in fact, that there might be some secret for him to let her into. And this prompted her to ask once again something she had asked herself quite often of late.

Who was she working for, really?

It was something she had wondered, vaguely, when she'd first been approached about a job at the Foundation, but it hadn't seemed, then, to demand a response. The Foundation for Freedom, its literature asserted, was a research institute, privately funded, whose purpose was "to provide in-depth economic and political analysis for a variety of institutional and corporate clients." And if the service thus provided extended (as she'd quickly discovered it did) to military analysis as well, and if the clients (as she'd also discovered) included the Pentagon and the CIA, these hadn't seemed reasons to give up a salary that was almost twice what she could make at a university and work that seemed to be fairly challenging and not to contribute, in any immediate way, to the world's pollution or destruction. And in regard to the challenge, at least, her expectations had been amply fulfilled. Indeed the work had been so absorbing, it had been easy to persuade herself, at first, that if it contributed to *anything*, it must be to the good; if the Pentagon and the CIA needed to pay someone to do their thinking, it ought to be someone—herself for instance—who'd do it with reasonable clarity and detachment. Recently, however, her faith in this reasoning had been shaken. She'd come to suspect she'd been burying her head in the sand, that thinking wasn't the only thing the Foundation did for its clients. There'd been whispers on the office grapevine that recently Rosenthal had been getting visits from "someone senior from Langley." And though visitors from Langley, even senior ones, were often to be seen at the Foundation's headquarters, it was troubling to hear that the recent visitor belonged not to Research, but Operations. Operations, it was fairly common knowledge, was known at Langley as "Dirty Tricks."

"You're very quiet." Rosenthal cut in on these thoughts. "What are you thinking about?"

She was almost tempted to tell him, but opted instead for a plausible half-truth. "I was wondering about this magical mystery tour. To be precise, the purpose of it."

"It's no mystery." He smiled. "You could say I'm indulging myself. . . . You've worked for us now for nearly eighteen months. I thought it was time I gave myself the pleasure of getting to know you better. Where we're going is to lunch. At a pub I know near here. It's fourteenth century, I think. It has good food, at any rate, and a pleasant ambience. Does that sound like a reasonable agenda?"

"It sounds like fun." It didn't, much. She continued to wonder, moreover, what she was letting herself in for. But whatever *his* motive, she owed it to *herself,* she thought, to be gracious. "I approve the location, too. I love old country pubs."

"I'm glad. Though the location, I'm afraid, was more or less dictated. I've got to make a detour on the way. It shouldn't take more than five minutes. I hope you won't mind."

"Mind what?"

"The detour." He shrugged "My killing two birds with one stone."

She shook her head. Though the words could have been better chosen—he didn't do metaphors well, she thought, ought to avoid them entirely—his mention of a detour aroused her curiosity. Though she wasn't sure exactly where, she knew they were now in Sussex. And Sussex—wasn't it?—was where the Foundation was said to own a sizable country estate. She'd heard rumors also that in the year prior to the Contra scandal this estate been the location for "seminars" whose participants came mostly from Latin America and had tended to dress in camouflage fatigues. When the scandal broke, the story had it, these seminars had abruptly ceased. It *was* only rumor, of course, the kind of vaguely plausible scuttlebutt people on the fringe of the Intelligence Community might concoct to suggest they weren't on the fringe. But on the other hand, it might be true.

It was time to stop burying her head, she decided. If there were secrets to be learned here, she'd better learn them.

She didn't want to work for the CIA.

The rumored country house, at least, seemed to reveal itself as real. Presently the Bentley, turning left off the A40, took a two-lane road on whose right, after maybe a mile, a red-brick wall appeared. It continued unbroken for several hundred yards, and though too high to see over, seemed to enclose a kind of park. Soon they pulled up at some wrought-iron gates, flanked on the right by a gatehouse. A gravel drive led off from the gates down an avenue of chestnuts and beeches. Some quarter of a mile down this stood a sprawling, early-Victorian pile. There was nothing to indicate who all this belonged to, but the concern for privacy was very evident, and not only from the wall. The gates were shut when the Bentley drew up, but a blast from the horn brought a man running out. He was wearing Levi's, sneakers, and a lightweight polo-neck sweater. In his late twenties or early thirties, he was visibly in very good physical shape and moved with the self-conscious spring and energy she tended to associate with PE instructors. He inspected and returned without comment the ID offered by the chauffeur, then produced a notebook, presumably a log, which he gave the chauffeur to sign. He then jogged back to the gatehouse. Moments later the gates slid open and the Bentley continued on its way.

Through all of this rigmarole Rosenthal gazed straight ahead with a distant, preoccupied expression that seemed intended to discourage questions. Chance, in any case, knew better than to ask them. Whether or not this place was the Foundation's, it clearly had some kind of intelligence function. She'd had enough contact with Pickett and others to know in the intelligence world curiosity was considered bad manners. If you needed to know, they would tell you. If you didn't, they wouldn't, and you oughtn't to embarrass them by asking. The other side of this coin, of course, was that they shouldn't tantalize by dropping hints. Rosenthal, by bringing her here, was guilty of a breach of etiquette himself. Presumably he was aware of this, which raised questions again about his motives. In the search for answers, however, she felt she'd already gone as far as unaided speculation could take her. More evidence was needed. She could only wait and see.

When they pulled up in the forecourt, however, and Rosenthal asked if she'd mind waiting in the car, it seemed unlikely that here at least she'd see anything very much. The house, an ivy-covered, two-story sprawl whose architecture made unconvincing gestures toward Gothic, was, in its exterior at least, as uninformative as the gatehouse. More so, in fact, since the security precautions evident there seemed here entirely absent. Rosenthal, briefcase in hand, simply walked up to the front door and let himself in.

The chauffeur got out of the Bentley and, lounging against its side, lit a cigarette. Chance would have liked to get out and stretch *her* legs, but Rosenthal's parting words, though ambiguous, seemed to indicate he wanted her to stay in the car. She was about to resign herself to an interval of tedious waiting—Rosenthal's five minutes, she thought, could easily turn into half an hour—when she noticed something she'd missed in her initial survey of the scene.

People.

The wing of the house closest to her connected to a boxwood hedge, some eight to ten feet high, in which was cut an open archway. Beyond the hedge and partly visible through the archway was an area of lawn (perhaps a tennis court, though she could see no lines), and on it, maybe thirty yards away, seated in a semicircle on the grass, men.

There were four of them. Four visible, at least. But there could be others, she guessed, because the four she could see—they were dressed like the one she'd seen at the gatehouse—were evidently watching something. What they were watching, she couldn't at first make out; but whatever it was, it was clearly entertaining, for they were grinning at each other, gesticulating, and from time to time applauding. And presently, when a shift in the action brought it into view, she saw that the entertainment was two other men, warily circling around each other as if wrestling. One was a big bearlike man wearing Levi's and a T-shirt with a message stenciled on the front.

The other one was holding a knife.

He seemed familiar. She'd seen him, further inspection convinced her, somewhere before and in a similar context. A second later she remembered where. It had been at the gym where she sometimes exercised. He was the Ukrainian, the fencer.

Adam Kalugin's buddy, Benko.

Why was he here? And what was going on?

The second question was no sooner asked than observation supplied an answer. Benko made a sudden lunge with the knife and was rewarded for his aggression, in a process too quick for her eye to follow in detail, by being flung headlong onto the turf. When this sequence of action was repeated in slow motion with pauses for commentary by the bearlike man, it was evident that what was going here on was some kind of combat training. It seemed that the scuttlebutt she'd heard in the office in London was not without some basis in fact.

But in 1986 it had been Contras. Now it was Ukrainians.

It was then, to complete her astonishment, that the group acquired a new member. He came into view from the left of the entryway, sat down on the grass beside the others.

Adam Kalugin.

CHAPTER TWENTY-THREE

(Sussex, England. August 4, 1990)

THE SPEAKER AT THIS AFTERNOON'S BRIEFING WAS THE MAN THEY CALLED the Moderator. He appeared, Kalugin thought, to be in charge of the training. It was he, at least, who'd addressed to the Knights on their arrival a laconic and somewhat chilly speech of welcome, and he'd since been apt to show up at the various sessions and observe silently from a seat at the back. He must have been in his early fifties but looked considerably older. American, to judge from his accent, he was dressed invariably with an English elegance. Today he wore a gray flannel suit of conservative but impeccable cut, a pale-blue shirt with French cuffs and starched white cutaway collar, a tie with stripes that looked regimental. His hair, brilliantined, was plastered tight against his scalp. Probably as a consequence of chain-smoking—he seemed to light one Camel off another—his voice emerged as a kind of raven's croak. His face, a leathery mask, yellowish in complexion and ravaged with lines of experience and care, wore an expression of permanent distaste. It looked as if it had witnessed more than its owner cared to remember.

"Are there any questions?"

An interrogative gaze was focused in turn on each of the Knights. A weary, faintly truculent emphasis placed on the word "questions" seemed to imply that these, though permitted, would not be particularly welcomed, that anyone needing to ask them had either not paid proper attention or suffered from some deficiency, probably irremediable, in his powers of comprehension. Questions as to concept or substance were clearly *not* invited. Given that in the course of this briefing at least one major bombshell had been dropped, the tone struck Kalugin as uncalled for. On the schedule, this afternoon's class had been advertised as a "Planning Session," but any suggestion this might have conveyed that the Knights would do other than listen was evidently unintended. Whatever else their roles here might be, it was not to reason why.

"I have a question." Benko raised his hand.

"Do you?" Condescending croak. "And what might that be?"

"It puzzles me that operational procedures and objectives will be withheld from the team until just prior to blast-off. What is the reason for this?"

A reasonable question, Kalugin thought, though Benko's use of the instructor's jargon implied an acceptance, no doubt unconscious, of precisely what was being questioned: that the Knights were so many guided missiles, mindless packages of destructive energy to be launched and targeted by others. Jargon, as it always was by secret services, had been used in the Knights' training as a subtle means of flattery and seduction. Since using it implied you belonged to a privileged elite, the temptation was hard to resist. But by using the jargon you adopted the mindset, thereby limiting your freedom to dissent.

"The reason is elementary security. Operational procedures and objectives are *never* revealed prematurely. You must realize that the need-to-know applies to *when* as well as to who . . ."

A wholly predictable response, Kalugin thought. If jargon was one seduction, secrecy was another.

Benko didn't buy it, however. "Does this mean that we are not trusted?"

"Not necessarily." The Moderator looked bored. "Trust has very little to do with it. Security leaks are mostly inadvertent. The principle is very simple. You can't let slip what you haven't been told."

Benko looked mollified. It was typical of him, Kalugin thought, that the issue of these people's trust in him, which he felt reflected in some way on his honor, should concern him more than the issue of his trust in them. He was willing to let them use him as a tool, yet he still didn't know, with any certainty, who they were or what plans they had for his honor.

Raina raised his hand.

"How long will we remain in the safe house in Kiev?"

"As little time as possible. Only pending final preparations. This decision, too, is dictated by security. You'll be far less likely to be noticed there than hanging around in the streets . . ." The Moderator paused, adding dryly, "I believe I mentioned this point in my briefing."

Kalugin raised his hand.

"Yes . . ."

"Why are we landing on the Black Sea coast? Don't we risk running into Border Guard patrols?"

Silence. The Moderator gave him a long, expressionless stare.

"Where do you think we should land? The Adriatic?"

Kalugin shrugged. "Why not the international airport in Kiev?"

Another stare, speculative this time. "You propose entering on tourist visas?"

"Why not? It strikes me as being far less risky than landing illegally on a beach at night."

"It's less risky then. At least in theory. But afterward you'd encounter problems. If you go in on a tourist visa, you're subject to regular surveillance and controls. Your freedom of maneuver is almost zero. You'd find it quite hard to plant your bombs"—quick, lizardlike smile—"with Intourist constantly on your asses."

"How about with Border Guards on our asses?" Vasa, who normally spoke little, seemed to share Kalugin's irritation with this attitude of do-as-you're-told-and-don't-ask-silly-questions.

"You won't *have* Border Guards on your asses. That's why I said 'less risky *in theory.*' " The Moderator looked enigmatic. "The Border Guard problem is taken care of."

The Border Guard problem is taken care of. Kalugin felt a sudden quickening of interest. For perhaps the first time in this mission, here was intelligence of genuine value. "The Border Guard problem is taken care of" could mean, surely, only one thing: These people had access to the Black Sea patrol schedules. Which must mean that the Border Guards had been penetrated; and probably, since the schedules were highly classified, at some fairly senior level. The alternative, that the crew of an entire Border Guard patrol boat had been somehow persuaded to look the other way, was improbable to the point of fantasy.

He had something, at last, to report to Atlas.

"It concerns me, too . . ." Benko again, "that you plan to include a stranger in our team. I don't see any necessity for this."

Silence. The Moderator waited, with bland courtesy, for Benko to continue. Benko waited for the Moderator to respond. The silence became uncomfortable before the Moderator broke it.

"Is that a question?"

"Yes." Benko rolled his eyes. "Will you *explain* the necessity, please."

More silence. The Moderator gazed at Benko with an interest that seemed almost anthropological, as if Benko belonged to some rare aboriginal tribe that he, the Moderator, hadn't before encountered.

"How long since you were last in Russia?"

Benko flushed. "I have never been there."

"I thought not." The Moderator smiled faintly. "Has anyone else on your team?"

"He has." Benko pointed to Kalugin.

"Recently?"

Kalugin shrugged. "I left Kiev in 1983."

"Could it have changed much since you were there? The Soviet Union, I mean."

"I'm sure it's changed quite a bit."

Kalugin glanced apologetically at Benko. It didn't much surprise him, however, that the Moderator had adopted this confrontational stance. Most intelligence bureaucrats he'd encountered exhibited this kind of military mentality. They expected unquestioning obedience from field agents and got upset when they didn't get it. The stated rationale for this attitude was simple: like generals in headquarters on hills behind the lines, they saw more of the battle than the soldiers in the trenches. The *unstated* rationale was somewhat different: they were smarter than field agents and the proof of it was this; they'd known much better than to *be* field agents.

"You see what I'm getting at, don't you?" The Moderator turned back to Benko. "Without someone with you who knows the score, you'd be more out of place than tits on a bull. Some silly piece of ignorance would give you away. Some fact that any Russian school kid ought to know would broadcast to the world that you're not what you claim. Next thing you know, you'd be explaining yourselves to the local chapter of the KGB. And that would be . . ."—he paused for effect—"uncomfortable, not to say painful."

Raina, surprisingly, came to Benko's assistance. "Clearly we shall need preparation to pass for native-born Russians. That, we thought, was primarily the purpose of this training."

"You thought wrong." The Moderator shook his head. "Prepping of that sort requires several months. We don't have time. Handholding is the only alternative."

"Handholding?" Benko's eyes narrowed. "Actually, it is much more than that. We would have to *depend* on this person. Which means in effect that he would be the leader."

The Moderator shrugged. "I guess you could look at it that way."

"I do look at it that way," Benko retorted. "You expect us to take as our leader someone we don't even know, someone . . ."—he paused—"we may not even trust?"

"Why wouldn't you trust him? *We* trust him, you presumably trust *us* or you wouldn't be here. Look . . ." the Moderator said. "We provide planning, training, and financing; you provide manpower. I thought that was clearly understood." He paused, then added, "We're offering you the chance to do what you've always dreamed of, a chance you wouldn't otherwise have had."

"I understand that. I know very well what you offer us. What I'm not sure I understand any longer," Benko said, "is what it is we offer you."

"That's easy. You offer us anonymity," the Moderator said.

"Anonymity? With a CIA agent on the team?"

"CIA?" The Moderator fixed him with a chilly stare. "Whoever said anything about CIA? We're operating absolutely freelance here. No links to any intelligence outfit. American, British, Israeli, or whatever. As to your new team member, we're talking to Mr. Disavowable himself. Nobody anywhere knows his real name. I doubt" —faint smile—"if he remembers it himself. And perhaps it's time you people met him."

Descending from the rostrum, the Moderator crossed the room and opened the door on the left. He opened it, stuck his head around it, called out.

"Will someone ask Leonid to spare us a moment."

He turned back to the Sailors. "Leonid offers us invaluable talents. He knows the Ukraine like the back of his hand. He's also an expert at making bombs."

Explosives, Detonators, and Timing devices . . . When Leonid presented himself some minutes later, Kalugin, seeing the matching checked jacket and cap, the polo neck, the too-tight pants, took satisfaction in a prediction fulfilled and felt simultaneously a pang of disappointment. The value of what he'd learned on his reconnaissance now seemed called into question. For if this man's name wasn't Leonid, it probably wasn't Gerhard Mueller, either.

CHAPTER TWENTY-FOUR

(London. August 5, 1990)

"ADAM . . ." CHANCE MUSED. "ADAM KALUGIN, MY RETICENT LOVER, what do you do with your life, really?"

She was snuggled up to him, her head on his chest. They were lying on her bed in a state of pleasured languor, clothes scattered all round the room.

"What do I do with my life?"

Questions again. He sighed lazily, affected to consider. "Maybe thirty percent devoted to sleep, ten percent to eating, forty percent to inventive and extravagant sexual fantasies whose focus, almost invariably, is a certain political analyst employed by a certain think tank."

"*Almost* invariably?" She propped herself up on an elbow facing him, knotted her eyebrows in mock severity. "And who might this certain political analyst share your inventive and extravagant fantasies *with*?"

"My grade-school teacher. Her name was Anna Sergeyevna. We were all completely in love with her. She had perfect breasts, amazing legs, and no control over her clothing. The buttons of her blouse kept popping open, granting us glimpses of her satiny brassieres; her slip would peek out from beneath the hem of her skirt, hint at unimaginable delights. I used to dream of being kept after school, receiving instruction of a very private nature."

"Poor woman. It must have been awful for her, being lusted after by a roomful of nasty little boys."

"She probably didn't even know. If she did, she didn't seem to mind. And we weren't nasty. Our behavior was always respectful." He paused. "You have to understand. The woman who arouses a young boy's first desire has a special place in his fantasy life. She becomes almost holy to him, a kind of sexual icon."

"Very edifying." She rolled her eyes. "But we're straying from the subject."

"What *is* the subject?"

"Your life. Your real life, that is, not your fantasy life. There's twenty percent still unaccounted for."

Questions still. And always on this topic. Just when his suspicions were starting to subside. Forcing him to ask himself similar questions about her. What was her connection with Randall Pickett? What did she do with her life, really?

"My fantasy life is more interesting." He paused. "Would you like to know what I'm fantasizing now?"

"Maybe later." She gave him a sideways glance, fluttered her eyelashes at him. "Stop trying to distract me. I want to know about that twenty percent."

"Of my real life?" He sighed. "I've *told* you. What I do is . . ."

"Translating . . ." She completed the formula. "Russian to English, Ukrainian to English, and sometimes the other way round. Mostly freelance, for corporations. Occasionally for the Overseas Service of the BBC."

"Exactly." He looked at her sharply. "You know this, so why do you keep asking?"

She seemed about to respond, then hesitated. He pressed the attack. They had reached the point, it seemed to him, when innocence would start to take offense. "Don't you see that this is a little insulting? When you ask the same question over and over, it suggests you don't believe the answer. This implies a view of my character which, to say the least, is uncomplimentary."

He gazed at her, unsmiling. She said nothing.

"You don't believe I do translating, is that it? You think I'm lying about that?"

She shook her head. "I believe you do translating. I just wonder sometimes if it's all you do?"

"Sometimes?" He stared. "What else would I be doing?"

"I don't know." She considered for a moment. "What were you doing yesterday, for instance? When not sleeping, eating, or fantasizing, that is."

"Yesterday? Yesterday I worked on a big commercial job. Regulations pertaining to the operations of foreign enterprises within the borders of the Soviet Union. Forty-three pages. Very technical, very tedious. Every other word had me reaching for the dictionary. I spent seven hours on only nine pages."

That part was true. It had taken him half the night.

"Seven hours *when?*"

She knew something. That much was obvious. It was obvious also he had only one strategy here. He could take offense, of course, refuse to participate further in what was now, nakedly, cross-examination, but that would neither allay her suspicions nor reveal exactly what it was that she knew. And he needed to know that—this also was clear—not only because his cover was in danger, but because what she knew about his yesterday's activities might shed some light on what he *didn't* know. She might know, for instance, where he had been. He must be evasive, he decided, provoke her to reveal what she knew.

"Why does it matter?" he added, disdainfully. "Which hours are you particularly interested in?"

She ignored the tone. "How about lunchtime, for instance? Where were you, let's say, around noon?"

He stared at her. "Obviously a loaded question. Where do you *think* I was?"

She met the stare. "I think you were in Sussex. Near Chichester. At some kind of country estate. A big Victorian-Gothic house, with fifteen-foot walls surrounding the park, all kinds of security on the gate." She paused. "I was there. I saw you."

"You mean you *think* you saw me."

She shook her head. "I was thirty yards away. In a Bentley parked in the courtyard. You couldn't see me because the windows were tinted. You were with a group of men. Training in some kind of combat. Your buddy Benko was there as well." She paused. "I'm not mistaken. I wasn't dreaming. It was you . . . Wasn't it?"

He sidestepped the question.

"And what were *you* doing there, in Sussex?"

"I was with Martin Rosenthal, my boss. He invited me to have lunch in the country, then told me he had to stop in somewhere on the way. When we got there he asked me to wait in the car." She paused. "It was obviously some kind of intelligence facility. That's why he didn't take me inside. But *you* were there. I saw you. And that's why I asked you who you are, though I'm not quite sure why I bothered. It's obvious you're some kind of spook."

Sussex. Rosenthal. The Foundation for Freedom. He had lots to tell Atlas now, he thought, and would call for a contact as soon as he could. In the meantime, the question was what to tell Chance.

She stared at him, accusing. "You are a spook, aren't you?"

He looked at her without expression. Maybe it wouldn't hurt to let her think so, he thought, provided she thought he was the right *kind* of spook. In the meantime, saying nothing might well provoke her to say more.

"Look . . ." she said. "It doesn't really matter what you do. I mean in *itself*, it doesn't matter. You could be a postman for all I care. Or the CIA's Director of Operations. What you do isn't the issue."

"What is the issue?"

She considered. "I think it's trust."

"You mean you don't trust me?"

"No," she flared. "I mean you don't trust *me.*"

He thought fast. She seemed genuinely angry. She was either very subtle or else completely innocent. In any case, the suggestion that he worked for the CIA was one he could safely go along with. Not explicitly, of course, because that was something she could check with Pickett. All he needed to do, really, was fail to deny it. Silence, he'd read, implied consent.

"Jesus." He sat up abruptly, threw his legs over the edge of the bed. "This is crazy. If I don't tell you everything I do, that means I don't trust you? Has it ever occurred to you that trusting you might not be my decision, that I might conceivably have other trusts to keep?"

He paused for a moment, delivered himself then of a thrust which should, he thought, if she was what she claimed to be, put a permanent end to her questions.

"Are we *married,* that I should have no secrets from you?"

CHAPTER TWENTY-FIVE

(London. August 6, 1990)

"BORDER GUARDS?" ATLAS QUERIED. "YOU THINK THEY HAVE SOURCES in the Black Sea patrol?"

Kalugin nodded. "The one they call the Moderator said, and I quote, 'The Border Guard problem is taken care of.' To me that means, at the very least, that they must have access to the schedules."

Atlas thought about this for a moment.

"I think you may be right about that. But I would like to go over, one more time, the reasoning process whereby you arrive at the conclusion that this training establishment is located in Sussex and connected in some way with the Foundation for Freedom."

"Go over it again?" Kalugin stared. "Is something not clear?"

There was something not clear to *him*, he thought, and that was why Atlas insisted on focusing on inessentials. This contact had taken some effort to accomplish. He personally had been on the move since ten, taking more than four hours to arrive, by various means and a highly circuitous route, at a destination less than an hour's travel from his original point of departure. Atlas had no doubt been equally careful. Eight to ten man hours between them, and all so that Atlas could treat as a footnote the most important information he, Kalugin, had yet discovered?

"It's clear," Atlas said. "I just want you to go over it again."

"Very well," Kalugin sighed. "I conclude that the training location is in Sussex because I saw in the house a copy of what I took to be the local newspaper, the Chichester *Gazette* or *Echo* or something. At any rate, it was published in Chichester. It's not conclusive proof, I agree, just a probable inference." He paused. "My other conclusion is similar, an inference based on observation."

"Observation?" Atlas queried. "Are you sure it was Rosenthal you saw? How did you happen to recognize him?"

"He arrived in a chauffeur-driven car," Kalugin said. "It drew up at the door and Rosenthal got out. I was thirty yards away, maybe less. As to how I recognized him . . ." He shrugged. "He is, or was, a public figure. I recognized him from pictures."

"And you knew he heads the Foundation for Freedom?" Atlas shot him a penetrating glance. "It's not a very well-known fact or, indeed, a very well-known organization."

"I guess I must have read it. *Time* magazine or somewhere. I do my best to keep myself informed." Kalugin shrugged again. "But in any case, does it matter how I knew? The important point, surely, is that I saw him. We now know that he is, or may be, connected with these people who are training the Knights."

The important point, actually, he thought, was to give Atlas as much information as he could without revealing the truth about how he'd got it. If he told Atlas about Chance, Atlas would want him to exploit her, to squeeze her for more information. Atlas would also want to know why he hadn't been told about her sooner. But he didn't want to exploit her. He didn't want Atlas to know anything about her. He was ashamed now of his behavior to her yesterday, his whole ignoble, manipulative performance. How he'd got up and started to dress. How he'd heard her apology in silence, allowed himself, grudgingly, to be cajoled back to bed. She deserved better, he thought. She was innocent—he was sure of it now—innocent of everything except caring too much about a KGB spy, a man without honor. Her innocence had been obvious, he thought, from her calm, sad response to his wounding question. "No, Adam, we're not married. We have no claims upon each other. And I won't ask you any more questions. Feel free to have all the secrets you want." He wasn't going to exploit her, he thought. Not for Atlas or anybody else.

"Tell me something," he said to Atlas. "Do I get the feeling you don't trust me?"

Atlas stared at him for a moment, then shook his head. "It's not a question of not trusting *you*. It's a question of assessing the accuracy of your information. Maybe you mistook somebody else for Rosenthal. Maybe you drew the wrong conclusions."

"I didn't mistake him." Kalugin shook his head. He was getting tired of Atlas and his questions. "And if you doubt my conclusions, check them yourself. It should be fairly easy to discover whether any estate like the one I described exists within the area surrounding Chichester. And if one does, it should also be possible to discover who owns it. It's just a matter of a little legwork." He shrugged. "After all, you've nothing else to do. And it shouldn't be too difficult or too dangerous."

He would wonder, later, on his way back to Hampstead, whether he'd been wise to take that tone. Though it had served to release his own feelings of frustration, Atlas had clearly been angered by it. Relations between agent and control, Kalugin thought, were on an accelerating downhill trend, and this did no one any good, least of all the agent. Ill feeling led to carelessness and mistakes. And mistakes, as they had never tired of stressing in the training, could cost lives.

It was only when he had actually reached home that he realized he already had been careless. The mistake was probably not serious and could easily be rectified at the next contact, but it was, nonetheless, a mistake. Though he'd told Atlas about the Knights' new team member, Leonid, he'd forgotten to tell him about Leonid's sportcoat, tailormade in Geneva, and the name on the inside of the interior breast pocket.

Gerhard Mueller.

CHAPTER TWENTY-SIX

(London. August 8, 1990)

PICKETT TOOK A SIP OF WHAT THE WOMAN WHO HAD SERVED IT HAD humorously referred to as coffee, shuddered, and to preserve himself from further memory lapses slid the cup across the table, out of his immediate reach. As he tried, without much success, to get comfortable in the only chair provided, a folding metal contraption the guiding principle of whose design seemed to have been to discourage its use, he wondered exactly what purpose this room had originally served. Vaguely coffin-shaped, tucked away in what had once been servants' quarters, with a window but no view because the sash wouldn't open and the window glass was frosted, it was small for a bedroom, large for a closet, oddly located to be cloakroom or pantry. But it had to have served some purpose, he thought. Some purpose other, that was, than the one it was currently serving. The eighteenth-century architect who'd designed this elegant terrace of houses could hardly have anticipated the use to which the twentieth century would put them. He could hardly have foreseen the need for an attic to hide Americans in while they read through the files of the British Secret Service.

This sudden helpfulness on the part of the Brits had taken Pickett somewhat by surprise. And for once they were not only being helpful, they were even, in their fashion, being gracious about it. It could only, he thought, have been Meredith's doing.

Faraday, for instance, had actually been waiting for him downstairs at the entrance. He hadn't ventured out himself into the brisk summer downpour that had coincided with Pickett's arrival, but he had sent the porter, armed with a small black umbrella, which he'd wisely used to stay dry himself, while Pickett, emerging from his taxi, had been soaked. Faraday then, tut-tutting over his visitor's dampened

condition, had personally escorted him up the sweeping marble staircase and into the dusty labyrinth beyond. His Lords and Masters,
he'd told Pickett on the phone, had elected to look with a favorable
eye on the US request for further information concerning a natural-
ized British subject, formerly a son of Mother Russia. If Pickett,
therefore, would care to pop over, he, Faraday, would find him somewhere cozy so he could browse at his leisure through the relevant
file.

Cozy? Pickett asked himself bitterly. One knew their views about
central heating, but was this really what the Brits considered cozy?

The relevant file, however, had materialized as promised. It was
dun-colored, moderately thick, a wallet-style folder tied up with or-
ange tape. An admonitory message on the top right corner read:
"TOP SECRET—UK EYES ONLY." The file also bore an index
number: 014 SU6 07/8I. Its title was simply: "Prospect."

Pickett had experience reading such files. Especially with ones that
were marked "No Further Action," it wasn't smart to start at the
beginning. The beginning was invariably devoted to background:
memos and documents from eager talent spotters explaining with a
wealth of redundant detail why the subject was so perfect for recruitment. Pickett wasn't interested in that, or rather in this case he knew
it already. He wanted to know what had scared the Brits off. He
would start, he decided, a dozen or so documents from the end,
somewhere in the final act of the drama.

Putting this resolve into practice, he was startled to find himself in
the midst of what seemed, at first glance, to be a long-distance literary discussion, the kind of thing diplomats used to amuse themselves
with before the advent of airmail and the telegram put them at the
mercy of their ministries at home and cut so deeply into their free
time. It began with a copy of a letter dated April 1984, from the
British consulate in Kiev to the Cultural Attaché of the Embassy in
Moscow. Pickett noted that though the original document had been
classified "Confidential," the copy in the file had been upgraded to
"Secret."

Dear Farrar,
    I am writing to respond to your request for anything I can dig
up on Russian translations of Malory for your forthcoming Literary Interchange Exhibit.
    The university here, as you know, has one of the strongest
Eng. lit. departments in the entire Soviet Union. They have

been responsible for preparing for publication by the State Publishing House many translations of our lesser known classics (lesser known here, that is), especially from the late Medieval and early Renaissance periods. It occurred to me that if a Russian version of *Le Morte d'Arthur* was ever prepared or projected, the man mostly likely to know about it would be the department chairman, Professor A. K. Sokolnikov. It happens that Sokolnikov and I have a mutual acquaintance, and I was able, through her, to convey to him the embassy's interest in Russian translations of the *Morte*. I have now, via this acquaintance, heard back from the professor.

It appears that in the mid-seventies a translation was undertaken, but never completed, by a K. V. Levchenko, a gifted young scholar in Sokolnikov's department. The project was brought to a premature conclusion by her death, apparently by suicide, at a time when the translation was less than half completed. According to the professor, Levchenko's work was not far enough along to warrant the project's being assigned to another scholar for completion, and in any case no one else in the department was believed to be capable of rendering into Russian what Sokolnikov referred to as "the noble simplicity of the original." Ms. Levchenko's manuscript and notes, however, are preserved in the department archive and available for inspection. Sokolnikov intimated that they might also be made available for inclusion in your exhibit.

Please advise whether, and in what way, you would like me to pursue this matter.

> With best regards,
> R. N. Sutcliffe.
> (Vice Consul)

Scrawled in ink near the foot of the letter, and followed by a totally illegible signature, was a terse comment, dated May 15.

"The name is wrong. Do I smell a rat?"

Underneath this someone else had written:

"Not necessarily. Couldn't she have been married?"

Following this was a cryptic memo also classified Secret:

014 SU6/07, our source for *his* version of the suicide story is silent re the sister's marital status. The fact that she shared a flat with her brother might seem to suggest, to those unfamiliar with local conditions, that she was single. But in view of his tender years and the chronic Soviet housing shortage, it seems unwise to build on this assumption.

P. A. Fairlie. May 19, 1984.

PS. Alternatively she could have been divorced.

Below this, in red ink this time, Mr. Signature Illegible had minuted, testily:

I suggest, in view of the importance, that we may want to stop speculating, take steps to find out.

By now Pickett thought he was beginning to understand. The process of vetting a prospect for recruitment was, as he knew from experience, very delicate, especially when a possibility existed that the prospect in question was actually bait. You didn't just haul him in for an interrogation and a polygraph test, because by doing so you would: a) prematurely reveal your intentions, b) risk scaring him off, and c) quite possibly disclose to the competition the identities and methods of your own personnel, especially those of your talent spotters. What you had to do was glean, in informal contacts with the subject himself, as much information about him as you could. This information you then checked for consistency and accuracy by consulting, where possible, independent and reliable sources. It was one such check, apparently, to which the documents on file related.

014 SU6/07, when consulted, confirmed the general accuracy of this guess. Since Kalugin was a Soviet citizen who'd applied to the British for asylum, he'd naturally been exposed to official scrutiny. 014 SU6/07, in fact, was the record of an interview he'd had, shortly after his arrival in 1983, with someone ostensibly from British Immigration but actually, Pickett guessed, from M15. In the course of this interview Kalugin had stated, in response to a comment on his flawless command of English, that English had been the language most often used at home by him and his sister, who had lectured in English literature at Odessa University and in fact had been engaged, at

the time of her death in 1977, in translating Malory's *Le Morte d'Arthur* into Russian. No doubt because Kalugin was a student refugee, with a documented history of dissidence in Warsaw, other and more dramatic claims about his life than the literary activities of his sister had received priority in the initial checking process. No one, at any rate, had thought to follow up on this lead until 1984, when the question of recruiting him had first been mooted and the checking had begun in earnest.

Had the KGB screwed up? In giving their illegal a brand-new identity had they somehow overlooked this detail of the old one? It was possible, Pickett supposed, but unlikely. He thought about the mechanics of creating a "legend," the identity an agent hid behind in his new home and country as he went about the work of uncovering its secrets. Invention was never the major problem; any pulp novelist, given a couple of hours, could dream up a credible persona and life history. The problem, always, was to fit invention to the contours of reality, to plant your shoots of falsehood in the flinty soil of truth. People had to come from somewhere—*that* was the problem—and ultimately, if you only dug deep enough, you'd get down to bedrock, the small but intractable discrepancy that marked like a fault line the boundary between fiction and fact. There were, he knew, two basic approaches to dealing with this problem. One was to invent almost from scratch, to give checkers as little as possible to work on, to bury the original identity so deep that the diggers would tire before they got close to it. The other was to invent almost nothing, to connect the new identity seamlessly with the old, to disarm suspicion by offering so much to check, by making checking so easy and unrewarding that in the end it hardly seemed worth the bother. It was the second of these approaches, Pickett guessed—if any approach had been taken at all—that the legend spinners had taken with Kalugin. They'd recruited (somehow) a young man from a family with a history of dissidence and turned him into a very public rebel and eventually a political refugee. The only things they'd needed to conceal were his recruitment and his whereabouts for the period of his training. The only thing they'd changed was his name.

Or had they?

The next few documents on file did little to clear up the question. Toward the end of May, as the memo writer with the illegible signature had suggested, inquiries had been made into why Kalugin's sister, who everyone had assumed was unmarried, had a different surname than he. Instructions had passed, Brit-style, through the proper channels: from the SIS to the Foreign Office proper, thence to the Cultural Attaché in Moscow, and from him to Vice-Consul Sutcliffe in Kiev. Had they passed a little quicker, Pickett felt, they might have yielded more definite results. Unfortunately, as Sutcliffe's Top Secret telegram explained, by June the hole in Kalugin's legend—if it *was* a hole, and if there *was* a legend—had been patched.

To: Farrar
From: Sutcliffe
Re: Ms. Levchenko's marital status

At a social gathering two weeks ago, Sokolnikov raised, un-prompted, the topic of my interest in what he referred to as "the Kalugin *Morte d'Arthur* translation." When I remarked that Ms. Levchenko appeared posthumously to have changed her name, he said that Kalugin had been her maiden name, which after her short-lived marriage she'd reverted to using. He went on to ex-plain that because her work was still indexed in the department archive under Levchenko, he tended to use either name indis-criminately. Shortly after this we were interrupted and the sub-ject was dropped. Since then he has been very cordial, twice extending dinner invitations which prior commitments unfortu-nately forced me to decline. Two days ago he phoned to ask whether *Le Morte d'Arthur* manuscript would in fact be needed for the Interchange Exhibit. He seemed disappointed when I told him it wouldn't.

It is hard to know what to make of all this; whether anything would be gained by checking Sokolnikov's story. I could perhaps gain access to the local bureau of records, but if, as is clearly a possibility, our interest in the matter has attracted notice in Moscow, this step, which would entail risking assets, is likely to be counterproductive. To a system that is willing, should the need arise, to rewrite whole chapters of its country's history, the falsification of marriage records would not present much of a problem.

Please advise.

The file did not record what Sutcliffe had been advised. Pickett hoped it had been to drop the inquiry. His own instinct to distrust Professor Sokolnikov's somewhat elaborate story had clearly been shared by Signature Illegible, who had minuted the file copy of the telegram:

"Sounds like a lot of cock to me."

What had followed had been six months of more or less round-the-clock surveillance of Kalugin (mercifully reported in summary form on the file) that had turned up no evidence whatever that he was not what he'd always claimed to be. Then, just as things were turning in his favor, when the talent spotters were arguing once more that the mix-up over names had no sinister implications, a bomb had been dropped on him by the Cultural Attaché in Moscow.

Either Farrar's Cultural Interchange Exhibit had been real, or else he had a lot of time on his hands and a genuine interest in Russian versions of the English classics. At any rate, one day he had happened to be reading a Russian translation of Chaucer, published sometime in the early seventies, and on page 56 had noticed a footnote he'd found interesting enough to be worth translating and dispatching to London by telegram marked: Top Secret/Flash. The footnote, which related to the interpretation of a textual ambiguity in *The Parlement of Fowles*, consisted of one sentence and read as follows:

"For the outlines of this analysis I am indebted to K. V. Stolypin in Kiev, whose projected translation of Malory's *Le Morte d'Arthur* is eagerly awaited by her colleagues."

It was shortly after this that the file had been marked: No Further Action.

Pickett was not surprised. He was not surprised now, either, that the initial British response to his query about Kalugin had been to issue a vaguely worded warning and to stubbornly refuse to get down to cases. For the file recorded an embarrassing near brush with disaster, what Signature Illegible, that hardened skeptic, would no doubt have called "a monumental cock-up." The Brits had been rescued by sheer blind luck from recruiting and reinfiltrating into Russia what Pickett would have bet his life savings was a KGB illegal. Thanks only to Farrar and his whim of reading Chaucer in Russian, there were men alive and at liberty today who might otherwise have found oblivion in the Lubianka.

But what about Kalugin? Apparently the Brits had done nothing about him. On reflection, Pickett found himself concurring. What else, he asked himself, *could* they have done? The evidence on file that struck *him* as so compelling would be more or less worthless in a court of law. And even if there had been a chance of convicting Kalugin of some crime or other—lying to Immigration perhaps— what was achieved by locking him away or by shipping him back to Mother Russia? Much better, from the Brit point of view, to leave him doing no real harm where he was than to tell the KGB that their agent was blown and worthless. For if they didn't know for sure that he'd been blown, there was always a chance they'd fall prey to wishful thinking, assign him eventually to some new operation, which you'd then be able to detect and abort.

From the Brit point of view it was better, but what about from the CIA's? That, he thought, was a whole different deal. He still wasn't clear why Meredith was interested in Kalugin, but the fact remained that he was. Chance Davenport, moreover, was now known beyond doubt to be screwing a KGB agent and was therefore a major security risk. From the CIA's point of view, Kalugin wasn't harmless, but a threat.

A threat everyone would be better off without.

CHAPTER TWENTY-SEVEN

(London. August 12, 1990)

IT WAS MOSTLY BECAUSE SHE SEEMED SO CAREFUL OF IT THAT KALUGIN noticed the woman's purse. A largish satchel in oxblood with a shoulder strap and a flap that fastened with a clasp of yellowish metal, it was leather, good box calf, sturdy and expensive-looking, the kind of purse that in Russia most women would have killed for, or at the very least waited in line for all day. It lay on the seat beside her at her table next to Kalugin's in the coffee house in Kensington High Street, but the shoulder strap was looped around her wrist as if she expected someone to snatch the purse, and every few seconds she glanced up from her magazine (which Kalugin suspected she wasn't really reading) as if to reassure herself that nobody had.

He wondered how much money she had in it.

She herself was less worthy of notice. Nobody, probably, would have stood in line for her. She was middle-aged—early fifties, he guessed—with fleshy features too heavily powdered, a dumpy figure, and straight coarse hair, cut into a kind of helmet, whose color suggested late autumn declining rapidly into winter. Her lipstick was scarlet and thickly applied; it had left a smear on the rim of her cup and on the filter of the cigarette she was smoking. He noticed that in the ashtray at her elbow there were several butts, similarly smeared, some of which had been stubbed out half smoked. She seemed impatient, if not actually nervous, and from time to time her eyes would flick to the clock. There were beads of moisture, he noticed, on her upper lip.

For a time he amused himself speculating about her. She was nervous, presumably, because of all the money which she'd just withdrawn from her savings in order to make a blackmail payment. And the reason she was being blackmailed . . . at this point imagination failed him; he couldn't think what anyone would blackmail her with. Presently, losing interest, he went back to the chess puzzle in the *Evening Standard.* (Fischer versus Larsen, 1972. "After White's next move, Black resigns. What was White's move?") When he next looked up, she had left.

Or at least he assumed she had left. She wasn't at her table, and the waiter was clearing it. But presently, happening to glance in that direction, he saw her emerge from behind the partition that screened the entrance to the restrooms. She walked briskly past him toward the cashier, her right hand holding her sturdy, expensive-looking purse by the shoulder strap.

Or rather, *not* her purse. One very like it.

It was *almost* the same. The color was oxblood; the size and shape were the same; the design was similar, satchel-type, with a flap and a metal clasp. Even the clasp was almost the same, a tongue that passed through a reinforced slot in the flap and twisted to shut. The only difference was in the finish of the metal: that one had been yellowish, this one was chrome.

So she'd taken the wrong purse by mistake in the restroom. It was a largish coincidence, perhaps, that women with virtually identical purses should be in the same restroom at the same moment, but stranger things had happened. The point about improbabilities, after all, was that even the very remote ones, if you waited long enough, would happen. Presently, when she came to pay the cashier, she'd no doubt discover the error. She'd be the blushing type, he figured, profuse with stammered explanations and apologies; the type who, because she'd invariably assume the worst about what others were assuming about her, would always manage to look guilty. But when the woman opened the purse to take out money to pay, she seemed to find nothing amiss, and when she left she was looking neither guilty nor embarrassed. If anything, he thought, she was looking relieved.

He realized then that he had witnessed a switch.

And presently, to confirm that conclusion, another woman exited the restroom. Her purse was identical in every respect to the other, except that this time the finish of the clasp was yellow. This woman was younger and much prettier than the first: good legs, a well-developed figure, a broad face with high cheekbones and a full, slightly pouting mouth, a glossy mane of deep chestnut hair. His reflex, admiring, inventory of features was cut short by the conviction that he had seen her before, a conviction promoted mostly by her walk, which without being obviously provocative or flaunting, conveyed an almost electric sexuality. She walked as if she expected to be watched, as if she wanted to assist you in the process of mentally removing her clothes, as if she wanted you to imagine her naked. He had seen a walk like this before, he thought. He had seen *her* before. He had even, it now dawned on him, seen her naked. The only reason he hadn't known her at once as his rival for top honors at the KGB Language School and his partner of several memorable nights in the earlier days of their training—the number of nights had been limited, he recalled, by her impartiality in bestowing her favors—was that her appearance had radically altered since then. Her hair, clothes, makeup had all acquired a transforming chic. But underneath the European varnish, there was no mistaking the Russian original.

Volkonskaya.

He assumed she had diplomatic cover, would therefore make for Embassy Row, the private street in which, as the name suggested, many foreign missions, including the Soviet Union's, were located. But instead she headed for the underground station. He followed her at as much distance as he could afford without running the risk of losing her entirely. She'd be on the lookout for surveillance, of course, but less so now, probably, than before. She'd never have gone through with the switch unless she was utterly convinced she was clean, and even if that conviction had been mistaken and she *had* been under hostile surveillance, they'd presumably have nabbed her as soon as the switch had been made. No point giving her a chance to ditch whatever it was she had in the purse. He could tag along for a while, he thought, without being noticed.

At the underground, since he didn't know how far he was going, he bought a one-day pass, good for unlimited travel on the system, and followed her to the platform for the southbound District Line. She might, he thought, be headed for Earl's Court, where the embassy maintained an apartment complex. He hoped she wasn't, because a Soviet Embassy apartment complex, where people were positively encouraged to mind other people's business, was not well suited to his purpose. What his purpose was, he wasn't as yet quite sure. To talk to her, perhaps, to ask about Zebo, to check out as much as he could of the curious story Atlas had told him. This was, of course, precisely what Atlas had told him *not* to do. The Residency was penetrated, Atlas had said; nobody in it could be trusted. But Atlas couldn't be trusted, either. And Volkonskaya was a friend, a link with home; they'd been students together, lovers. And though none of this constituted much of a basis for trust, it was more of a basis than anything offered by Atlas. The problem was, of course, that she probably wouldn't trust *him.* KGB rules, indeed, utterly forbade it. Unless they were colleagues and had diplomatic cover, officers in foreign countries were forbidden, except in the line of business, to meet, communicate, or even to acknowledge each other's existence. If they ran across each other by chance, they were bound by rule to ignore each other. Volkonskaya wouldn't talk to him, therefore; if he tried to talk to her she'd probably report him.

But even if she did, the thought suddenly struck him, that might not be entirely to his disadvantage. What people *did,* after all, was usually more revealing than what they said.

Especially people like Atlas.

When her train arrived, he took the same car as she did. By the ordinary rules of surveillance this was an error. You got into an adjoining car and stood by the doors where you could observe and, if the target unexpectedly got off, follow. But the rules were devised to promote discretion. Indiscretion, here, might suit his purpose better.

There were seats empty in the row next to her, but he ignored them, stationing himself instead next to the automatic doors and diagonally opposite where she was sitting. He stood turned toward her, hanging on to the handrail and shooting glances at her over the top of his *Evening Standard,* which between glances he went through the motions of reading. He had snatched it up without thinking on his exit from the coffee house, but now he was glad to have it with him. In the plan that was starting to take shape in his mind, it would play an important role. For a while, though he kept shooting glances at her, willing her to look at him, she simply stared abstractedly ahead. Presently, however, she looked.

When their eyes met, she at once looked away. He, on the other hand, redoubled his stares. He knew she was used to looks from men, but a barrage such as his, he figured, she would hardly be able to ignore. In this he was right. A moment later she looked again.

She was probably a good card player, he thought. Her second look, at any rate, was hardly longer than the first and as expressionless, or almost. Her eyes wandered toward him, rested on him half a second, then wandered away; but for that half-second, it seemed to him, they widened just very slightly, registered a flicker of something—surprise perhaps, or even dismay. He couldn't be sure, because in these situations one tended to imagine. But what would clinch it, he thought, would be what she did now. A woman aware of being stared at by a man could seldom resist stealing the occasional glance, if only to confirm she was still being stared at. This was likely to be true, especially, of Volkonskaya, whose interest in men had always been constant and compelling. If she didn't look at him again, or not soon, it would only be because her reason not to was compelling. It would mean, in fact, that she had recognized him.

A minute passed, then another. The train boomed and rattled through the bowels of Southwest London. She stared ahead, apparently lost in her thoughts. Earl's Court arrived in a squeal of braking. The automatic doors hissed and trundled open. Some people got off, others got on. She stayed where she was, didn't move, didn't look. The automatic doors hissed and trundled shut. The train lurched, shuddered into motion.

She had definitely recognized him.

It was time to put his plan into practice.

Taking a ballpoint from his pocket, he turned to the back page of the *Evening Standard,* where the crossword was located. He folded the paper in half longways and stared with seeming intensity at the puzzle, assuming the mentally constipated look he'd often seen on the faces of crossword addicts. Meanwhile, he watched her from the corner of his eye. Presently, when he saw her glance flick toward him, he started filling in blanks in the puzzle. He filled them in in fits and starts, as if writing in solutions to the clues: five letters across, six down, five across, seven down, four down, five across, four across. When read in sequence they formed a cryptic message:

PURSE SWITCH NOTED PROBLEM NEXT TRAIN
BACK

When he'd finished, he walked over and sat on her left, leaving an empty seat between them. Now he was sure that he had her attention, he ignored her completely, pantomimed absorption in the puzzle. Presently, appearing to lose interest, and still without looking at her, he placed the paper casually on the seat beside her, with the puzzle facing up and turned toward her, so that without moving more than her eyes she could read the message.

She got off at the next stop.

CHAPTER TWENTY-EIGHT

(London. August 12, 1990)

"I THINK YOU MUST BE MAD. OUT OF CONTROL ENTIRELY."

There was no one in earshot, but she spoke in English, quietly, not looking at him, in a tone she might have used for commenting on the weather. She was sitting next to him, on a District Line train as before, but returning now to Kensington High Street. At Putney Bridge, where they'd both left the eastbound train, it had been a matter, merely, of crossing to the next platform to catch the westbound one. Only one other person had got off when they did, and since *he* had left the station forthwith, it was safe to assume they were now surveillance-free.

"Out of control?" he queried. "Do you mean personally or professionally?"

"Probably both." She still didn't look at him. "Your extraordinary behavior could have jeopardized my mission. If anyone but me had been watching that foolishness with the paper, we could be under arrest right now."

"Possibly." He shrugged. "But console yourself with this thought: You could also be under arrest if anyone but me had been watching that foolishness with the purses."

She said nothing, continued to inspect her reflection in the window facing them. Her expression was petulant, resentful. They could have been some married couple, he thought, quarreling over whatever it was that married people quarreled over: money, perhaps, or sex.

"I must have scared you," he said. "I'm sorry."

"You didn't scare me, you annoyed me. I agreed to this contact only to prevent you becoming an embarrassment, making an even bigger spectacle of yourself."

"I was forced to improvise on short notice." He felt somewhat offended. His approach had not, admittedly, been subtle, but "spectacle," surely, was overstating. "In any case, relax. There was no one watching."

"If not, I can hardly thank you." She frowned. "You were *forced* to improvise? What forced you? Your message implied some problem with the switch. Was there?"

He shook his head. "Except for the fact that the purses were not identical and the switch could therefore have been noted by any halfway observant bystander, like myself, there was no problem." He paused. "The woman looked nervous, however. Did she volunteer, or did you seduce her?"

She ignored the question. "If there was no problem, what was your reason for making contact? I'm assuming the purpose of this breach of procedure was not to engage me in prohibited discussion."

"Breach of procedure . . . prohibited discussion." He shot her a look of reproach. "Would you please stop talking like a training manual. We used to be friends at one time. We used to mean something to each other."

Now she did look at him, sharply. "I wouldn't say so. We shared a bed once or twice, twelve years ago, to satisfy a need which on my side at least was temporary. I can see no reason to get sentimental about it." She paused. "I see no reason to talk to you at all. If you have something of professional importance to say, say it."

Say what? The trouble was, he didn't know. He was fishing here, and probably without bait. He could only cast at random, hope for some kind of strike.

"I'm assuming you're a member of the Residency staff," he began, "operating under diplomatic cover."

"Make what assumptions you like." She went back to looking at her reflection in the window. "Don't expect me to comment on them."

"I have information," he persisted, "regarding penetration of the Residency by a hostile service. I need to transmit it somehow."

Again the deadpan stare. "I have no knowledge of that subject. This information you claim to have, I suggest you transmit it through your normal channels."

No knowledge? But if, as Atlas had claimed, the Residency had been extensively penetrated, all members of the staff would surely know about it. On the other hand, of course, her denial might be a lie, based on her obvious mistrust of him. He tried again.

"I *have* no channels. That's why I risked this breach of procedure. My normal contact is unavailable."

"Unavailable?"

He nodded, thought of Zebo. "I don't know why I said unavailable. What I should have said was dead."

"Dead?" She was suddenly still. He sensed that her irritation had changed into something else. He wasn't sure what. Watchfulness, maybe? Fear? "Your normal contact was Gryazin? You were under *his* control?"

He nodded. A thought struck him. Atlas had said that the CIA killed Zebo. He wondered, if he could get her to say *anything*, what Volkonskaya would say about that. "He was murdered, as you know. I presume by the Americans."

"You presume . . ." She broke off, her look suddenly guarded. "You weren't assigned a replacement?"

"If I had, would I be bothering you?"

He could have told her about Atlas, of course, but that would have involved him in further explanations. This whole thing was looking like a mistake. He'd thought talking to her might make a difference, that the very fact of their former relationship might thaw at least some of her distrust. But as far as he could tell, she was chillier than ever. She was KGB through and through now, he thought: KGB right down to the bone marrow.

"You weren't assigned a new control?"

He nodded impatiently. "I just told you."

"And you wish me to transmit a message?"

"I told you that, too."

"And your code name is Cobalt?" Her voice was scornful, icy, her question less question than accusation.

"I didn't tell you *that.*"

He felt a lurch of apprehension. He hadn't told anyone that. In the Residency only Zebo had known it. Zebo and the Resident himself. So how come she knew it? Did the whole world know it?

"You didn't *need* to tell me." She paused, turned round in her seat to face him. She was looking at him now with a curious expression. A mixture, perhaps, of fear and revulsion. And something else. Something, he thought, very close to hatred. "I am breaking off this contact. At the next station I shall leave this train. There will be no point in your following me, because I will not transmit your message."

He was too stunned to speak. She continued:

"You say you presume Gryazin was killed by the Americans, but you are lying. Gryazin was killed by his own agent. The Resident himself told us this. He was killed by the only agent who, after his death, didn't respond to his regular call sign, and who couldn't, therefore, be assigned a replacement. The agent in question was code named Cobalt. In other words . . ." her voice was as sharp as an icepick, *"You."*

CHAPTER TWENTY-NINE

(London. August 13, 1990)

"WHAT I DON'T ACTUALLY SEE," CHANCE SAID, "IS WHERE MY PRIVATE life gets to be any of yours or the Agency's goddamn business."

Though she spoke with a smile, the words were delivered with a steely mildness in which there was no hint of compromise at all. It reminded Pickett forcibly of his mother, who throughout his adolescence and beyond had ruled her children with an iron firmness and without, to the best of his recollection, ever once having to raise her voice.

He inspected the crystal depths of his martini, gave it a moody stir with the olive. This was turning out tougher than expected. Maybe he'd misjudged his talent for diplomacy. Or maybe he'd simply misjudged her. What he'd planned, at any rate, as a friendly chat over lunch, he dispensing sage and kindly advice, she gratefully receiving, had turned, at the mention of Kalugin, into something reminiscent of the START negotiations.

"Let's be realistic," he said. "You have high-level access to Agency classified; your private life gets to be Agency business the moment they find out you're seeing a Soviet defector. They're entitled— wouldn't you agree?—to *protect* their secrets." He paused. "As to its not being *my* business, you're right. Strictly speaking, it isn't. What I had hoped, however, was that by *making* it a little my business, I might be able to stop it becoming the Agency's."

This didn't seem to impress her much.

"In other words, you're warning me off. Letting me know that unless I stop, you'll feel obliged to make sure the Agency finds out that I'm—how did you so delicately put it?—'seeing' Adam."

He shook his head. "You're misinterpreting. I'm not here to issue warnings. I merely want you to know certain facts, so whatever decisions you make about your private life, which I agree is entirely your business, are at least *informed* decisions." He shrugged. "Be fair, Chance. I don't deserve this. I'm not acting here as an Agency narc, I'm doing this purely out of motives of friendship."

"Maybe you are." She didn't sound convinced. "But in that case tell me this . . . How do you *know* that I've been seeing him?"

"You forget." He smiled. "I'm a disappointed rival. Remember that drinks bash at the Bayswater Hotel? Thrown by the Anglo-Hungarian Alliance or some such? He cut me out when I wanted to ask you to dinner."

"That was weeks ago. What makes you think I've been seeing him since?"

"Usually well-informed sources . . ." Seeing in her expression the beginnings of outrage, he cut her off before she could voice it. "Now don't go getting your nose all out of joint. Nobody's been following you around. You just happened to be noticed, that's all."

Her look was glacial. "Just happened to be noticed *where?*"

"Christ, I don't know. The exhibition at the Royal Academy. Some restaurant or other. The tea room at the Ritz." He shrugged. "Someone saw you and mentioned the fact. He didn't mention where. I didn't ask."

"And this someone who mentioned seeing me. Who was it?"

He shook his head. "It wouldn't signify if I told you. But I will tell you this much. You weren't the primary focus of interest."

"I wasn't?" She pondered this. "In other words, Adam was. Or *is.*"

He shrugged. " 'Was' would be closer to the truth. It wasn't, in any case, any big deal. I'll put it this way. Since that bash at the Bayswater Hotel, I've had reason to interest myself in Kalugin. When I found out a) that he was a Soviet defector and b) that he'd been seeing you, it struck me that you ought to be apprised of a and consider the risks inherent in b." He paused and smiled, he hoped disarmingly. "And there you have it. The whole story."

She eyed him thoughtfully.

"The whole story? Are you saying, then, that he's no longer the focus of interest?"

He met her gaze squarely. "Yes."

"Then why do you keep calling him a Soviet defector?"

"Because that's what he is . . ." He saw her start to protest and cut her off. "I know you'd rather call him a political refugee, a victim of repression and the wicked KGB, but the fact is, he came from behind the Iron Curtain at a time when there still was an Iron Curtain. In our book that makes him a Soviet defector. And from the standpoint of security, guys like him are suspect. Always and irrevocably suspect."

"Like homosexuals, in fact?"

"Or former members of the Communist Party." He nodded, ignoring the irony. "Oh, I know what you're going to say next. The presumption of innocence is a wonderful thing, and I'm all for it, in a court of law. In security work, however, it's a luxury you can't permit yourself. You're forced to operate on mere suspicion. And of course we know that maybe ninety-eight percent of all Soviet defectors are exactly what they seem, but we also know that two percent aren't. The two percent are what we can't afford."

"Injustice, in other words, rather than disorder?"

"If you want to put it that way, yes."

She thought for a moment.

"And so what you're saying, when we get right down to it, is that though you have no evidence at all, Adam is nonetheless under suspicion of being a Russian spy and always will be. And because of that, if I continue to see him, I'm probably going to lose my job."

He considered.

"I wouldn't say under suspicion. That goes way beyond the facts. It's a possibility, merely, that we can't afford to ignore. As to losing your job, that's overstating, too. I'm saying that if the Agency finds out, it may want to cancel or limit your access. Whether in those circumstances the Foundation would want to continue to employ you isn't a judgment I'm able to make."

"Isn't it?" She looked skeptical. "But I imagine you can guess."

He took a pull at his martini, sighed.

"Chance, look. I've told you something I thought you ought to hear. If you don't want to hear it, that's your decision. Let's drop the matter, forget I raised it."

Moment of silence.

"I don't think it's quite that simple, is it?"

He shrugged. "Why wouldn't it be?"

She didn't answer at once, gave him instead an appraising look.

"You said *if* the Agency finds out. Does that mean you're not going to tell them?"

He thought about this. Actually he hadn't been sure what he meant. His side of this dialogue hadn't been planned in advance, but improvised from moment to moment. Now it was taking a promising direction. It was going to depend on his finding the right words. But then that was always the problem, wasn't it? People were governed by language, mostly. Find the right words, and you could make them do anything.

Almost anything.

"To be honest," he said, "I don't know. My inclination is to use my own best judgment. And my judgment is that he's part of the ninety-eight percent. I also believe that, regardless of whether *he's* unreliable, *you're* not. On the other hand . . ." He paused. "If the Agency finds out that I didn't report what I knew about you and Mr. Kalugin, *I'm* the one who's going to be out of a job. Officially, I'm not given any choice. Security officers are not at all keen on people using their own best judgment."

"You're contemplating, in other words, going out on a limb for me?" She gave him a somewhat skeptical look. "Purely out of friendship?"

"That wasn't the point I was trying to make."

"What was it then?"

"I don't know . . ." He shrugged. "Maybe this, that since my neck *is* out a little here, I would hope that at some point you'd remember that fact."

"At some point? When?"

He hesitated, thought for a moment. "If at some point, let's say, you should come to suspect, for some reason, that my judgment of Kalugin was mistaken." Christ, he thought, I need to go back to the States. I'm starting to sound like bloody Faraday.

"And if that should happen, what would you hope that I'd do?"

"If it happened I would hope that you wouldn't leave me in the dark, that I wouldn't get to learn about it from some security officer and only about half an hour before they requested my head on a platter."

"You'd want me to warn you, in fact."

He nodded. "I'd certainly appreciate that."

She was silent for perhaps half a minute, time she spent toying with her fork and gazing out of the window. When she turned back to him, her look was opaque.

"And you'd appreciate it, too, no doubt, if in the meantime one kept one's eyes open?"

"Open . . . For what?"

"For reasons to suspect that your judgment about Adam was, in fact, mistaken."

He shook his head. It was tempting, but "keeping your eyes open" was only a short step, semantically, from "spying." Whatever the right words were in this case, that, clearly, wasn't one of them. In any case, he thought, the seed had been planted. Whether she wanted to or not, from now on she would watch Kalugin like a hawk. It was possible to wonder, moreover, whether her feelings for her lover could survive the strain of that suspicion. On the whole, he tended to doubt it.

"If you mean am I asking you to keep an eye on *him,*" he said. "I'm absolutely not. As I thought I'd already made clear, I don't think there's anything to keep an eye *on.* Ideally, of course, I'd prefer you didn't see him, but failing that . . ." He shrugged. "What I'm asking you, since you force me to put it bluntly, is, if necessary, to give me some warning so that I can *try* to cover my ass."

The arrival of their waiter, inquiring, intrusively, how everything was, put the conversation temporarily on hold. It was only when Chance's glass had been topped up, dessert refused, and coffee ordered, that the subject could be taken up again. It was Chance who did so. She continued to look troubled.

"You know what I have a hard time believing?"

He shook his head.

"That your suspicions of Adam are merely general. That you don't, in fact, think that there's anything to keep an eye on . . ." She paused. "You mentioned that party at the Bayswater Hotel, when Adam and I went out to dinner. Do you happen to remember what you said about him then?"

He thought for a moment. "I can't say I do."

"You called him a young thug. It struck me at the time as an odd thing to say. Uncalled for, really. Unless, of course, you were trying, then, to *hint* at suspicions you're now more willing to voice. In any case, it's clear you were interested in Adam before I ever knew of his existence." She paused. "I think you ought to tell me, at least, what made you call him a young thug."

Pickett considered. This was a tough one. He'd prefer, of course, to stonewall or tell her some comforting lie. But she was too clever to be fooled by obfuscation, and telling lies involved an obvious risk: Kalugin might already have told her something different. The safest thing was to tell just enough of the truth to answer her question.

"You know that he's Ukrainian, of course?"

She nodded.

"Well, I started to get interested in him—it was shortly before you met him—when he joined this emigré group. They call themselves the Knights of Vladimir. Their burning ambition in life is to bring about Ukrainian independence, and the way they think they're going to accomplish that feat is by murdering people in the Ukraine."

"Murdering people?"

"Terrorism. Assassinations of leading Party members, high-ranking KGB officers and the like." He nodded. "Not very nice people, perhaps, but people nevertheless. Of course they're crazy, these Knights, and in all probability harmless. But part of my job was to keep tabs on them to make absolutely sure they were harmless." He paused. "Thuggery, in my book, is a state of mind. You don't have to do it, necessarily; you just have to be willing. I think this guy is willing. That's why I said what I said."

It sounded plausible. At least, he thought, it ought to satisfy *her*. It explained his remark, his interest in Kalugin; it oughtn't to raise further questions. The conversation had turned out quite well, in fact. She would watch Kalugin now, mistrust him. And because she mistrusted him, in all probability, she wouldn't, for fear of alerting him to the fact, tell him she'd had this conversation. For a moment Pickett considered warning her about this but decided not to. Downplay everything was the indicated strategy here. In diplomacy, as in architecture, Mies's dictum held good: Less is more.

Her next remark, however, forced him to wonder whether his success had been quite as complete as he'd thought.

"And of course," she said, "when you checked into his background and discovered he'd come from behind the Iron Curtain, you naturally wondered if his job might not be duplicating yours."

"Duplicating?"

"Keeping tabs on these Knights of Vladimir." She nodded. "But in his case not for the CIA, but instead for the wicked KGB."

"It crossed my mind." Since he'd raised the possibility himself, he thought, he'd be more than idiotic to deny it. "I made some inquiries, as I told you. I even, I'll admit, had him watched for a while. I came to the conclusion this particular suspicion was probably groundless. In the course of my inquiries, however, as I also said, I was made aware of his possible relationship with you. Which brings us back"—he shrugged—"to where we came in. I wanted you to be aware of the facts."

"That was thoughtful of you." For the first time in fifteen minutes she smiled. It might have been more reassuring, he thought, had it not been tinged with what looked like mockery. "And let's both hope you're right."

"Right?"

"Right that this particular suspicion was groundless." She nodded. "Because if he *is* with the KGB, somebody—you perhaps—is in a lot of trouble." He was about to speak, but she cut him off. "You were right to say that I've been seeing him. And you want to know where I saw him last week? At that place down in Sussex, that ugly Victorian country house which allegedly belongs to the Foundation. Fifteen-foot walls and electronic gates manned by muscular young men who don't look particularly the gatekeeper type."

"Sussex?" He stared, his amazement genuine this time.

"Don't pretend you don't know what I'm talking about." The mockery in her smile was open now. "That place down in Sussex that you guys, or *some* of you guys, or someone *connected* with some of you guys, used to use for training Contras."

CHAPTER THIRTY

(London. August 13, 1990)

CHANCE SAT AT THE KEYBOARD OF HER TERMINAL, GAZING WITHOUT focus at the log of operations displayed the screen and trying, without much success, to kid herself she was working. It was now seven-thirty. A full hour ago the last of her colleagues had signed out and gone home. The log had been on screen for some minutes. She was thinking about Adam Kalugin.

To be specific, Adam Kalugin and the Ukraine.

Adam and the Ukraine. Rosenthal, the log informed her, had recently gamed a scenario that in some way involved the Ukraine. And Pickett had told her at lunch that Adam was involved with Ukrainian emigrés, a wannabe terrorist group. And Adam had told her . . .

She didn't often work late. Though willing to grant exceptions for emergencies—she'd several times worked past midnight to make a deadline—she believed that employment was a limited transaction, involving on both sides a limited commitment. They, employers, bought a given amount of your time and shouldn't, unless they were willing to pay for it, get in the habit of expecting more. The other side of the coin, of course, was that *you* shouldn't get in the habit of giving less. Which was why, tonight, she was still in the office, for though in the hours since lunch she'd been more or less constantly at her desk, she hadn't succeeded in doing much work. She'd tried hard enough, God knows. She'd tried her damnedest all afternoon. She just hadn't been able to keep her mind on anything for more than ten seconds at a time. On anything other than Adam, that was. Or rather, what Pickett had told her about him.

Adam Kalugin and the Ukraine.

But what *had* Pickett told her exactly? That, of course, was part of the problem. In conversations connected with his work, Randall

Pickett tended to be opaque. The whole was often more than the sum of the parts, reading between the lines obligatory. It was best to start, she thought, with what Pickett had actually stated. One could next compare this with what Adam had actually stated, then assess both statements, in turn, in the light of whatever—there was, when you got right down to it, precious little of this—she knew for certain to be fact.

Adam, Pickett had said, belonged to a Ukrainian terrorist group. What had Adam said about that? When she cast her mind back (again) to her last conversation with Adam, she was struck (again) by how little he'd said on *any* subject. He'd not even admitted, not in so many words, being in Sussex. But he had been in Sussex—she had seen him—and at least one of the men she'd seen doing combat training at the country house, namely Benko, had been Ukrainian. So it looked as if, in this respect at least, what Pickett had said might be the truth.

But what about his insinuation that Adam might be spying for the KGB? This was another subject on which Adam had made no direct statement—he hadn't, admittedly, been given a chance to—but he had hinted at an intelligence connection ("I might, for instance, have other trusts to keep."), which she'd naturally assumed at the time must be with the CIA. But if Adam's intelligence connection was with the CIA, why would Pickett be warning her against him?

But perhaps, she thought, Pickett didn't *know.*

And that was quite possible, wasn't it? Because if, for the sake of argument, you assumed that what Adam had hinted was the truth and he *was* involved in some Agency business or other, Pickett wouldn't know it unless he was involved in it, too. So it was at least conceivable, wasn't it, that both men had told (or hinted at) the truth? Adam, for instance, might be engaged in some piece of Agency skullduggery involving this Ukrainian terrorist group and re-quiring his presence at that place in Sussex. And Pickett, encounter-ing him in the course of his own routine contacts with the Ukrainians and not being aware of the Agency connection, might well have been alarmed by his early history and felt duty bound to pursue the matter further. It was a *little* hard to conceive perhaps that, in any *normal* enterprise, two employees could be separately instructed to cultivate the same contacts and not be informed of each other's existence, but the Agency in that respect was decidedly *not* normal. It had elevated to the status of an art, in fact, not telling the right hand what the left was doing.

But unless—and this was what really disturbed her—Pickett's suspicions about Adam had some kind of basis in fact, would he have felt obliged to warn her about him? He said he had done it out of friendship, but that was obviously nonsense. That Pickett would risk his career to save yours was next to impossible to swallow, unless you also accepted his claim to be convinced that Adam was harmless and the risk therefore negligible. But unless he believed the risk *wasn't* negligible, he'd hardly have gone to the trouble, not to mention the potential embarrassment, of warning her. It crossed her mind, here, that his motive mightn't have been professional at all, but personal and ulterior, but she tended to doubt it. Not that she'd put it past him, she thought, but she doubted he'd be so unsubtle. No. What she kept returning to, against her will, was the uncomfortable conviction that in spite of his various disclaimers, Pickett had alerted her to real misgivings. And not because he cared about her or her job, but because he knew she was close to Adam and hoped she might be induced to spy on him.

She might, in other words, be in love with a KGB illegal.

The "might" didn't refer to her. And this was why, since lunch with Pickett, she'd found it so impossible to work. The knowledge that Adam might work for the KGB—the absolute, heart-stopping void that had seemed to open beneath her when she'd first confronted this possibility—had forced her to acknowledge her feelings. She had fallen in love with this Adam Kalugin, this Soviet defector, who didn't have a real job (or not one in any way commensurate with his talents), who was never home in the daytime and frequently not in the evening, who made no commitments for more than a few days in advance, who resolutely declined to talk about the future, who disappeared mysteriously for days at a time, and who had recently mysteriously reappeared (among a group receiving combat training) at a country house in Sussex probably owned by the Foundation.

The man she'd fallen in love with—there was no getting around this, at least—was mixed up in something rather strange.

He was mixed up in something *very* strange. For here, on the screen of her computer, was a record showing that Martin Rosenthal, unregenerate Cold Warrior that he was, had recently been gaming a scenario which in some way involved the Ukraine. This, at least, was what the entry in the log on the screen suggested:

SATURN. 8:10:90 SOVCOM2. PARAMETERS CURRENT.
SCENARIO CODE 5. IMP POLMIL GLOBAL. MTR.
17431824/40.16

Saturn was the name of the simulation. SovCom2 was the geo-
graphical area primarily covered by the simulation. For gaming purposes the world was always divided, since Pentagon dollars had
largely financed the program, along military lines. Sector 2 of the
Soviet Military Command roughly coincided with the borders of the
Ukraine. Parameters referred to the assumptions made by the scenario to be gamed; for the most part they described social, economic,
political, and military conditions currently prevailing in areas affected by the scenario. (It was a large part of Chance's job, as one of
the more than two dozen analysts employed by the Foundation, to
ensure that these parameters were kept as current and accurate as
possible.) Scenario referred to the hypothetical situation whose
global political and military implications the gamer, in this case Martin Tausig Rosenthal, had used the computer to explore. He had used
the simulation for forty minutes and sixteen seconds between five
forty-three and six twenty-three PM on August 10. What scenario he
had actually gamed was not apparent from the log. What *was* apparent was his desire to keep the scenario in question to himself, since
Code 5, the security classification of the game, was one to which only
he, at least among the Foundation's employees, had access.

What exactly had he been gaming?

She wasn't likely to find out. Access to each security level of the
system was governed by identifying codes. If you knew the codes and
the sequence in which they were to be entered, it was as easy as
unlocking a series of doors. However, since the codes all involved
seven digits, and since they and the sequences had been randomly
generated, your chances of stumbling into, or using trial and error to
gain access to, the Code 5 level were almost astronomically remote.
If the proverbial six monkeys were chained to keyboards and
punched in numbers nonstop, twenty-four hours a day, three hundred and sixty-five days a year, for twenty years, the probability of
their generating the sequence even once, so the man who had briefed
her on the system had told Chance, was only fifty percent. If, moreover, you did use trial and error in your effort to break in, you
needed to get lucky very quickly, because mistakes not immediately
rectified by the Error Correction Code, which of course was also
secret, would immediately shut the system down and leave an inerad-

icable audit trail. The entry procedures to Code 3, her own level, were complicated enough that she was always afraid she'd forget them. Those for Code 5 were no doubt more so.

She wondered how Rosenthal managed to remember.

If there *was* a precise moment when she formed the intention to break her employer's trust—and maybe the law, though she wasn't at all clear exactly what law she'd be breaking—it was, she thought afterward, then. For as soon as she wondered about Rosenthal and remembering entry codes, it was clear beyond possibility of doubt that Rosenthal *didn't* remember. Rosenthal couldn't even remember the PIN number he'd needed to use to get money from the automatic teller on the day he had taken her to lunch. She remembered his searching his wallet, with a mixture of embarrassment and that inexplicable pride which literate men often take in being innumerate, for the scrap of paper on which he'd *written* his PIN number. There was no way he'd memorized the entry codes, she thought. He would have them written somewhere.

This was strictly forbidden, of course. It made a total mockery of the system. Security systems, like chains, were only as strong as their weakest link. And the weakest link, as her regular security refresher courses had never tired of stressing, was always the Human Element. The most impregnable safe in the world was no good at all if you omitted to lock it, or if, as she was confident Rosenthal had done here, you hid the combination in the security equivalent of a shoebox. And she was confident about Rosenthal, she thought, because she had never met anyone who embodied the Human Element, at least as it applied to security, with quite the determination he did. She recalled some security officer somewhere proposing almost as a law of his profession that carelessness about security increased as you went up the bureaucratic ladder. And that Rosenthal, who had climbed that ladder to the topmost rung and whose consequent disdain for the rules governing ordinary mortals made him a security officer's nightmare, had actually put himself to the trouble of memorizing the codes and entry sequences for a system he personally seldom operated struck her as stretching probability beyond the breaking point. He would have them written somewhere.

The question was where?

By the time she'd got as far as asking this question, she thought afterward, the next step had been an almost foregone conclusion. For added to the almost irresistible emotional compulsion to know the worst about Adam was the intellectual challenge this now presented: could she, from her knowledge of Rosenthal's character, figure out where he might have hidden the sequences? And besides, she told herself, it wasn't as if she would really be spying; anything she learned would be kept to herself.

For her own peace of mind she *had* to know.

All the same, once the decision had *consciously* been taken and she found herself in the corridor that led from her office to Rosenthal's, she was scared. Granted she was Rosenthal's assistant, or one of them, that didn't give her the right to poke around in his office. There was, moreover, a security guard on duty, and though his patrols were sporadic and perfunctory and one of them had happened barely five minutes ago, this wasn't going to help her if one of these sporadic and perfunctory patrols *discovered* her in Rosenthal's office. As she crept through the outer office and approached the twin doors at the entrance to Rosenthal's sanctum, she was conscious of entertaining quite strongly the chickenshit hope that something would happen to thwart her, something as simple as Rosenthal's door being locked.

The door was open, of course.

The thing she had going for her—she told herself this to boost her evaporating courage—was the fact that there was still some daylight. The velvet curtains serving the sets of French doors hadn't been drawn all the way. They admitted strips of grayish phosphorescence which, though not illuminating the office fully, at least mitigated the gloom enough to let her prowl without knocking furniture over. If she drew the curtains just another few inches, she would have enough light by which to conduct at least a preliminary survey. The security guard, when he checked again, would probably not notice that the light was less dim. And indeed since it was now getting on for eight, if he left it very long, as she fervently hoped that he would, it might very well be dark outside, in which case there'd be nothing to notice. Only if she needed to read something, she decided, would she take the risk of turning on a light.

Rosenthal's terminal was in a small anteroom adjoining his office. But he wouldn't hide the codes there, she thought, not that close to the terminal, because physical proximity suggested too naturally a link between terminal and numbers. Rosenthal wouldn't go for anything *that* obvious or stupid, because whatever else you might think about him, he wasn't obvious or stupid at all. Actually he was rather clever.

And that was the key to him really, she thought: the self-conscious

cleverness which, reaching always for brilliance, fell short occasionally of common sense. He wouldn't do anything obvious, and that
included hiding the codes in the pages of a book, or taped to the
underside of a desk drawer, or anyplace else where, to anyone stumbling across them, they'd look conspicuously hidden. What he'd do
was hide them in full view, put them where anyone could see them
without ever suspecting what they were. He would hide them, in
other words, among other numbers, numbers that looked exactly like
them.

But what other numbers looked exactly like them?

She tiptoed over to the huge mahogany desk. In spite of her caution, her footsteps on the parquet sounded, to her oversensitized
ears, like amplified castanets. She took off her shoes, pushed them
under the desk. Since her only warning of the guard's approach
would be noise, it was vital she make none herself.

There was nothing interesting on the surface of the desk. Nothing
much at all, actually, except the blotter, the two phones, what looked
like a diary or address book bound in morocco leather, and an over-
size fountain pen. She tried the drawers. All but two were locked. Of
the two that weren't, one was empty and the other contained only a
stick of underarm deodorant and a laundry box in which there were
no less than three clean shirts. The shirts brought a smile to Chance's
lips. To the image Rosenthal went to such pains to achieve, perspira-
tion was a constant enemy.

No numbers anywhere.

When she paused then, baffled, the reality of what she was doing
reasserted itself with brutal clarity. She must have gone mad. She
must be literally, certifiably crazy. What the *hell* was she doing in
here, presuming to search her boss's desk, presuming (even more) to
read his mind? How could she be so certain she was right—about the
scenario and its relevance to Adam, about Rosenthal's not memorizing the codes, about how he would hide them if he hadn't? What she
was doing—the response took no time at all in coming—if not actually criminal, could cost her her job. It could subject her, moreover,
to a thoroughly intrusive and hostile investigation by the CIA, or at
least the FBI, whose upshot, since the Agency's links with academe
were known to be extensive, would no doubt be that she'd find it
almost impossible ever to get a university job. The hell with finding
out about Adam. The hell with Adam, in fact. She needed to get out
of here. Now.

It was just as she was making this eminently sensible decision that she heard, in the outer office, the sound of a door being opened.

The guard had come back.

For an instant her mind seemed to stop. She just stood there, stupid with terror, the purest terror she had felt in her life. Then instinct and adrenaline took over. Before she had even begun to consider options, almost before her mind could start functioning again, she found herself behind a curtain in the alcove that served the nearest set of French doors.

Footsteps approached Rosenthal's door. They paused for a second. The door opened with a muffled creak. The footsteps resumed, clacking hollowly on the hardwood floor. They stopped for a second —crossing one of the rugs, probably—then they sounded again, closer.

They stopped again. The guard was halfway across the room now, she judged. He ought, if he was merely looking around, to come no farther. She was filled with a desperate urge to peek around the edge of the curtain, to see him, to know where he was, to know exactly where he was looking. But she daren't move, hardly dared breathe. All she could do was stand there, blindly hoping, ears straining for the slightest sound and hearing only the pulse at her temples, the insane pounding of her heart. *Please,* she prayed. Please *God* make him go away. But when the footsteps sounded again they were not receding.

They were coming directly toward her.

He must have spotted something. Her outline behind the curtain, perhaps, or some unconscious, involuntary movement. But the curtains were velvet, lined with poplin, far too thick for light to pass through. She was positive, moreover, she hadn't moved.

The footsteps kept coming.

Less than a yard from her they stopped. She held her breath. He was so close now she could hear his breathing on the other side of the curtain: stertorous, adenoidal gasps, taken in through the mouth.

A hand came snaking round the edge of the curtain.

Oddly, she felt no temptation to scream. She didn't even gasp. It was as if, in this moment just prior to disaster, her panic mechanism simply shut down. Or perhaps, though in her perceptions the next few seconds expanded to fill an eon, everything just happened too fast. She watched with an appalled fascination as the hand, followed by a skinny wrist, a frayed shirt cuff, and a forearm clothed in black serge, slid past within six inches of her arm. It grasped the brass handle of the French doors, turned, tugged, released, and withdrew.

Chance thought she was going to faint.

The footsteps moved off to her left. The process of checking the locks was repeated, to judge from the sound, on the other set of doors. The footsteps receded. Then suddenly, startlingly, a voice broke into song. It was hardly more than a whisper really, a kind of melodious cockney croak:

> It's the rich wot gets the pleasure,
> It's the poor wot gets the blame.
> It's the same the 'ole world over.
> Ain't it all a bleedin' shame?

Then the door closed and he was gone.

Chance found she was trembling quite badly. She felt weak, needed to sit down. She stumbled over to Rosenthal's desk and collapsed into the big high-backed leather chair. A moment to collect herself, she thought, then on with her shoes and out of here.

It was when she was putting on her shoes that her eye fell again on the phones and the leatherbound notebook beside them. And a train of thought, which must have been driven from her consciousness by her recent near collision with disaster but had kept on going anyway, resurfaced. Numbers that looked exactly like the codes? Seven-digit numbers? Phone numbers! Phone numbers in the leatherbound notebook!

For the leatherbound notebook—she remembered now quite clearly his writing her number in it—was Rosenthal's personal little black book.

And very shortly the whole thing was clear. Because in the index for the letter S, there was only one name, Sam, to which no surname was attached. And the seven-digit number next to it, though presumably a London number (since it had no area prefix), belonged to no London exchange she could recall ever using or seeing. And the same thing was true of an Alex under A, a Thomas under T, a Una under U, and a Rhonda under R. The fact that there was no similar entry under N more or less clinched the matter, it seemed to Chance, because although SATURN had six letters, its highest security level, Code Five, had only five entry codes.

*   *   *

What made the whole thing worse, she thought later, was the fact that her effort was entirely wasted. She could have spared herself the trouble, the necessity for brilliance, the terror. For when she returned to her office, armed with the sequence of seven-digit numbers, she discovered she had stolen the key to a safe that had never been locked. Either Rosenthal had made an error in the log, or else he'd simply spared himself the trouble of looking up and entering the codes, assuming—the extent of his carelessness and arrogance, she thought, beggared imagination—that his initials on the entry in the log, together with the Code 5 classification, would be enough to discourage snooping. But whatever the explanation, she discovered when she sat down at her terminal again that what was booked in the log as a scenario gamed at Level Five had actually been gamed at Level Three. She didn't need to use the special entry codes—which was just as well, she thought, because she'd have had her problems erasing the audit trail—the scenario was open for anyone (authorized at her level) to see.

It took her about a minute to call up and read the scenario's starting assumptions. And when she had done that, at least two things were clear:

If the scenario Rosenthal had spent forty minutes gaming was more than just a figment of his sick imagination, it *should* have been gamed at Level Five.

And Adam Kalugin had a lot of explaining to do.

CHAPTER THIRTY-ONE

(London. August 14, 1990)

"So . . ." Meredith said, "our friend Kalugin is a KGB illegal." This was the second time in as many weeks that Pickett had found himself in Ackerman's office, talking to Meredith about Kalugin. Meredith, it seemed, had come over on the Concorde, must, Pickett thought, be racking up some useful frequent flyer mileage. And Kalugin must be a lot more important than he looked.

Pickett nodded. "That was certainly the Brits' conclusion."

"Which we, however"—this from Ackerman—"are not necessarily compelled to share."

Necessarily compelled? That was a redundancy. Necessity—wasn't it?—*was* compulsion. Pickett didn't point this out, however. He suspected that, especially in front of Meredith, Ackerman wouldn't appreciate it.

"We're not compelled to, but I think I do," he said. "I figure what happened was something like this. Kalugin attracts KGB attention in college, because of his talent for languages and fluency in English. Then afterward, when he's already enrolled in the Sleeper School, it transpires that his sister has a record of support for the Ukrainian separatist movement. Now, normally this would make them back away from him fast, but in this case some wise guy at Yasenevo has the bright idea of taking advantage of the family background—the half-Polish father, the sister's history, her suicide—to build him a history as a dissident. They arrange for him to be sent to Warsaw, tell him to join Solidarity, demonstrate, throw bottles or whatever, get himself into so much trouble he has no choice but to flee to the West. The object, of course, is to lure us or the Brits into recruiting him and sending him back him into Russia. If it works the KGB have themselves an absolutely devastating double; if it doesn't . . ."—he shrugged—"good try, no points. A little tough on Kalugin, perhaps, but what the hell, you can't win 'em all."

Silence. Ackerman looked skeptical. But then Ackerman, Pickett thought, would. He tended to be skeptical of any theory not advanced by him. Meredith, on the other hand, looked thoughtful.

"Question." Ackerman moved to the attack. "Given the family history of dissidence, why would he let himself be recruited?"

"Search me," Pickett said. "I don't know his motive exactly but I can think of half a dozen. It happens all the time—doesn't it?— different loyalties in the same household. Take the Civil War, for instance. All those families with brothers or cousins fighting on opposite sides."

"Sure." Ackerman shrugged. "But would the KGB, once they learned about the sister, trust him for something with that kind of backfire potential? An unreliable double is a bitch."

"They probably fluttered him," Meredith offered. "It's what *we* do —isn't it?—when the vetting process turns up a problem? They used him because of his background, let's say, trusted him because the polygraph told them they could."

"But if they used him because of his background," Ackerman objected, "why change his name? That strikes me as untypical of the KGB. Untypically dumb, that is."

"I guess they screwed up," Pickett said. "Maybe his legend was already built when they learned about the sister. Maybe they thought they could tack on this extra bit without rebuilding the whole structure from scratch. Perhaps they assumed that because the sister had been married, no one would question her not being called Kalugin, so no one would think of asking what her maiden name had been. Then when someone did, they improvised."

"I don't buy it." Ackerman shook his head.

"Why not?" Pickett said. "It was sheer blind luck that the Brits stumbled onto that footnote. It's not as if she was at all well known in academic circles. She published nothing before she was married. Actually, so far as the Brits were able to discover, she published nothing, period. There was just some friend of hers, some guy, let's say, who hoped to get into her pants, giving her a plug in a book he wrote that was going to be read by maybe fifty people. So when the Brits started asking why Kalugin's sister was called Levchenko, the KGB, not even suspecting that footnote existed, thought all they'd have to do was front Sokolnikov with a reasonably plausible story, and follow up by falsifying the records, just on the off chance the Brits thought of checking. And it nearly worked," he added. "Let's not forget that. The Brits came damn close to recruiting him. And if they hadn't, *we* might have. It was something, you'll recall, that crossed our minds."

"I'm not denying it." Ackerman frowned, none too pleased by this reminder of his own first reaction to Kalugin. "I'm merely saying all this theorizing strikes me as overelaborate."

"But what does it matter if it's right in detail?" Meredith stepped in to head off hostilities. "We've got to assume it's right in principle. Who cares *precisely* what the Russians did or intended? No matter what he actually is, we have to *treat* him as if he were KGB. We can't, prudently, do otherwise." He turned to Pickett. "What about him and the Davenport woman?"

Pickett considered. An awful lot was obscure to him here, not least Meredith's reasons for interest in Kalugin. But whatever they were, what *wasn't* obscure was that Meredith's reasons had little or nothing to do with a possible security breach. The CIA's Deputy Director (Operations) didn't cross the Atlantic (on the Concorde) four times in two weeks just because someone with access to Agency classified was linked romantically with a KGB illegal. There were people in London, security people, who could deal satisfactorily with that. What bothered Pickett, given all this high-level interest in Kalugin, was the possibility that he himself had screwed up. He hadn't approached Chance when they'd first told him to; but once he had gotten the lowdown on Kalugin, he'd probably blundered in approaching her at all. His handling of her, moreover, struck him now as less than adroit. It was obvious from her parting remarks that she wasn't inclined to be helpful, and certainly not to the extent of placing her love life at the CIA's disposal. But that wasn't really the problem. The problem was that, in trying to be subtle, he had failed to make the situation clear. She might well ask Kalugin for clarification and, by so doing, spook him. Meredith wouldn't appreciate that.

"She's sleeping with him. She more or less admitted."

If he felt a pang at throwing Chance to the wolves, it was for himself, not her. He could kiss goodbye to any hopes *there*. But then again they'd been more or less dead already. And so, of course, was her career with the Foundation. He wouldn't go out on a limb for her. No point bleeding for lost causes.

"More or less?" Meredith frowned. "You've spoken with her then?"

"As instructed at our last meeting." It might be as well, Pickett thought, to remind them early and as often as possible of what, at some future point, they might find it convenient to forget. "I sounded her out about her possible relationship with this Kalugin. When it became clear that there was a relationship, I told her that, although there was no present reason to suspect him of being anything other than he seemed, he was a Soviet defector. So her relationship with him, if continued, might conceivably become of concern to the Agency."

"And what was her reaction?"

"Basically that who she slept with was her business and no one else's. In the circumstances, I thought it best not to pursue the Honeytrap suggestion." Pickett gave Ackerman a sidelong glance. "It didn't seem quite the moment to ask her to screw for her country."

Ackerman frowned at the allusion. Meredith ignored it.

"Do you think she believed you?"

"About him not being under suspicion? As a matter of fact I do." Pickett's nod, medium-emphatic, conveyed a lot more confidence than he felt. But if he was fudging a little here, it wasn't about anything they could check. He was the sole authority, after all, on the state of his own convictions. He was, moreover, starting to feel better about this conversation. No one had asked him *when* he had spoken to Chance; if he steered the conversation right, no one would. "I actually think . . . I got the distinct impression, at least . . . that *she* thinks he's working for us."

Afterward, particularly after he received the cable from Personnel announcing his unexpected transfer and promotion (on very short notice) to New Delhi, Pickett would find himself looking back on that moment. When you'd been in the business as long as he had, you got to be something of a connoisseur of reactions. Especially suppressed ones. Neither of his listeners batted an eyelid. Nobody suddenly breathed or stopped breathing. Nor did Meredith, as Pickett related to him Chance's account of her trip to Sussex, let slip any hint of extraordinary interest. But in spite of all of that, and without his ever being quite able to put his finger on what caused it, he got the feeling he'd hit them with a bombshell. What the moment reminded him of most was poker—that electric moment in a high-stakes game when someone pushes his whole stack of chips into the middle, and for just an instant everyone is conscious, acutely, of everyone else *not* reacting. And that was what Chance must have done, he'd thought. Whatever the game they were playing here was, she, unwittingly, had raised the stakes.

CHAPTER THIRTY-TWO

(London. August 17, 1990)

"I'M SORRY," BENKO SAID. "I CAN'T TELL YOU HOW MUCH I'D RATHER have you with us than some others I could mention. Raina, for instance."

Kalugin didn't comment. It seemed safest not to. He wasn't sure that his acting abilities were up to expressing with any conviction the feelings that Benko expected of him here, or to concealing the welter of conflicting emotions that, against his will, he actually was feeling. He was glad, of course, that he wasn't going. On the other hand, however, now that this business was nearly done with and he ought to be feeling profoundly relieved, what he actually was feeling was guilty.

"When do you leave?" he asked.

"I don't know." Benko's eyes were shining with an excitement which, from consideration for Kalugin, he was trying to keep out of his voice. "Within the week, I expect. They haven't finalized the details yet, or if they have, they haven't shared them with us. They only told me yesterday that they wanted the team quarantined. Security reasons, they said. Only those who are actually going can take part in the final briefings." He paused. "I really am sorry, Adam. Maybe the next time."

Maybe the next time? Kalugin was seized suddenly by the urge to take Benko by the shoulders and shake some sense of reality into him. It seemed incredible that he could be standing here, in the "operations room" of Benko's apartment, listening to this kind of solemn lunacy. Was it possible, he wondered, that an otherwise fairly intelligent man could be led by mere wanting so deep into fantasy land? Maybe the *next* time . . . Couldn't this idiot see that whatever else was going to happen here, *this* was not; that even if Atlas and his

KGB masters had not, right now, been making arrangements for their betrayal, the Knights would have stood no chance whatever? Couldn't he see that their plan was misconceived, they themselves were unqualified, unprepared, that all they had ever been was cannon fodder? Next time? There wasn't going to *be* a next time. There wasn't even, he thought, going to be a this time.

Later he would wonder why he hadn't said so. All it would have taken was a few words of truth, and so much that turned out badly would have been different, especially for the Knights of Vladimir. Maybe some last reflex of duty or patriotism stopped him. Maybe, offered a choice of betrayals—and his life had consisted, he sometimes thought, of little else—he had chosen the one that would stain more deeply. Or maybe he had known it wouldn't do any good, that the words of truth he had to offer weren't words that Benko (on the verge, as he thought, of accomplishing his dream) could bring himself to accept. In any event, he didn't say them. He just shrugged and nodded.

"Maybe the next time."

"So this is goodbye for now. At least"—Benko looked suddenly awkward—"let's hope it's just for now."

He hesitated a moment, strode over to the cupboard where he kept the Kalashnikov and the Mauser. Unlocking it, he produced a bottle and two glasses.

"Glenlivet." He poured a healthy shot into each of the glasses, handed one to Kalugin. "We should drink to this moment, I think. And to friendship."

As they faced each other, glasses in hand, Kalugin wondered if Benko would remember this moment. Would he lie on bare boards in his cell in the Lubianka and feed his bitterness on memories like this? They would shoot them, of course, Benko and the rest of his team. First they would try them, with maximum publicity, and then, when the inevitable verdict was brought it, the prosecutor would demand the death sentence. And he would get it, Kalugin thought, because any move toward clemency would expose the government to the charge of softness, invite the fury of hardliners.

"To your safe return." Kalugin raised his glass. "To our next fencing match."

"Fuck our safe return. And fuck fencing. Drink to the success of our mission." Benko raised his glass. "To the Knights of Vladimir. To a free Ukraine."

He drank.

"To success . . ." It was hard to look Benko in the eye. Kalugin raised the glass to his lips, hoped that nothing of what he was feeling showed.

"To the Knights of Vladimir. To a free Ukraine."

He wondered if Katya was watching him from somewhere.

When he got home there were messages on his answering machine. One was from Chance, her fourth in as many days. He would have to call her soon, he thought; he couldn't keep ducking her forever. Another was from the Fairchild Translating Service; they needed his services, if available, for a fairly sizable commercial job. The third message was anonymous. A voice, male, said simply: "White plays knight to knight five. Wriggle your way out of that, if you can."

The game was set up on a board in his bedroom. He made the Knight move, considered its implications. On the board, he could see no problems. White was launching a premature attack; it would fail because the knight was inadequately supported. Off the board, things were more complicated. In one way this move was expected. Five days had gone by. Plenty of time for Volkonskaya to report; for the Resident to cable Moscow, requesting advice; for someone in Moscow to contact Atlas; and for Atlas, who still played lousy chess, to leave this message on the answering machine, demanding a face-to-face contact. In another way, however, things were not at all clear. Though Atlas would know that he'd disobeyed the order to avoid all contact with the Residency staff, how seriously he would take such disobedience would depend on how far he thought it extended. And this in turn would depend on what Volkonskaya had reported.

Kalugin thought about Volkonskaya. In retrospect she'd have realized, almost certainly, that she'd told him more than she should have. Since her instinct for self-preservation had always been well developed, mention of her indiscretion perhaps had been omitted from her report. So though Atlas would know that his agent, Kalugin, couldn't be trusted very far, what Atlas might *not* know was that Kalugin, on his side, knew exactly how far Atlas could be trusted.

And that was no distance at all. For Atlas and his KGB masters were clearly the authors of this lie that he, Kalugin, had murdered Zebo. And while their motives remained inscrutable, the implications for him were painfully clear. His usefulness to them was strictly limited. He could, indeed, have outlived it already.

Then maybe he should duck this contact. But what would that do for him? he wondered. Atlas would always know where to find him. It was better to face him now, when forewarned was to some extent forearmed, than to wait for Atlas to act at his leisure, for the silent bullet in the back of the head.

And maybe, he thought, he would even learn something.

CHAPTER THIRTY-THREE

(Sussex, England. August 18, 1990)

THE PUB, KALUGIN NOTICED, WAS THE FOURTH IN THE LAST FIFTEEN MILES that called itself The Royal Oak. Some English king, he seemed to recall reading, had hidden in an oak tree somewhere near here to avoid being captured by his loyal subjects. Since then all oaks in England had been "royal"; and every second pub in the area, it seemed, had been named to celebrate the famous evasion. There was no doubt at all, however, that this was the right pub. Five and a quarter miles on the right side after the turn off B289, the instructions had read, and a glance at the odometer confirmed their accuracy. Not that they'd needed to be quite so precise; this was the only pub he'd so far encountered on this road, and the only building of any description he'd seen for the last three miles. He noticed, as he pulled into the parking lot, that a restaurant stood next to the pub—the sign promised fine French cuisine—and across the road was a bed-and-breakfast, presumably part of the same enterprise. Since the road was hardly a bustling thoroughfare, more a lane than a road, in fact, just a single track with occasional passing spaces, he wondered what kept all this in business. Tourists, he guessed, readers of guidebooks, looking for English country charm but not necessarily English country cooking. And they would get the charm, at least, for the pub, with its whitewashed walls, thatched roof, and tiny windows, was picturesque as well as ancient. Tucked cozily into a fold in the downs, with a garden in front, a meadow at the back, and thickly wooded hills all around, it was about as far off the beaten track as one could imagine this close to London.

Which presumably was why Atlas had chosen it.

There was only one other car in the lot, a gray Fiat, no doubt Atlas's rental. Atlas himself was in the garden. A half-pint beer mug, three-quarters empty, stood on the table in front of him. The day was overcast, not raining but threatening, the temperature a little chilly. Not ideal conditions for sitting outside, but no doubt Atlas had his reasons.

As Kalugin approached, he got up, smiled, drained his beer, and extended a hand in greeting. Kalugin took it. Atlas's palm was dry and smooth. His grip, Kalugin noticed, was like iron. His dress was properly nondescript, the kind of outfit no one would remember: beige gabardine slacks, rubber-soled loafers, a faded blue work shirt in some kind of rough cotton, and over it a beige windcheater which zipped up the front but which Atlas had left hanging open. It had side pockets a little above waist level, but there seemed to be nothing in them. Nothing, at least, the size of a gun.

"I thought we might take a walk in the country." Atlas gestured to a narrow track that led up the hill from the lane to their right. "I'm told there's quite a view to be had from up there. The hike would give us an appetite for lunch."

Lunch? Except at their first meeting, when they'd visited the night-club, they hadn't eaten or drunk together. Atlas was being affable, Kalugin thought. Remarkably affable, in the circumstances.

"Is the restaurant any good?"

"I don't know. I thought we might try it."

"Sounds like a plan." Kalugin shrugged. "Let's investigate this view of yours."

They set off, side by side, up the track. It climbed steeply, wound to the left, and was flanked on both sides by thick hedgerows. Within a few minutes the buildings were lost from view. Kalugin stole a sidelong glance at Atlas. If he *wasn't* armed, or not with a gun, that might be indicative of his intentions. For Atlas, having no doubt read his file, would know to respect his talent for hand-to-hand combat. Had *he* been Atlas, he thought, and planning violence, he wouldn't have come here without a weapon. Atlas might have the advantage of strength, but almost certainly he was inferior in speed. And in a contest between strength and speed, commitment being equal, speed was favored.

Especially when the speed had a knife.

"You're certain you weren't followed?" Atlas asked suddenly.

Kalugin eyed him. "I am if you are."

"Ah . . ." Atlas smiled slightly. "I sense a rebuke. You wish to remind me that you are a professional; such enquiries are therefore uncalled for."

"Perhaps." Kalugin shrugged. "And a little late."

"The latter point is well taken." Atlas's smile became a little chilly. "As regards professionalism, however. It's hard to have much confidence, professionally, in a man who willfully defies his orders, who contacts a member of the Residency staff, in public, in a clumsy and amateurish manner, and in doing so jeopardizes her mission."

Moment of silence. Kalugin considered.

"Volkonskaya reported me, then?"

Atlas stared. "Did you really think she wouldn't?"

Kalugin hadn't, of course, but he knew that the chess game had started—though what they were engaged in, on second thought, was probably closer to fencing. The outcome might be determined, at any rate, by how well each read the other's intentions, while managing to conceal his own. If Atlas did have violence in mind, it wouldn't hurt if he could be persuaded that the intended object didn't expect it.

"I didn't know." Kalugin shrugged. "The mental processes of women are notoriously difficult to follow."

"Women?" Again Atlas looked surprised. "She's a KGB officer. Gender is irrelevant."

"If you knew her, you wouldn't think so." Kalugin smiled faintly. "Did she also report that she and I had been lovers?"

Almost certainly she hadn't, he thought, because sex between members of the training program had been absolutely forbidden. She'd have told herself, no doubt, that their brief affair was no one else's business. And that was largely true, he thought, because mind and body, with her, had never interfered much with each other.

"That's also irrelevant." Atlas frowned. "You defied your orders. I want to know why."

Kalugin shrugged. "Why do you think?"

"I've no idea. That's why I'm asking." Atlas's voice was patient, his face expressionless. "The officer who reported you gave it as her opinion that stress had affected your judgment. I find that implausible. I think you had some purpose in mind. But as to what that purpose might have been, I'm waiting for you to tell me."

He glanced ahead and fell suddenly silent. From around the corner there appeared half a dozen black-and-white cows. They were plodding down the middle of the track, with a placid, somewhat preoccupied air, yawing slightly from side to side but showing no sign of yielding to oncoming traffic: a disorderly, inexorable procession. Following them was a man with a stick. Kalugin and Atlas moved into single file and onto the verge to let them pass. As the man drew

22 John Griffiths

level he nodded at Atlas, smiled, and mumbled some kind of greeting. Since he spoke with a twang and half swallowed his words, Kalugin wasn't sure what he'd said. He thought it sounded like:

"Quite the hiker, I see."

Atlas returned the nod but not the greeting. He fell back in step beside Kalugin.

"Friend of yours?" Kalugin inquired.

Atlas shook his head.

"He seemed to know you."

"He was being friendly. Country people generally are." Atlas frowned. "You seem determined to be flippant. This attitude is unfortunate. You disobeyed instructions that were given for a reason. People in Moscow are seriously displeased."

"People in Moscow?" Kalugin queried. "Would those be the people who informed the Residency, presumably in the full knowledge that their allegation was false, that it was I who killed my former control?"

Silence.

Atlas had stopped dead, turned toward Kalugin. His gaze had suddenly become opaque, his features as expressionless as stone.

"*She* told you this?"

"Volkonskaya?" Kalugin nodded. "She was indiscreet, as no doubt she also omitted to report. She was scared, no doubt, or angry. When she learned that I was the treacherous illegal, Cobalt, she spoke without thinking." He gave his voice an edge of irony. "I expect you're going to tell me she was lying?"

It was done now, he thought. His disaffection was out in the open, declared, like a gauntlet thrown down between them. He hadn't planned to do it this way. He'd expected they would probe, feel each other out, that neither of them would force conclusions. But the conversation had turned this way and suddenly he had wanted it over. He had let the words slip, deliberately reckless, almost without thinking, certainly without caring. He was sick of it all, he thought: of Atlas, of Moscow, of the Knights of Vladimir, of the suffocating fog of lies that had taken over and stained his life. But most of all he was sick of himself, because everything that had happened to him had happened with his permission; because as Katya, quoting Malory, had said: "Once shamed may never be recovered." So if Atlas wanted to kill him now, he was welcome.

He was welcome to try, at any rate.

Aggression, however, seemed remote from Atlas's thoughts. He was looking at Kalugin like a doctor, with a grave but kindly concern. "You expect I will tell you she lied? But why would she lie about something like that?"

"Good question." Kalugin smiled bitterly. "The question that really interests me, however, is why would you?"

Silence. Atlas continued to inspect him. The patient expression didn't change.

"The normal reason for telling lies," he spoke calmly, as if to a fractious child, "is to stop people learning the truth. And the normal reason for withholding truth from people is that they don't need to know it. You were told what you needed to know. The Residency staff were told what they needed to believe. The fact that what they were told happened not to be true should neither concern you nor disturb you. However, since you now know and evidently are disturbed, this changes the situation." He paused. "First, I will hear your report, then I will explain the reason for this deception."

Kalugin was tempted to demand the explanation, withhold his report till he got it. He found himself angered by Atlas's patient air, his calm insistence on controlling the conversation. But nothing would be gained by that kind of verbal sparring; it would only distract him, he thought, scatter his energies when they needed to be focused. And did he, in any case, want to hear Atlas's explanation? It would probably just be more lies.

So he reported on his meeting with Benko, the quarantining of the Knights' team and the likelihood of its imminent departure. Atlas listened impassively. When Kalugin had finished, he said: "What you're telling me, in effect, is that the team is leaving, but you don't know when, you don't know from where, and you don't know the specific targets."

"Benko himself doesn't know," Kalugin said. "It seems they don't intend to tell even him until the last possible moment. Their security, as I've told you before, is extremely tight." He paused, then added: "The professionals, it's obvious, lack faith in the amateurs' ability to keep secrets. That doesn't surprise me. The only thing that surprises me here is that they trust them for anything at all."

Atlas ignored this.

"I have the impression Benko didn't expect this," he said. "Is that your impression also?"

"He expected the team would be quarantined," Kalugin said. "He didn't expect it would happen so soon."

Atlas thought about this.

"From our point of view it's inconvenient," he observed. "Since you don't know where the team will be quarantined, how will we get the intelligence we lack."

It sounded like an accusation of negligence. Kalugin shrugged.

"I don't see that more intelligence is needed. This operation poses no threat. If it doesn't founder on the team's incompetence, we can nip it in the bud without any problem. We may not know the exact date, but we know it near enough. We know they plan a landing on the Black Sea coast near Odessa. We know they must have access to the Border Patrol schedules. All we have to do, it seems to me, is strengthen the patrols and change the schedules."

Atlas considered this.

"It sounds as if you're saying, in effect, that you consider your mission accomplished."

"As to 'accomplished,' I wouldn't know"—Kalugin shrugged—"since I never understood what I was meant to accomplish. What I'm saying is that, due to circumstances beyond my control, I think my mission is ended."

Atlas regarded him gravely for a moment. "In this at least we agree. I think so, too."

"Good," Kalugin said. "I've made my report. Now you owe me an explanation."

They were close to the top of the hill. To their left, a few yards ahead, was a gap in the hedgerow and a stile that served a narrow pathway which led off into a copse. Atlas didn't speak until they reached the stile, then he stopped and turned to Kalugin.

"The view I mentioned . . . to reach it we take this path. In about a hundred meters we come to a field. And a view, so I'm told, of three different counties. Also in the field are Saxon barrows, burial mounds of some archeological interest. Now that we're here, we should see them, don't you think?"

Burial mounds . . . Kalugin said nothing. He had a sudden, paranoid suspicion that Atlas was deliberately playing with his mind, that somehow he could read his hesitation, that he sensed his fears and was taunting him with them.

"Let us go and inspect this view," Atlas said. "As we go I will give you your explanation. Then we will have lunch together like friends. Nothing is gained by hostility and suspicion."

"Why are you so insistent on seeing this view?"

Atlas looked at Kalugin calmly. He shrugged. "I heard about it at the pub. I thought we would be more private out of doors, so I asked if there was somewhere interesting to hike to. They directed me up here. They told me about the view. Also," Atlas smiled, "about the burial mounds."

Kalugin looked at Atlas and back at the path. Within a few yards it disappeared from view, lost itself between bushes. The copse was gloomy, thickly wooded, the undergrowth in places very dense. A body dragged just a few yards off the path could go weeks, maybe months, before being found. But whose body? He pictured himself lying there, starting to rot, his body a breeding ground for insects, a larder for small animals. He pictured Atlas in the same context. Neither image was acceptable. A sense of unreality came over him. Could this calm, smiling man really be waiting to kill him? Could he himself really be considering the reverse? Maybe Volkonskaya was right, he thought, maybe he *was* unbalanced. For people in his profession, after all, paranoia was an occupational hazard.

"You look like Hamlet," Atlas joshed him. "But what is there to contemplate exactly?" He turned and headed for the stile. "I'll go first, you follow."

He hopped over the stile. Kalugin followed. He felt hypnotized by Atlas's calmness, drawn after him as if on a line. His sense of unreality grew, and with it his sense of danger. The inner debate intensified. If Atlas intended to kill him, why had he come here unarmed? But if he didn't intend to kill him, why had he brought him to this lonely wilderness? Why had he insisted on his seeing the view? But why would Atlas *want* to kill him? This, of course, was the crucial question, the one on which the others hinged. He didn't know the answer to this. Any more than he knew why Zebo had been killed. He only knew that someone in Moscow, who knew very well that the accusation was false, had been telling people that he, Kalugin, had killed Zebo. And whatever else this might mean, it didn't bode well for the future.

The best defense was attack. He contemplated Atlas's back, the thick torso, the bull neck, the powerful, sloping shoulders. Maybe he should just kill him. It would certainly be safer than waiting to be attacked. He had the knife in a sheath in his pocket. Maybe he should just slip it out, slide an arm around Atlas's head, and with one quick slash put an end to uncertainty. It would surely be safer. And if the roles here were reversed, Atlas, just as surely, wouldn't hesitate to do it to him.

It would be safer, but he just couldn't do it.

"It's up ahead." Atlas looked over his shoulder. "There's a gate and a field beyond it. I think I can see the mounds."

There was no alteration in his tone, but it seemed to Kalugin that he'd quickened his pace. The gap between them, at any rate, had widened from two or three paces to more than half a dozen. Kalugin looked up the path. Ahead, about fifteen meters away, was a dry stone wall and a gate. Someone, he noticed, had left the gate open.

Atlas glanced back over his shoulder.

But not at Kalugin. At least there was no eye contact. Atlas just stole a quick look behind. Like a distance runner, it struck Kalugin, checking his lead on the closest pursuer. And then, in a moment of frozen clarity, he heard in his head, quite clearly, an echo of what the man with the cows had said, and not to *both* of them, to Atlas:

"Quite the hiker, I see."

It had happened to Kalugin once or twice before in his life that a complex process of deduction had been compressed into a instant, so that what were actually separate steps presented themselves to his mind as one, a single stroke of revelation. Quite the hiker? When Atlas had been only five minutes walk from his car? And why just Atlas? Why not *hikers,* plural? Because—the answer was as plain as the nose on his face—it had not been just the one encounter that had prompted the cowman's comment.

The cowman had seen Atlas before.

Kalugin knew suddenly why Atlas was unarmed, why he'd insisted on coming up here, why the gate was open, why he'd quickened his pace, why the distance between them, even now, was lengthening.

Atlas had a weapon stashed up here.

It was to the right of the gate, probably. On the far side of it. Perhaps in a crevice of the wall. For a couple of hypnotized seconds, Kalugin just stood and watched while the scenario he was imagining unfolded before his eyes. Atlas's movements were quicker now, but there was nothing hurried or furtive about them. He acted like a man with a job to do, went calmly and deliberately about his business. Now he was at the wall . . . now through the gate . . . turning right at once but still not glancing at Kalugin . . . a couple of steps along the far side of the wall . . . reaching down . . .

Kalugin didn't wait any longer.

CHAPTER THIRTY-FOUR

(Sussex, England. August 18, 1990)

THE UNDERGROWTH WAS THICK, BUT HE PLUNGED INTO IT, DODGING branches and crashing through bushes, heedless of noise and the thorns that clawed at his clothing. He held himself low, half running, half scrambling, using his hands as much as his feet, kept going until he was in the densest part of the copse, in a tiny clearing thirty yards off the path and certainly invisible from it. Then he crouched down and waited, motionless, taking air in quick shallow gulps and exhaling through his nose to minimize the noise of his breathing.

"Kalugin . . ." Atlas's voice sounded from the path. Not a shout, Kalugin noticed, something lower and conversational, irritated, a kind of carrying half-whisper. It came, as nearly as Kalugin could tell, from roughly the point where he had left the path.

"Kalugin. What the hell are you *doing*? Playing cowboys and indians? Come out of there."

Kalugin stayed where he was. Perhaps he had made a mistake in not just running. He'd have had to offer Atlas a twenty- or thirty-yard shot, but by dodging and weaving he might well have made him miss. And had he succeeded in making it to the lane he'd have been home free; Atlas would never have risked attempting to kill him in the open. But now, though safe for the moment, he was trapped. He had forfeited, perhaps for good, the option of flight. The underbrush gave cover, but it would slow him down. Any noise he made would give away his position. But it was done now, and maybe for the best. For what would running away have achieved? A stay of execution, nothing more. Atlas could simply have hunted him down at his leisure.

He could do that now, of course. He could just turn around and go home, leaving him, Kalugin, skulking here, terrified to come out. But somehow it was hard to see him doing that. It would mean confessing failure, for one thing, and Atlas, who prided himself above all on being a professional, wouldn't want to do that. He would want to finish what he had started. He would come in here, calm and deliberate, to find his quarry and dispatch it. And when he did, Kalugin promised himself, his quarry was going to kill him.

The only problem was how.

"Kalugin. What are you hiding from? Stop playing around and come out of there."

This time the voice sounded farther off, more to the left than it had been before. Atlas must still be on the path, since Kalugin hadn't heard him enter the bushes, but he'd gone a short distance back toward the stile. A few paces from where Atlas now seemed to be, Kalugin recalled, the path veered sharply to the left. It seemed that Atlas was hoping to work around his flank, to get between him and the stile and cut off his escape to the track. His answering strategy therefore, one dictated by the fact that he didn't have a gun, must be to get around behind Atlas. And since moving through this undergrowth was hard to achieve without noise, he would have to get Atlas to do the moving. Somehow, he thought, he would have to lure Atlas into an ambush.

How?

"Kalugin, I'm tired of this." Atlas didn't seem to have moved. "If you want to hide in the woods all day, that's your decision. I'm going back. If you want to join me for lunch, I'll wait for you at the restaurant. If not . . ." The voice trailed off.

Going back? If anything had been needed, Kalugin thought, to confirm his suspicions of Atlas's intentions, this was it. Atlas was going *back*? Atlas who'd been so insistent on his seeing this view was going to wait for him *at the pub*? Why not at this so fascinating view where he'd so far spent about fifteen seconds?

"Kalugin, I'm going now. I want you to know I consider your behavior unbalanced. Goodbye . . ."

Then there was silence.

Atlas hadn't gone, of course, but now there would be no more talk. The rest of this drama would be played out in silence. Atlas would be waiting on the path, hoping that he, Kalugin, would think he'd gone back to the pub. But sooner or later, when he failed to fall into this trap, Atlas would come in after him. It was simply a question of patience, Kalugin told himself. Wait until Atlas got tired of waiting.

In the meantime, he took stock of his position. The liabilities were many and obvious. Unless he wanted to depress himself, they were not worth enumerating. What about assets? They were mostly intangible, he thought, and perhaps imaginary: He was smaller than Atlas and more agile, should be able to move around more easily and with much less noise. Also the undergrowth gave quite good protection; it wouldn't stop bullets, but it would deflect them. Unless Atlas got a clear shot, the effective range of his weapon—presumably some light-caliber pistol, its accuracy almost certainly reduced by a silencer —would be not much more than a couple of yards. But these assets were purely defensive. What potential did he have for attack? The knife, of course, if he could ever get close enough to use it, but otherwise nothing. Nothing except . . . He had one thing, maybe, a small psychological edge, if he could only figure out how to use it: *Atlas wouldn't expect him to attack.* Atlas didn't know that he had the knife, or that he intended to use it. And this, Kalugin thought, was perhaps his chief asset here: that mistaken assumptions might make Atlas careless.

How to exploit it?

What was needed, clearly, was some capacity to operate from long range, to affect the situation from a distance, to mislead Atlas about his position.

In other words, something he could throw.

He looked about. The ground was mostly covered with a damp mulch of rotting leaves, in which, in the prevailing gloom, it was hard for his eyes to discover anything. Here and there, however, his hands, exploring, encountered promising bumps, two of which, on further investigation, proved to be rocks about the size of his fist. He also turned up several sticks of about an inch in thickness and eight to ten inches in length. They were sodden with moisture and thus heavy enough, when thrown, to carry a reasonable distance. He put the rocks in the pocket of his jacket, held the sticks in a bundle with his left hand, leaving the right free for throwing. Then he settled down to wait, listening intently.

What struck him most was the stillness. It wasn't absolute; noise from outside was more or less constant—an argument of rooks in a nearby wood, the whisper of a jetliner passing overhead, the distant grind of a tractor—but such sounds seemed only to enhance, indeed almost to encapsulate, the silence within. There must have been animals in here, he thought, or birds at least, but nothing was calling or moving. The bustle of ordinary life was suspended; everything in here seemed to be holding its breath. And in consequence his hearing became specialized, hyperacute, able to filter out background interference and amplify anything immediate or unusual. So when Atlas did finally get tired of waiting—it was close to half an hour later—he might as well have broadcast his decision. What announced it was only the snapping of twig, followed by an urgent rustling of branches, but to ears accustomed to silence the noise seemed almost shocking, like a drumbeat followed by the clash of cymbals.

He was interested to discover, now that the hunt was on, that he wasn't really scared. Or rather, considering the matter with one half of his brain while another monitored Atlas's progress, he found himself afraid but detached from his fear; using it, in fact, to sharpen his perceptions. He had the expected physical responses to the flood of adrenaline danger pumped into his system—he was sweating, and not from exertion, and his heartbeat was noticeably elevated—but in the midst of them his mind was cold. It noted the possibility of its own imminent extinction but refused to dwell on it, preferring to focus on practical issues: How to get Atlas close enough to kill him? How not to get spotted, and killed *by* him, first?

To judge from the sounds, Atlas was doing as expected: working round his left flank, cutting off retreat to the stile. Since Kalugin himself hadn't yet moved, the distance between them, he thought, must have shortened considerably. He couldn't see Atlas, didn't know exactly where he was, but an intermittent rustling to his left suggested he was less than twenty yards away. It was hard to determine from sound alone the precise direction in which Atlas was moving, but he didn't dare stand up to take a look. He could do it, certainly, without making any noise, but he might end up staring Atlas in the face. On the other hand, he thought, he couldn't just sit here doing nothing, waiting for Atlas to blunder upon him.

It was time to throw one of his sticks.

He threw it to his right and away from the path, ahead, he figured, of the line in which Atlas was moving. It traveled in a looping parabola up through the frame of bushes that surrounded him and down a narrow alley between the neighboring trees. For perhaps ten yards it flew cleanly, then striking an overhanging branch, it dropped, noisily, into the bushes.

The result was immediate and startling. From fifteen yards to the left came a kind of muffled thump, then a pause, then another thump. It was a sound like someone hitting a pillow with a stick, a sound Kalugin instantly recognized from the days of his small-arms training.

A shot from a silenced .22 caliber pistol.

Atlas must have fired at the source of the noise, for neither shot had come in Kalugin's direction. He had fired twice, blindly, into the bushes. This was promising, Kalugin thought. Atlas, it seemed, was getting jumpy.

He threw another stick, in the same direction as the first.

As he did, there was movement in the undergrowth up ahead.

It was closer than he'd expected. Much closer. Barely ten yards away and heading right for him.

Kalugin's heart stood still. He had to master an impulse to bolt. Atlas must have happened on a clearing, crossed it without making a sound. Since he hadn't reacted to the stick, it had obviously landed while he was moving. If he kept on in the direction he was headed, he would see Kalugin in the next few seconds.

Kalugin's mind churned. He had to do something. But what? Frontal assault. It was the only thing now. Stay down until the last possible second, until Atlas was almost on top of him, then thrust with the knife from below.

Atlas stopped.

Kalugin crouched lower, holding his breath, straining to see beneath the screen of bushes, the four or five yards of undergrowth that separated him now from Atlas. He thought he could make out Atlas's legs—through the gloom and the lattice of twigs and leaves he could see strips of beige that had to be gabardine slacks—but not clearly enough to determine which way Atlas was facing. With clear ground between them, he thought, and if Atlas was looking the wrong way, he might have been able to get to him with a rush, but the bushes were too thick; he would have to let him get closer. But seconds passed and Atlas didn't move. He was listening, Kalugin knew, listening and waiting.

Kalugin could feel his self-control going, a kind of hysteria starting to take hold. He knew that if he didn't act soon his nerves, overstretched, would simply snap. He would hurl himself screaming on his enemy, or bolt, blindly, in the other direction.

It had to be now.

Transferring his remaining stick to his right hand, he took a rock from his pocket with his left, then he threw the stick over Atlas's head. It looped up, clipping a branch just beyond where Atlas was standing. As it fell, Atlas whirled. Kalugin heard the thump of his pistol.

Kalugin rose. In a single continuum of motion, he switched the rock from his left hand to his right, drew the right back, and right at the instant he sighted his target, let fly.

Atlas had already started to turn. The rock, directed at the base of his skull and hurled with all Kalugin's force, caught him slightly below the left ear. He staggered sideways and dropped to one knee, like a boxer taking an eight count.

Kalugin could never remember crossing the intervening space. Even before the rock found its mark he was following up, reaching for the knife in his pocket. Later, a long, shallow gash on his cheek, multiple scratches on his legs and forearms, and various rips in his clothing would tell him that part of what he tore through had been bramble. At the time, however, he had no awareness, no sensation of pain or hindrance. All he could feel was the urgency, the need to get to Atlas before Atlas could use the pistol.

Atlas's powers of recovery were amazing. Even as Kalugin burst out of the bushes he was rising, turning, trying to focus, almost by instinct bringing the pistol to bear. Kalugin's flying kick caught him high on the forehead, whipped his head back as if it had been on a hinge. He went down, dropping the pistol.

Kalugin retrieved the pistol. It was a Luger-style .22, tubelike silencer attached to the barrel, the classic assassin's weapon. He backed up a couple of yards and sat down with his back against a tree, covering Atlas with the pistol.

What now?

What he ought to do, he knew, was put a bullet in Atlas's head and get the hell out of here. But now that it was over and he was safe, a curious inertia had come over him. He felt faint, light-headed, as if everything that had happened in the last forty minutes had been an unpleasant hallucination, a dream from which he would shortly wake up. The anger and fear that had driven him up to now had drained away. He didn't *want* to kill Atlas, he thought. He didn't want to kill anyone.

Except Zaitsev.

Atlas stirred, opened his eyes. When he saw Kalugin, he sat up groggily, and then lay back again, propping himself on one arm. He shook his head, as if to clear it, screwed his face into a grimace of pain.

"They were right about you," he said.

"Right?"

"Unreliable." Atlas nodded. "Potentially a first-class agent, but subject to some curious sense of honor. Which presumably is why I'm still alive." He paused. "How did you know?"

"Instinct." Kalugin shrugged. "A bunch of little things. But I never trusted you from the start. I knew you'd lied to me about Zebo. I knew the Americans didn't kill him. You did it, didn't you?"

Atlas ignored the question, but his shrug, Kalugin thought, was answer enough.

"What are you going to do now?"

"For God's sake *why*?" Suddenly Kalugin was filled with anger. "What's the *point* of all this? Killing Zebo, killing me, sending Benko and the rest of those fools to be killed as soon as they set foot inside Russia? What good does it achieve? Just tell me that."

Atlas didn't answer. "What are you going to do with me?"

Kalugin thought. There wasn't any choice. And in any case it was payment for Zebo.

He looked Atlas in the eye.

"You were going to kill me. I'm going to kill you."

"Then stop talking," Atlas said. "Stop talking and do it."

He closed his eyes.

Kalugin shot him in the middle of the forehead.

CHAPTER THIRTY-FIVE

(London. August 20, 1990)

"ADAM, WHAT IS THE *MATTER* WITH YOU? YOU LOOK AS IF YOU'D JUST been told you had cancer."

Kalugin was sitting hunched up on Chance's picnic blanket, his arms clasped round his shins, his knees drawn up to his chin, gazing broodingly across the park at the ornamental excess of the Albert Memorial and the massive domed pillbox of the concert hall beyond. It had been a mistake to call her, he thought, a mistake also to come here. Hyde Park, though not exactly country, was near enough to it to provoke unwelcome thoughts.

He shrugged. "I guess I got out of bed on the wrong side."

"Oh, right." Chance's tone was withering. *"Fell* out of it, by the look of that scratch on your face, and *into* a bed of brambles." She paused. "Look, Adam. I know I'm not supposed to ask questions, but I've never seen you like this. Something's bothering you, isn't it? Something bad."

Something bad. Bad, he thought, was not quite the word for it. It wasn't guilt he felt when he thought of Atlas—Atlas, after all, had planned the same fate for him—but a kind of nausea. And nausea not for the deed itself, but for everything that had led up to it: the whole sickening process, started years earlier in Kiev, of which this killing was merely the latest outcome. "Once shamed may never be recovered." Malory had been right about that. And that was what was bothering him, he thought: not what he'd done yesterday, what he'd *not* done years ago.

He didn't answer.

She looked irritated. "I suppose you're going to say you can't tell me about it."

"I'm sorry." He nodded. "But I *can't* tell you about it."

"Why can't you tell me?"

"Lots of reasons." He frowned. "One is, there's too much to tell."

"Too much to tell? Too much to tell about what?"

He had to find something to tell her. She deserved it, he thought. He owed her. "Let's just say there are days when I wish I could start my life over, build it differently, straighter and taller. Let's say today is one of those days."

"I see." She thought this over. "I get that feeling, too, sometimes. I imagine everyone does. But why you, today, specially?"

"That's what I can't tell you."

She gave him an odd sideways look, a mix of affection and concern, tenderness and wry humor, resignation and a touch of sadness. It was the way a mother might have looked at him, or a sister.

"Here we go again." She rolled her eyes. "Exit Adam, enter the Iceman."

"Enter the Iceman? What's *that* supposed to mean?"

"It means this," she said. "There seem to be two of you. There's Adam, who's wonderful, sexy, and funny. Warm. Someone I really like, someone I think I could fall in love with. Someone . . ." She hesitated. "Someone I think I *have* fallen in love with. But then there's always the Iceman, getting in the way. Him I don't like at all."

"The Iceman? Who is this Iceman?"

"You tell me." She shrugged. "He's the guy who keeps me at arm's length, the guy who won't ever say what he's thinking. He's the guy who when Adam vanishes, sometimes right in the middle of a conversation, shows up in his place. He's the one who has bad dreams." She paused. "This is the guy I compete with for you, and since most of the time I lose, I want to know who he is, why he wants to start life over."

"You *don't* want to know." He looked at her steadily. "You think you do, but I promise you you don't."

"Trust me," she said. "What can there be in your life that's so bad you can't tell me about it."

He said nothing. He pictured Atlas, lying in the bushes, a bluish hole in the middle of his forehead; probably the animals had got to him by now. He thought of Zebo on the bed in the Raleigh Apartments, a similar hole just in front of his right ear. He thought of Benko and the Knights of Vladimir who would get theirs sooner or later, probably in the base of the skull. He thought of Katya, twisting on a rope in the stairwell. What could there be that was so *bad?* The problem, he thought, would be where to begin.

"I can't tell you," he said. "I'm not at liberty."

"Okay," she said. "Then tell me something you are at liberty to tell. Trust me with *something*, for Christ's sake, something personal. Just one small thing." She paused, her eyes pleading with him. "Please."

He shrugged. "I don't know what you want me to tell you."

"Tell me why you have that dream," she said. "The one you have that's always the same. Tell me why you blame yourself for your sister."

"My sister?" He stared. "Who says I blame myself?"

"You do," she said. "You told me once she fell foul of the KGB, but when you dream you always say the same thing. You always say, over and over, 'I'm sorry.' Tell me why you always say that."

Once shamed may never be recovered. It would do as well as anything, he thought; it would do as well as anything to show her who he was. His mistake—yet another of his many mistakes—had been to think he could be different people and keep them separate. Chance and he had no future together, and precisely for the reason she'd stated. If he'd been one person, they might have had a future, he thought, but as she'd said, there was always the Iceman. She might as well know about the Iceman.

"I say I'm sorry because I failed her. The KGB killed her, or caused her death, but I was her brother and I betrayed her."

They'd announced themselves by kicking in the door.

Afterward, looking back on this moment when his life, as it were, jumped tracks, exchanging one direction and motion for others, darker and swifter, what Vadim would remember most vividly was the abruptness. There was no transition; no time to adjust, nor even, in those first stunned seconds, to be scared. One moment he and Katya were home, secure in its comfort, its apparent privacy; the next, in an eruption of violence as sudden and shocking as the bursting of a bomb, the door was off its hinges, comfort and privacy were memories, home nothing more than a poky, three-room apartment, property of the District Thirteen Peoples' Collective, a fiction exploded by this sudden intrusion of the state.

That much, at least, that it was the state whose servants slouched in through the shattered doorway, was never in question. As even fifteen-year-old schoolboys knew, only one sort of people in the Soviet Union announced themselves by kicking in the door.

There were two of them, dressed identically: belted blue topcoats, gray felt hats, black leather shoes with heavy soles and rounded stubby toecaps, shoes designed for kicking in doors, or people. One, presumably the door kicker, belonged to the type Vadim would come to recognize as standard-issue KGB gorilla: short, heavyset, bull-necked, with features that seemed molded out of putty and afterward flattened with a mallet, and a set, unfocused stare that suggested habitual drug use and/or mental deficiencies. Even at the time, how-ever, he seemed to merit no more than a glance. It was the other, the tall one, who from the first commanded Vadim's attention, who so totally dominated subsequent proceedings that, in time, all memory of the door kicker faded, mingled with images of the countless other gorillas to form, in the end, a kind of composite mental portrait of mindless violence. His memory of the tall one, on the other hand, seemed with the years to get only more sharp and vivid. Thin and angular this other one was, and hawk-faced, with restless, intelligent eyes, projecting not just a physical threat, but a more elemental men-ace.

For several seconds no one spoke. Vadim, catatonic with shock, could only gape at the intruders. Katya, too, seemed turned to stone. She'd been reading in one of the armchairs that flanked the room's only window; now she sat there, pale and rigid, her eyes riveted on the taller man, her book, forgotten, open in her lap.

The taller one, skirting the table where Vadim had been doing his homework, strode over to confront her. He stood looking down for a moment, then, abruptly, not taking his eyes off her, he dragged the other chair round to face hers. Unbuttoning his coat, he sat down. Leaning back, he pushed his hat to the back of his head and stretched his legs out in front of him so that, though not actually touching Katya's, they flanked them. The action troubled Vadim more than anything so far, more even than their kicking in the door. Familiar and insolent, it was also proprietary. As if this man had taken over their lives.

"You are Katerina Stolypin?"

"You know very well who I am." Katya glared at him, chin in the air. "And you, as I wish I didn't know, are Alexandr Zaitsev, a major in the KGB. Let's not start by pretending with each other."

He shrugged. "By all means not."

"You *might* start . . ."—her glance flicked over to the wreckage of the door—"by explaining this uncivilized invasion, this quite unnec-essary destruction of what is, after all, public property."

He ignored this.

"As you say, let us not pretend, for instance, that you were not present at the unauthorized gathering of dissidents and subversives, calling themselves Ukrainian nationalists, which took place this morning on Taras Schevchenko Boulevard."

She met his gaze squarely.

"It's not a question of pretending. I wasn't there."

"We can produce eyewitnesses."

"You people can always produce eyewitnesses. In this case they are blind or lying. I wasn't there. Furthermore," Katya said, "You Viktor Zaitsev, major in the KGB, *know* I wasn't there."

Their eyes locked. Vadim was really scared now. Not least by this defiant tone Katya was taking. Surely she knew that truth was irrelevant. Power alone meant anything to these people, and power was always on their side. He tried to will her to look at him, but she wouldn't. "For God's sake, be polite, Katya," he wanted to implore her. "Don't anger him for no reason."

Zaitsev shrugged.

"Your denial will be entered in the record. You were aware, nonetheless, that such a march occurred."

"Of course I was aware. The news was all over the university. Two hundred students, carrying Ukrainian flags, assembled for a peaceful demonstration. Your people broke them up with baton charges and water cannon. You beat them, arrested them, stamped on the flags, confiscated or smashed the cameras of anyone trying to take pictures." She paused. "If it's a crime to know about this, half of Kiev is guilty."

There was no response. It almost seemed that Zaitsev had had no interest in her answers, as if they—and his questions—had no bearing on the issue. Vadim didn't know what the issue was, but he sensed that somehow, in some way profoundly disturbing, the issue was not political, but personal.

Something had happened between Katya and this Zaitsev.

"Vadim . . ." Katya turned to him. "Go outside now and leave us alone. This doesn't concern you. I'll call you when these gentlemen" —the word was loaded with irony—"have left."

"He stays." Zaitsev spoke sharply. He motioned to the gorilla, who moved immediately behind Vadim's chair. "Maybe he will learn something. After all"—Zaitsev smiled—"one's education . . . one's *political* education . . . is something one can never start too early."

He leaned forward, took the book from Katya's lap.

"Sir Thomas Malory . . ." Examining the spine of the volume, he pronounced the title in passable, though accented, English. *"The Death of Arthur.* You make a habit of reading foreign writers? Aristocratic foreign writers?"

Katya shrugged. "I'm a teacher of English literature; it's necessary I should read English writers, even *aristocratic* ones. The book is one I assigned to my class at the university. Even your informer, if he wants to maintain his cover, will have to read it." Pause. "Since it deals, among other things, with chivalry and honor, we can hope it will teach him something."

"We can *always* hope . . ." Zaitsev seemed less than optimistic. "But this chivalrous, honorable book of yours, it was written in prison, wasn't it?"

"It's possible." She nodded. "What about it?"

"And the author, Sir Malory, what was he in prison for?"

"The records of that time show that a Sir Thomas Malory was accused of rape." Katya flushed. "It's not known whether it was the same Sir Thomas. It's also not known whether he was guilty. If there was a trial, the record was misplaced. He was imprisoned for a while, then released."

"And what significance do you attach to this?"

"Significance?" She stared. "Did you break down my door to engage me in literary discussion? Wouldn't it have been easier to consult your informer? Or better yet, enroll in my class?"

He ignored this. "I would like to have your opinion."

"Then my opinion, since you've asked for it, is that most people— most decent people—fall short of their own ideals. They fall short necessarily, if the ideals are worth anything. What matters, therefore, isn't the failure, but the struggle." She paused. "No doubt you will find this ridiculous. From the Marxist standpoint it is, of course, nonsense: Honor and chivalry are propaganda, virtues to which the aristocracy laid claim in order to justify their privileged position, but which they signally failed to practice in their lives."

He shrugged. "Your statement of the Marxist position is no doubt correct. And given the accusation of rape, it would certainly seem to apply in Sir Thomas Malory's case. From a personal standpoint, however . . ."

"From a personal standpoint . . . what?"

"Actually, I find this story very simple. It tells me that in six centuries nothing much has changed. Records are still misplaced. People are wrongfully accused. Imprisoned without trial." Pause, in which his eyes seemed to wander the length of her body. "Raped."

Silence.

"Threats?" Her chin came up.

He shook his head, his face expressionless.

"Facts."

More silence.

"As a matter of fact, I have read Malory's book." Zaitsev dropped it back into her lap. "Parts of it. I find the psychology implausible. At the end especially. The King dies nobly, forgiving everyone. The Queen retires to a convent, devotes her life to prayer. Her lover is reconciled with his enemy. Everyone preserves dignity in defeat. People fail, but values triumph."

He paused.

"Which is all nonsense, of course. It's nonsense that pride conquers fear, that dignity endures in the face of pain. In the last analysis all of us, you and I, him"—he turned and pointed suddenly at Vadim—"are nothing but bodies that bleed and hurt. Everything else is propaganda."

He stood up.

"You are to come with me now to answer questions regarding your involvement with the organizers of this so-called march, these subversive elements which, according to our information, have taken root in the university."

"My involvement? What proof do you have for this accusation?"

He shrugged. "Your name appears on certain lists."

"Lists. Of course . . ." The irony was palpable. "But who wrote them? You?"

Another shrug.

"Your lists are a pretext. We both know why you are here, to press on me attentions that nothing would ever induce me to receive." She paused, eyes blazing with contempt. "You, Alexander Zaitsev, major in the KGB, are a liar and a coward."

Silence. Zaitsev forced his lips into smile. His eyes, Vadim saw, were colder than stones.

"You think you can be heroic, like the Queen in your story who went proudly and with dignity to be burned at the stake, knowing that Lancelot would ride to her rescue. You will find you are mistaken." He leaned so close, their faces were almost touching. "Where we are going, pride and dignity mean nothing. No Sir Lancelot will ride to your rescue. I predict that in time you will welcome those attentions which nothing, you say, would induce you to receive." He paused. "I predict that you, Katerina Levchenko, associate professor of English literature, lover of honor and chivalry, will be happy to go down on your knees before me and beg for the privilege of sucking my dick."

Vadim erupted from his seat. His fear swamped by a wave of anger, he hurled himself at Zaitsev, kicking him, scratching him, pounding him with his fists.

A blow to the back of his head sent him spinning. His mind fogged. He was caught from behind, his arm twisted behind his back with a force that threatened to tear it from its socket.

"So . . . Sir Lancelot to the rescue." Zaitsev inspected him, smiling nastily, furious. Livid scratches tracked his face from cheekbone to jaw.

"Another would-be hero." He turned to Katya. "But heroes are dangerous. For the safety of the state, not to mention the individual, aspirations to heroics must be nipped in the bud."

Reaching forward, he grasped Vadim's crotch. He squeezed. The pain was like a blow, knocked the breath out of Vadim. He gasped and retched, strained to cry out, but couldn't.

"Coward!" Katya's cry was compounded of fury and panic. "Bully. Pervert who takes his anger out on children."

"Anger? Anger has nothing to do with it." Zaitsev looked surprised. "It's a matter of education. Heroism comes at a price. Would-be heroes must understand this."

He turned to Vadim.

"Repeat these words after me . . ." he said. "My sister sucks dicks for a living."

Vadim spat in his face.

Zaitsev wiped his face on his sleeve. He squeezed again, twisted, kept squeezing.

Vadim wanted to scream but couldn't. He bucked and writhed, but the gorilla held him fast. The agony surged through him, enveloped him, swamped him. It was as if he were choking, drowning in it.

"Say it, Vadim! For God's sake, say it." Through the roaring in his ears he heard Katya imploring him. "It won't mean anything. They're only words."

Zaitsev stopped. He turned to Katya.

"Shut up. I won't tell you again. If you interfere, I will maim him for life."

He turned back to Vadim, his voice conversational. "In a sense, she's right, of course. They *are* just words. Objectively, they don't mean a thing. But heroism is *subjective.* What's at stake here is your opinion of yourself."

He paused.

"So now you need to stop and think. You can try to be a hero and have your testicles crushed like eggs. Or you can say the words, stop the pain, and admit to being what you really are—A sniveling schoolboy, with snot running out of his nose, whose sister," he paused once again, smiled mockingly, "sucks dicks for a living."

He pulled up his sleeve, inspected his watch. "I shall give you ten seconds. If you want someday to be able to call yourself a man, I advise you to do as I tell you."

Vadim tried to imagine resisting but couldn't. His mind cringed from the memory of that pain. Nausea and aftershocks swept through him still, but compared to *that,* they were less than nothing. He looked over at Katya, tears streaming down his face. Help me, he silently pleaded. Don't let him do this to me again. Forgive me.

"Five seconds . . ." Zaitsev said.

A sense of his powerlessness overwhelmed Vadim. In the end what difference would it make? If he said the words, who would it hurt? The only issue was self-respect, and weighed against the pain, what did *that* matter? But along with these thoughts he could hear in his head an echo of words Katya was always quoting. They were from her beloved Malory, of course; Lancelot's words, words that now seemed to come from another time altogether, from a world he wasn't sure had ever existed: "Once shamed," Lancelot had said, "may never be recovered."

He saw that Katya had tears in her eyes. From deep in his chest a sob forced itself to the surface.

"So . . ." Zaitsev said. "It seems Sir Lancelot has made his decision."

Vadim looked away. Zaitsev caught his chin, forced him to look him in the eyes.

"Well . . . ?"

Vadim nodded.

"Say it then." Zaitsev ordered. "Look at her when you say it."

Vadim looked at Katya. There was no reproach in her eyes, just sadness.

She said, "You're too young to be tested. You weren't ready. Forgive me, Vadim."

She had tried to give him his honor back. She had tried both then and later. But what Malory had written for Lancelot was right. If you lost your honor, you lost everything. And age was irrelevant. Ready or not, he'd been put to the test, and ready or not, he had failed it. So he'd known even then, even as he'd uttered Zaitsev's lie, that this surrender was irrevocable, final.

When he finished the telling, Chance was silent for some moments. Finally she said: "What happened to your sister?"

"She killed herself," he said. "They interrogated her for a couple of days, then they released her with no charges. When she came back, she wasn't the same person. She wouldn't talk about what had happened. She wouldn't go to the university to teach her classes, wouldn't write, wouldn't read. She just sat all day next to the window. She was like that for a week. I stayed with her most of that time, but one day I had to go out to go shopping. When I came home, she had hanged herself in the stairwell. She said in her note there were things she had learned about herself that she found herself unwilling to live with."

More silence.

Presently Chance said: "Why do you blame yourself? For leaving her alone?"

"For leaving her?" He shrugged. "Not just for that, for everything. For leaving her, for not seeing what kind of despair she was in, for betraying her."

"Betraying her?" She looked incredulous. "Are you serious? You betrayed her by saying what he *forced* you to say?"

He nodded. "Betraying seems to me an accurate description. For lacking the courage to endure a little pain."

"You were fifteen, for Christ's sake, and it wasn't a little pain. It was a lot of pain." She stared at him, seemed almost angry. "Have you been blaming yourself for this all these years? When was it, fifteen years ago? My God, you were just a baby."

He shook his head. "You're making excuses for me. It's generous of you, but it doesn't do any good. They're the same excuses I tried to make for myself, the same excuses Katya made. The trouble is, I don't accept them. I didn't then. I don't now."

"Obviously, or you wouldn't still be dreaming. The thing is, you have to. For your own sake you *have* to accept them."

He didn't answer.

"Adam, look at me." She reached over and took his hands, forced him to meet her eyes. "It wasn't your fault. There was nothing you could do that would have made a damn bit of difference. What happened would have happened no matter what, whether you gave in at once or held out till he maimed you. And you didn't give in. You held out as long as you could. You were *fifteen,*" she repeated. "Just a baby."

"I was fifteen," he said. "I was not a baby. There were boys my age who fought in the war against Hitler, who were killed defending Leningrad and Odessa. It wasn't a question of age, it was a question of courage." He paused. "Some writer, Conrad maybe, wrote of a man's need to be faithful to his 'ideal conception of oneself.' That's what I blame myself for. I was not faithful."

"That's just stupid," she said. "Forgive me, but that's plain fucking dumb. You *were* faithful. Nobody ever lives up to their ideal conception absolutely; they live up to it as best they can. What was it you told me your sister said? 'Decent people fall short of their ideals; they fall short necessarily, if the ideals are worth anything.' Faithful doesn't mean succeeding, she was saying, it means trying. You have been faithful." Chance shook her head as if in disbelief. "My God, have you ever been faithful."

He shook his head. "If only you knew."

"If only I knew . . ." She gazed at him, speculating, for a moment. "Maybe I do," she said. "Or maybe I can guess."

He stared. "Guess? How could you?"

She ignored the question. "This Major Zaitsev, what happened to *him*?"

"Nothing happened. At least, not for what he did to my sister."

"Then he's still in the KGB?"

He shook his head. "No. Two or three years later he got involved in some scandal, some black market thing. He defected to the West."

"So where is he now?"

"I don't know."

"You don't know . . ." Her eyes rested on him for a moment. "Two or three years later he defected to the West, and two or three years after that, so did you. With the KGB . . ." she paused, "hot on your tail."

"Yes," he said. "Why are you asking me this?"

"You don't know where he is." Again she ignored the question. "But that doesn't mean you wouldn't like to find out."

He shrugged. "Why would I want to find out?"

"I think it's obvious," she said. "You want to find out because you want to kill him."

He made a face. "That's fantasy," he said. "Pure melodrama."

"It's not fantasy." She shook her head. "I know because you've told me. We've slept together, remember. You do a lot of talking when you dream."

Silence.

"All right," he said. "I want to kill him. He defected to the West, so that's why I came to the West. I want to kill him, and sooner or later I will. Wouldn't you say he deserves it?"

She shrugged. "I don't know what *he* deserves. I'm not good at that kind of moral arithmetic. I don't think *you* deserve it."

"Deserve what?"

"What you've done to yourself all these years. You've devoted your life to getting revenge on him, and in the process you've been punishing yourself. He defects to the West, so you come here, too, as if you were linked, like convicts on a chain gang." She paused. "Is *that* your idea of faithfulness, to find him and kill him, no matter what happens to you?"

"That's right," he said. "No matter what happens to me. I came here to find him and kill him, and that's what I'm going to do."

She gazed at him sadly.

"And was that also," she asked him, "why you joined the KGB?"

CHAPTER THIRTY-SIX

(London. August 20, 1990)

"KGB . . ." He stared at her. "You must be totally crazy."

"I don't think so." She returned his gaze calmly. "Randall Pickett doesn't think so, either."

"Pickett." He gave a dismissive shrug. "What would he know about it?"

What *would* he know about it? Kalugin was outwardly calm, but his mind was in turmoil. If Pickett knew about it, he was really in trouble. He knew he ought not to argue his innocence—innocent people didn't—but arguing, on the other hand, would force her to support her accusation, reveal exactly how much she, or Pickett, knew. He needed her to do that, he thought; in the interest of self-preservation, he badly needed to know how much Pickett knew.

"He'd know this much at least," Chance replied. "He'd know—wouldn't he?—whether you were CIA."

"Not necessarily. They don't just hand out lists. Anyway," he added, "what's that got to do with it?"

"It has this to do with it," she said. "When I ran into you at that place down in Sussex—the one with electronic security, fifteen-foot walls all around, and an obvious heavy on the gate—you gave me to believe you were CIA—."

"I gave you to believe nothing," he cut in. "You assumed. There's a difference."

"Where's the difference?" She shrugged. "You knew what I believed and you didn't contradict it. But why would you let me believe you're CIA when you aren't? To cover, perhaps, the fact that you're working for someone else? Pickett thinks you're working for the KGB. He suspects you enough, at any rate, that he asked me to spy on you."

"He asked you to spy on me? When?"

"A few days back. And not in so many words. He pretended to be warning me about our relationship, the security implications and danger to my career of shacking up with a refugee from the Evil Empire. He made like the whole thing wasn't a very big deal, claimed to be convinced that you were clean, but then he asked me, just as a personal favor, to let him know if I came across anything to suggest that you weren't."

He claimed to be convinced that you were clean. It suggested Pickett had done some checking. And if he'd asked her to take over the checking, that suggested, in turn, that he hadn't been very convinced. Things were looking bad, Kalugin thought. His own people had already tried to kill him. Soon the Americans might join the hunt.

"And what did you tell him?"

"I told him our relationship was none of his goddamn business. Which was what I believed at the time. But now . . ." She looked at him searchingly for a moment, shrugged.

"Now you think I'm a KGB agent." His tone was withering. "Simply on the basis of Pickett's casual suggestion. Ten minutes ago, if I remember rightly, we were talking about trust."

"It wasn't a casual suggestion." She shook her head. "Maybe he thought it *looked* casual, but it didn't. And it isn't just that. There are other things, too. The look on his face, for instance, when I told him I'd run into you down in Sussex. He looked as if he'd been sandbagged."

So Pickett knew she'd seen him in Sussex. And Pickett suspected him of being KGB. Things, Kalugin thought, were beginning to make a bit more sense. Pickett's suspicion would explain, at least, why the Knights' team had been quarantined so abruptly, removed from the reach of *his* prying eyes. But if things were beginning to make a bit more sense, further reflection told him, they still were not making a lot. Pickett, it appeared, had been shocked to learn of his presence in Sussex. But why *shocked?* Pickett knew of his connection with the Knights, and probably that he was on the Knights' team. Why otherwise had he been checking into his background? But then perhaps it had not been *his* presence in Sussex that shocked Pickett. Was it possible that Pickett hadn't known that the Knights were training in Sussex? Was he looking into the background of Adam Kalugin for some other reason entirely? But if so, what other reason? And there were still other parts of the puzzle that didn't seem to fit: Why had Atlas wanted to kill him? And why had Atlas, as it now seemed clear he had, killed Zebo? Why would Moscow, if it planned a provocation involving the Knights of Vladimir, willfully deprive itself of its only source of intelligence about them?

"You're very thoughtful all of a sudden." Chance's voice cut in on these reflections. "It makes me wonder what about. There's something else makes me wonder, too. I tell you that Pickett thinks you're KGB, and all I hear from you are a bunch of arguments. What I *don't* hear is a denial."

"Why would I bother?" He shrugged. "If I did you wouldn't believe me. But can't you see it doesn't make any sense? The KGB killed my sister. How can you think I would join them?"

She shook her head. "It wasn't the KGB who killed her, it was Zaitsev. He's the one you wanted to kill." She paused. "And you needed *them* to do it."

"The KGB? Why would I need them?"

"How else were you going to find him? You forget I'm a student of your country. It's a fact—isn't it—that the KGB deals harshly with its defectors? They're tried in absentia, usually sentenced to death. And because of this, they always go into hiding. When the CIA, or whoever, gets through squeezing them, they're given new identities and sometimes police protection. Some of them even have plastic surgery to alter their appearance. On the other side, of course, there's a KGB unit whose mission is to track them down and carry out the sentence." She paused. "I'm only guessing, but I think that's why you joined. You made some kind of devil's bargain: you'd work for them if they'd find him for you and let you kill him."

For a moment it was all he could do to conceal his surprise and dismay. He managed it, however.

She continued: "And actually it strikes me as psychologically plausible, too. It's obvious you despise yourself for what you're convinced was cowardice and betrayal. What more fitting than to be forced, as part of your atonement, to belong to an organization for which normally, I'd guess, you'd have nothing but contempt? You get to revenge yourself on Zaitsev, and in the process you punish yourself."

He continued to look skeptical. "It strikes me, you're doing an awful lot of guessing."

"I am," she admitted. "So tell me I'm wrong."

"You're wrong," he said. "You're smart and imaginative, but you're wrong. But I don't expect you to believe me, and I'm not going to argue anymore, because arguing, apparently, only strengthens your suspicions. And now, I expect, you'll be wanting to take those suspicions to Pickett. And Pickett will take them to MI5. And MI5 will reopen the file they closed half a dozen years ago, and I'll have to drag myself round to Queen Anne's Gate to answer, one more time, questions I've answered ad nauseam already." He paused, stood up abruptly. "But for now I've had enough. So I'm going to say goodbye. In the circumstances, you won't be surprised not to hear from me in future. In any case, I'm sure you won't want to."

He started to walk away. This had always been coming, he thought. He'd always known, because he didn't own his life, that their feeling for each other would come to nothing. However much he might come to love her, the KGB, his sleazy mistress, would always stand in his way. But though he had always known that, what he hadn't known, until now, was how much it would hurt.

"Iceman . . ." She called out after him. "Adam, wait."

He turned. Their eyes met.

"How would you know what I want?"

He was startled. "How would I *know*?"

"Yes," she said. "You've been so busy keeping your distance, making sure I couldn't get close, how the hell would you know anything about me?"

"I know this," he said. "You think I belong to the KGB, that I'm therefore an enemy of your country. Are you're really going to tell me you'd want to continue to have for your lover someone you think is an enemy of your country?"

She didn't answer at once, inspected him instead with a look that expressed the same odd mixture of emotions he'd noted in her earlier: concern, affection, sadness, exasperation.

"For an otherwise intelligent man, you do think a lot in boxes."

"Boxes?"

"Yes," she said. "Boxes labeled 'American' and 'Russian,' or 'Friend' and 'Enemy.' And every box fits neatly into some other box, into that one and that one only. Since I'm American and you're Russian, that puts us forever in the box labeled 'Enemies.' "

"The box you put *me* in was labeled KGB," he said. "That makes things a little different, I think. That's not a box, it's a coffin."

She shook her head. "I haven't put you in a box. If you feel you're in one, you put yourself there. For me you're mostly a question mark. If you are KGB, you're not *just* KGB. You're that, but more important, you're Adam. Adam"—she shrugged—"or whatever your name really is."

"Vadim," he said. "My name is Vadim."

The words were out before he'd thought, but as soon he heard them, he knew how badly he'd blundered. How could he have been so careless? But then maybe it hadn't been carelessness at all. Maybe something in him had simply rebelled. Maybe, after so many years of repression, his real self had seized the moment to rise up and proclaim its independence. Or maybe he'd fastened so thankfully on her suggestion that things between them were not necessarily over, that he'd failed to notice the trap. In any case, the words were said; it was too late to unsay them.

"Vadim?" She raised an eyebrow. "An interesting admission."

It was too late to unsay the words, but he should, he thought, make an effort to recover.

"Phonetically Adam is the closest English equivalent. I thought, when I came here from Poland, that if from then on I was going to be English, I should at least have an English name."

"Of course," she said dryly. "Kalugin, for instance."

He shrugged, said nothing.

"Vadim," she said, "or Adam . . . Iceman. Shut up and listen to me, will you? Sit down, hear me out, and then you can leave if you want. I have no intention of going to Pickett."

"No intention?"

She shook her head. "What could I tell him that he doesn't suspect already? But in any case, that's not the point."

"Not the point?" He stared. "Then what *is* the point? What are you trying to tell me?"

"I'm trying to tell you," she said, "that I hope you are a KGB agent."

CHAPTER THIRTY-SEVEN

(London. August 20, 1990)

"You hope I am a KGB agent?" Kalugin was utterly astounded. "Why?"

She nodded. "Because that way, at least, I'll know they've no chance of succeeding."

"They?" He looked blank. "Who's they?"

"Oh, for Christ's sake!" she flared. "Don't tell me you don't know that. One way or another you just have to. I'm talking about the Knights of Vladimir. The plan Martin Rosenthal's been gaming on the Foundation's computer, their criminal, frivolous, *stupid* plan for murdering hundreds of innocent people."

Hundreds of people? His mind whirled. Hundreds of *innocent* people? That wasn't what the Knights had planned, what their anonymous benefactors had claimed to be training them for. Ten or a dozen surgically executed strikes against leading Ukrainian Communists and KGB high-ups could hardly be stretched, even by the grossest exaggeration, into "murdering hundreds of innocent people."

"Look," he said. "Please don't be angry, but you need to listen, and listen carefully. I really don't know what you're talking about."

"You don't *know?*" Her disbelief was plain. "You mean you don't know about the Knights of Vladimir? You're telling me those Ukrainians I saw you with in the garden of that place in Sussex are *not* the Knights of Vladimir? You really expect me to believe you?"

They were at a moment of decision, he knew. If he denied everything, she'd clam up on him and he'd learn nothing. And anyway, he thought, if he kept denying until he was black in the face, she wasn't going to believe him. His slip with "Vadim" had seen to that.

"I know about the Knights of Vladimir." He nodded. "Actually I am one, or was. It's the rest of it that has me baffled."

For some seconds she inspected him, eyes narrowed, then she shrugged.

"Okay," she said. "I'll buy that. I have no choice. Tell me what you know about these Knights. I'll tell you what I saw on that computer."

He hesitated.

"Jesus . . ." She gave a disgusted sigh. "You still think I'm trying to trap you, don't you? But think about it for a second, will you. If you aren't a KGB spy, if you really *are* working for the CIA, then I've laid myself open to prosecution for treason. If you are a KGB spy, on the other hand, I'm in a position to give you information. You may know it already, of course, but if you don't, you desperately need to."

He shrugged. "If I were a KGB spy, why would you, an American, give me information?"

"Look," she said. "Let's get rid of the boxes. The Cold War is over. The Soviet people and the American people are sick to death of that bullshit. The only ones who aren't jumping for joy are the guys that made a living off it. Generals and spies and Pentagon contractors. And politicians like Rosenthal, of course, whose view of reality has suddenly turned into mirage." She paused. "But it seems that some of those people aren't quite ready to call it quits. That's why we're having this conversation. Why I'm risking prosecution. Why I hope you're a KGB agent. There's something going on here that needs to be stopped. But if it's going to be stopped, we need to pool information. We're going to have to trust one another."

Trust one another . . . He considered for a moment. Distrust was so much a reflex with him it was hard, even now, to overcome it. But what did it matter if she *was* out to trap him? The Americans would close in, eventually, whether or not she told Pickett about him. His own people would close in, too. Atlas's fate would be known in due course, and then they would send someone else. His life was a sandbar, and the tide was coming in. The ocean was rising all around him.

"Okay," he said. "Here's what I know. The Knights of Vladimir are training to send terrorists into the Ukraine. They plan to assassinate Party officials and high-ranking officers of the KGB. They're hoping thereby to provoke a popular uprising. Someone, the CIA or some group connected with it, is providing help, using the Foundation for Freedom as a channel. The KGB is aware of this plan, but intends for now to let things develop. They intend to arrest these Knights when they land, then exploit the incident for propaganda." He paused. "In other words, business as usual."

She stared at him. "But that doesn't make any sense. The terrorism plan, I mean. Killing Communist officials won't provoke an uprising. An outpouring of joy, perhaps, but not an uprising."

"Of course." He shrugged. "But we're talking about idiots. Political idiots, that is. They think the killings will provoke harsh reprisals, which in turn will provoke the uprising they hope for. It's conceivable in theory, I suppose. In practice, however . . ."

He broke off, suddenly ambushed by thought.

"In practice, what?"

He didn't answer. In practice, he thought, facts—facts that had earlier, taken in isolation, seemed to make no sense whatever—were coming together in his head. The Knights' inexperience, their political naiveté, the utter impracticality of their plans, the unsuitable nature of their training. It amazed him that he hadn't seen it earlier. He'd been misled, he thought, mesmerized by the farcical ineptitude of the Knights, the absurd, fantastical quality of their aspirations. He'd assumed that these qualities, the same ridiculous aspirations, were shared by their so carefully anonymous sponsors. Because *they* had seemed to be taking the Knights at face value, he'd made the mistake of doing it with them.

"They're not *meant* to succeed," he said. "They have no chance and their US sponsors know it. They're intended to fail. They were programmed to fail from the start."

"Programmed? But who on earth would program them to fail?"

"The only ones who aren't jumping for joy," he thought. *"The spies, the generals, the Pentagon contractors, people whose lives have been made redundant, and so-called statesmen, like Rosenthal, whose view of reality has suddenly turned into mirage. And it seems those people aren't ready to quit."* She'd said it herself—hadn't she?—only a moment or two before, and in doing so had echoed, more or less, what Atlas had remarked at their very first meeting. *"The Cold War is over? Who told you it was over?"* And with that, other pieces of the puzzle seemed to fall neatly into place: Atlas's far too prescient prediction that the Knights would be offered US assistance, Zebo's murder, Volkonskaya's extraordinary revelation, Atlas's abortive bid to kill him. Because there were spies in Moscow too, he thought; spies and generals and politicians, too, whose vision of reality had suddenly turned into mirage. Especially the vision of reality, he thought; and especially in Moscow, where a world view of more than seventy years standing was threatening to blow up in the politicians' faces. So the politicians on both sides had got together, shelved their differences and pooled

their resources, to make one last, despairing attempt to invest their grim vision with the trappings of reality.

"It's a provocation," he said. "It's clear to me now. They're programmed to fail, but not right away. People are going to get killed, all right, but not to provoke a Ukrainian uprising. What the people behind this are hoping for is a nasty little crisis, a nasty little *international* crisis. Like the Berlin Wall or the Cuban business. You know the kind of thing"—he shrugged—"the usual mix of melodrama and farce: Bush and Gorbachev trading accusations, ambassadors at the UN pounding their shoes on the table, forces worldwide on round-the-clock nuclear alert, all the Cold Warriors nicely back in business. All totally phony, of course, the whole thing completely stage-managed, the KGB and the CIA in comfortable collusion, pulling off a confidence trick with the world as its victim . . ."

He happened to glance at her, then, and broke off. She was staring at him with something like horror. He remembered now that she'd promised information. In the flood of his own revelation that promise had slipped his mind.

Hundreds of innocent people, she had said.

"What's wrong?" he asked her. "You know something I don't know? Something you saw on the Foundation's computer?"

She didn't answer his question, not at once.

"It's not going to fail *right away*? People are going to get killed?" All the color had left her face. "You mean your side is going to *let* them be killed?"

He nodded. That had to be it, he thought. It was the only halfway plausible explanation for what had happened to Zebo, for what very nearly had happened to him. Whoever was planning this in Moscow was cutting all links with the Knights of Vladimir. When the killings took place there'd be no one able to point fingers at them, to reveal that these killings, the whole vicious project, could so easily have been strangled at birth.

No wonder Atlas had been ordered to kill him.

"Phony crisis, real blood." He shrugged. "To make it more convincing, I suppose."

She closed her eyes as if the thought was painful, as if to blot out the image his words had conjured up.

"It's not going to need to look more convincing." She spoke quietly. "And it isn't going to be phony. The CIA and the KGB are in collusion, you say, but someone isn't playing by the rules. Someone on my side has rewritten the script. Unless someone stops it, it's going to be real."

"Real?" It was his turn to stare. "That's what you saw on the computer?"

She nodded.

"How?" he demanded, "Where?"

"In Kiev." She paused. "Does September fifteenth mean anything to you?"

He thought for a moment, shook his head. "Should it?"

"It's some Ukrainian anniversary, I forget which, but there are rallies planned, especially in Kiev. Tens, maybe hundreds of thousands of people, plus leading Ukrainian nationalists and bishops of the Catholic Church. A mass demonstration of anti-Soviet sentiment." She paused. "And someone's going to bomb it. The Knights of Vladimir, actually. At least that's what I saw on the computer. Casualties projected in the hundreds. And that's just the beginning, before the rioting starts."

"Rioting?"

"Of course," she said. "In the heat of the moment, who will people blame? The KGB, of course, the Communists, the Russians, anybody and everybody they've always hated. Later, it may occur to some of them that this wouldn't have been a smart thing for *any* of their enemies to do, but by then it will be much too late. All the old hatreds will have been rekindled. The Ukraine will be in turmoil. The authorities will have to send in troops. Gorbachev, under pressure from the Stalinists, who'll be brandishing intelligence obtained from the KGB, will be forced into a confrontation with the US. We'll have your little crisis, but this time not phony. And not carefully stage-managed, but out of control."

"Out of control . . . You mean possibly leading to war?"

"Cold War, not hot war. At least the computer didn't think so, though the Doomsday Factor was up around thirty percent. The trouble is, people who play with computers tend to think of themselves as rational, so they set up their programs that way. Because men like Rosenthal are rational, at least in *their* twisted sense of the word, they expect rationality from other people. And that's what they're counting on here. They think, since no one could win a war like that, that no one would ever start one. I'm afraid I don't share that conviction. They forget just how close we've come on occasion."

She paused. "This has got to be stopped. War or no war, hundreds of people in Ukraine and Russia are going to die needlessly for this.

That's why I'm telling you about it. You have to get word to your people."

Get word to his people. *Which* of his people? he wondered. How was he to know if he'd got the right one? And how was he to get word to them? His people were trying to kill him, weren't they? They probably had orders to kill him on sight.

"This game," he said, "couldn't it just be speculation? Rosenthal or someone daydreaming on the computer?"

She shook her head. "You don't use it to daydream. Not that computer. And it was too highly classified and too specific. It wasn't just anyone setting off a bomb. They were mentioned specifically: The Knights of Vladimir."

But Benko wouldn't, he thought, not voluntarily. He was a lunatic and homicidal, perhaps, but he'd never kill his own people. Nor would any of the others. Not any of the other *Knights*. . . . It was then that he remembered the handholder, Leonid, alias Gerhard Mueller. But Benko and the Knights wouldn't *have* to do it. They were not the operation, they were simply cover. They were there to get to go through the motions, to show Moscow what Moscow expected. And while Moscow watched and laid its traps for the Knights, Leonid would go about his business. It was clear enough now, Kalugin thought, why there wouldn't be a problem at the border.

"It wasn't daydreaming," Chance repeated. "You have to stop them."

"I know that." He nodded. "I understand perfectly now. The trouble is, I can't."

"You can't?" She stared. "Why not? How hard can it be to get word to your people?"

"Harder than you think," he said. "My people are trying to kill me."

CHAPTER THIRTY-EIGHT

(Moscow. August 20, 1990)

"STILL NO WORD FROM ATLAS," LEM SAID. "THIS MAKES THE THIRD transmission he's missed. Do you think he may have fucked up?"

Rakowski sighed. He shut his eyes. Placing his hands together, he rested his elbows on his desk, placed his forehead against his finger-tips—an attitude that struck his assistant as suggestive of prayer.

"Let's review the facts." He spoke wearily. "A week ago we sent him instructions to liquidate the illegal, Cobalt, who according to Atlas's own reports, had been showing symptoms of distrust and disloyalty. This Cobalt, whose personnel file reveals him to be highly intelligent and unusually adept at most forms of violence, had good reason, moreover, to be wary of Atlas, since his recent unfortunate chance encounter with a member of the local residency staff had alerted him to the fact that he was viewed with suspicion, also that he'd been systematically lied to. And now Atlas, who was ordered to act at once and to report back to us as soon as he had, has not been heard from for five days." He paused. Opening his eyes, he examined Lem bleakly. "What do *you* think?"

Lem shrugged. "I think he fucked up. I think he's going to show up in a ditch with his throat cut from ear to ear."

Moment of silence. Rakowski inspected him with distaste.

"Have you ever *seen* anyone dead in a ditch?"

Lem shook his head. "I can't say I have."

"I have," Rakowski said. "I saw it a lot in Afghanistan. It's not a thing to be taken lightly."

Their eyes met. Lem flushed. "I'm sorry, General."

"It's okay." Rakowski's stare relaxed. "But people like you and me, we need to remember that sometimes. We sit at our desks and play chess with men's lives, and too often we forget what it is we're playing with. In the end we can lose sight of why. Those are two brave men, Atlas and the other one. Or they *were,* because I, too, think one of them is dead. And like you"—he paused—"I'm afraid it's the wrong one."

He was silent for a moment, then he resumed: "If we're right, this Cobalt is a dangerously loose cannon. If he doesn't know now what's going on, he will before long, as soon the killings begin. It's lucky we don't need him anymore." He paused. "Do you think we should alert the Americans to this problem?"

Lem thought for a moment.

"Why not?" He shrugged. "They must have known we weren't going to trust them. And after all, he's their problem, too. They can employ the resources we lack . . . MI5, Special Branch. And actually . . ."—he thought a moment more—"why not the ordinary police? We give them photographs of both men, and they put out a countrywide alert: Cobalt wanted by Scotland Yard for questioning in connection with the murder of Atlas."

"It makes sense." Rakowski nodded. "I think we have to try it. I'm afraid I'm not optimistic it'll work. He's intelligent, and resourceful, and he knows now that we're after him. He's probably gone into hiding already. We'll get him eventually, of course, but eventually may be too late."

"We've got until September fifteenth. That still gives us . . . What?" Lem glanced at his watch. "Give or take eighteen days."

Rakowski frowned. "It's not enough. He could have gone to Europe. He could have holed up somewhere in the country with a television and a month's supply of food. We can't rely on finding *him* . . ."

He broke off, swiveled his chair around so it was facing away from Lem and toward the view. For several minutes he sat staring out at the parkland, the ornamental lake, the distant prospect of Moscow. Then abruptly he swung round again. He was looking, Lem noted, distinctly more cheerful.

"We can't rely on finding him. There's no guarantee we'll do it in time. He'll have to be made to come to us. And I think," Rakowski said, "I know just how to do it."

CHAPTER THIRTY-NINE

(Connemara. Republic of Eire. September 3, 1990)

"BUT WHY?" CHANCE DEMANDED. "WHY DOES IT HAVE TO BE YOU?"

"You know why," Kalugin said. "It has to be me because I'm all there is."

They were in the kitchen of the cottage Chance had borrowed from a girlfriend in Washington, DC. On the table in front of them the remains of a meal: bacon and eggs, soda bread, plum jam, sweet country butter, tea. A peat fire smoked in the grate. Outside it was raining. The cottage was thatched, whitewashed, primitive, four hundred yards from the next habitation, five miles at least from the nearest town. Country people were inclined to be nosy, but she'd been here often enough before, she'd assured him, for their presence not to occasion much comment. So long as he kept out of sight, let her do the shopping and running around, they'd be safe for a couple of days at least.

"Are you sure?" she persisted. "Are you sure there isn't somebody we could warn?"

"I'm quite sure." He nodded. "Look, we've been through this . . . If I knew how, believe me I would. But I can't get hold of Benko, and I can't think of anyone else. At least, not anyone I can trust."

"Not *anyone?*" She looked skeptical. "Not even in the KGB?"

"Tell me who?" he demanded. "This is a conspiracy of both sides, remember, a conspiracy reaching to the very highest levels. There must *be* people who could help us, but how do we find out who they are? How do we get to the good guys before the bad guys get to us? And even supposing we can find them, how do we get them to believe us?" He paused. "Just think about *that* for a moment, will you. You're some midlevel officer, let's say, in the CIA or the State Department, with a pension to protect and a bureaucrat's horror of looking foolish, and out of the blue you're confronted with these two flakes, some ivory tower academic and a guy who claims to be a Soviet illegal, and they tell you this utterly incredible story: shadowy cliques in the CIA and KGB conspiring in a sinister scheme to restore the Cold War. Can you really see yourself believing that? Can you even see yourself *listening* long enough to give yourself a chance to believe it?"

He paused rhetorically. When she didn't respond, he continued: "You don't think I *want* to go, do you?"

But he did, of course. He did now, at least, now that he'd heard the broadcast. He wanted it more than he could have imagined.

"You must see that I *have* to go," he said. "What you told me you saw on the computer really leaves me no choice. I can't just sit back and let people be killed."

Silence.

"I'm afraid *you're* going to get killed," Chance said. "I'm afraid I'm not going to see you again."

"You're going to see me." He gave what he hoped was a reassuring smile. "Don't even worry about it. I'll be gone ten days, two weeks at the most. There's a cruise makes a two-day stopover in Odessa beginning the fourteenth. I'll join the ship in Istanbul, take the overnight train to Kiev. I'll have plenty of time to complete my business there and be back on board in Odessa the next evening."

It sounded easy, he thought, and in theory ought to be. He knew that it wouldn't be, though. Something was bound to go wrong. Nothing was ever that easy.

"Adam . . ." She studied him intently. "Are you being honest with me? Is there any chance at all of your succeeding? Or is this just some despairing gesture, something you feel you have to do?"

"Of course I feel I have to do it." He met her gaze and held it. "But it's not a gesture and it's not despairing. I think I stand an excellent chance of succeeding . . . I know exactly who to look for, remember. I know when, and I know where. They, on the other hand, *won't* be looking. At least they won't be looking for me."

"Maybe . . ." She looked dubious. "But what if something goes wrong? Suppose you get delayed and miss the ship. How are you going to get yourself out?"

How was he going to get himself out? It was a good question, he thought, and not one to which he currently had an answer. Not that in the long run it mattered very much. Getting out, after all, was not the main objective. If he achieved the main objective, did what he'd gone in to do, then so far as he was concerned the long run could look after itself. What was it that economist, Lord Someone or Other, had said? "In the long run we are all dead."

He shrugged. "I'll think of something."

"Somehow that doesn't reassure me," she said. "The more I think about this, the less I like it. I think the risks are enormous."

He shook his head. "It's risky, perhaps, but not suicidal. In any case, the risk is not the point. The alternative to going is doing nothing. Both of us know that's not an option. We're speaking of innocent people, remember. I'm trying to save hundreds of innocent lives."

And not just to *save* lives, he thought, but also—though the life in question was hardly innocent—to end one.

Leonid the Handholder.

Alexandr Zaitsev.

The broadcast had been meant to trap him, of course.

He still wasn't sure whether he owed his having heard it, this message it seemed he'd been waiting for half his life, to luck or judgment. When Chance asked him why he'd brought the short wave radio, why he was always so adamant about listening through a veritable blizzard of static to a classical music request program from an obscure station in Moscow, he'd shrugged and said it was mostly habit. In the past they'd used it to send him instructions; he kept listening now in case they were trying to reach him. He hadn't really believed they would, of course, hadn't even known if they knew enough to try.

As he'd said, it had mostly been habit.

So when he'd heard the Mozart—it had always been one of Katya's particular favorites—though he'd known at once why they'd chosen this moment to air it, he'd hardly been able to believe his ears. *Five years* now he had listened to this program, four PM faithfully, Tuesdays and Thursdays. Five years he had waited, confidence gradually waning, to hear them air this little wisp of music, these thirty-two measures of learned polyphony, classical grace, and wit. But what had completely stunned him was the message. *Eine Kleine Gigue,* K 574, was broadcast this evening, so they'd said—in Moscow, of course, it *was* evening—by request of a listener in Geneva, Switzerland.

A Gerhard Mueller.

And he'd realized at once he knew something they didn't.

It was a little insulting, of course, that they'd even tried it. Did they really think he was that stupid? Or did they hope he'd believed what they'd told him years ago at the Sleeper School, before they'd arranged his defection: that his superiors in Directorate S (Illegals) would be kept in the dark about his one-shot assignment for Service A (Active Measures)? Or perhaps they'd known he'd suspect it was a trap, but had banked on his not be able to ignore the proffered bait. In any case, it really didn't matter. Because luck—or was it destiny? —had been on his side for once. For the something he knew that they apparently didn't was that Gerhard Mueller, formerly Alexandr Zaitsev and now Leonid the Handholder, wasn't *at* the address they had given for him in Geneva, and wouldn't be there for the foreseeable future, indeed, (if Kalugin had his way) not ever again. He had spent at least the last several weeks, in fact, at a well-protected country house in Sussex, offering, to a handful of aspiring terrorists, instruction in the basics of their trade. And then he'd gone with them on their mission.

So while whoever in Moscow was behind all this put out bait, set careful traps for him in Geneva, he, Adam Kalugin, would be more than a thousand kilometers east.

Where they least expected him.

In Kiev.

BOOK IV

(September 13 to 19, 1990)

CHAPTER FORTY

(Odessa, Ukrainian SSR. September 14, 1990)

IT WASN'T UNTIL IT WAS HIS TURN IN LINE THAT KALUGIN STARTED TO GET nervous. There had to be something in the national character, he thought, some deep-seated, inherited subservience that made Russians want to cringe when confronted by someone wearing a uniform. There had to be in the Russian character, too, characteristics that *wearing* a uniform brought out: an officiousness aroused by the subservience, some obverse of the tendency to cringe that expressed itself as a tendency to bully. From the way this officer was looking at his passport, you'd have thought it was an imperial thousand-ruble note. A forged one, at that.

It didn't help the way *he* felt, of course, that the passport subject to such hostile scrutiny wasn't his.

The *picture* was his, taken only ten days ago in Dublin, though the way the official was inspecting it—examining the image minutely, then the face, feature by feature, then back again to the image—you'd have thought that was open to question, too. The transit visa was genuine also. Issued by the Dublin consulate at short notice (thanks to the good offices of the travel agent who'd booked his passage on the cruise from Istanbul), it was good for a forty-eight-hour stopover in Odessa. But the slim green booklet with the eagle in gold on the cover had cost him, in cash, five hundred dollars. He had got it from a dealer in Blackrock, who served, or so he claimed, as a regular supplier of documents to the IRA. US was best, this gentleman had assured him, easiest to come by, easiest to fix. Since the document itself was genuine and current and the page substitution indiscernible, at least to the unaided eye, the risk of detection, he'd asserted, was near zero. But though that claim had sounded bankable in Dublin, here, with this sharp-eyed bureaucrat checking every page, it seemed flimsy, mere paper and promises.

Thank God, Kalugin thought, that being nervous didn't make him sweat.

"James Whitcomb?" The official pronounced the h as a strangled g, voiced the silent b, wrinkling his nose in distaste at the barbarism of the sound sequence resulting. On his lips it seemed like an accusation.

"Yes."

"What is your reason for visiting the USSR?"

"Tourism." Volunteer nothing, Kalugin had told himself, answer their questions but volunteer nothing. To his ears, however, this answer sounded a little curt. He added, "I came on the cruise ship from Istanbul. Leaving Wednesday."

Leaving Wednesday with any luck, that was. Leaving Wednesday if still alive Wednesday.

"Where will you be staying in Odessa?"

"A hotel, if rooms are available. If not, I'll come back to the ship."

"I do not think there will be rooms available." The officer seemed to take some satisfaction in this. He tore off the first part of the three-section visa. "When you return to the ship, you surrender your exit permit. You will not be permitted back on shore. In any case, you may not stay longer than forty-eight hours." He paused, then added, "It is my obligation to inform you that, under Soviet law, the renting of unlicensed accommodations by foreigners is forbidden."

The usual official catch-22. Kalugin made no comment. At least, he thought, this much hadn't changed, though for people so desperately in need of foreign currency, they were notably unwelcoming to tourists. Hotels would not be a problem, however, nor would renting unlicensed accommodations. Odessa to Kiev was overnight both ways. He would sleep on the train.

The officer handed back the passport.

"Enjoy your visit to Odessa."

He didn't make any effort at all, Kalugin noted, to look as though he meant it.

Customs was next and ought to be no problem. Ought, that was, unless for some reason they took it into their heads to rip out the lining of his toilet kit in the overnight bag, which was, all the luggage he was taking ashore. He'd brought no weapons, of course—given the ubiquity of metal detectors, that would have been suicidal—but a full set of Soviet papers had seemed vital to ensure him a freedom of movement which, at least when he'd last been here, was unavailable to tourists. And that, his ignorance of how and how much things here had changed, was what bothered him most, he thought. Maybe now, with *glasnost*, tourists were not hamstrung with restrictions the way they had been in the 1970s. Maybe his transit visa would have taken him anywhere he needed to go. He hadn't known that for certain, though, and hadn't been able to risk, therefore, relying on tourist papers. The Russian documents had cost a lot of money; two thousand dollars, in fact, to the Russian emigré in Paris (a walking encyclopedia on Soviet documents and an artist at their fabrication) who'd provided an up-to-date domestic passport, a residence permit for Kiev, *spravkas* for travel to and from Odessa, and also—something of a masterstroke, this—ID as Vladimir Stepanovich Grusha, lieutenant in the Second Chief Directorate of the KGB. But with this as his fallback identity, he thought, his ignorance of how things were done would work with, not against, the identity he planned to assume. The mistakes expected from a foreign tourist would also be expected, surely, from someone *posing* as a foreign tourist—a KGB officer working under cover, seeking to entrap black-marketeers.

Customs *was* no problem. The officer handed him a card, listing items whose import into the country was prohibited, poked perfunctorily through the carry-on bag, expressed his approval at discovering there a volume of Pushkin's stories in translation, wished him luck in finding a hotel room, and waved him through.

He was home.

It didn't feel like home. As the taxi carried him, by a route expensively circuitous, from the port to the station through streets he'd not seen for close to twenty years, he was surprised both by how little things, physically, had changed and by how unfamiliar they nonetheless seemed. Odessa was the same; it had all the features that existed on the map he had somewhere stored in his mind—the long, vertiginous flights of steps made famous by the crowd scene in Eisenstein's movie, the Monument to the Potemkin mutineers, the Richelieu Monument, Shevchenko Park where Katya had taken him for picnics, the yellow beaches, the Monument to the Unknown Sailor at the foot of Dzerzhinski Boulevard (was it a law that every Soviet city had to contain at least one reminder of the KGB's founding father?) —but somehow his sense of it had changed. In memory it existed as a kind of enchanted snapshot album, the images suffused with a golden glow of childhood visits and lazy summer vacations; now, in early autumn, with the leaves in the parks and boulevards already beginning to turn, it seemed alien and chilly.

It came to him that he no longer had a home.

CHAPTER FORTY-ONE

(Kiev, Ukrainian SSR. September 15, 1990)

LOOKING AHEAD, OUT OF THE WINDOW, IT WAS ALWAYS THE STATUE YOU spotted first. That was how he'd remembered arriving on the train from Odessa, and though the feeling this time was completely different, in this respect at least his memory hadn't lied. Long before you got to the Dnieper, before the skyline of the older parts of the city on the steep, wooded right bank of the river came into view between the modern shoebox apartment buildings of the left bank residential areas, you saw *her:* Motherland, in some Soviet architect's conception, a stainless-steel figure, megalomaniac-neoclassical in style, holding aloft a sword and shield, and standing (if you counted the granite plinth) more than a hundred meters high. Katya, he recalled, had always hated her, the totalitarian assertiveness, the way the huge figure laid hold on the eye, wrenched it away from the old Kiev, from structures more worthy of attention: the Andreievsky Church, the Vydubichi Monastery, the elegant golden-domed bell tower of the Lavra. Even in the seventies, when saying such things had been perilous, Katya had maintained to anyone willing to listen that "Motherland" was ultimate *poshlost,* the essence of that pretentious sentimentality whose sporadic occurrence in the Russian sensibility was apt to be blamed on the German influence. Monumentalism, she'd been fond of saying, was what happened when politics meddled with art, when the state intruded into areas of feeling that ought to be kept strictly private. If she'd failed to make the obvious comparison with Hitler's Reich, it had been because, even for her, indiscretion had its limits. Kalugin himself, having little interest at the time in the links between politics and esthetics, had been mostly indifferent to the statue. Now, however, with the station rapidly approaching, he found himself greeting her with something like relief. She was ugly,

but she heralded arrival. Within five minutes, give or take, this nightmare journey would be over. He would know, at least, whether his
stupidity had earned its just reward.

If the KGB was waiting at the station.

His stupidity, his *first* piece of stupidity, had been perpetrated in
Odessa. In view of his obviously foreign appearance—the Levi's, the
Nikes, the Italian leather jacket—he'd assumed that by keeping his
tourist's identity he would minimize the need for explanations. Before half an hour of the journey had gone by, however, it was clear
he'd just traded one set of problems for another. His traveling companions turned out to be friendly Ukrainians who insisted not only
on his joining their conversation, but also, in the process, on his
learning their language. Ignorance of a language, he'd discovered,
was harder to fake than its opposite. Maintaining the fiction of in-
comprehension demanded a very high level of alertness, and mispro-
nouncing, convincingly, words that had rolled off the tongue since
childhood taxed his linguistic skills to their limit. He had also pro-
voked raised eyebrows from the car attendant checking tickets,
who'd demanded of him (and the company in general) why anyone,
even a crazy tourist, would make a twenty-six-hour round trip to
spend something less than a day in Kiev, a city whose charms—the
attendant was from Yalta—paled in comparison to those of the Black
Sea resorts. The question gave rise to lively debate in the compartment, but Kalugin had managed to lay it to rest by explaining: first,
that there were no hotel rooms in Odessa; second, that he liked
traveling in trains because one always met such charming people;
and third, that he'd heard Kiev was a beautiful city, well worth making a detour to see. This triumph of diplomacy, though somewhat
garbled in translation, had mollified the attendant, delighted the
three Kievans present, and flattered everybody. It had the unfortunate consequence, however, that retreat into silence became thereafter impossible, at least without giving serious offense. Kalugin was
promptly declared to be "kulturny," and presently someone produced a bottle of brandy. It wasn't until long after midnight, though
the effort of maintaining his cover had been utterly exhausting, that
he, or for that matter anyone, had been able to sleep.

Sleeping had been his second piece of stupidity.

He had dreamed—in retrospect it seemed almost inevitable—and
he had dreamed of Katya. Not the usual dream with Zaitsev, but a
dream he'd never had before, and not one dream but several: a

disjointed sequence of images from his past, some welcome, some not, like reflections in a badly fractured mirror. Awakened, around four, by voices and the sound of the compartment door slamming shut, he'd opened his eyes to find himself staring into the face of a now-unsmiling car attendant.

"Your papers. Now." The voice was flat, uncompromising, hostile; the language, not English as before, but Russian.

Russian? What the hell was going on?

"Ya ni panimayu." From instinct, or habit, he responded in halting, phrasebook Russian, repeating in English for clarification, "I don't understand."

"He doesn't understand. Sure." The attendant looked around the compartment. He was smiling unpleasantly, sharing his skepticism with the others. They were all awake, Kalugin saw, these friends of the previous evening, their eyes fixed accusingly on him, their faces utterly unfriendly. "At least not when he's awake, he doesn't. When he's asleep, however, he understands just fine."

He'd talked in his sleep. He could have kicked himself for not thinking, not guarding against this by staying awake. He'd talked *Russian* in his sleep, fluent colloquial Russian, just as he always did. And his traveling companions, hurt by his abuse of their friendship and trust, and furious at the way he'd made them all feel foolish, were not only outraged but deeply suspicious. An American who claimed to speak no Russian but actually spoke it like a native? One didn't have to look very far for an explanation of that.

"You're a spy." A woman in the corner supplied it. "A spy for the CIA."

Murmurs of assent from the others.

He had to do something.

Now.

Before these people got completely out of hand.

He reached under the seat for his bag, then stood up. Ignoring the other passengers, he fixed his eye on the car attendant, jerked his head in the direction of the corridor. This, the representative of officialdom, the man in uniform, was the one he needed to convince. The others, their cultural reflexes conditioned by centuries of obedience to men in uniform, would take their lead unquestioningly from him.

"I have something to say. But for your ears only . . ." Kalugin spoke to the attendant in Russian, adding after a pause and with a certain emphasis: "Comrade."

Silence. The attendant looked uneasy. That "comrade" had given him something to think about, it and the official ring to the phrase: "for your ears only." His right to command here had been tacitly challenged, and in consequence the instinct to bully was competing with an instinct to cover his ass.

"I will come with you," the man sitting opposite Kalugin suddenly announced to the attendant. "For your protection. In case he tries anything."

"You will stay where you are." Kalugin spoke with icy authority, fixed the man with an unblinking stare. "You will stay where you are, or you will find you have reason to regret it."

More silence. The man met Kalugin's stare for a moment, struggled to hold it, shrugged, and looked away.

Kalugin turned back to the attendant. "We will talk in your compartment. Tell these people to stay where they are."

Brief pause. The car attendant nodded. In what looked like an effort to retrieve lost face, he spoke to the man who'd offered to come with him. "Thank you, but I prefer to handle this myself. It would seem to be a matter that needs to be handled discreetly."

At the door, Kalugin turned back. "What I said to one applies to all. Stay put until I tell you otherwise."

The attendant's compartment was a narrow, pantrylike space at the end of the car. An upholstered bench seat ran across one wall. Beside the window was a fold-out table on which sat a samovar, aromatically steaming.

Kalugin plopped himself down on the bench, placing the carry-on bag beside him. He looked up at the car attendant.

"You could offer me tea . . . if you have a clean glass."

The attendant didn't move.

"You could offer *me* an explanation . . . if you have one."

Kalugin shrugged. "I'll offer you better than that."

"Oh?" The tone was guarded, but not indifferent; in the eyes a sudden gleam of interest, "What could you have to offer me?"

"Wait and I'll show you."

Kalugin opened the carry-on bag, rummaged inside it for his toilet case, a leather container, like a miniature valise, that snapped shut and zipped across the top. Opening it, he removed the articles inside, placing them one by one on the seat beside him and not so much as glancing at the car attendant. An old-fashioned cutthroat razor, a bowl of shaving soap, toothbrush, stick deodorant, toothpaste, brush, comb. Unfolding the razor and still not looking at the attendant, he cut a long slit in the waterproof lining of the case. Then he shut the razor, placed it on the seat, and inserted his hand in the slit.

"What do you think you're doing?" The attendant's voice rose in what, Kalugin guessed, must be simulated outrage. "If it's money you've got in there, I should warn you that attempting to bribe an official of the railways is a very serious offense."

"So you don't take bribes? That's unusual." Kalugin grinned at him without humor. He removed his KGB officer's ID from beneath the lining, shoved it under the attendant's nose.

"Take a look, official of the Railways . . . Lieutenant Grusha. Second Chief Directorate, Black Market and Racketeering Section. How lucky for you that you don't take bribes."

"Second Chief Directorate . . ." The car attendant took a step back. His whole manner had abruptly changed. He looked like a man who'd cracked a safe and found it harboring a cobra. "But the American passport? The visa?"

"Cover . . ." Kalugin shrugged. "An operation against the black market. I was posing as an American tourist, but thanks to the misfortune of talking in my sleep, I seem to have torn a hole in my cover. How much of a hole depends of course on you. If you're intelligent, no harm may come of it. If not . . ." He paused, subjected the attendant to an unfriendly stare. "It takes time and money to set up something like this. My superiors won't be pleased to see their efforts wasted."

"Your superiors won't be pleased?" The attendant showed a flash of spirit. "I think that mostly they won't be pleased with *you.*"

"That's true. But my mistake was inadvertent. Yours, if you make it, will be stupid."

Silence. The attendant was faced with an uncomfortable dilemma. Here was a man with two sets of papers, at least one of which had to be false. But since it was impossible to tell which one, what the issue reduced to, by a reasoning process instinctive to petty officials, was this: Which mistake would land one deeper in the shit—screwing up a KGB operation or failing to apprehend a foreign agent? This was not, on the face of it, an easy choice to make, but one of the alternatives offered a loophole, which Kalugin counted on the attendant's being smart enough to spot.

The attendant, having considered for a moment, vindicated Kalugin's judgment by making the bureaucratically correct decision.

"What do you want me to do?"

"First I need to see your papers. Domestic passport, *propiska,* work pass, the lot."

The passport contained the attendant's name and particulars, which Kalugin made a show of recording in his notebook. If his threat of KGB reprisals was to carry any weight, the KGB had to know—didn't it?—against whom to take its reprisals. The other documents, especially the *propiska,* or residence permit, were irrelevant to any purpose he could possibly have here, but demanding them, scrutinizing them with furrowed brow and an air of menace, was something the attendant would expect, something *he* would do if the roles were reversed. As any minor official knew, the proper response to an act of submission was a prompt and conspicuous dominance display.

"Good." Kalugin handed back the documents. "Now get back in there and pacify those people. Tell them that until we reach Kiev they're forbidden to leave the compartment. Tell them that if they have to leave it, for instance to answer a call of nature, they're strictly forbidden to speak to anyone. Failure to comply with these orders may result in charges of obstructing justice."

The attendant nodded, went back to the compartment. Kalugin, close behind, heard him repeat the instructions, heard him add, in a kind of admonitory whisper: "KGB."

For the rest of the journey Kalugin had stood in the corridor. In those more than two hours no one had ventured out. It appeared that his fellow passengers, at least, had taken at face value the warning given them by the car attendant. The attendant himself, however, was a question mark. Given that he'd had time to reflect, he might now, if he hadn't before, have spotted a way through the horns of his dilemma. A quiet call ahead would cover his ass both ways, allow the station authorities, before the train arrived, to check on this questionable lieutenant with KGB headquarters in Kiev. If he checked out, no harm would have been done; if he didn't, the attendant would be spared the embarrassment, and worse, of having been duped by an American agent. The more Kalugin had considered this possibility, the less likely it had seemed that the attendant could fail to spot it. It was surely what anyone halfway intelligent would have done. It might also explain, moreover, why a short time after relaying Kalugin's instructions to the others, the attendant had emerged from his cubbyhole and headed up toward the front of the train. When Kalugin had asked where he was going he'd responded with noticeable self-assurance:

"I don't hinder you in the performance of your duties, Comrade. Don't hinder me in the performance of mine."

He'd returned looking pleased with himself.

They were at the river now, reducing speed for their arrival. In another five minutes they'd be in the station.

It was no time to be taking chances.

Kalugin walked up to the attendant's compartment. He knocked softly.

"Oh, it's you." The attendant's manner had undergone a subtle alteration. No longer deferential, he seemed now almost patronizing. "What do you want?"

"A word in your ear, Comrade, if you please."

"Come in then." The car attendant sighed, turned back into the compartment. "We're about to arrive, so make it quick. I've work to do."

When Kalugin hit him, a short clubbing chop to the side of the neck, delivered with the edge of the hand, the attendant didn't make a sound. His eyes rolled upward, his knees buckled. Kalugin caught him as he slid to the floor, heaved him on to the bench seat, facedown, checked to make sure he was breathing.

He was. This was something of a relief. The blow he'd received wasn't normally a killer, but accidents sometimes happened. One didn't want to add, to risks already present, that of being charged with murder. Nor did one want on one's conscience the death of an essentially innocent man.

But restraint was another matter entirely. One needed something to restrain him with. A belt, for instance. Luckily the attendant himself was wearing one. Kalugin removed it, crossed his victim's arms behind his back, ran the belt around them and his chest, and, pulling it as tight as he could, buckled it firmly. It wouldn't hold for long, but with luck it wouldn't need to. Silence was another a requirement. Kalugin took a handkerchief (clean) from the carry-on bag, stuffed it into the attendant's mouth, checked to make sure he was breathing. Then he removed the attendant's shoes. Finally, as an afterthought, he unbuttoned the man's trousers and pulled them down around his ankles. As a method of hobbling this fell short of ideal, but in the short run it would probably work. There was no more effective deterrent to action than the prospect of looking a total fool.

Now to disguise himself a little . . . Without the attendant to help with identification, they'd have to depend on a physical description. Nobody, even a trained observer with the descriptive powers of a Pushkin, could paint a verbal portrait accurate enough to use as the basis for making an arrest. And since Kalugin's physical attributes—medium height, brown hair, gray eyes—were shared by half the male population of Kiev, the attendant's efforts at a verbal portrait would have to have been made in terms of clothes. They'd be looking for someone in Levi's, Nikes, an Italian leather jacket. The Levi's he could get away with, in a pinch. They were common in Kiev, or had been the last time he was here. The jacket would have to go—sadly, for it had cost him a bundle. So would the Nikes.

The conductor's shoes were lace-ups, clodhoppers, in some kind of black synthetic leather. They were half a size large, but when he had a chance, Kalugin thought, he could fix that with an extra pair of socks. Better this way, at any rate, than half a size too small . . . He inspected himself in the mirror on the wall of the compartment. Still too foreign. It was the shirt, he decided; it was pure Egyptian cotton and far too stylish to be keeping company with synthetic leather shoes. He needed to cover it up with something, but what? He had a sweater in his bag, but it, being cashmere, would merely aggravate the problem. What then? The conductor's off-duty jacket was hanging on a peg beside the mirror. A wind cheater in some shiny gray fabric, it was cheap, undistinctive, obviously Russian, just what was wanted. He put it on, left his own jacket on the peg. It was far more than a fair exchange, he thought. At least the attendant would get something for his headache.

He let himself out of the compartment, thankful that there was no one in the corridor to see him, started to move up the train.

He knew he was lost if they checked every passenger's papers, but probably they wouldn't. It would take too long, for one thing, and unless—highly unlikely—the system had been changed in the last twelve years, it would also present formidable logistical problems. Where, for instance, would they run such a check? There was no ticket collection at the gate, nor indeed any gate to collect tickets *at*. Passengers just got off the train, swept in a kind of wave along the platform, poured down the broad marble steps to the terminal's main hall, then stampeded for trolley buses, metro, or taxis. Stemming this flow to check passports would pose quite a problem in crowd control, and given the low esteem in which the KGB was held by the public, might very well cause a minor riot. Since *perestroika,* he'd heard, the KGB kept a lower profile. They would try to spot him in the crowd, he guessed, waylay him discreetly and whisk him away.

When the train pulled up at the platform, he was in the corridor of the second car from the front, four cars up from his original compartment. He shouldn't, he figured, be among the first passengers off; that would make him needlessly conspicuous. To avoid awkward encounters, on the other hand, he should stay ahead of his former traveling companions. Above all he needed to avoid looking furtive, like a man looking out for the police.

It was hard, all the same, to keep from hanging back or hurrying, keep his eyes from wandering, from scanning, furtively, the platform up ahead. Pressure from other passengers—"Let's not be blocking the corridor, young man. People are trying to get off this train"— forced him to exit sooner than he'd wanted. He was in the first wave to reach the head of the platform. He felt vulnerable, exposed, almost naked.

They were there, too, just as he'd expected. Two of them at the head of the platform, two more at the top of the stairs. They weren't in any ordinary way conspicuous, no regulation heavies in felt hats and trenchcoats. One of them, indeed, the one nearest the engine at the head of the platform, was dressed more or less as Kalugin had been, in Levi's, sneakers, and a soft leather jacket. You could almost have thought he was meeting someone, waiting eagerly for a wife or girlfriend. Except, Kalugin thought, that he wasn't eager. He didn't look eagerly down the platform, avid for a glimpse of familiar features. Instead he restricted his looking to the nearest few feet of foreground. There was something too systematic, moreover, in the way his eyes flicked from one face to another. He was looking for someone he *didn't* know, checking particulars against a mental list. Male, Caucasian, early thirties, medium height, brown hair, gray eyes; Levi's, sneakers, black leather jacket. Kalugin, coming into range, saw the eyes flick onto him, scan up and down, from the face to the feet, away . . . then back again, narrowing.

You did not look away. Elementary principle this, familiar from the schoolroom: trying to avoid the teacher's gaze merely invited his attention. But there was danger, on the other hand, in meeting it too boldly. He made himself hold the appraising stare a moment, then, with apparent indifference, he let it drop. He kept walking, heart in mouth, expecting at any moment the peremptory summons, sharp, accusing: "*Ty,* you . . . Over here . . . Now!"

It didn't come.

He was through. Over that hurdle at least. There'd be others to come, though. More than one, no doubt. Had he been in charge of this search, he thought, he'd have set up a series of filters, posted his men at intervals between platforms and the exit, stationed them at the tram stops and taxi lines outside. He shouldn't count himself safe, therefore, until he was well clear of the station. And not even then, probably; because someone, before too much longer, was going to discover the car attendant.

The two KGB men at the head of the stairs were hardly bothering to conceal their purpose. One of them had a walkie-talkie, from which there issued short bursts of Russian punctuated by crackles of static. Kalugin, figuring that someone watching and listening had less attention to spare than someone simply watching, steered closer to him than his colleague. He felt it was now legitimate, moreover, since these two were clearly cops of some kind, to show curiosity about them. Indeed, he thought, it would be almost suspicious not to. Up in front, at any rate, heads were swiveling as the exiting passengers returned, with more or less unanimous hostility, the stares of appraisal to which they subjected. From behind Kalugin came mutters of resentment: "KGB" . . . "Bad news for some poor sucker" . . . "Rather him than me" . . . "Bastards." As he drew level with the man with the walkie-talkie, Kalugin made eye contact, held it for a moment.

He held it, perhaps, a fraction too long. Or maybe like so many policemen, the man had a nose for uneasiness or guilt. Either way, he seemed to sense something. He lowered the walkie-talkie, started toward Kalugin.

Kalugin froze, tugged by conflicting instincts. Should he stand his ground and bluff it out, or bolt? Before he could make a choice, however, there issued from the walkie-talkie, through the crackle of static, a terse, triumphant message: "Got him!" And at that exact moment a man in Levi's and a black leather jacket came plunging through the crowd toward them, scattering passengers in his wake. Spotting the man with the walkie-talkie he cut sharply right, sprinted toward the other staircase.

Kalugin never learned who he was. Some wrongdoer, no doubt, maybe a black marketeer, who'd chosen the wrong outfit to travel in. Accosted by a KGB officer and faced, as he thought, with the prospect of arrest, he must have decided to run for it. But whoever he was, he saved Kalugin. The man with the walkie-talkie and his cohort gave chase, as did their colleagues at the foot of the stairs. The latter, indeed, came barreling up the marble staircase, taking the worn steps three at a time and elbowing people out of their way. And Kalugin, almost light-headed with relief, was able to descend unmolested. When he reached the main concourse he headed for the men's rooms, where, in the privacy of a stall, he abandoned the windcheater and exchanged his Egyptian cotton shirt for a T-shirt more in harmony with the car attendant's shoes. Then it was back to the main concourse and out, past the statue of Lenin, to the street.

Three minutes later he was in Boulevard Taras Schevchenko, heading on foot toward Kreschatik. It was then eight-fifteen.

That gave him three hours and forty-five minutes.

CHAPTER FORTY-TWO

(Kiev, Ukrainian SSR. September 15, 1990)

EXCEPT FOR THE FLAGS, THE CITY WAS THE SAME AS HE REMEMBERED. There were still flower sellers outside the station, still chestnuts, leaves not quite turning yet, lining the streets and boulevards. At the head of Taras Schevchenko (where instead of making directly for Kreschatik, he'd kept on for a while, prompted by some instinct for indirection, before turning left toward the river) the bronze Lenin on his pedestal of granite still surveyed, with a fatherly, ironic eye, the comings and goings of his people. In the streets of Pechersk there was still the same insistence on color; the buildings, disdaining the plain brick and concrete of London, stuccoed and painted: pale pink, saffron, ochre for the walls, white or cream for the trim. In the squares and gardens where babushkas, plying brooms, lavished their domestic instincts on the city, there were still the same splashing fountains, the same squadrons of pigeons disputing rights to food, the same neat circles and rectangles of grass carefully protected by low white railings.

It was all the same, except for the flags.

The flags astonished him. Everywhere, any place you looked, were the blue-and-yellow Ukrainian colors: fluttering on the masts of public buildings, draped from the upper windows of houses, fastened to sticks and sold on street corners, worn as lapel pins or ribbon buttonholes. Here and there, of course, you could still spot red Soviet banners, but today at least they seemed a tiny minority, straggling survivors of an endangered species, stubborn remnants of a crumbling status quo. He'd wondered what Benko and the Knights of Vladimir, always supposing they had seen it, had made of this explosion of blue and yellow, this amazing expression of patriotism as color. Maybe they *hadn't* seen it. Maybe they were still quarantined, holed up somewhere in their safe house. Maybe they hadn't even made it to Kiev. Or maybe, he'd thought, they'd seen it but hadn't found it amazing. They hadn't been here before, after all, hadn't lived here in the seventies when flying the flag had been frowned on if not banned, or in Stalin's day when even a lapel pin could win you a trip to the gulag or a bullet in the back of the head. So perhaps they hadn't grasped what they were seeing: how completely the blue and yellow had swallowed up the red.

But if they had grasped it, he'd thought, they must surely have grasped something else: that their enterprise served no conceivable purpose; that since there *existed* a Ukrainian nationalist movement with the depth and momentum manifested here, acts of terror to jolt it into motion (such acts, at least, as *they* had been planning) were irrelevant to the point of frivolity; they would no more influence the course of events than hand grenades dropped into it would alter the course of the Dnieper.

They *would* have grasped it, he'd thought. Even they couldn't be that blind. And if they hadn't, Zaitsev would have. Zaitsev, seeing the flags, the thousands of people already gathering, would have known at once that this was history speaking. So rather than risk letting Benko and the Knights read what was clearly spelled out—not on any figurative wall, but literally, on placards in Kreschatik—he'd no doubt kept them away from all this. He'd kept them in a cellar, perhaps, rehearsing: going over street plans, memorizing timetables, practicing with detonators and timing devices.

Or else he'd gotten tired of it and killed them.

But in any case, the Knights weren't important right now. What *was* important was calling the police.

He was starting to worry that he'd left it too late.

The first two hours he had spent reconnoitering, trying to find out about security arrangements, checking points of access to the square. At ten it had still been open to motor traffic, but around eleven, he'd learned, it would be cleared of all except official vehicles—police cars and TV equipment vans—and barricades would go up at the exits. He'd gathered this, in the course of purchasing a volume of Chekhov, from the owner of a sidewalk bookstall, who based her information, she'd said, on what had always happened in the past, most recently at the rally held here in April to mark the anniversary of Chernobyl. If she was right and they did what they'd done in the past, as given the inertia of the system there was every reason to believe they would, it meant that Zaitsev would wait until after eleven before attempting to plant his bomb.

That was when Kalugin would nail him.

He hoped.

Chance, from the start, had told him it was crazy. What did he figure to do? she'd demanded. Wander around and hope to get lucky? In a city of more than two million, hope against hope to stumble upon one? It was madness, she'd argued, utter madness, especially given the lack of time. In three and three-quarter *months,* perhaps; but three and three-quarter *hours?* Plus you had to reckon with timing devices. The Pan Am disaster was a case in point. A suitcase loaded in Athens or Cairo had exploded over Scotland more than half a day later. Zaitsev could be safely back in Geneva before his bomb brought chaos to Kiev.

Kalugin had disagreed.

You had to reason this coldly, he'd argued; not indulging in wishful thinking, but also not giving in to premature despair. If you looked at this from *their* perspective, considered the problem in practical terms, then most, if not all, the features of their plan could be deduced from its intended outcome.

This bomb was going to be very big. That, it had seemed to him, was the crucial given. *Hundreds* dead, Rosenthal's scenario had specified. And even allowing for overstatement, this argued something orders of magnitude bigger than a man alone could lug around (wrapped up as a parcel perhaps) and deposit in, say, a garbage container. It would furthermore have to be exploded *outside,* right in the middle of the crowd. Setting it off in a nearby building, unless you used literally tons of explosive (making the building itself the bomb) would blanket the impact, not enhance it. But if you set it off outside, you not only had to make it big, you also had to confine it. Blast by itself wouldn't kill hundreds; to accomplish that you needed shrapnel. So added to the problem of size—hence of concealment and transportation—was the problem of finding a suitable container. You needed, in other words, a car or a van.

But using a van created other problems. Kreshchatik was the busiest street in Kiev. Even at the best of times parking was restricted. If you wanted to leave a vanload of explosive at the point where it would do most damage—adjacent, that was, to the speakers' platform—you would need to obtain a special permit (for instance, to transport TV equipment) and, since you would have to show it to someone, to arrive after the square had been closed to normal traffic. This argued that Zaitsev *wouldn't* be home in Geneva, and he, Kalugin, *wouldn't* be just wandering around, hoping to stumble upon him. At some time after eleven Zaitsev would be parking his bomb, probably disguised as a TV equipment van, near the platform in the October Revolution Square. And Kalugin would be there to nail him.

It was simply a question of watching for the vehicle.

Simply.

Back in Ireland, when he'd still been euphoric at knowing that Zaitsev was at last within his reach, it had all seemed simple enough. A whole lot simpler than it did here and now. Back then (given that no alternative seemed to offer), each step of this logic had seemed solid and compelling. Here and now, however—here being the ice-cream café on Kreschatik, now being twenty minutes to eleven— doubts were beginning to gather.

Chance hadn't placed much confidence in logic. Logic, as she'd tartly observed, was mostly the art of going wrong with confidence. Suppose his assumptions were wrong? Suppose he'd overlooked something? Did he really, seriously mean to entrust, to some rickety structure of premise and conclusion, the lives and futures of hundreds of people? The moment he got to Odessa, she'd insisted, the moment he could contact them directly, without any risk of his message being sidetracked, he had to call in the police.

And he hadn't disagreed, not openly, mostly because he'd known that morally at least she was right. He wasn't entitled, in pursuing a private vengeance, to roll the dice with other people's lives. But actually, he'd thought, it wasn't much of a gamble. Police assistance wouldn't be needed. *He* would find Zaitsev, take care of him himself. Besides, Chance hadn't known that the would-be bomber *was* Zaitsev. And if she had, she wouldn't have understood . . . For half his life he, Kalugin, had lived for the moment when Zaitsev would recognize, in the man about to kill him, the boy he had shamed so many years ago. He had sacrificed everything for this, embraced an occupation he despised, endured the loneliness of exile. He had pointed his life like a rifle at this one target. Was it reasonable to expect him now to forgo pulling the trigger? This was owed to him, he'd told himself, and owed to Katya. It was owed to both of them for what they had suffered.

He still felt that way. But what had changed was his confidence. Chance had been right, he now saw, about assumptions. He *had* overlooked something. Something important.

The crowds.

He ought to have known. He'd seen them on TV—hadn't he?— images of that spreading revolution which, in a matter of weeks, had changed the political face of Europe: the massive gatherings in Vilnius and Riga, the hundreds of thousands in Wenceslas Square. But somehow he'd hadn't expected them here. What "an independence rally" had conjured for him here were images from the remoter past: a couple of hundred glum-looking dissidents waiting forlornly to be arrested. This time, as the flags should have warned him, it was different. When he'd last looked, half an hour ago, there must have been ten thousand people in the square, with more flooding in every minute. Speakers on soapboxes, haranguing their audiences. Sellers of lemonade, cakes, and kvass. Dancers in Ukrainian dress. Musicians leading groups in song. Entertainments breaking out, impromptu, all over. Strangers talking and laughing together because for these hours they would not be strangers. Everyone exuberant, optimistic, joyful.

One wasn't entitled to take risks with these lives.

And the risks, it was clear now, were not minimal. The square covered a sizable area. Perhaps, in ordinary conditions, hoping to spot someone there was feasible, but now, with this turbulent mass, it looked hopeless. Unless he saw Zaitsev actually parking, the odds were he would miss him altogether. And if he missed him, how was he to find the van (or car, or truck) in which the bomb was hidden? Zaitsev would hardly advertise, stick the bomb in plain view in a crate marked, helpfully: Danger/Explosive. He would hide it somehow, wire it to the chassis, or cache it under the floorboards. And he, Kalugin, could hardly go from one vehicle to another, openly checking. And even if he managed to find it, he wondered, what was he going to do then?

He wasn't an expert in explosives. He didn't know the first thing, in fact, about disarming bombs. He would have to get help. And the police, of course, would waste time asking questions. They'd have to call in bomb disposal experts, and that would take more time. There might not be that much. He needed to call the police. He needed to call them right now. He ought to have done it hours ago.

He prayed he hadn't left it too late.

It took him half an hour to find a call box.

The problem wasn't finding one, but finding one not occupied, no line of callers waiting to use it. Kreschatik itself was hopeless. Far too many people, most of them, it seemed, needing a phone. Kirov Street wasn't much better; no empty call boxes there. Heroes of the Revolution had fewer people but no call boxes, none visible, at least, from the corner of Kreschatik. Desperate now, he recrossed Kreschatik, cut through the archway into Engels Street, headed for the residential area beyond it. Surely somewhere in this city was a public telephone with fewer than ten people waiting in line? He could have tried cutting in, he realized, at one of the booths on Kirov or Kreschatik, claiming (quite truthfully) an emergency need, but that would have earned him a lot of unwanted attention. Call boxes were not that private, and Soviet citizens, especially the women, were not noted for minding their own business. He hadn't wanted to find himself explaining to a crowd this bomb threat he just got through reporting.

When he found what he needed, on a side street off Engels, it was ten minutes after eleven. A call box with a man just about to hang up, and only one person, a woman, waiting.

As Kalugin approached, the man hung up. Before the woman could replace him, Kalugin intercepted, flashing his KGB identity card.

"Excuse me, Comrade. I need this phone. Official business. An emergency. It shouldn't take more than a minute."

She inspected him for a moment with narrowed eyes, shrugged, stepped aside. But not very far aside, he noted. When he dialed the police emergency number she was hovering well within earshot.

He stuck his head outside the booth.

"If you don't mind, Comrade, this call is confidential."

She shrugged again, moved a little farther off.

The operator, a woman, came on the line.

"What is your emergency, please?"

"I wish to report a bomb threat."

Even to his ears this sounded odd. Was he *reporting* the threat or *making* it? This ambiguity, however, seemed lost on the operator.

"Hold the line, please, while I transfer you."

"I don't want to be transferred." Or left on hold while you put a trace on the call. "I want to report a bomb threat. It's urgent."

"If it's urgent"—placidly—"I suggest you stop wasting time. My job is not to take messages, it's to route calls to the appropriate emergency service."

Click.

He'd stay on no more than two minutes, he thought. They couldn't trace that quickly. But longer might be dangerous and was certainly unnecessary. He could tell them everything in twenty seconds.

Transferring him took half a minute.

Involved some suspicious-sounding clicks.

"What is your name and where are you calling from?" A man's voice, calm, the tone slightly bored.

"That's irrelevant. What isn't is this. Sometime shortly after twelve noon today, that's to say during the independence rally, a bomb will be exploded in October Revolution Square. I don't know where, exactly, but my guess would be in a parked car or a van. Unless it's found and removed, it will kill a great number of people. I can't give you any more detailed information, but please believe me this is not a hoax."

Silence. His watch said it lasted five seconds. It seemed longer.

"Did you hear what I said?"

"I heard it." Another pause, shorter this time. "But I have to inform you, Comrade, that anonymous phone calls don't inspire much trust. Unless you tell us who you are, explain how you came by your information, you can hardly expect us to act on it. Please state your name in full, your domestic passport number, your precise location at this moment."

Kalugin hung up.

The response had been inevitable, he supposed. Police were the same everywhere. The nature of the work shaped the nature of the animal, and the nature thus shaped was above all untrusting. Statements anonymously volunteered were not to be taken at face value; the identity of the messenger determined, more than did anything else, the credibility of the message. Any experienced policeman knew, for instance, that ninety percent of all bomb threats were hoaxes, but that people who amused themselves with that kind of joke were, whatever their motive, probably safer behind bars. In addition, of course, there'd been that business on the train. Whoever had taken his call would have known that somewhere at large in the city was a man, fluent in Russian and Ukrainian, whose papers claimed he was a KGB officer but who more than likely was a foreign agent. What more natural than to make a connection, to treat this call as a case of Greeks bearing gifts?

But they couldn't risk ignoring it, could they? Surely they *had* to act on it. And no doubt they would, he thought, in some fashion. But at this late hour their options were limited. In theory they ought to have cleared the square, conducted a systematic search, but the practical implications were daunting. You didn't just *move* tens of thousands of protesters, not when *you* represented the system *they* were there to protest against. Imagine the outrage if you cleared the square and the threat—as the probabilities suggested it would—turned out to be phony. What they'd do, no doubt, was alert the bomb squad, then sprinkle the square and the neighboring streets with plainclothes officers all unobtrusively searching. And maybe they'd find it and maybe they wouldn't. But if they didn't, he thought, hundreds of people would be killed. And he would be responsible. Because he had called too late, put his own wishes first, trusted too much in his own misguided logic, all those deaths would be on his conscience.

"Did I hear you say something about a bomb?"

Christ. The woman must have eavesdropped after all. Turning, he confronted her chilly stare. She was heavyset, thick-limbed, her round red face wrapped in a headscarf. From under black eyebrows shrewd eyes glinted suspiciously. The tone, he noted, was hardly polite, the manner verging on belligerent.

"You did not." He shook his head, eyed her coldly. "But you did hear me say that my call was confidential. I'm afraid I must ask you, Comrade, not to interfere in official business."

She was not buying this, neither the message nor the tone. She came closer, stepped in front of him as if to bar his way. Jesus, he thought, this was all he needed, some officious bitch making a public scene.

"You dialed zero two," she accused, "the police emergency number. Don't try to deny it, I *saw* you. And I heard you say something about a bomb threat."

"You're mistaken. I'm obliged to remind you, moreover, that you're speaking to an officer of the KGB. Please step out of my way, Comrade. I assume you don't wish to be charged with obstruction?"

She didn't move.

"Your papers may say you're KGB. But the radio says a that man of your description assaulted a car attendant on the eight o'clock train from Odessa. The radio says also that this man, who's suspected of being an American spy, was using forged KGB papers." She smiled nastily. "I think it's my duty to call the police, see what *they* have to say about your papers."

Kalugin considered for a moment. Something would have to be done about this cow. Browbeating clearly wasn't going to work. His eyes flicked up and down the street. There were people farther up,

less than fifty meters away, but they were not, or not obviously, paying attention to him. In any case, he really had no choice.

He hit her in the solar plexus.

The punch was solid, all his weight behind it, and it caught her
unprepared. The air came out of her in an audible rush. She doubled
up, and as she did so, he caught her, pulled her toward him and into
the phone booth. She sank to her knees, gasping and retching. He
stuck his head out of the booth, glanced swiftly in both directions.
Still no one seemed to be paying attention.

He stepped around her, inspected her for a moment. She was still
gagging, clasping her stomach. She must have been raised on a farm,
he thought; obviously she had the strength of a horse. In fifteen or
twenty seconds, half a minute at most, she'd have got enough breath
back to start a racket. He needed much more time than that.

He purchased it with a blow to the side of her neck, chopped
downward hard with the edge of his hand. Her head snapped sideways and her eyes rolled upward. She slid to the floor without a
sound. As he left her there, he wondered how badly he had hurt her,
and by some sideways skip of the imagination found himself thinking
of Katya.

Now he was making war on women.

Some Lancelot.

He started for Engels Street, walking briskly, taking care not to
glance back, but listening carefully for cries of discovery, any sound
of imminent pursuit. As he turned the corner into Engels Street, his
watch told him it was twenty past eleven.

Behind him, in the street he'd just left, someone started shouting.

CHAPTER FORTY-THREE

(Kiev, Ukrainian SSR. September 15, 1990)

WHAT TO DO?

Instinct told him to bolt, sprint up the street and through the archway, attempt to conceal himself in the crowds on Kreschatik. Reason told him this wouldn't work; if he ran he would just draw attention to himself, add, no doubt, to the ranks of his pursuers. What he needed was somewhere to hide. He looked around. To his right was a short flight of steps leading into an apartment building. Sprinting up it, three steps at a time, he found himself in a gloomy foyer. It was tiled in marble but totally unfurnished, with an elevator shaft opposite the entrance and next to it, leading off to the right, a staircase. Standing by the elevator doors was an elderly woman. She was carrying a violin case, supporting herself with a cane. He noticed one of her ankles was bandaged.

"You seem to be in a hurry."

Not phrased as a question, but plainly interrogative. Jesus, he thought. Did they always have to be busybodies? He scouted the notion of ignoring her, decided against. If he did, she might start yelling.

"Not really." He forced himself to smile. "It's my normal life tempo. *Molto allegro.* Put it down to youthful exuberance."

"Ah . . ." Wisp of ironic smile. "And who, Mr. Youthful Exuberance, are you *not* in a hurry to see?"

Who indeed? Think of a Ukrainian name. A *common* Ukrainian name. His mind was a blank, then a word popped into it.

"Martov . . . Viktor Martov." Not Ukrainian but better than nothing.

"Martov . . . Viktor Martov." She frowned, apparently in

thought, then shook her head. "No Martov here, Viktor or otherwise."

"You wouldn't know him," he improvised. "He's a visitor, a guest.
Staying with some people on the second floor. I forget their name.
Krav something or other, I think . . . Kravchuk, Kravchenko." He
pantomimed an effort at recollection. "I remember it begins with a
K."

"Kyrilenko?" she offered.

"Kyrilenko . . . that's it."

"No Kyrilenko here, either. Not on the second floor, nor the third.
Not on any floor in fact." She cocked her head, grinning, enjoying
her triumph. "Not a very accomplished liar, are you? That was quite
an obvious trap. My late husband, a *very* accomplished liar, would
never have fallen for anything like that. You had to be subtle to catch
him."

She paused, inspected Kalugin with an amused, appraising glance.
She must have been lovely once, he thought: huge gray eyes, chis-
eled, aristocratic features, a delicate, slender neck. A delicate neck,
he sincerely hoped, he wouldn't shortly find himself having to break.

"You look honest enough, but you're obviously running from
something. What are you? A criminal of some kind or other?" She
lowered her voice to a melodramatic whisper. "A *desperate* criminal?"

"Desperate is right." He nodded. "A desperate man with a talent
for violence, but no real wish to inflict it on you."

"Threatening me now." This seemed almost to amuse her. "It
won't do you the least bit of good. I'm far too old to be frightened."
She paused, considered. "I'll tell you what I'll do, though. I'll make
you a bargain."

Make him a bargain? This was not happening, he thought, this
absolutely was not happening. But outside in the street, reminding
him that it *was* happening, he heard people calling out to one another: "He's got to be around here somewhere. Maybe hiding in one
of these apartments."

Then footsteps approached the entrance.

He looked around wildly for somewhere to hide.

"Over there!" she hissed. "The staircase. Quick!"

Three strides took him to the foot of the stairs. As he started up,
the foyer door banged open.

He froze. The staircase was marble, no carpet. If he moved, he'd
be heard. For now a corner screened him from whomever had en-

tered, but if the newcomer—the footsteps sounded like a man's—
took ten paces forward, this hiding place would be clearly visible.
Kalugin could only crouch and hold his breath, trusting to luck and
this extraordinary woman.

Footsteps approached a few paces, halted.

"Hey, Granny." A man's voice, rough and peremptory. "Did you
happen to see anyone come in?"

Pause.

Slowly she turned, her eyes sweeping past Kalugin, to confront the
source of this insolence. Coldly she inspected the newcomer. She
had, Kalugin thought, amazing presence, had obviously once been on
the stage.

"Who are you calling granny, flatfoot? Didn't your mother teach
you any manners?"

The man—to judge from her "flatfoot," a cop—advanced a few
more paces. Another two or three, to judge from the sound, would
bring him to where, if he turned his head, he would instantly spot
Kalugin. Kalugin tensed himself for the encounter. Things were
starting to get hopeless. One startled cop he could no doubt deal
with, but after he'd dealt with him, what then?

"I don't have time for manners just now. I'm after a dangerous
criminal, a fugitive from justice."

"Believe me, there is *always* time for manners." She paused. It was
easy to see what was coming. "What's he wanted for, this criminal of
yours?"

Kalugin held his breath. When she heard what he'd done to the
woman in the phone booth, she wouldn't want to protect him any
longer. He tensed himself for the inevitable. Flight was not an option
here; it would have to be fight.

"He's a spy, a suspected American provocateur. Guilty of assault
and impersonating a government official."

Another pause. She gave a dry laugh.

"Guilty of impersonating a government official. If that's a crime,
you're *all* guilty." She paused. "I haven't seen him."

He sounded unconvinced. "You haven't seen *anyone?* Are you
sure?"

"Do I look blind? Of course I'm sure. I haven't seen a soul. No
one but you in the last ten minutes." She paused, added with some
asperity, "Which is how long I've been standing here waiting for the
elevator. If you want to talk about criminal, let's talk about that."

"I don't have time to talk . . ." Wearily.

"I know," she cut in. "You told me. You're in hot pursuit of a fugitive from justice. You don't have time to talk, you don't have time for manners. Yours must be a very limited existence."

It seemed the policeman could think of no suitable response. There was silence, shuffling, then:

"Yes, well . . . Thank you for your cooperation." Heavily sarcastic.

Then footsteps retreating, the door opening and banging shut, then silence.

She turned, with a sort of flourish, to Kalugin.

"So much for him . . . We were speaking of a bargain. I've done my part."

"You did. I'm very grateful." He descended to the foyer. "May I ask you why?"

She shrugged. "I'm not sure. Instinct maybe. I don't like flatfeet, especially when they call me 'granny,' and yours seems a reasonably honorable face." She paused, subjected him to a sudden penetrating look. "Who are you running away from, Chekists?"

"Among others."

Nothing could have been more indicative of her political sympathies, he thought, than her use of that pejorative name for the service that had formerly employed him.

"Then I've no doubt my instinct was right. But anyhow, that's beside the point. I did what I did and you owe me a debt. The question is, are you going to pay?"

He hesitated. "I don't have much time. What is it you want?"

"I can't manage the stairs by myself, not with a bad ankle, and the elevator, clearly, is taking a vacation. I need someone to help me to my apartment." She paused. Her gaze was clear and steady. She wasn't pleading, merely stating facts. "It's on the next floor, but I'm rather slow, I'm afraid. I should think it will take you about five minutes."

Five minutes . . . And it must be close to eleven-thirty. The square had been cleared now for half an hour. And every minute wasted reduced his chances of finding Zaitsev. But a lot of minutes had been wasted already. By now Zaitsev's bomb could already have been planted. This woman, moreover, had taken a considerable risk for him; but for her, he might have been arrested. He was struck suddenly by how fragile she was, how tired she looked. What she was asking of him wasn't, it was clear, some mere coquettish whim. A kind of fatalism came over him. He had botched this, botched it completely. Nothing but errors from start to finish. If it was also an error to help someone who'd helped him, just how much, at this point, could one more error matter?

He said, "I'll be happy to help you."

"Take my arm then." She handed him the violin case. "And remember, I'm old and frail. So, Mr. Youthful Exuberance, *molto adagio.*"

It took at least five minutes to get her to her apartment. By the time she'd fumbled through various pockets for her keys, found them, negotiated the double locks that secured the front door, it was eleven thirty-six. As he turned to leave, she stopped him.

"Better come in for a minute."

He shook his head. "Thank you, but I don't have time. I'm very grateful . . ."

"I'm not suggesting tea and conversation"—cutting him off with considerable asperity—"but common sense, which you seem to lack. You can see the street from my front window. Maybe there are flat-feet still lurking."

It made sense. Better to waste another minute than dash headlong into the arms of the police. He nodded his thanks, followed her into the apartment. It was dark, to his taste overfurnished, crammed with furniture, bric-a-brac, and books. He noticed several framed photographs, most of them of her in theatrical costume. He'd been right then; she *had* been an actress or a singer, and also very beautiful. One of the photos was a studio portrait of a man in doublet and tights, tall and rather self-consciously handsome.

"My husband as Don Giovanni." It appeared she'd noticed him looking. "If ever there was type casting, that was it. A magnificent baritone, also systematically unfaithful. Actually a philandering pig. I'm ashamed of it now, but I was crazy about him."

She crossed over to the window. "If I stick my head out of here, I can see the whole street in both directions. It's better *I* do it. Some cop might take a notion to look up."

He nodded agreement. She raised the sash, pushed aside the muslin curtain.

"It seems clear. On this side at least. The other side you can't see too well through the trees. I don't hear any shouting, though. I think they've gone."

She was just about to turn away from the window when she stopped. Her attention had been caught by something in the street.

Her eyes widened. "That's very odd."

"What's odd?"

"That man down there. It was most extraordinary. He seemed to be just walking along. Then suddenly, quite deliberately, he dropped something—it looked like his keys—and kicked them into the drain."

"Keys?" Kalugin stared. "What kind of keys?"

"How should I know?" She shrugged. "House keys, safe keys, car keys. I'm sure they were keys, though. They were on a ring."

Keys? Someone had deliberately dropped keys in the gutter? *Car* keys? Kalugin went over to join her at the window.

"That's him." She pointed to a figure passing below the window, a tall thin man in a polo neck sweater and sportcoat. Seen from above, his head was narrow, balding on top, the scalp showing palely through wisps of hair. "He dropped the keys in that drain behind him. I didn't see him take them out of his pocket, so he must have had them in his hand already and then just casually let them fall. But it had to be deliberate, because when they fell they got caught in the grating and he stopped to nudge them through with his foot."

She paused and turned to face Kalugin, her eyes alight with mischief and pleasure.

"There's obviously a story here, some fascinating scandal. That man just murdered his mistress, perhaps. Locked the body in a trunk and sent it by rail to Siberia. Now he's attempting to cover his tracks."

Car keys. . . . Something clicked in Kalugin's mind. Someone had locked his car and deliberately thrown away the keys. There *was* a story here, he thought, but it had nothing to do with cut-up mistresses in trunks.

He leaned out of the window, called down: "You down there . . . Comrade. I believe you dropped something."

The man stopped dead. He turned to look, first behind, then up. When his gaze met Kalugin's there was a moment of blankness, then a frown of puzzlement, then recognition, then alarm.

On Kalugin's side there was no doubt at all. It was the face he'd first seen in a hallway of the country house in Sussex. The face of the man who'd lectured them on explosives. Leonid the Handholder. Alexandr Zaitsev.

On both sides there was an instant of indecision. Then Zaitsev broke into a loping run. After four or five steps he looked back over his shoulder, as if to confirm that his eyes had not deceived him, but by then there was only the woman at the window. Kalugin was already out of the apartment, halfway across the hall outside.

It seemed to him he had never moved so fast or taken so long to cover so short a distance. His descent to the street was a single surge of acceleration. He took the hallway at a dead run, the stairs three and four at a time, not breaking stride, constantly on the edge of falling, but somehow managing to keep his feet. Then he was out across the foyer, bursting through the door at the entrance, sidestepping a woman coming up the steps. He was in the street in less than twenty seconds.

But by then Zaitsev had disappeared.

"He went left at the corner," his ally called down to Kalugin from the window. "I don't think you'll be able catch him, though. Too many places to hide." She paused, then added in a tone of exasperation, "You're getting to be very confusing, you know. First escaping, now chasing. It's as bad as the movies. Do you even know *why?*"

He'd been about to set off in pursuit. Her question stopped him. Something in her voice, some trick of emphasis, reminded him of how Katya had questioned her students, especially when she knew they didn't have an answer. It reminded him now of what he'd been about to forget: that while *he* was chasing some fantasy of vengeance, a timer attached to a carload of explosive was ticking down to zero in Kreschatik Square. *Why* was a question he hadn't asked himself recently. In fact, he hadn't asked it in years. He'd just taken it for granted that the goal of his life was and ought to be to find and kill Zaitsev, and maybe because this had never before seemed close to achievement, it hadn't occurred to him to question that belief, to ask what it was he hoped to achieve. And now that he did ask, he found he didn't have an answer. Maybe he'd catch Zaitsev and maybe he wouldn't. But even if he did, what difference would it make? If he killed Zaitsev, tortured him to madness, exactly what would that do for Katya? Would it add so much as a second to her life, cancel any fraction of her pain? And what would it even do for him? Would it alter anything that had happened? Would it really help him to recover his honor, when the cost could be hundreds of people dead, a nation plunged into chaos? "Once shamed may never be recovered." Malory had known about shame. Once you had it, you had it. The best you could do was not add to it.

He didn't have time now to think about Zaitsev.

He desperately needed to find that bomb.

This meant, first of all, finding the vehicle. He ran over to the grating in the gutter where Zaitsev had discarded the keys. It was metal, immovable, bolted into the concrete, the spaces between the bars too narrow to get a hand through. He knelt beside it, peering into the drain. Light reflecting on a trickle of filthy-looking liquid revealed that the channel ran parallel with the gutter and about half a meter underneath it. He couldn't see well enough to make out the keys, but since the trickle was barely moving, and certainly not enough to carry them away, he thought they must be directly under the grating. What he needed was a flashlight. A flashlight and some wire.

"What are you *doing?*" the voice from the window impatiently queried.

"I don't have time to explain." He stood up, strode over to the window. "Do you have a flashlight? And some wire?"

She considered for a moment.

"I think I have a flashlight. I don't know about wire."

"Will you find the flashlight and drop it down here to me please? And see if you can find wire, any wire. A coathanger would do."

She hesitated. "Will you tell me what this is all about?"

"Please," he said. "It's a matter of life and death. You trusted me once. Trust me again."

Some urgency in his voice must have convinced her. She nodded and disappeared.

She was gone for what seemed like half an hour. In fact, it was less than five minutes. When she returned, she was holding a flashlight.

The time was eleven forty-five.

"I found this, but no wire, I'm afraid."

No wire. But without it the flashlight was useless. He looked around desperately. There were chestnut trees, apartment buildings, one or two cars (which were probably locked); nothing that at first glance seemed a likely source of wire.

"It doesn't have to be wire necessarily. Something I can use to fish for the key ring with. Anything. A crochet hook maybe."

"I know what you need." Patiently. "I don't to have anything like that. Do you want the flashlight?"

"Yes. Drop it down please. Don't throw it. Just hold it clear of the window ledge and drop it."

She did exactly as he instructed. He caught it easily, shone it into the drain.

The keys were there, two of them on a ring, lying in the trickle and tantalizingly close, no farther than the distance from his wrist to his elbow. Car keys.

"Can you see them?"

"I can see them." He nodded. "But seeing's no good if I can't get at them."

Suddenly he felt weary. It came to him that he was not going to make it. He was ten minutes at least from Kreschatik, with these crowds maybe more. If he snagged the keys right now the rally would begin before he got there. And even when he got there he would still have to find the vehicle and move it, *if* that was possible, and there was no telling how long that could take. But the bomb could go off anytime after twelve. It could go off now, he thought, and still cause untold havoc.

It was hopeless.

His slide into despair was arrested by a question from above:

"That car down the street . . . Does it have a radio?"

A radio. What on earth was she thinking of? How would he know if it had a radio? And anyhow what did it matter? But automatically his eyes flicked over, registered (without much interest) an ancient black Zhiguli much in need of bodywork and a paint job. On the driver's side was what looked like the knob of a retractable radio antenna.

"Well, does it?"

"I guess so." He shrugged. "It has an antenna, at least. . . ."

The antenna . . . Of *course*. That must have been why she'd asked. Not wire but as good as: long, thin, metal, bendable. Waving his gratitude to his remarkable accomplice he sidled over to the Zhiguli. Taking a quick look to make sure no one was watching, he pulled out the antenna, broke off the top section.

He was grateful that the street was almost empty. No gathering of bystanders to get in the way, inquire what the hell he was doing, wonder whether it was legally permitted, offer advice on how to do it. Still, it took him several minutes to retrieve the keys. The problem was mostly that the hook he had fashioned from the antenna was shallow, while the angle of attack—he was coming at it from directly above—was steep. Also he was in a hurry. Twice he succeeded in hooking the key ring only to lose it before he could get it to the grating. On the third attempt, however, he succeeded.

"Got them." He showed them to his friend at the window. "I don't have time to return your flashlight. I'm sorry."

"Forget it. Leave it at the bottom of the steps. There's always a chance it won't be stolen . . ." She smiled. Surprisingly, she blew him a kiss. "Take care of yourself, Youthful Exuberance. Good luck with whatever it is you're up to." She paused for a moment, then added, "If you get a chance, come back and see me."

"Thank you, I will." He knew he wouldn't, and the knowledge filled him with sudden regret. "I never even asked you your name."

"Ludmila . . . Ludmila Feodorovna Menshikova."

"Then Ludmila Feodorovna, permit me to say this. Your husband, the philanderer, must have been crazy."

He turned toward Kreshcatik, breaking into a run.

It was five minutes before twelve.

CHAPTER FORTY-FOUR

(Kiev, Ukrainian SSR. September 15, 1990)

IT WAS TEN AFTER TWELVE BY THE TIME HE MADE IT BACK TO THE SQUARE, worked his way around the fringes of the crowd to arrive at a point behind the platform. The dignitaries—leaders of the independence movement and assorted bishops—were all assembled. One of the bishops was speaking to the crowd.

In one way this was good, Kalugin thought. Since most of the people, including the police, were focused on receiving benediction, he'd be less likely to attract attention.

In another way, of course, it wasn't.

There must have been in this part of the square alone fifty or sixty thousand people. In the immediate vicinity of the platform, they were packed together like sardines. If the bomb went off, the carnage would be unbelievable. The square would become a slaughterhouse, a literal bloody shambles. And already it was *after* twelve.

For ten minutes now they'd been living on borrowed time.

Excluding two marked police cars, there were six vehicles in the cordoned-off area behind the platform: a Chaika (presumably belonging to the churchmen), two Volgas (presumably belonging to the independence leaders), and three TV equipment vans. One of them, almost certainly one of the vans, would unlock with the keys he'd retrieved from the drain.

But which one?

And how to find out? In theory it was simply a question of matching keys to locks, but in practice things were less straightforward. There were uniformed cops all around, no doubt plainclothes KGB, too, and though no one seemed to be guarding the vans, he could hardly hope to engage, unchallenged, in a lengthy process of trial and error. He would have to get lucky right away, guess right the first or second try. And this meant he would have to be smart. By looking at the problem from Zaitsev's angle, he must see if he could figure this out.

Presumably Zaitsev had thrown away the keys mostly in order not to have in his possession anything that could link him to the vehicle. But probably he had locked it when he'd left, partly to discourage theft or curiosity, also to make it harder to move. It seemed to be a reasonable assumption, therefore, that if any of these vehicles was not locked, it probably *didn't* contain the bomb.

Which might not be very helpful, of course—if they were all locked, he was back to square one—but it seemed to dictate, at least, a strategy of elimination. He could check to see which ones were locked, reserve his key matching for those that were.

But neither process was going to be easy. Indeed, he thought, it was hard to decide which would look more suspicious: trying vehicle doors at random or fitting keys into locks that wouldn't turn. What would help him was the fact that were the people behind the platform; at least he could hope to get close to the vans without making himself totally conspicuous.

Which one to try first? The vehicles were all parked, nose to tail, facing Kreschatik and the Monument to the Heroes of the Revolution. At the head of the line was the Chaika. It was followed by two vans, then a Volga, then another van, finally the second Volga. Up ahead of them the closest way into Kreschatik was blocked off by a barricade manned by a couple of policemen. In order to get out of the square, therefore, he would have to burst through this barricade, and to give himself the best shot at that, he needed to give the policemen as few shots at him as possible. The best choice from this point of view was the van immediately behind the Chaika; it had the shortest distance to cover, and there was also enough room between it and the Chaika to allow him to drive off without backing up.

On the sound gambling principle that when risks were equal one should choose the one that offered the greatest reward, it would have to be the van behind the Chaika. And it would have to be now.

And now, suddenly, he was afraid.

He hadn't been before, perhaps because he'd been too busy. What earlier events had required of him mostly was what he was best at: spur-of-the-moment decisions, under-the-gun reactions. Now, for what seemed like the first time in days, he had a choice.

He didn't have to do this. He could simply walk away.

When he thought about it, when he allowed the reality of where he was and what he was doing to hit him, he could hardly believe he was doing this. All his instincts protested. Imagination and reason both balked at the prospect of their own extinction. It would be so easy *not* to do it. He could get himself the hell away from here, catch the eight o'clock train to Odessa, turn his back on these people who were not, or *ought* not to be, his problem. This bomb plot, after all, was not of his making. It wouldn't be his fault that people had been killed. And anyway, he had tried, hadn't he?

It was then, as fear eroded his resolve, that he seemed to hear Katya, speaking from a place and time he didn't want to remember. "It's not your fault. You were too young to be tested." And with the memory, hesitation left him. She'd found an excuse for him then, but there was no way she'd do it here. He didn't have a choice. He did have to do this.

He had to do it now.

The trick, he told himself, was to act with confidence, to avoid at all costs looking surreptitious. People mostly took you at face value. If you looked commanding, they would let you command them.

He marched up to the van behind the Chaika, tried the handle of the door at the back.

It wasn't locked.

Just as he was making that discovery, someone spoke behind him.

"What do you think you're doing, exactly?"

He forced himself to turn round slowly, assumed a hostile, officious stare. The man he confronted was not a policeman or not at any rate a policeman in uniform. Nor did he look the KGB type. He looked, in fact, like a student or an artist. Dressed in jeans and a denim jacket, he was prematurely balding, sported a wispy fringe of beard of the same dirty blond as what was left of his hair. His stare, however, was very direct.

"What did you say?" Kalugin let some truculence into his tone. Act with authority, he reminded himself. Don't answer questions, ask them.

"I *said*, what are you doing, trying to get into my van?"

The tone of this was truculent, too. This was clearly someone not easy to intimidate. Unless he was disposed of fast he might also be someone who'd draw a crowd. There was only one option here. It could be courting disaster, especially if this guy had been listening to the radio, but at this point everything was courting disaster.

Reaching into his pocket for his KGB identification, Kalugin thrust it under the other man's nose. It had, he was relieved to note, the intended effect. Visibly the man's self-confidence ebbed. His body language became submissive. He didn't actually back away, but he held himself as if he'd like to.

"Is this *your* van?" Kalugin demanded.

"It's the crew's, actually." Modification of the previous statement brought mollification of the previous tone. "Since I'm with the crew, I'm responsible for it."

"Then why have you left it unlocked?" Note of stern accusation here, exploiting the initiative just gained. "It's a standing invitation to thieves."

"There isn't anything much in it to steal. We're using most of the equipment." The man shrugged, endeavored to recover lost face. "Is it a *crime* to leave a van unlocked."

"It's not a crime, just stupid."

Kalugin paused. He had his opponent on the run, but meanwhile time was wasting. It seemed to him he could hear his heartbeat, ticking off the seconds of his life. He was gripped by a fierce irritation, alternating with waves of panic. He didn't have time for this nonsense. He had to get rid of this guy.

Somehow he managed to stay calm. Panic achieved nothing but delay. You had to deal with what actually happened. There might even be something to be learned from this guy.

"These vans, they all belong to your crew?"

"Just these two here. Not that other one." Pause. "I guess it belongs to some other crew, though I don't see another one around."

That was the van then. It *would* be, he thought. It was farthest from the barricade, sandwiched between the two Volgas. It would take some maneuvering to get it out. And that was going to be a bitch.

"Okay." He nodded curtly. "I want you to lock both your vans. Now. I'll go check that one over there."

He didn't wait for a reply, just turned and walked away. He was conscious, as he did so, of the other's eyes following him thoughtfully; conscious also that his cover story wouldn't stand a lot of scrutiny. His control here was resting on a knife edge of consent. Any suggestion of wavering on his part—looking back, for instance, to see if his order had been followed—could tip obedience into mutiny.

The driver's side door of the third van was locked.

Now he allowed himself a glance at the crewman. He was at the driver's side door of his van, apparently locking it as instructed. He was also, it appeared, keeping an eye on Kalugin. When their eyes met, he shrugged and looked away.

Kalugin walked round to the back of the van, out of sight of the crewman. Checking doors was one thing; checking them with a *key* was something else.

The back doors of the van were also locked.

The lock opened to one of his keys.

A microsecond *after* he twisted the door handle, it occurred to him that it might have been booby-trapped. He was washed by a wave of retrospective panic that threatened for an instant to swamp his will. It didn't last, however. Perils survived were of minor interest, offered no assurance for the future.

The van was filled with what looked like TV equipment.

No bomb.

None visible, at least. But then he hadn't expected to find it in plain sight. Probably it was under the floor. He climbed in, pulling the doors shut behind him. Since there was no partition between the front and back, he'd be able to reach the driver's seat from inside. As he crawled over the jumble of equipment, most of it metal and probably intended for shrapnel, it occurred to him that he was literally on top of the bomb. If it went off now, he'd be instant vapor.

Not a bad way to die.

If you *had* to.

If there actually *was* a bomb. . . . For a moment the two sides of his mind disputed. Logic told him doubt was crazy: Zaitsev had come here to plant a bomb; he'd attempted to ditch a set of keys; they fitted this van; ergo, the bomb was in here somewhere. Imagination, on the other hand, proposed a series of plausible-crazy alternatives: Chance had misread the Code 5 Scenario; he himself was dreaming or hallucinating; Zaitsev had experienced a change of heart. None of this was real, in other words. It just wasn't happening.

Outside, however, he heard the bishop call for a moment of prayer.

Exactly, Kalugin thought, what the moment called for.

And then in the ensuing hush, as he sat enclosed in his capsule of loneliness and fear, steeling himself to do what logic told him he must, he heard from beneath the jumble of equipment a sound that told him logic was right.

Something ticking.

He inserted the key into the ignition.

This, too, could be booby-trapped. He'd thought of this earlier and, relying on logic again, dismissed the notion as improbable. It would have to have been done, he'd told himself, *after* Zaitsev had driven the van here, at a time when any terrorist's most fervent wish would have been to get clear as soon as possible; it would also have necessitated running two sets of wires to the detonator, an arrangement both cumbersome and dangerous. Zaitsev wouldn't see the need, wouldn't take unnecessary risks. Ergo, the ignition *hadn't* been booby-trapped.

Logic insisted.

Imagination, however, disagreed. And because of it he sat paralyzed, palms sweating, mouth dry, steeling his will to send his hand the message that might be the end of both. Do it, he urged himself. Just do it. He hadn't any alternative anyway. He had to finish this now that he'd started. The only freedom left him was the freedom to commit.

He turned the key.

As the motor turned over, caught, and he realized with a kind of dazed relief that he hadn't yet been turned into vapor, he happened to glance out of the window. Coming toward him with a purposeful step and an air of distinct self-satisfaction was the crewman.

With him was a policeman.

The van was sandwiched between the Volgas, the clearance at each end barely more than a meter. There was no time now for careful maneuvers. He slammed the gearshift into reverse and let out the clutch, gunning the motor. With a squeal of tires, a sudden explosion of breaking glass and metal, the van surged into the Volga, driving it back several meters, crumpling the front like cardboard. He threw the van into first, swung the wheel hard and took off, burning rubber, clipping, as he passed, the rear of the other Volga. Ahead of him people scattered in panic.

The two policemen at the barricade ran forward, waving him to stop and fumbling for their pistols. Glancing in the side mirror, he saw others behind him sprinting for their vehicles. Ahead, the barricades were coming up fast. They were wooden trestles, symbolic only. One of the policeman, however, had managed to draw his gun. He held his ground, and as the van came up on him, aimed at the windshield and fired.

A hole surrounded by a spiderweb of fractures appeared as if by magic in the middle of the windshield. Something hummed past Kalugin's ear. There was a snapping sound. He ducked down till he could just see above the dashboard and veered the van toward the marksman, straightening up at the very last second. He had the satisfaction, as he burst through the barricade, skidded through the right hand turn that would take him up Kreschatik, of seeing this idiot hurl himself out of the way.

Behind him sirens started to wail.

He had no real plan. Except to get this deathtrap the hell away from people, drive it to the closest unpopulated space and ditch it. But where an unpopulated space was to be found, on this day when all Kiev had taken to the streets, was unclear. There were stretches of riverbank that might suit, but they were down beyond the Lavra, two miles away, maybe more. There was no way of knowing how much time he had left, but it was almost certainly not that much.

He needed somewhere a lot closer.

In the end it was circumstances that chose his route. As he hit the top of Kreschatik, going way too fast to negotiate safely the sharp right-hand turn into Kirov Street, he found it in any case blocked by pedestrians. Apart from stopping—unthinkable among so many people—his only alternative was to make a left, up Heroes of the Revolution Street and past the Andreifvsky Church to the Podol district behind it. Now that he was *doing* something—acting, not thinking about it—he found himself calm, almost fatalistic. It was almost as if, in this turmoil of sirens, tires squealing, engines racing, he was totally caught up in the physical business of driving; as if, in what could be his life's final minutes, his mind had become a spectator at this drama, content to watch his body act it out. He didn't know what he would find up here, how or where this thing would end. He only knew it would end very soon. Where, at this point, seemed hardly to matter.

It ended at the Lenin Museum.

He remembered it about the same time as he saw it. Halfway up Heroes of the Revolution on the right. Another of the monuments Katya had hated. A modern, secular version of devotional architecture: a tall pillbox of glass and concrete enclosed by a cube of the same construction, white structural columns discreetly suggesting the pillars of a temple, broad steps in front leading down to a spacious forecourt.

A spacious, currently *unpopulated* forecourt.

No people in sight, at least. There were tour buses parked, but all of them seemed to be empty. The tourists and drivers, no doubt, were at the rally in Kreschatik. On this day of exuberant nationalism, there was not much enthusiasm left for Lenin.

He swung right, skidded into the forecourt.

The police were right on his tail. Since the barricade they'd refrained from shooting—presumably to avoid hitting bystanders—but now that there were no bystanders to hit, this was no doubt going to change. The problem was how to ditch the van while somehow managing not to get shot as he made a dash for cover.

What he had to do was to muffle the blast.

He slammed the van into the space between two buses. Then, almost before it had come to a halt, he was out of it, sprinting around the front of the bus nearest, heading off at an angle for the steps and the shelter of the building, keeping the bus between him and the van, and shielding him temporarily from the guns of the police.

He had no real sense of how much time he'd borrowed since he crashed the barricade into Kreschatik—in fact it had been less than five minutes—but he knew that his credit must be almost exhausted. But in spite of this, when he reached the steps, he turned to his pursuers to shout a warning. It seemed important that no one, not even police, should be injured.

Important that Zaitsev should fail completely.

The police, however, misunderstood. Three shots were fired, and one of them hit him, knocking him down by the foot of the steps.

And an instant later the van exploded.

CHAPTER FORTY-FIVE

(Kiev, Ukrainian SSR. September 17, 1990)

LATER IT WOULD SEEM AS IF HE'D BEEN ON A JOURNEY, DRIFTING for weeks on some underground river through caverns of almost impenetrable dark. Now and then, he'd seemed to hear voices, and here and there, punctuating the journey as dreams will punctuate sleep, there'd been moments when clarity had almost broken through, intervals not of light, but of thinned-out darkness, in which he had seemed to catch glimpses of men in uniform, women in caps and long white dresses. They had leaned over him, faces pushed close to his, had seemed to be speaking, calling him back to life, but he had floated past them, unheeding.

Reality returned to him as pain.

That at least was how it seemed when it happened, a sudden flooding of the head with pain. Almost at once, of course, the self began making the normal separations; acknowledging otherness, marking off cause from effect, sorting, ordering, explaining, confining. Sash windows, framing azure patches of sky, fitted themselves into walls of saffron which, connecting in turn with floorboards and ceiling, defined a space that seemed pleasant and airy. One by one, *things* presented themselves to the eye. At first they seemed alien, almost threatening, but brought into focus, labeled, placed in the appropriate verbal boxes, they took on aspects of the known and familiar. That on the right was a table. Another one stood against the wall. On it was a vase of freshly cut flowers. Adjacent, a washstand with towel, jug, and basin. Above this, a framed reproduction of "Boatmen on the Volga." Beyond the windows, a city and a river.

Kiev?

It came to him then, almost as a discovery, that he was alive.

He felt, if anything, disappointed.

Investigation revealed that he was on his back in bed, his movement restrained by covers stretched across the chest and tucked at the sides with military firmness and precision. His head was supported by pillows, his arms by his sides but outside the covers.

One of his arms was in a cast.

His head, he learned next, was wearing a helmet of bandage. Raising it produced hammer shots of pain, which the bandaging did nothing to muffle. He was just resolving to defer for the moment further exploration of his predicament, when the door opened and a young woman entered. She was dressed, like the women of his interrupted dreams, in a cap and a long white dress. As she closed the door behind her, he caught a glimpse, just outside and to the right, of a uniformed soldier sitting on a chair. A rifle was resting against the chair.

"I see you finally decided to wake up."

He gazed at her weakly. She was crisp, white and pretty, but the look on her face, like her tone, was unsympathetic. She was evidently one of those martinets, familiar from childhood visits to the doctor, to whom all sickness was a form of malingering.

"Where am I, exactly?"

"In hospital." She paused a moment, added with disapproval, "A private room, all to yourself. Just as if you were important."

"In hospital? Then who's that outside?"

"Outside? Oh, him. You *must* be important. A room to yourself and also a guard."

"But who is he guarding? Me or the others?"

"The others?" This seemed to go right by her.

"Is he there to stop people getting in, or me getting out?"

"I really couldn't say." Her lips pursed primly. "You should know that better than I."

He should, of course, and did. He'd remembered now what he'd been doing in Kiev: the search for Zaitsev, the chase, the bomb. The guard on the door was to keep him in.

Reality was a box and he was in it.

"How long was I out?"

"Three days. You were amazingly lucky." Her tone conveyed that he didn't deserve it. "Severe concussion and a radius fracture. The bullet through your shoulder missed everything important. All things considered, I'd say you were fine."

"All *what* things considered . . ." Something in her tone invited his question, a hint she knew something he didn't. "What things?"

"All sorts of things . . . Considering, for one thing, that those buses were totally demolished." She hesitated a moment, smiled unpleasantly. "Considering, for another, that the newspapers reported you dead."

"Dead?" For a moment he was utterly dumbfounded.

"Yes . . ." She smiled again, teasing. Now her ascendancy had been established, she was almost friendly. "How does it feel?"

How did it *feel?* That was his cue, he thought, to say something mordant and witty, to bring forth some pearl of gallows humor. For some reason, however, he didn't feel humorous. Nothing occurred to him except the obvious: *Why* had the newspapers reported him dead?

It didn't take a Lenin to figure out the answer.

"What kind of hospital is this?"

"With private rooms and guards on the door?" She seemed surprised he should even ask. "A military hospital, of course."

"How long till I'm able to get out?"

"That's not for me to say. Or you." She produced a thermometer and stuck it in his mouth. "No doubt, in due course, they'll send someone to see you."

They sent someone the next afternoon. He was from the KGB. Perhaps to emphasize that fact, he was in uniform: standard gray-beige, with the Prussian-blue collar tabs and shoulder boards, sword and shield insignia on the tabs. You didn't need the stars on his shoulder boards, moreover, to tell you you were dealing with a big shot. The man's bearing, his air of authority, were an eloquent testament to that. He was powerfully built, of medium height, with a broad strong-featured face, penetrating greenish-hazel eyes, and thick waves of fiery red hair. In spite of his stars he was civil, even courteous. He knocked, and waited to be asked, before entering. On entering, he nodded a greeting, then, fetching a chair from beside the table, set it down, facing Kalugin, at the foot of the bed.

Then he stood, studying Kalugin for a moment. He seemed stern, not much given to smiling but not, or at least not obviously, hostile.

"May I?" He tilted his head in the direction of the chair.

"Of course." Kalugin nodded.

The visitor settled himself into the chair, allowed another moment for mutual appraisal.

"Are you able to answer questions? Well enough to, that is?"

"I'm well enough." Kalugin paused for a moment, added, "Reports of my death have been much exaggerated."

"Oh. You heard about that?" Suggestion of a smile. "Somebody seems to have made a mistake. It can easily be corrected."

Can be corrected, Kalugin noted, not *will.* Apparently it depended on something.

His visitor continued: "Do you know who I am?"

An interesting question. One could hazard, Kalugin thought, an educated guess. One wasn't about to do so, however. The situation was already hazardous enough.

"Your uniform says you're a KGB general. Beyond that . . ." He shrugged.

It was hard to judge how this was received. He seemed to sense it was welcomed. In any event the visitor, if he took at face value this claim of ignorance, took no steps whatever to dispel it.

"Do you know who *you* are?"

"My enlistment file identifies me as Vadim Stolypin." Kalugin nodded. "In the course of my work I have sometimes used other identities. I don't mean to be impertinent, General, but it's not yet clear that I'm entitled to tell you what they are."

"James Whitcomb, for one." The eyes registered, briefly, what might have been amusement. "Vladimir Stepanovich Grusha, for another."

Kalugin said nothing. This was expected. They'd checked his Soviet papers at origin. Finding them phony, they'd then traced his movements, guided, no doubt, by the rail ticket stub in his pockets.

"I could ask you," the general continued, "to explain why you entered the Soviet Union on one set of forged papers, journeyed from Odessa to Kiev on another. I could point out that this puts you in an awkward position with Immigration, just as the fact that you drove through the streets of Kiev in a van containing high explosive and registered to a foreign import-export company puts you in an awkward position with the police. For the moment, however, I will confine myself to stating that your cover name is Kalugin, your code name Cobalt, and that you hold the rank of lieutenant in Directorate S of the First Chief Directorate of the KGB." Pause. In the stare now aimed at Kalugin there was neither warmth nor humor. "I hope it is now sufficiently clear that you are—how did you put it?—entitled to answer any question I may care to ask you, and on any subject whatever."

Kalugin thought about this. Displaying knowledge of his personnel file had also been Atlas's method of establishing credentials. But this fact by itself, though possibly significant, proved nothing. This general might be an enemy or he might not. There was no point whatever in *making* him one.

"It is clear, General."

"Good. Then explain some things to me: Why did you return to the Soviet Union under false identity and without proper authorization? How did you come to be driving around Kiev in a van filled with high explosive?"

Kalugin considered. How to answer without jeopardizing himself? Big shots in the CIA had conspired with big shots in the KGB, etc? That was all well and good, perhaps, but what if this general (as was more than likely) was one of those big shots? What if his purpose (as was more than likely) was to find out precisely how much one knew, especially about the identities of the plotters? What one had to do, Kalugin decided, at least if one wanted the reports of one's death not to become cold, sober fact, was to think smart but act a little dumb. A little dumb, but not too much. One should tell the truth, but not *all* of it. Above all, one could let slip no hint of one's suspicions, at least about this general and why he was here.

"Is the question so difficult that you need to think so long?"

"Not difficult, General, but the answer is complicated. I'm thinking how best to summarize." Kalugin paused. "What happened was this. . . ."

About the next half hour's conversation—in fact, it was mostly monologue—there were two things that chiefly struck Kalugin: the general's powers of concentration, and his failure to take notes. From time to time he interrupted to ask for details or clarification, but mostly he just listened, and with the kind of attention that suggested he was weighing every word. It was possible, of course, that note-taking was redundant because the room was wired for sound. The attention, on the other hand, and the grasp, evident from the occasional questions, of the story's twists and turns were remarkable. It was easy to see why this man had made general. And if it was also possible to suspect that the quick comprehension was not all due to intelligence, that the general followed the story so well because parts of it, at least, were already familiar to him, *entertaining* this suspicion, it seemed to Kalugin, served no useful purpose at all. The diplomat's strategy was called for here:

Hear no evil. See no evil.

Make no ill-considered statement.

When Kalugin was finished, the general reached into his briefcase. Extracting a sheaf of photographs, he shuffled through them, glancing briefly at each, then handed the sheaf to Kalugin.

"You mentioned Knights of Vladimir. Would these be them?"

Kalugin examined the first photograph. A man's face in close-up, it was taken from slightly above, the head thrown back and angled to one side, the features twisted in a rictus of agony. In the eyes was a look of surprise and horror.

Raina.

"The rest are the same," the general said. "They were found, all five of them, locked in an apartment in the Podol district. They were killed by a nerve gas, presumably released by some timing device. It had dissipated when the bodies were discovered. Death, I understand, was more or less instantaneous."

More or less instantaneous . . . Kalugin flicked through the other pictures. Vasa . . . Beloff . . . Kaminsky . . . Benko: each had the same wide-open eyes, the same horrified, ambushed expression. Zaitsev had left them in the apartment, no doubt, told them to stay put while he reconnoitered. They had served their purpose; now they were redundant. He remembered with shame his own last encounter with Benko, the insincerity of his words at parting. But it was better this way, he thought, better this "more or less instantaneous" than the fate that otherwise would have been theirs: a lingering disintegration in some cell at the hands of men the KGB called "debriefers." But it hadn't had to be either, he thought. Benko and the others could still be alive. All he'd had to do was warn them. But that would have taken something he had lacked. He wasn't quite sure what it had been. Courage maybe? Imagination?

He handed the pictures back. "They're the Knights of Vladimir, all right. They were harmless really. Or left alone, they would have been. Politically they were nothing more than children." He paused, hearing an echo in his head, quoted in the English of the original. " 'Children ardent for some desperate glory.' "

"Ardent for some desperate glory . . . ?" To judge from his accent, the general's English was fluent. He looked blank, however.

"It's a poem," Kalugin said. "About dying for your country. The poet advises against it. It seems to fit the Knights of Vladimir. They didn't know the Cold War was over. Perhaps they didn't want to know. They were living in the wrong decade, maybe in the wrong century. They thought they were patriots, whatever that means."

"Whatever that means . . ." The general looked at him sharply. "You don't believe in patriotism then?"

"I thought I was meant to believe in Marxism-Leninism." Kalugin shrugged. "Party before country. Not that it makes any difference. Neither seems to mean much anymore."

For a moment his visitor examined him without speaking. Almost, Kalugin had the impression, without *seeing* him, at least as a person. It was less an inspection than an appraisal, an assessment of a problem.

"Yet you risked your life to remove that bomb." An observation, not quite a query.

Kalugin said nothing. There seemed nothing he could say that wouldn't to some extent misrepresent his motives. Not that his motives were at this point important. But if one couldn't achieve honesty, one could at least avoid its reverse. Why misrepresent if one didn't have to?

"Allow me to summarize," the general said. "You believe that officers in the KGB conspired with their counterparts in the CIA to provoke a resumption of Cold War hostilities by means of a complex provocation involving a campaign of terror to be carried out by these so-called Knights. Is that approximately right?"

"In a nutshell." Kalugin nodded.

"But who stood to gain from all this?"

"I think it was more a question of not wanting to lose." Kalugin shrugged. "People made careers from the Cold War, General. Apparently some of them weren't willing to let go."

His visitor regarded him gravely.

"You're overcynical," he said. "I cannot believe that any of my colleagues, however ambitious, would be parties to an outrage such as that; that simply to protect their careers, they'd wantonly sacrifice so many lives."

Extended silence. They'd arrived, Kalugin gathered, at a crux. The general continued to gaze at him steadily, but his look, like the tone of his statement, was hard to read. There was something dogmatic in it, an air of official pronouncement, not to be disputed, but there was also something else. Something more personal, it struck Kalugin, a kind of sincerity, almost a kind of appeal.

He nodded. "I agree with you, General. I, too, find that impossible to swallow. What happened, I think, is that the Americans tried to cheat, added their own murderous twist to what was originally no more than theater. That, at least, is what I *want* to believe."

The general frowned.

"If you're right," he said, "if there ever was a conspiracy, then *clearly* the Americans attempted to cheat."

"*If* there was a conspiracy?" Kalugin stared. "Do you think I'm inventing this, General? Do the facts I've given you lead to any other conclusion?"

"I don't think you're inventing. But as to your conclusions, it's hard to know." The general paused, gave a ghost of a smile. "I will tell you *one* thing I think. Even if you're right, it will very be hard to prove."

More silence. And again, Kalugin noted, that ambiguous look, the same odd mix of assertion and appeal.

"Again I agree." Kalugin paused for a moment, added, "Indeed I would say *impossible* to prove. I don't know your opinion, General, but I would think it pointless to try."

His visitor considered this.

"You may be right," he said presently. "That decision is not mine, of course. But since, thanks to you, no lasting harm was done, it may be that those whose decision it is will find it impractical to pursue an inquiry whose chances of success seem so slim."

No lasting harm . . . Kalugin thought of the photographs. What about Benko? What about Zebo? Vasa, Beloff, Kaminsky, Raina? What about Atlas, even? All those eyes sightless now, staring, with that look of mingled surprise and horror, into nothingness and silence. But what could he do for them? he wondered. Make some quixotic gesture of solidarity? Join them in their futile comradeship of death? He thought not. If this general, as he seemed to sense, was offering him his life, he was going to take it. He was going to take it and do something with it. He hoped that Benko and the others would forgive him; but if not, he thought, perhaps in time he could manage to forgive himself.

CHAPTER FORTY-SIX

(Athens. September 24, 1990)

"I DON'T UNDERSTAND IT," CHANCE SAID. "HOW COULD HE JUST LET YOU go?"

"Easy," Kalugin said. "It was the bureaucratic neatness that appealed to him, I think. The tourist, James Whitcomb, who entered the country legally, left the country legally, a little behind schedule perhaps, but with all the paperwork in order. The illegal agent, Vadim Stolypin, who died preventing the bombing in Kiev, was buried with appropriate honors." He paused. "I'm not quite sure what they put in the coffin. Rocks probably."

"That's all very interesting," Chance said. "But it doesn't really answer my question. What I still don't see is why?"

It was ten o'clock. Chance and Kalugin were in bathrobes, eating breakfast on the balcony of their hotel room. The balcony offered a view of the Acropolis, on which, on this relatively unpolluted day, the Temple of Athene, though under restoration and partially obscured by scaffolding, gleamed like a promise in the morning sun.

"What I mean is, why take the risk? Wouldn't it have been safer just to kill you?"

"Perhaps." Kalugin shrugged. "But what was he really risking? I may know, more or less, what they were all up to, but how much can I actually prove? There are no independent witnesses, no corroborating evidence. It would simply be my word against theirs."

"No corroborating evidence?" She frowned. "There was a bomb, wasn't there? The bodies of five Ukrainian emigrés? You might not be able to prove anything, but you sure as hell could embarrass some people. The general who let you go, for one."

"Maybe, if I knew who he was." Kalugin gave another shrug. "I think that was the point he was delicately making. That I couldn't prove much, and trying would be harmful to my health. When I talked to him in that hospital room, the newspapers had already reported my death, a fact that was brought to my attention. They were letting me know, if I got out of line, they could easily make the report come true. They still can, of course, anytime they want. But I don't think they will, unless I provoke them." He paused. "There was something else, you see, a feeling I got from the general. I think he felt they owed me a debt. I believe he wanted to pay it."

"A spook with a sense of honor?" She looked skeptical. "In view of what they tried, that's a little hard to swallow."

"It shouldn't be." He shook his head. "I think most spooks have a sense of honor. If you see them as merely cynical, I think you miss the point. In their view they're always the good guys, and given man's talent for self-deception, that's mostly what makes them so dangerous. Since they firmly believe they're serving their country, they come to see its interests as identical with theirs. So preserving themselves is always justified. They never notice when their means turn into ends, when the process, as it always does, usurps the purpose." He paused. "I think my general will pay his debt, if only because he owes it mostly to himself."

They were silent for a moment. Chance looked out across the modern city, across the canyons of steel and concrete that spread out as far as the eye could follow, across the lines of midmorning traffic that wound and writhed, like a tangle of snakes, between the buildings, across the brownish haze of exhaust fumes that had compromised already the brilliance of the day, to the citadel which, standing above it all, bore witness to the existence, somewhere in human affairs, of some capacity for clarity and order.

"But Zaitsev got away." She raised, obliquely, the issue that was really on her mind. "It seems the real villains often do."

"I guess so." He shrugged. "Maybe now that they don't need him to help control me, the KGB will deal with him themselves. But so much has changed in the last few months, I wonder if they care anymore. If he's got any smarts, which he obviously does, he'll get the hell out of Geneva, find somewhere safer to hide. I don't know where . . . Paraguay, perhaps."

"And what about you?" The question sounded casual, but she asked with her heart in her mouth. "You sound as if *you* don't care as much as you did. If he gets away, how will you feel about it?"

He thought for a moment, shrugged.

"I won't care very much. At least I don't think so. And if I do, I just won't let myself. I got very lucky in Kiev. Lucky in all sorts of ways. I'm going to do my damnedest not to waste it."

"Lucky?" she queried. "You mean that the bomb went off when it did. Not half a minute earlier?"

He nodded. "That, but also something more. The real luck was finding the bomb in time to move it. If people had died, it would have been my fault. I think I'd have found that difficult to live with."

There was more silence. Presently he said: "But that's all over. The question is, what do we do now?"

What do we do now? It was not a question he had ever asked her before. It was not a question she was sure she understood.

"Maybe we should get dressed." She shrugged. "Have the hotel call us a taxi. Wander around the ruins a bit. Find somewhere nice to have lunch. Somewhere outside, perhaps, tables shaded by vines. Lamb souvlaki, a salad with olives and feta cheese, the whole thing washed down by a bottle or two of . . ."

He cut her off. "I didn't mean now, this minute. I intended a more general reference, a 'now' extending beyond the moment."

"Extending?" she queried. "Extending how far?"

He smiled. "I guess that would be the topic of the discussion."

"I see," she said. "Extended discussion of an extended now. Maybe we should schedule that for lunch."

He shook his head. "I don't think we should wait that long."

"You mean it should happen here and now?"

"Now." He nodded. "Not necessarily here."

"Oh? If not here, then where?"

"Inside." He gestured with his head.

"Let me get this straight," she said. "You want to take me back to bed to discuss how long 'now' should last?"

"Yes," he said. "It's an important discussion. I'll need any advantage I can get."

She thought about this.

"Are you saying what I think you're saying."

"I *think* I am." He nodded.

She looked at him for a moment without speaking, then she reached across the table and took his hand.

"But you'll have to twist my arm," she said.

EPILOGUE
(Geneva, Switzerland. December 4, 1991)

IN THE DARKEST CORNER OF THE DOWNSTAIRS BAR OF HIS HOTEL, MAJOR General Rodion Rakowski, Head of Directorate R (Operational Planning and Analysis) of the First Chief Directorate of the KGB, sat staring into a half-empty tumbler of whiskey, trying not to think about the future. On the seat beside him was a copy of yesterday's *Financial Times,* one of whose headlines—UKRAINE VOTES YES ON INDEPENDENCE—was, though the news it reported was far from unexpected, what he was trying not to think *about.* His method of doing this was to think about something else, specifically the minor semantic problem of whether his glass—his third this evening, though it was still some minutes short of six—could more properly be described as half full or half empty. This question, he decided, was not really very difficult. Nor was it fraught with the deep existential significance that pop psychologists and self-help gurus, Americans naturally, frequently attempted to give it. The answer depended not on one's temperament or one's attitude to life, but simply on the direction of change. If the contents were being increased, the glass was half full; if reduced, it was half empty. This analysis, it further struck him, could be extended to much in life besides tumblers and single malt Scotch.

One's career, for instance.

One's future.

Such analogies, however, weren't altogether precise. Tumblers of Glenlivet could always be refilled; one's cup of life, once overflowing but now reduced to what looked suspiciously like dregs, was a different kind of receptacle altogether. But this, of course, was where temperament came in. One could either despair at the one-shot nature of existence or rejoice in the renewable blessings of single malt Scotch. And in this respect, being Russian offered a decided advantage. For while the people of most other cultures were enslaved to the tyranny of either/or, a Russian, with happy flexibility of spirit, could despair and rejoice at the same moment. Gulping the remainder of his drink, he signaled to the waiter for another.

"I'd count it an honor, General, if you'd let *me* buy that."

The voice behind him was American, familiar, unwelcome.

He looked up. Approaching from the entrance and wearing a wisp of a smile, his patrician air enhanced, as always, by the tousled hair and rumpled Brooks Brothers suit, was Turner Meredith.

Drinking with the enemy . . . For a moment Rakowski hesitated, but it was only for a moment. Nothing was gained by being churlish. And a drink, whoever bought it, was a drink.

"Thank you. You'll join me, of course." He gestured to the chair next to him, feigned a good humor he was far from feeling. "What brings the CIA's deputy director of dirty tricks to Geneva?"

"Consultations." Meredith plopped into the indicated chair, gave his order to the waiter. "One of those tiresome interservice conferences organized by our intelligence bureaucrats, mostly to justify their own existence. I'm supposed to be guest speaker: 'What next for the CIA?' 'Whither spying in the post-Cold War era?' I'm sure you can imagine the kind of thing."

"I can imagine." Rakowski nodded. "What are you going to tell them?"

"I'm sure you can imagine that, too." Meredith gave him a twisted grin. "I cribbed most of my speech from the Joint Chiefs of Staff. With the evident decline of the Soviet Union, blah blah, we now face a world of dangerous instability, offering new challenges, unforeseen threats, blah blah. We therefore need to maintain our capabilities, remain, more than ever, armed and vigilant. In other words, don't cut our budgets; there are still plenty of bad guys out there."

"Saddam did you a favor, then." Rakowski gave a perfunctory smile. "And Herr Doktor Rosenthal, what news of him?"

"On the lecture circuit, where else? 'Whither *security* in the post-Cold War-era?' In addition to which I gather he's writing a book. Provisional title: *The New World Disorder,* or *Don't Say I Didn't Tell You So.*" He paused. "What about yourself? What are you doing in this haunt of the bourgeoisie?"

"Rest . . ." Rakowski shrugged. "And contemplation. Whither

Rakowski in the post-Cold War era?" He held up his *Financial Times* so Meredith could see the headline. "The Soviet Union exists now on paper only. Since the Revolution is finally dead, it seems to me legitimate to wonder what will become of its sword and shield."

At this point the waiter arrived with their drinks. Meredith paid. Rakowski, with only a token demurral, let him. One could consider it a modest first installment, he thought, of the aid the US, in the flush of victory, would sooner or later surely offer. For a while they sipped in almost companionable silence.

"If you're contemplating a career move," Meredith presently offered, "I hope you'll seriously consider us. A man of your experience could virtually write his own ticket. There'd be publishing contracts, talk show appearances, guest lecturing all over the place. And that's all quite apart from what *we* could offer."

"Thank you, no." Rakowski shook his head. "I'm afraid I can't see myself in a safe house somewhere, narrating my story to relays of CIA debriefers, each statement checked, re-checked, cross-checked, double-checked until I myself can no longer tell truth from fiction. I can't see myself being shuttled from talk show to talk show, a captive commander in a gilded chariot, gracing the conqueror's triumph. That would be too . . ." He paused, searching for the word he wanted.

"Too demeaning?" Meredith supplied.

"Not demeaning." Rakowski thought for a moment. "Too bitter."

"Bitter?"

"You sound surprised." Rakowski stared at him. "Did you think that what we fought *for* didn't matter? Did you think that for us it was just a matter of *jobs?* Did you think that we, the heirs of Lenin, could watch without regrets while his revolution collapsed in chaos, that we could witness without shame the Russian people trading socialism for consumer goods, betraying their dream of dignity and freedom for Budweiser, Big Macs, and MTV? Did you think . . ."

He broke off. Now he was making idiot speeches, giving this American encouragement to gloat. The drinks must have affected him more than he'd realized. He needed to pull himself together, make an effort not to seem—what was the American phrase?—"a sore loser."

"Those fools bungled it in August," he said sourly. "They tried to intimidate people by force, but lacked the courage to *use* it. In any case it was too late for force. Our idea was better: use patriotism. It could have worked."

He paused for a moment, turned suddenly to Meredith. "You didn't win, you know. The Germans and the Japanese won. The Europeans won. You nearly went bankrupt paying for their defense, but *they* saved their money, used it to rebuild. And now that the Communist dragon has been slain, don't look to them now for obedience. . . . or gratitude."

He looked at Meredith for some response.

Meredith said nothing.

"It could have worked," Rakowski repeated. "It could have worked for our mutual benefit. Why did you people have to try and cheat?"

"Ignorance mostly," Meredith said. "Ignorance and a kind of reflex. We weren't equipped with a good enough crystal ball. We didn't know how things were going to work out. We thought you guys were stronger than you were; that was the mistake we always made. We didn't know you were going to fold up. We thought we saw a chance to zap you . . ." He paused, looked at Rakowski, shrugged. "It seemed like a good idea at the time, but then doesn't it always?"

They were silent for a moment. Meredith looked at his watch.

"I have to go, I'm afraid. A dinner engagement."

He stood up, extended a hand. Rakowski shook it.

"Until we meet again," he said. "I'm sure we shall."